"Pete's vision encompasses a wider scope than simply telling grand tales. He's a storyteller in the truest sense of the profession — that is, he weaves together the past and present, the true and mythological, in a seamless tapestry that matters to his readers.

In *Sunday Rain*, Pete maintains his consistent themes of masculine friendship, father-son relationships, and budding romance, but he also moves into what is, for him, virgin territory. Pete is recreating the classic Western, and he's doing so with remarkable skill."

–Holland Webb, author, and international editor

SUNDAY RAIN

PETE LESTER

Burning Bulb
PUBLISHING

Sunday Rain
By **Pete Lester**

Burning Bulb Publishing
P.O. Box 4721
Bridgeport, WV 26330-4721
United States of America
www.BurningBulbPublishing.com

PUBLISHER'S NOTE: This book is a work of fiction. Names, characters, places, and incidents are either the product of the author's imagination or are used fictitiously, and any resemblance to actual persons, living or dead, events, or locales is purely coincidental.

Copyright © 2023 Burning Bulb Publishing. All rights reserved.

Cover paintings by Pete Lester.

First Edition.

Paperback Edition ISBN:978-1-948278-67-6

Dedication

This book is for Debra, Drew, and Carson,
the best loving family in the world.

Dedicated to a father of greatness, Larry, the one who turned my attention to good books and Western movies.

For my loving mother, Donna, I will always remember the great meals and big hugs, especially when I was in school.

For my cool sister, Angela, we had a blast in our neighborhood when we were young. My memories go back to you and the fun we had with the one and only Clifford "Petom" Green, the best friend anyone could hope for in life.
I miss those days.

I love you all.

Chapter 1
Kentucky Sons

Shortly after a warm October sunrise in 1863, Chas Bellew carried a letter in his pocket that spoke of his father's death at the Battle of Chickamauga. His cousin, Jackie Ray Monroe, turned twelve that day and saw his father's name printed in the newspaper. The column listed fallen troops who would soon be transported to Kentucky and other towns. Teenaged and too young to fight, Chas and Jackie Ray were old enough to rage against bloodshed and found themselves fatherless at the end of the Civil War.

Now, seven years later, two cousins, restive and ready to fight, dusted by lengthy war stories from old timers and veterans, felt it was time to carry guns for the sake of freedom and protection and had their own keen intentions.

In a snow-white church on Sunday morning, tucked in the wilderness of the Appalachian Mountains, Chet Bellew preached before his congregation, spirit-filled and hopeful, not far from the Cooksey Creek Cemetery, where he'd walked among tombstones and prayed, just as he did every Sunday morning.

"Each Spring, I am reminded," said Preacher Bellew, "of men who marched and especially those who perished, like my brother, Charles Bellew, did. But today, as I see your beautiful and young faces and the next generation of sons and daughters left behind by the Civil War, my heart is hopeful. Let us recall, there's a time to mend, a time to speak, a time for war, and a time for peace."

The sermon and Spirit changed Denton, Kentucky, on that day, and everyone in it. The year was 1871.

It was the time young ladies became women, seemingly overnight. Mothers aged in the same manner; old men yearned for their youth, and slick-faced boys became rugged and raw. Preacher Bellew knew young men had reasons to fight and wander, just as he did in his youth, finishing the undone work of their rugged fathers.

"I hope to have God on my side," said the preacher, "but I must have Kentucky." The preacher raised his hands. "As we try to overcome loss, Heaven must be a Denton, Kentucky kind of place."

Tombstones of fallen soldiers dotted the hillsides of Carter County. The names and faces of soldiers made newspapers, memories of the past lingered, and names once on the church roll were now on gravestones. Brother beside brother, slowly fading into the pages of history, yet strong names and bloodlines carried beyond the field of battle became unsettling times. Wounds and scars ran deep in the hearts of mountain folks. Young men stood ready for the next great Civil War, and women worried about tomorrow; hope stirred among the flesh, strengthened by the Word and labor, proud daughters and sons picked up where their fathers left off.

Indeed, the high mountains were places with music and song, beauty, and virtue, with heritage and strong traditions, deeper than the roots of shadowy trees, and as old as the earth itself, and truly, it was a Kentucky kind of place. The frontier was a place of grace and manners, spread of wavy bluegrass and smoky rolling hills, swept by the Lord's own hand. Streams weaved in a timeless landscape and had not withered much since the beginning of time, where lush valleys grew ready for harvest, and mountains stood tall and rugged as the people of its day in Eastern Kentucky.

On a cool spring morning, thunder clouds darkened, and walked across the sky, drifting and waving skyward the shade of worn Confederate uniforms. High winds bent trees; broken limbs tumbled over dusty country roads in Denton. Pathways were made narrow that led to Straight Creek Presbyterian Church, where dozens had gathered for worship. Women screamed when lightning split the trunk of a towering oak into a dozen pieces at the time of invitation.

Without a tug of rope, church bells sounded. The steeple swayed from the vibration and agitation of the harshness of unpredictable spring weather. Whinnying horses broke free from buggies, uprooting newly sunken posts. Animals raced to the nearest shelter. Livestock slowed to a halt. Roads became soft. Flash flooding rushed across the terrain. Forked roadways were turned into blockades; still today, it's said whinnying horses are heard in the deepest valleys and caverns of Carter County, Kentucky, the place they called home.

Young boys outraced their grandfathers to rescue horses and pulled buggies from soft, sunken roadways. Girls joined their grandmothers and stood at doors and windows, sang hymns, and prayed for peace far from nature's wrath on the mountains as they watched their small community crumble and fall.

The Sunday rain subsided. Men soiled by earth and water was the day life changed the residents of Denton. Forces and hardships changed boys into men, and when they returned to the little church, respect was granted by the congregation. Those who braved the Sunday thunderstorm had changed, returning rugged, faces scruffy, shoulders broad, and arms muscled, now admired. No longer unproven but acts of valor pinned with hugs and handshakes, they became men in the smoky Sunday rain. Preacher Bellew kept the Word alive, louder in Spirit and song when the thunder rumbled and lightning flashed. He felt uneasy about ending service without a benediction, especially with a churchhouse full of prodigal sons and daughters.

"Though the church may tremble, and the earth may crack, worry not," as he held the Bible in both hands and gazed at the congregation. "We are troubled on every side, yet not distressed; we are perplexed." He sounded, "We are persecuted, but not forsaken; cast down, but we are not destroyed."

Suddenly, the storm drifted away, the wind stopped, and the blazing morning sun broke through the thin curtain clouds. Rainbows arched above the town smiles lit up the service, and warmth shined on faces through drenched windows. Seven people, four old men, and three women, dropped to their knees in prayer as the preacher saw the congregation. "Would there be one today who knows not the Lord, just one daughter or one son who will meet me here at God's altar, just one? God will take the daughters and sons of war and honor them just the same as the eldest of His saints. Who will be called?"

"I will, preacher," said a young man in the back pew.

"Awe, well," said Preacher Chet, stunned. "Amen to my nephew, Charles "Chas" Bellew."

"Glory be to God and all His angels," said the congregation.

"Did hell freeze over?" mumbled Jackie Ray, best friend to Chas.

Chet held out his hands. "Yes, for sure. Oh, Mr. Chas Bellew, my nephew and one of the sons left behind by the Civil War. I knew your heart would begin again," said the preacher, who hugged him at the altar. "Maybe you can bring Jackie Ray with you because God has a certain sense of humor about Him. He's another son left behind by the bloody Battle of Chickamauga, Tennessee. Both their fathers fought for the Great South and were killed, joining God's army in heaven, so we carry on."

"Heck, no, Preacher Bellew," chuckled Jackie Ray, who covered his mouth with his hat and sniffed. "Not me."

"Stand up when you speak, son," said Preacher Bellew.

"My granddaddy said I was hell-bent on playin' poker and fun for girls." With a goofy voice, he said, whispering low to Chas Bellew, "Or was it pokin' funny girls and hell-bent, I forget the joke?"

"Well said, my friend."

The congregation heard him and laughed.

"Would there be another who needs the Lord?" begged the preacher. "One with obedience and character, just one more?" Chet held out his hand and said, "God has room for one more sinner on this Sunday."

The pastor gripped his nephew's stout shoulders, turned the young man toward the happy faces of the congregation, and smiles ran across the faces of all who attended.

"Okay. Well, in this Sunday rain, the Lord has found only one sheep," said Preacher Bellew, "left behind by the brokenness of a bad war."

"I'm not being baptized in a muddy river, though, preacher," Chas murmured, "and a handful of water never hurt anybody, and it won't hurt me."

"Likewise," said Preacher Bellew, raising his hand. "I say unto you, there is joy in the presence of the angels of God over one sinner, our son, that repented. My nephew wants to be baptized in the muddy river next Sunday." He laughed and grinned. "Said he would not want to be washed of his sins in any other way than a Kentucky way of life."

"Amen and amen!"

They sang. "He's washed in the blood, washed in the blood."

"Hallelujah!" shouted Jackie Ray in a deep country accent. "Glory be to God and Jesus and that beautiful siren, Mary Magdalene."

***

After service, Chas and Jackie Ray walked two ladies to their log cabin, and then the sun broke through the paper-thin clouds as they walked around the edge of a bluegrass field where cattle grazed and a big barn stood. The sky was filled with blue, red, and orange streaks after the rain passed and the sun warmed their faces. The two young men were more than eager to show their new neighbors the countryside of Carter County. Jackie Ray walked Alice Brooks to the barn and fed the horses.

"Look, there's a second rainbow," said Kate, walking beside Chas. "Pastor Bellew told how the rainbow was a sign that God would not flood the world again."

His hand blocked the sun. "Wise man."

"Have you ever thought about what kind of man you would be, Chas?"

Chas leaned back on a downed tree and laughed.

"What do you mean, the kind of man I want to be?"

"Work on the railroad, cut timber, be a blacksmith in Grayson or Huntington?"

"I thought of being a banker or running a saloon."

They stood close.

"It doesn't suit you, being all dressed up, behind a counter, or working at a tavern. I see you as a rugged man of the big mountains, roping wild horses and killing bears."

"Alice and Kate. Ladies!" her father yelled from across the field. "Time for supper, ladies."

Alice jumped up from the barn, straw in her hair, kissing Jackie Ray before she buttoned her shirt. Kate raised her hand, strolling back to her house with Chas, laughing and flirting with each other as they ran across the field.

"I might own a saloon or be bank president. Hard to predict any man's future." He stopped and picked a handful of flowers. She loved flowers. "To see me in dark clothes might suit me just fine; see what you think of that, Kate?"

She grabbed his hat, full of flowers, and ran through an open field.

"You would make a great cowboy, Charles Bellew, with those bright blue eyes and new hat."

He mumbled, "Uncle Chet warned me about chasing women with green eyes." She slowed down to let him catch up, out of breath by the time he'd reached the barn. "Kate," said Chas, breathing and laughing, "you impress me."

She walked him through the barn and stopped.

"Kiss me, cowboy," said Kate, smiling. "How's that?"

"Not bad for your first time, Chas," said Kate, laughing.

"First time?" he stepped back. "Ha-ha, you think that was my first kiss?"

The door swung open. "Alice and Kate, supper's getting cold," said her mother. "Let's go, ladies."

Then, Mr. Brooks stepped outside to hug his daughters. He gripped the axe handle, ran his finger slowly down the arch of the blade, and stood in silence, eyes on Chas and Jackie Ray, grinning.

"Good day, sir," said Jackie Ray.

"Gentlemen, gentlemen," said the man. "Stan Brooks. It's good to finally meet two strong lads. God, I can surely sharpen an axe blade, can't I? Look at that edge, young man."

"That would split a thick oak," said Jackie Ray, careful with his words.

"Fine edge, sir," said Chas, finger on the edge. "But this side needs some work."

The young man hesitated when he took his hand and saw the dark eyes of Mr. Brooks turn cold. They looked at each other.

"My wife, Linda, and I, two daughters, of course, spoke about having you two gentlemen over for dinner next Sunday. How about it, boys?" said Mr. Brooks, who whipped the axe into a slab of wood. "Potatoes, chicken and chopping wood, right, boys?"

Chas and Jackie Ray looked at each other and witnessed the older man, hands about the axe, half-drunk, one eye closed.

"Yessir," said Jackie Ray, surprised, head bobbing. "We'd love to have dinner next Sunday. Do ya like good ole bourbon, Mr. Brooks, sir?"

"Yeah, yeah, if you're buying, son," said Mr. Brooks, eyes squinted, pulling the axe from the stump. And he chuckled. "Guess I do favor a snort at bedtime," he said, slowly cutting hair from his left forearm and whipping his axe into a stump again, grunting and staggering.

"Good. I like bourbon myself," said Jackie Ray, with a smile in the corner of his eyes. "Since we are friends, I'll drop some off this week. Had it since my Pa died."

"That is if we're still in town," said Chas, hand on his chin. "We'd love dinner with you and your daughters." His face tilted toward the fading sun. "It's getting late, Jackie Ray, and we gotta run, sir."

"Might have some cards and tea for you boys," said Mr. Brooks. The man winked.

"Looking forward to a good supper, Mr. Brooks," said Chas, hands in his pockets. "And we thank you for the invite, sir."

They saw their breath when the two young men ran up the road, far down the valley, and laughed about Mr. Brooks being drunk. Jackie Ray stopped to rest at a boulder the size of two wagon wheels, and Chas rested beside him.

"He might like us," said Chas.

"What the heck was that all about if we're still in town?" Jackie Ray yanked the shoulder of Chas. "Hey, talk, I'm tired of running! It's rude not to take up a man's invite for dinner with his daughters." He reached for his pocket. "I need some tobacco."

"Those are beautiful ladies back yonder, goodness, boy, they are natural as honey and eye-catchers," said Chas. "But all I see is castration, Jackie Ray. Two bachelor men cut off from any hope of carrying on the family name."

"Nope. He's a friendly man who knows his bourbon," said Jackie Ray, who stood tall. "And the man likes good company and a late snort. He can't be all bad."

"He'll make you a gelding by Friday night," said Chas. "You get that axe if he catches you and Alice in the barn." He bent and laughed and pointed his hand at his friend's pants and said, "Your barn door is open, bud." He covered his face and laughed.

"Hey, he'll have to catch us in a compromised position first, right?" said Jackie Ray, laughing. Then his face relaxed. "I'm gonna ask you again, bud, what was all that 'if we are in town' bull crap you pulled back there? You know we are always in town."

"Nothing."

"I know there's something. My old man said, when a man says nothing, expect something and soon."

Jackie Ray downed his wet hat, and water fell from the brim. The sun's warmth faded behind the tall mountains, and the evening was gone. The road forked at Straight Creek and Williamson Creek, so the young men divided, and each man walked home.

Jackie Ray's father, Jack Raymond Monroe, was killed at the Battle of Chickamauga and fought alongside troops from Denton and good men from other parts of Kentucky. Jackie Ray's mother refused to pack after he died for Grayson and died of a bad heart in the spring of 1865.

Preacher Chet, Charles, and Carl were born and raised on Straight Creek. Charles, the father of Chas, was a fighter who was killed in Chickamauga, Tennessee. The Lord called Chet into ministry as a missionary, and he had done nothing else in his life but served the church since he was twenty-four. God had always provided for him. Carl Bellew, the youngest of the bunch, was an evil man and moved to Texas after the Civil War.

Later, cornbread and beans were cooked by Preacher Chet when Chas arrived, still muddy from the Sunday rain. Good cuts of fried ham and bacon, coupled with freshly picked greens and black coffee hot brewed on the stove. Uncle Chet saved the best meals for Sunday supper so he could spend his day with his nephew.

"Good message today, Uncle Chet, except for the storm and the muddy creek."

"Worst thunderstorm I've seen since your Daddy was killed, but it saved your tail and got you to the altar on time, didn't it?"

"Yeah."

"Scared the daylight out of the congregation, too. People jumped up and down when the lightning popped and cracked." The tubby man blessed the meal and stacked more cornbread and bacon inside his hands. He chewed the bacon and talked. "I loved your father and miss him very much. He was my favorite brother, too. Carl and I never saw eye to eye on anything. The meanest man I have ever seen in my life. He was lazy and cursed the world when I went off to seminary school, and he had to labor my part on the farm."

"Pa has been dead for ten years. Hard to believe." He stared into his empty plate, then sipped coffee, face slim and ghostly white.

"Loved your father, and I hated Carl Bellew!" He stabbed the table, sniffing and gritting his teeth. "I graduated from Divinity School at Bacon College in 1851, twenty years ago," said Chet, nodding and chewing. "I saw Carl in Waco, Texas, back in the summer of 1862." Bacon crunched in Chet's mouth. "Carl was not a man who valued me or Charles. Carl is evil to the bone, so I'm glad he moved on."

Chas broke his cornbread and listened.

"You never spoke of Carl much."

"Seven years apart from Carl Bellew, a bit of a wild cat, more of an outlaw type and a man with no manners. We're not friends. Never were as kids, either. Not close like me and your father were growing up."

"What caused him to ride west to Texas?"

"Spanish woman, gold, cattle, I reckon." The pastor clasped his hands. "He wanted to see the Wild West, be a cowboy, and he's the luckiest man alive," said Chet, who poured more coffee and held it. "He made it big in Texas, I guess."

Blue eyes filled with curiosity, Chas tilted his fine jaw and leaned back in his chair.

"Is he still in Texas?"

"Yeah, I reckon. I wrote to him when your father died out of respect. No other reason." The preacher wiped tears from his red eyes, "He wrote back, said your father fought for the wrong side, and he said your father should have been a Yankee soldier, buttoned up as a Blue Blood."

"What part of Texas?"

"He lives in Hewitt," said the preacher. "Carl is a Texan now. Owns 1500 head of cattle and drives them to market in Abilene. Guess he made himself a lucky cowboy and said, "Well, if I died, he'd see me on the other side of Hell. That's the last I heard from that man."

"What makes a man so evil, sir?"

His uncle leaned forward, lips tight.

"Son, he chooses to drink from the well of unhappiness," said Chet, face turned, head shook in discontentment. "When he wakes in the morning and plans to harvest a bucket of sin, the sight of another day makes him hate the faces he sees. He had a blade of hatred as a boy. I have known Carl too long to say anything kind about my worst brother, so I won't."

***

Weeks later, Chas lit a candle upstairs and studied his figure in a broken mirror; and his face was black from a hard day's labor. The bawl of a cow poked holes in his imagination about being on horseback in Texas, high riding on the rim of some canyon. Rifle in hand, lips dry, and Chas saw himself on the banks of the Brazos River. He saw tornadoes and how the wind rolled across Central Texas and cattle pressed further west. Time and cattle moved steadily across the Devil's Backbone in Central Texas, and he felt the sun burn a hole atop his hat. Chas thought about driving Longhorns and prodding a thousand head of cattle from Waco to the cattle market in Fort Worth. He drew a good picture of a Texas Longhorn on a page and pondered about a land he'd like to dust his boots on soon.

He told himself, "Texas, that's where the real cowboys ride after the war." He brushed his hair three different ways and steadied his eyes in the mirror. "I can see myself in a new pair of boots, slick Texan hat, saddled on atop a black horse in San Anton, headed for the Stockyards of Tarrant County or somewhere else."

After supper on the first Sunday in March 1871, Chas kicked up his legs, and the fireplace popped with dry wood, and he talked more with his Preacher Chet on the Lord's Day than any other time of the week. His home was always open to visitors. I knocked on the door.

"Atohi," said Preacher Chet, who looked through the small opening in the door. "Come in, get in here and eat," he said, smiling.

Did I miss the soup dinner?" I spoke.

"Plenty of soup left," said Preacher Chet.

"Words I like to hear!" I said excitedly.

Chas talked half the day about Texas and cattle. I could tell when a man was troubled and had something on his mind, and an ember of thought and curiosity burned inside of him, and he was full of questions about Texas. I felt the young man was about to reveal his plans.

"Heard about some raiders in Mount Savage, Uncle Chet," said Chas, seated at the hearth. "Two men stole money and chickens from the Blackstone Farm on Thursday night."

"They will keep moving on, farm to farm, and the devil is always moving and working at night," said Chet, eyes closed, half asleep.

"They'll steal a few things, ride out, and keep stealing until they get shot. That's the best thing for a thief."

"They'll patch themselves up," I said. "Find something new to steal in the next town. Sorry way of life."

"I can find those guys," said Chas, who stood and smiled and had a smile in his eyes. "Jackie Ray knows their hideout and saw 'em both. Bet there's a big reward for two outlaws in Grayson."

"You will get yourself shot or killed, boy!" I told him. "What they want is a gunfight. You are too young to be messing around with outlaws."

"I ain't no boy!"

"I meant you haven't proven yourself with a gun yet. There's no reward for a bunch of carpetbaggers. Sit down, Chas!" said Preacher Chet, knocking his chair over.

"This is my big chance, Uncle Chet."

"You are making me nervous spinning a loaded revolver in my house. You are too young to compete with a bunch of proven Civil War veterans. They are pure outlaws, Chas. Sit down."

I wet my lips with a tall bottle and wanted to say more. Chas was about twenty-one or twenty-two when I had that soup and listened to them disagree. Chet was right as usual; Chas was unproven with firearms. That was not my home, and Chas was not my nephew. He was my good friend, though. I cared enough to look after him.

"Chas, that's good stuff." I tucked something into a small bag and sat it behind a stack of books. "Is that bourbon from Jackie Ray's house?"

"Yeah," said Chas, who sat down at the table. "How did you know, Atohi?"

"Everybody knows his family are scalawags and drunks!" said Preacher Chet, who overheard the conversation. "Rumors spread wide and far, and people gossip when there's a low-life paddling hooch on Straight Creek." His uncle planted his feet on the floor, stood flat-footed, and said, "When did you start drinking, anyways, Chas?"

"When my father was killed," said Chas, taking another snort, sniffing. "Death makes a young man like leather and some flavor. My veins have become cold toward evil, and I watch my back more than I did years ago, even as a sinner."

"What? You say you have been drinking since you were ten years old!" said Chet, surprised. "O God help you, son. I thought you had put this world behind you. You got yourself redeemed today."

"Sadness cannot be washed away from a young man's mind in one Sunday sermon, sir," said Chas, arm turned to his uncle. "Plus, I still need to be washed in the blood."

"Drinking hooch has never solved anything," said the pastor, examining the color of the bourbon in the bottle. "You think since you're a big man, you can drink your problems away, tote a revolver, huh? Bourbon and bullets never solved anything. Think you are better than Jesse James, huh?"

Chas paced around the room, tucked one hand under his armpit, and his neck turned red.

"You think you can preach and pray your problems away, Uncle Chet, huh?" said Chas, "Being saved doesn't make my problems go away. It seems nothing new has happened to me."

His uncle charged him to the center of the log cabin and pushed his hat off his head.

"Not always, son!" yelled Chet. "My problem is you, the way you provoke me!" His teeth shone, and he pressed his fist against his nephew's shoulders.

Chas stepped back.

"Hands off me!" said Chas, neck turned red. "Men died in the Civil War who prayed the same as you did." He walked to the doorway. "That didn't work for either side during the big war, did it, preacher? They prayed. They humbled themselves. They felt redemption. One side prayed against the other, and men still died in the line of battle. The problems of a man will not disappear because of his faith and prayer. They just get worse because of the nature of sin."

"Men who fight battles are exposed to cannons and guns, but when one slug fired in hatred, it will kill a redeemed man, same as anyone else," said the preacher, who tried to find the right words to say. "Brothers and fathers make young men like yourself curious and restless to fight and to finish the job of your father who'd fallen in battle. I begged him not to volunteer. The problem is, life gets worse when men are far from God." His eyes of truth found his nephew in agreement. "Ever since you have become a son left behind by a senseless Civil War, that's when life changed you, and you don't feel different, huh?" Chet held his coffee close to his face, eyes steady, and he said, "Atohi, I need that bourbon."

"I don't think you do," I said. "Why do you say those words?"

"Lost on the sauce. Sin. Anger," Chet told us.

We crowded around the table. I overheard Chas and Chet talk for a while, and they apologized to each other. Chet did not strongly drink, either. I listened as they spoke about the Civil War, building pine boxes, and shooting guns. There was no better man to share time with than Chet Bellew, who chopped wood, read Scripture, ran barbed wire up steep hillsides, and broke green horses. He came to Christ in his mid-twenties after his seventh bare-knuckle fight in Kentucky, mainly to raise money for his first church, known as the "Pope of the Right Cross," in the mountains. His fists had resolved many problems, and he hated the thought of some who tried to take advantage of him.

"We can do away with the lawless," said Chas, who stood at the window. "Is that what the Word says, Chet? Is it an eye for an eye in the Old Testament? Leave some wrath for the Lord in the New Testament, right?"

"Yeah. I taught you well, Chas."

The preacher found the Scripture verse by the lantern. "It's not the best way, but I have done it between here and Texas. I can't say that I was always a redeemed man. Anger was my biggest problem."

Chet held his nephew's shoulder tight, and he tilted his head toward the door and said, "Where's your revolver, Chas?"

"Why?" said his nephew.

"Someone has been stealing from the barn," said Chet, the revolver spun in his hands. "I have turned my cheek for the last dang time! I counted two saddles, one good saw, the one owned by my grandfather, and a heck of an axe, all missing."

"What are you doing?" I spoke. My hand was on the door.

"They are big thieves, Atohi," said Chet, grinning. "Watch out from the door, please!" He blew out the lantern. We all stepped outside.

"See, there's no one out here," I said, voice low.

"Listen," Chas said, and his eyes searched.

We all did.

"A thief must be punished, Atohi," said Chet. With his dark coat around his back, the preacher paced across the porch jumped to the ground, and whispered, "My father hated a thief. The best thief is underground, and a man who does not work steals for a living is just taking up good space."

We stepped across the yard, and light appeared inside the barn. Tools from Chet's blacksmith days rattled.

"Robber," said Chas, arm extended to the barn.

Chas pointed his gun at the barn. I stood low behind the wagon. Preacher Chet waited at the doorway, broadsided, hidden in the shadows, and suddenly, fog lifted from the stream to the barn. The night was cold. I was with Preacher Chet when several men followed, and he was the last person they trailed, and he defended himself for much less than what he'd spoken about over coffee.

Preacher Chet stepped in the doorway and smiled.

"Pow!"

The thief fell to the ground, got up a wounded man, and ran the length of the barn, and the robber was outside in the dark screaming for help. I am not sure how anyone could have found their target in that dark night.

"Pow!" Preacher Chet's gun smoked. Then, a third shot was fired. "I got him good, Chas!" said Chet, shoulder against a post.

"You're bleeding, Preacher Chet," I said, hands outstretched. He fell into my arms. "Sir, you alright?"

The preacher dropped, body doubled over, and he rested in the hay. "This is not my first bullet, boys," said Preacher Chet, hand on his side, face in pain, and his eyes were hidden under his dark hat.

"But I hit that dang thief and hit him good, boys," said the preacher. His eyes opened wide, and he said, "Who's the robber, boys?"

I flipped over the robber.

"Mr. Brooks!" I ran back inside and told the preacher. "I would have bet my good horse on a crook like him."

"I knew it." The preacher whispered, moaning, voice faded low. "Take the farm, Chas. Find my brother in Texas, tell Carl that I am sorry, and I hope he finds God."

"You'll make it, Uncle Chet," said Chas, arms around the preacher. "You got my word, though." Chas wept and held his uncle.

"I see the lights of glory," said Preacher Chet, grinning, head tilted. Blood ran down his best Sunday shirt. "My wife is calling me for dinner, Chas. Headed home, Atohi. Love you, boys." His eyes found us both for the last time.

My heart cracked and was never the same after the night of the robbery.

I held his hand, and Chas held his shoulder. The preacher faded away between us. We had lost a great part of our lives that night.

"He's home, Chas," I said, weeping.

"Nooo!" yelled Chas.

Somewhere between my words to Chas, the world lost a good man, and heaven gained a saint. Chet was truly home, resting in the home he'd spoken in his sermons, and he'd finally found it. I watched Chas close his uncle's thin eyes, and we knew the world had lost a great friend.

"I didn't care too much for his sermons, anyway," said Stan Brooks, laughing.

His jaw was struck by my right hand.

"How would you know your face was never at the Presbyterian church?" I said.

After I chimed the bell of Stan Brooks, the man met Jesus not long after his pilferage in the barn. Deep down, I hoped the Lord cleaned his temple, and John the Baptist prepared the way for him.

Lightning struck the ground where the thief had moaned and crawled, but Stan Brooks failed to object against the church, and his hands lifted nothing else. I bet Hell held a special place for dirty dogs and robbers, men such as him.

Later, out of the fog stepped a black horse and rider with a bucket in his hand. The rider wheeled his reigns and circled his horse as if he knew we were at the barn. "Hey, Chas, your barn door is open, bud," said Jackie Ray, laughing.

"We have serious times, Jackie Ray," said Chas.

He dismounted his horse and stood in the dark.

"I need to talk seriously to Preacher Chet about the Lord and Heaven, Chas," said Jackie Ray, being followed by his horse. "Got some questions for the preacher man."

"My uncle is dead, Jackie Ray," said Chas, who washed blood from his hands and face by the well in front of the barn.

"So you have been washed in the blood, Chas," I said, surprisingly.

"Did Stan Brooks shoot Preacher Chet?" asked Jackie Ray, who removed his hat.

"Both men are dead," I said, arms folded.

I am Atohi, and this is the story of my family.

Chapter 2
Blood Brothers

The evening was still and foggy as Chas Bellew stood in the doorway of an empty log cabin built by his Uncle Chet in 1852. Chas and I listened to green frogs croaking in the mud, like an unskilled symphony, who acted like they knew Uncle Chet had passed away, and more creatures sounded like a choir from the valley. It was a sad time for songs and to be alone, anyway.

Streams merged at the fork in the valley and rolled rapidly downhill to Denton, Kentucky, our first spring rain alone without the Godly voice of Chet Bellew directing our journey. So, in the quiet times, we noticed nature more than usual, such as chicken hawks, crows, and birds in flight at twilight. Hounds chased rabbits and raccoons into the blackness of the dense woods, and the animals spent the night on the hunt. Chas mounted his dark horse, Black Sam, the one he had traded for the year before, and rode under silver moonlight. We listened to hounds trail raccoons, valley to ridge, crossing over the next ridge until the dogs could no longer be heard and we could close our eyes.

"Just let the hound run, Atohi," said Chas, mounted on horseback. "Let them work out their own sin toward raccoons."

"Sometimes, you must let the dog run his own race and learn how to be a hunter. See you in the morning, blood brother."

"Sleep well, Atohi."

I had known Chas Bellew since he was a young boy. It was the time Buchanan was president. Anyway, it was the year I left my Cherokee land in North Carolina for Kentucky. I could see Chas from my track of land still slowly pacing Black Sam into the barn. Preacher Chet had welcomed this Cherokee writer to his land and church after the Civil War. However, I refused to live like the white man in a log cabin, and there was little sleep beside the horse barn, anyway. So, young Chas helped me build a more traditional home out of rock and clay. My Cherokee name is Atohi, which means "In the woods," and not into the log cabin.

Across the mountain from Preacher Chet and Chas, I had my own land, my homeplace, property given by the Bellew family, and I felt at home. Land that could never be taken away by the white man, a land free from evil spirits and mostly free from barking dogs and smelling cows.

I saw how Chas was haunted and broken when he left the Bellew Cemetery that afternoon at sundown, uncle and father buried. We were two blood brothers grafted with broken promises, and my friends were buried no more than the length of a spear apart, resting in the sunlight. The Great Spirit ushered them into Heaven with peace and joy. Each man's headstone angled toward the West to feel the warmth of the evening, like the end of a hard day with coffee as we watched the sun disappear.

My ears heard voices that made a man stall and listen, calling voices more native to the West. Will I see the Wild West? I asked the voice. There was no answer.

War cries and brokenness had no boundaries in a man's head, and there was no hiding from the past. I'm not sure why Chas decided to bury the preacher in a blazing hot sun. The rock of the earth was hard at high noon, and I dug for hours and hours because Preacher Chet Bellew, as close as he was to others in the community, was my greatest friend. But the ground was still hard during the day. Friends or no friends, ground was ground, rock was rock, and my back hurt from the labor. The Great Spirit of the Calling Voice said not to dig in the open air of the day. I sat in the dirt and hoped "digging angels" would offer a hand to a Cherokee man, but no angel did. The Lord sent no angels to help with the digging. Since the Lord called no one to my side, I dug at night, and the earth broke easier by the light of the moon, but it was still hard earth, and the nights were cool in the spring of 1871.

Beans and water were my friends on the mountain. Chas was at the home of Kate, kissing. Lonesome after dark, the sound of a barn owl hooting high in a tree was a friend of Chas, and that is why he kept his open window to the noise of natural things. He spoke a lot about how his Uncle Chet taught him to fish and hunt and learn more than just animal names but how to survive in the wild. I could have taught him a better way, the way of the Cherokee tradition, but young men are stubborn fools. He recognized trees and plants by sight and how to live off the land and rely on the Lord, too. Picture books of artwork were flat pages on the kitchen table. Other pages were of chalk and pencil drawings of owls and other birds, signed by his uncle's hand, a man of redemption who could write and draw with either hand.

Chas was crazy about maps but not as crazy as his friend Jackie Ray Monroe. Each morning, Jackie Ray showed up to work with us on the farm, and he could never make it at Sunup, so we painfully waited on him each morning, men in angst.

"Hey, Chas," said Jackie Ray. The front porch creaked, and the door slapped when he knocked. "Chas, you home?"

He stood at the door.

"Yeah, Jackie Ray, you are early, bud." said Chas, legs crossed." Come in," eyes popping. "Come in, piano player. Where in the heck did you get that ugly hat?"

"Ugly hat? It is the new style from the city, they say," said Jackie Ray, grinning. "My gambler's hat, bud, is one to be admired, and it's not ugly." He spun it on his hand. "I will forgive you for those fighting words. This hat, right here, well, it's black leather and handmade by a true gambler from Chattanooga, Tennessee. Look."

"I like the hat, Jackie Ray!" I said as I admired myself in the mirror. "Who was the lady that sold you this hat, holding you inside that private room?"

"Umm, I swear she was a third-generation palm reader, and her name was Claire Voyance," said Jackie Ray, face tight, rubbing his mustache.

"Claire Voyance, huh?" I held that ugly hat.

"Yeah, yeah, Claire Voyance, that was her name, Atohi." Jackie Ray scratched his head and chased his memory.

"Boy, that's a fine name for a seeker, right?" said Chas, laughing.

"It sure the heck is," said Jackie Ray, taking back his hat. "And man, she pretty as a dancer when she takes off her eye patch."

"A seeker with an eye patch, huh?" I said, and could not hold my gut from laughing any longer.

My friend with the ugly hat smiled, face in the mirror, humming, and we told Jackie Ray no different. We let him believe that her name was the one that her parents had given her.

"Claire Voyance makes a fine hat," said Chas, brim bent on his own hat, and his eyes smiled from across the room, coffee in his hand.

"There's no demand for a gambler's hat in the mountains, Jackie Ray," I told the young man.

"Claire Voyance said you'd say those very words of jealousy," said Jackie Ray. "I paid her well to hear the truth, and here it is among my friends. Jealousy."

"You think I have envy!" I said.

"Yessir." Said Jackie Ray, hat over his heart. "My eyes see the pangs of pure jealousy among us this morning."

I paced toward the man with the ugly hat.

"Hey, Atohi, we got work to do. Let him alone, Cherokee."

"Yeah, Cherokee, he knows his place." Jackie Ray said, grinning.

"I'm about to place my foot…" I told him.

Interrupting me, Chas yelled, "Atohi, let it go!"

"Claire Voyance said that good style on a man is rare, like pearls and diamonds on a puppy," said Jackie Ray, adjusting his coat. "Hey, sure, there's a need for style in the mountains, Cherokee." Jackie Ray insisted. "If Jesus would have had a hat this fine, our Savior would have had it with him on the cross, gents." The boy who admired his face in the mirror had tilted his hat over his eyes and combed dark hair again and grinned, just as if he'd found pearls and diamonds on Straight Creek.

"Wish Uncle Chet was here to pray for that gambler's hat," said Chas, and he poured more coffee and handed me a cup.

I held out my arms like Christ.

"Lord, let this ugly hat and cup pass from me," I said.

Chas spilled his coffee when he laughed.

"Boys, go ahead, laugh it up, make fun. Claire Voyance said there would be strife and envy among friends over this gambler's hat. At first, Claire didn't want to part with the hat; said it had been in her family for years. I offered her double what it was worth, so I convinced her to make a sale. She said she saw that coming. Tell me she ain't the best seeker you've seen, boys."

With a straight face, he added, "It was her honesty that sold me to beat it all."

"Honesty, huh?" I said and looked at Chas behind my coffee cup. I felt Jackie Ray had given away his marbles in the private room, and his money followed shortly after his marbles.

I mumbled, "Claire Voyance. Claire Voyance."

"Hush, Cherokee. Stop it right there!" said Jackie Ray. "If you say her name three times, she might appear. I don't think it's such a good idea, Atohi."

"Maybe, Jackie Ray, out of respect, I'll stop," I replied.

"Thank you. This powerful hat needs no more prayer, gents," said Jackie Ray, walking around. "It's a true work of art." He adjusted the brim in the mirror, down on his forehead, tilting his head and teeth shone, and said, "Plus, this hat is my good luck charm to win as a big-time gambler."

That's what Jackie Ray paid to hear in the Chattanooga Witch Doctor's private room.

"Atohi, she has feathers from an Eagle," said Jackie Ray, face as serious as a member of the church. "You should see had a crystal ball and everything."

"Atohi could have told you the truth about the ugly hat for free, Jackie Ray," replied Chas, face long when my friend laughed.

"I could have told you the truth for half the cost of that hat," I said. "But I like the hat better on you than me."

"I knew you could get over your place of envy and strife, of course, if you put your heart into it, Atohi," Jackie Ray said it with a slow voice.

***

Later, we huddled around the fire, and Jackie Ray told more stories about restless women in Chattanooga. Chas lit a lantern, and the candles waved and righted when the door slapped from the windstorm that whipped into Carter County. Jackie Ray's jaw stopped chewing beans, and he grabbed his pistol and checked for another thief. No one was there.

"The hound," I said and pointed at the door.

"We have not seen each other much since Preacher Chet passed away," I said, and the fire warmed my hands. "

"Place looks like a bat cave, Chas. Dust. Mud. Do you own a broom?" I thumbed the tabletop.

"It's been two weeks since Uncle Chet died," said Chas, head up. "I was a better man when he was alive."

"No offense," said Jackie Ray, hat off, "but all he did, Chas, was tell you how you needed to prove yourself and experience life like he did when he was your age."

"He was more than that." I insisted. "He was a man that you could depend on when it rained, and it rains trouble every day in this world."

"Atohi is right," Chas told us. "He gave more of himself than any man I know. All I have are memories of death. Maps and drawing keeps me company when my dog hunts. Uncle Chet did his best to teach us how to live in Kentucky, but you both are right."

"I find my advice to be relatively useful, like a squirrel who finds his nuts and eats them. I should've been like Aristotle, boys, right?" said Jackie Ray, the man who thought he could have taught college.

"I am sure that was painful for the squirrel," I said, closing my eyes to rest. "What's the plan, men?" I said, lips tight, head canted toward my friends.

Jackie Ray snapped his fingers and said, "What you need is to marry Kate, get a life, get a wife, have a boy, cousin. Teach your son how to hunt and trap and pass on the tradition. Keep the mountaineer's life alive, just like your forefathers did. Your Pa and Uncle Chet were legends in Kentucky and known as far as Texas."

"I got dreams of my own," said Chas, who slapped his revolver and held his coffee. "I can no longer stay in these Kentucky hills. I need to see a few places so I can tell my son what life is like beyond Denton."

"What dreams, Chas?" I said and sat up straight. "I know you have big dreams. Adventure that is what you want, right?" I walked over to the kitchen table. "Heck," laughing at my best friend, "I dreamed last night that I rescued seven Cherokee women from a burning building."

"Do you get burnt, Atohi?" asked Jackie Ray, head titled.

"It was a.." I thought, but I was kind with my words. "No, friend, I was without an injury."

"You're a lucky man!" said Jackie Ray, hand extended.

"Did I say it was a dream, Chas?" I was confused.

"Yeah."

Jackie Ray jumped up and said, "I bet you Claire Voyance could decipher that dream for you, Atohi."

"I will keep that in mind," I said. "I am pretty sure the dream was about seven women, seven horses, or seven days. Something like that."

"I get it," said Chas, and he finally cleaned.

"Hey, what you need, Atohi," said Jackie Ray, hand pointed, "is a deeper measure of what Claire Voyance has to say about your desires for a nice woman. You should not covet another man's mule. It's a verse in Scripture."

"I won't," I told him with confidence. "I believe my dreams are natural for a man and somewhat predictable."

"My dream is to ride, take a long trip away from here," Chas said, mumbling.

"Found gold nuggets in Charlotte, North Carolina. Might get you rich and famous." Jackie Ray waved his fork and said, "They dig coal in West Virginia, boys, and mining. That's a real adventure."

"My horse is aimed to the West, Jackie Ray?" said Chas, with an honest face, and his boots were in his hands, toes out of his socks.

I saw my friend work his chin and famous eyes a few times and nodded; he settled his face, and I knew an honest face. We had many good days in our time in Kentucky, but I was no Claire Voyance, gold digger, or coal miner.

"Listen," said Jackie Ray, chewing his beans. "You got a lady who keeps you warm on weekends, so why do you need to run off, find trouble out in the Wild West? You're gonna get yourself killed by some drunk bandits!" He covered his face, hands dirty from a day with an angry green broke horse.

"I guess you might be right," said Chas, who stood and walked around the room, toes eating his socks. "Well, I could take Mad Bill Benning with me to Texas. That man is a good shot, too."

I loved to see Chas when he poked the bear.

"Mad Billy Benning!" shouted Jackie Ray, eyes rolling, and he threw his hat across the room. "He's scared of a mouse, bud!" said Jackie Ray. "He can't stand in a washtub and hit the bottom without shooting his toes off." He stopped chewing.

"He's an ace with a buck knife, though," I said, just to stir the pot. "Useful man."

"Forget that dream, Chas. Get married, bud, and bring that dream to life at home," said Jackie Ray. "No rings yet, but Alice likes my rugged way of livin', and she's hungry for a mountain man. You know what I'm aiming at, right?"

"Yeah, I know," said Chas. "I know you are not partial to Mad Bill and his mountain man skills."

"Lots of good years left, you know what I mean?" said Jackie Ray, cocking his chin. "I'm the best-lookin' man in Carter County."

"I have not heard your name mentioned, but I heard other stories about Shetland Pony, per se," I said, smiling.

"Women pull their hair back and say 'Jackie Ray is a handsome man, momma,' and I treat 'em right," said Jackie Ray. "So, I have to court a few ladies... and decide when I'll settle down after the next crystal ball.

I paid ahead for her to find out, too. She is studying my future endeavors, so she said, and needed a little to get by."

"Ugly or handsome, women will keep looking for a good man while you two ride out West," I said and held the coffee pot. I stirred the milk and said, "While you are dreaming here and Claire rubs her crystal ball, I will be sharing dessert and buying gifts for all the ugly women who need love from a lonely Cherokee."

"This Cherokee has had too many peace pipes," said Jackie Ray, bending over laughing.

"Texas," said Chas. "That is where I headed, men."

"Texas!" yelled Jackie Ray. His eyes stared into the warm fireplace, and he chewed on day-old cornbread. His eyes widened, and he stretched out toward the flames. "I swear, Chas, you ride to Texas, and men will be at Kate's door the day you leave Denton. What do you aim to get out of the trip to Texas, anyways, huh?"

"I'll take what I can get," said Chas.

"You will get tricked by the locals!" said Jackie Ray, slapping his leg.

"I guess Tom Buck will help Alice with her horses while you are gone to your crystal ball," said Chas, who grinned.

I remembered how Alice had a crush on Tom Buck three years earlier, in 1868, and I saw Jackie Ray's neck flash red when the name Tom Buck was mentioned. Some folks thought they would jump the broom. Jackie Ray was the right man for her, though. They were both right, and a woman won't wait too long for a man when someone else is picking her daisies.

"You had to go and mention Tom Buck, didn't ya!" yelled Jackie Ray. "You're tryin' to piss me off, bud?" He rolled his eyes and slapped the table. "Jesus, Tom Buck, he ain't no help on a farm. His little arms can't tote a feed sack across the general store without calling me for help."

"I guess Atohi will ride with me, right?" said Chas, face looking for an agreement.

"Am I invited, huh?" I said, nodding. "Yeah, I guess you need a good scout." I leaned forward for an answer.

Chas held his rifle, door opened, long arm pointed west.

"Don't need no deadweight holdin' us up complaining when we are getting up early on a hunt in Texas," said Chas, who walked across the room. "I hope both of you good men will ride to Texas with me, though."

Jackie Ray stood, adjusting his gambler's hat, coat on his arm.

"You are dead on chasin' your dream, huh, Chas Bellew?" said Jackie Ray, tapping his gambler's hat.

"Mark it down," said Chas, "I will leave shortly for Texas. Uncle Chet took three trips to Texas. I aim to follow his map and do what he did. I have some things already packed for the trip."

"We've been friends since we walked mules together on Palm Sunday, Chas," said Jackie Ray, hands on his buckle, "and I am proud to be invited, but..."

"But, Jackie Ray, you mean your horse won't make it to Texas," I said.

"My horse can ride as good as your horse!" yelled Jackie Ray.

"You're welcome to say go, put the animal to the test," I said.

"Are you going to leave that lady, Jackie Ray," said Chas, "ride off in confidence?

"Hey, looks like Chas has made up his mind, and it's Texas," I told both of them.

They locked eyes and laughed at each other. Each one with his own ideas about life and adventure. And my own were unspoken. I could see anticipation in their eyes, but wanted to hear their words.

"The ladies will wait on us, Chas, that is, if they really love us and aim to marry us," said Jackie Ray, laughing at himself. "I am a man of too many choices when it comes to Carter County women."

"Choices?" said Chas. "Name three ladies, huh?"

"Now, Chas, I don't aim to put you on the spot," said Jackie Ray, grinning. "Don't wanna talk right now."

"The choice is stay or go," I said. "You can't take women to Texas. If they love you, they'll wait on you two cowboys to change a baby's bottom. The choice is yours: ride or stay home."

"Chas, can you ride the open plains of Texas, shoot some outlaws, and leave that beautiful lady in Denton for a year or two," said Jackie Ray, checking his hat in the mirror.

"Are you going to ride out West or not, Jackie Ray?" asked Chas, who listened. "Stop beatin' around the bush."

Jackie Ray covered his face with his hat and moaned and groaned.

"Jesus, guys, two long years, Chas, two long, long years, huh?" said Jackie Ray, hat on his chest, and he held the door. "Thank you, my friend, for supper, but I just cannot ride to Texas right now."

"You might find another place to eat, Jackie Ray," said Chas, "well, I will lock the cabin on Saturday morning, give my dog to Kate, or to some old timer who can hunt him a few times a week until I get back."

"Until we get back," I said, holding the door.

The face of Chas was as serious as a graveside service. "Saturday morning at Sunup, if you see this Cherokee with me, we are packed for Texas. See if Alice will let you join us, Jackie Ray. That lady will wait," said Chas.

"Or she won't, huh, Jackie Ray?" I said, grinning. "She might enjoy pie with another man."

I remember how we walked out on the porch.

"Two days, Chas," said Jackie Ray, sighing. "You might be gone for two years, cousin."

"See you when we get back, Jackie Ray," I said, slapping his shoulder.

"Well, I will spend my last night with Kate on Friday," said Chas. "Atohi said his horse is packed and ready, so we will ride out on Saturday morning. Sunup."

"Long way to Texas, men," I said. "No one waits for me."

"You watch your back in Texas, Cherokee," said Jackie Ray, shaking hands. "You got that look in your eyes, so I know you well enough to say that you two men ain't kidding about this ride."

"I don't kid about death and dreams," I said and walked around.

All three of us men stood on the long front porch of the cabin and looked out over the farmland and talked about what Texas must be like and if it was like Kentucky or some dry land that everyone had to see at least once.

"If you stay, take my hound, Jackie Ray," said Chas, "hunt him as much as you can."

"I will sleep on it and talk to Alice," said Jackie Ray, who downed his gambler's hat and leaned on the porch post, not sure about the trip.

"We won't be at church Sunday, Jackie Ray," said Chas. He didn't smile, lips tight, a man with certainty in his eyes. "We are going."

"You will be here," said Jackie Ray. "Kate won't let you go far, will she?"

"I promise you, I won't be here, and she don't own this man," said Chas, who stepped down to the ground.

Jumping off the porch, "I'm headed West, Jackie Ray Monroe, bud!" I said, in assurance. "I am the best-looking scout in Carter County, and my horse will easily make it to Texas! How about you?"

"I'm curious," said Jackie Ray, removing his hat. "What reason do you have to ride so far away, huh?" He looked beyond the mountains.

"I got reasons to be in Texas, Jackie Ray. Big reasons! See a Cattle drive, for one, and learn more about the things the preacher saw as a young man," said Chas, arm waving.

"Open plains. Land. Cattle, huh?" said Jackie Ray, hand on his chin.

"I can see a thousand head of cattle in front of my horse. God knows they're no better place to be after the Civil War than Texas. All those Spanish women are waiting for your crystal ball, Jackie Ray. They say we are in some post-war Reconstruction after thousands of men were killed and a million horses died. Things must change. Gettysburg and Manassas and a hundred other places on the map are growing."

The hound dog ran up to Chas, and he rubbed the ears of the dog. It seemed to me like the hound knew we were about to be without him and far away from the hunt.

Jackie Ray mounted his horse, pulled the reins, and reared his favorite horse a few times.

"Show off!" I told him.

"We leave Saturday at Sunup," said Chas. "Pack your bags and join us, cousin. Leave all this Carter County politics and pseudo-romance behind you for a while and play that piano."

Jackie Ray yelled, "You are two crazy men! I just can't go."

Later, Chas rolled a pocket map across the kitchen table, and his hand followed the wagon train trails with his finger. Hundreds of men, men who had known, old timers, men who had dodged death, trailed across the Wild West for gold and land and who fought Indians crossed our minds. Some became legends. Towns were built like Denton, Grayson, Louisville, and St. Louis. All of these towns, places he'd seen, were written down by Chet Bellew.

Beside a lantern, I saw the blue eyes of Chas run across the page, and how his hands angled southward beyond Missouri and Oklahoma, and how he marked rivers and big towns along the cattle drive, the trails his uncle saw years earlier, where people became redeemed by the Good News of the Gospel. We spoke of forts and Chiefs and generals and how wagons were defended against outlaws. Chet told how he loved Louisiana and Texas and would see them again. Chas arched his hand across the paper, and nothing would be in his way headed West, a man out to prove himself. We expected to face no different life for ourselves, a hard life, but would we return home.

Chapter 3
The River

Less than a mile from his log cabin Kate Brooks knew Chas Bellew, inside and out, the good and bad, and she knew what he dreamed about and why he had nightmares, too. His hound, Dan, barked and followed Chas, nose down, and prowled around with an endless passion to hunt until they reached Kate's home. The front of her property had roses and lilies, blooming flowers along the fence and horses were tied to posts. Lots of visitors came to Straight Creek for revival. To the West, two small towns, Mount Savage and Grayson, and east were the rugged mountains of Kentucky and the Mountain State of West Virginia.

Kate's mother, Linda, was still broken and embarrassed about the way her husband had died. His life was a lie. Stan Brooks was considered a thief, and the man who shot Preacher Chet Bellew and the man of God defended himself in the spring of 1871. Chas barely had the heart to keep her chores up on the farm since the shootout. I remember it being the only year that we did not farm the land together.

Hat in his hand, Chas gave the door a knock of courtesy and respect, and Kate somehow knew he would show up.

They saw him ride down the hill.

"Chas, come in," said Mrs. Brooks.

There was a glow of serenity and peacefulness on Kate's land, and it had always been that way, but not on that day.

"You should leave right now!" said Kate. "How could you, Chas Bellew?" Tears rolled down Kate's face as she ran him out the door. "Need some time to express my feelings, Ma."

"Take as long as you need, honey," said her mother and held her daughter. "How could you, Chas?"

Hands raised on his hat, Chas said, "What did I do now?"

"You are going to ride off to Texas without saying goodbye, right?" Kate said, face wet. "Leave and not talk about where you are going or when you would return home."

"Jackie Ray told you everything, didn't he?" said Chas. "Didn't he? Dang him!" He walked closer to the Kate. "I wanted to tell you in person."

He followed her to the barn as she paced fast, face tired from crying, and her hands cleared her eyes, more than once in a rage. Red covered her green eyes, hair disheveled, and the time had come for her to hear his side of the story. They walked over to the fence, and the horses moved toward them.

"Why do I hear town gossip from Jackie Ray and not you?" She turned her back to him. "Is this Texas trip true? When did this enter your mind, anyway?"

"That's why I'm here, to talk this out and get it out in the open, see what you think." He held her hand, but she withdrew, and her lips were tight. "Something I have to do, Kate, something for me."

"That is a selfish thing to say, Chas," said Kate, tears rolled down her face. "We only have two days together. No more."

"That's right, Kate. I plan to leave early Saturday, pack my horse, and ride out of Kentucky on Black Sam. Got some ground to cover, and I might as well get started." He nodded with a face of certainty.

He propped his boot on the fence rail.

"This relationship will not work, Chas." Her voice was broken, her face wet. "And I hoped it would. I'm sorry. Most good women will settle for a man's compromise, but I won't. Gotta plan of my own. All of us are leaving Denton soon, like you."

***

Not much gets by a good Cherokee, not even the wind or heavy rain, especially when two people parted ways. Chas had no guess about a woman, and neither did any man alive. I could feel the cold of her voice, and it was no different than the last snow that fell that day, and not even the sky could decide to stay blue or grey in Denton, Kentucky. I could blend in with the bark of the trees and made a promise to Preacher Chet Bellew: I was to keep an eye on Chas Bellew, and I kept my promise. I was stationed on the top of the barn, half asleep. My eyes slept when I could find a dry place in the barn, and if there was not a dry place, I had no choice but to call it a bad day.

By the look on the face of Chas, a face of ice, he felt cold, like winter flakes of snow covered him, and it did. Time rolled by, and Chas stared at the mountaintop and turned to the horse pasture, walking and talking to himself. For the first time in a long time, she kissed him, and I saw it from the hay barn. It was a good kiss, too.

"This is it," said Chas, and his hands held her face, "our last day together. You are not strong enough to last a year, are you?"

"Yeah, I can last. Can you?" said Kate. "Jackie said, two years or so. What if a Union captain gets drunk and fires off at the mouth, and you get into a gunfight? Then what?"

"I'll be alright," said Chas, smiling. "Might be two years, but I was hoping you would wait for me." He held her hands. "I was hoping we could start a family when I return. I can work the field and start a grain mill or a lumber yard. My arms are strong and got a good mind about business."

"What about me, Chas? How is my household supposed to survive without my father and… without you?"

"What about you, Kate?" said Chas, who turned his eyes on him. He threw his hat against the barn door. "Mrs. Brooks says the Lord will provide. I don't have all the answers."

"Wait! Wait," said Kate, who dropped her head. "What about us? Are you joking? You going off to God knows where taking whiskey and women upstairs in some dark saloon in St. Louis. I know what happens when sporting women find young men and how they unlock the belt of a soiled dove like yourself to handle his revolver. And you somehow just lose your money and make friends. How will you handle the next woman who winks at you, Chas?"

Hat over his face, Chas grinned and knew how Jackie Ray spent his time in Chattanooga, Tennessee.

"My revolver will stay in my hostler, Kate," said Chas, smiling.

"You will seduce the next lady you see, Chas, like you seduced me. Women are your downfall."

"Seduced you? Women are not my downfall, little lady."

"Remember the river, Chas?"

Some things, the private things, I did not need to hear, but Chas did not know where I scouted.

"O' the river, yeah. I recall the river and Denton mountain."

She rested against his chest and said, "Are you in love with me?"

"Yeah. You have my word and loyalty. And love."

"Or are you in love with the man you think you should be, Chas Bellew?"

I was curious to know his thoughts, not his answer. Her lips puckered, and she needed an answer. That moment was the only moment he had to define himself.

"I am crazy about you. I love you, Kate, like I have never loved another woman. " He stepped back. "But…"

He was about to blow it. I held my breath.

Chas rubbed his thick hair.

"But I must go to Grayson tomorrow, trade some things. Swap. Sell. If I have some luck and get some money for the trip, then I will go to Texas. It has been a family tradition. I got to give Texas a try."

They walked to the front of her house.

"I promise to wait for you until the lilies bloom… next spring. That's it," said Kate, and her smile was sincere. "After the lilies bloom, if you are not back from Texas, I'll know you are not serious about us. I'll marry another. Someone will pick me flowers."

"Fair. Okay," said Chas, nodding and smiling. "That is some luck and some love. I'll hold you to that promise, dear." He kissed her. "Knew you loved me, little lady."

"Chas," said Kate, who stopped and turned. She had stopped crying and said, "If you are not back by spring, I promise you, I'll marry another man."

***

From where I stood in the woods, the stillness of the earth and the quiet of nature were as if Chas jumped into the depths of the rush of a cold river, ice about his neck. I imagined how it was cold in his boots, and his heart was frozen with her words. His long face felt like a winter snow. Thank God for her mother, or he would still be standing outside, left as a snowman. I shook my head and returned to my land. I knew the young man had a rope tied to his heart, and his mind wanted to ride to Texas, just like his father and his uncles had done. I covered my ears when her mother spoke, and her harsh voice was like a worried crow.

"Kate!" yelled her mother. "It's kind of late. Look at the beautiful snow. Chas, are you alright?"

"Yes, Mrs. Brooks." He snapped out of the thought of her with another man.

"Be right there, mother," said Kate, shivering in the spring snow.

Chas walked her to the door. The night was cold, the moon full.

"How about one last kiss, Kate?"

"How about we save it and wait until next year?"

"It will be worth the wait," he told her.

The next day was late as I trailed behind Chas to Grayson and back. The sun melted the snow, and when we returned, it was the same barn owl who welcomed us back home. Chas had a stop to make. I returned his horse to the barn.

"Kate," said Chas, "You home?"

"Yeah," Kate replied. "How did it go in Grayson?"

"Great!" He removed his hat. "The good news is I met a mountain man, fur trader, Grizz Moore, who had been to Texas, spoke of seeing big heron birds at the Rio Grande River, hundreds of free-range cattle along the Brazos River in Waco, Texas, and he even fired upon raging Comanche Indians, hunted around the Pecos River long before he was in the Civil War."

Her long face said that she was not impressed.

"Is this the kinda life you want, Chas Bellew, to be a cowboy, ride the open range?"

"Will you just let me finish?" said Chas, with a face of uncertainty.

"I think we are finished!"

"Hear me out, Kate. Dang it."

Kate crossed her arms, tightened her face, and said, "Don't tell me how you will live or the way you will stay warm with women during cold nights. This is just a trip to enjoy your manhood while I barely survive the next year."

"Hear me, Kate, huh?" said Chas, water bucket in his hands. "Grizz Moore told how the hills in Texas rolled across the thundering countryside, how he saw far away lightning strikes that hit the desert, and how the flatland goes as far as the eye can see. He stood his horse in deep snow, but in the distance was dry, barren land."

"Snow does not worry me, but girly shows and whores happen in big towns. I am not stupid, Chas! You cannot stay true to me for a year and keep your pistol in your pants, huh?

"I can see there is no convincing a stubborn woman, especially a lady unaware about life outside of Kentucky."

"I knew you would not bet me. Chas, you cannot stay true for a year," said Kate, who stopped walking to hear him. "I am more social and cordial about life than you think."

"What's that supposed to mean?"

He walked inside her log home and told her about how Grizz Moore rode his horse into the red hanging cliffs of a Texas canyon, where mesquites buzzed like hummingbirds, and wolves followed him until he fired his rifle at them. Chas told how prairie dogs popped out of the earth like groundhogs lived inside the mountains of Kentucky, how howling coyotes were spooky animals at night, and how trees were no taller than horses on the desert landscape. Grizz Moore told about the canyon of the Sangre de Cristo Mountain range in New Mexico, a place with dew still on it at breakfast, and how he flushed game and bathed among fish and frogs in a wavy pond. Grizz Moore traveled as far west as Oregon and bathed beneath Silver Falls, a mountain waterfall that fell from heavenly clouds; seven eagles rested in tall cedars and watched him disappear under the ice-cold mountain river. Later, he told how Grizz traded with a kind mountaineer from Baileysville, West Virginia, a man with many wounds and scars from the war, and how he had ridden from the beach of the Atlantic Ocean to the Pacific Ocean shore.

Kate walked beside him and listened.

"Sounds like no place for a man considering a family next year, like yourself, Chas."

"I'll be fine."

"A bad man hunts for you, Chas," said Kate, watching it snow. "My uncle wants you dead."

He sat the water bucket in the dirt and asked, "Who's huntin' me, Kate?"

"Pistol Miller-Smith," said Kate, facing him. "The man was released from the Army in Fort Marion, Florida, after seven years of fighting the Indians and Confederate soldiers. He wants you buried."

"Why?"

"You killed my Pa; My father was Pistol Miller-Smith's favorite brother, a close brother, and he plans to do the same to you." She turned around in the doorway. "Go on your way 'for you bring more trouble to my family."

"I did not kill your father," said Chas, who crossed his arms.

"I heard what happened," said Kate. "Preacher Chet pulled the trigger. But to Pistol Miller-Smith, to kill a Bellew, it makes no difference to him who he buries."

Chas reached for her, but she turned away. "In the morning, Kate, I'm gone," said Chas. "Pistol Miller-Smith can follow me and find trouble." The young man removed his hat and spoke with certainty about his intentions to defend himself. "I'm no killer, but I will pull the trigger. And it's all the same to me, too."

She faced him.

"Ma told her brother-in-law the whole story this morning, how it happened," said Kate, who wept. "My uncle said his Henry rifle has no preferences about what "Bellew Boy" takes a bullet, and in due time, guns will settle the score. My mother agreed."

"How do you feel about it?"

"My father is dead. Chas, it is all the same to my mother, too."

She never answered him.

"Tell your mother," Chas said, pointing at the lady in the window watching him, "my heart is broken about what happened to her husband." He mounted his horse and said, "See you next year, Kate."

With her hand over her heart, Kate cried and said, "May the Lord be with you, Chas."

The door slammed.

***

In my smoke-filled home, my eyes were closed, thoughts hung above my head about the Great Spirit, and faces rolled over inside the wavy gray smoke. The land was lush green and full of game in the spring of 1871. The clever owl became my friend and rested on my saddle the night before we left on our journey.

Yapping coyote pups kept my eyes open, but they knew no better than young, hungry hound pups. The worst part was the untamed bitter wind that blew across Carter County and snow spit from cotton clouds that shifted like heavenly doors. The pelt of an ice storm layered long, tall pines and pearl-white snow layered the hillside, nearly a foot deep, high above boot strings. The time was when God showed off his power and covered the landscape in snow. Winter was the worst time we had seen since 1863.

Chas had no grievance against Pistol Miller-Smith, the half-brother to Stan Brooks. The small place in Denton had never seen him before and would not know his face on a poster. However, revealed in my dreams, his face and I danced in smoke while Pistol Miller-Smith rode through the snowy mountains with an evil spirit of death in his heart, like the first kill of the lone wolf. In the wavy smoke, many things came to life, and Pistol Miller-Smith had gathered his old gang; some had served in the Army, and others were promised money for the death of Chas Bellew.

A time of danger drifted over our land, and tracks of many horses were found in the deep snow but disappeared into the High Country of the snow and smoky fog. Outlaws could be followed; five horses carried evil men and an aged dog. Deep down, Pistol Miller-Smith, the man, was the fox in a hen house, and I was the scout, a predator unknown to him.

Chas Bellew needed more help than Jackie Ray Monroe, so it was my time to keep my promise to Preacher Chet, protect Chas, and be his scout and blood brother, too. It was not my choice to volunteer, but from my word, I kept it in the winter of 1871. To be honest, I was a lazy Cherokee scout before I met Preacher Chet, but I had improved somewhat. I remember how I broke a wild, green horse for Chas Bellew, and it was the day we became friends, hands of blood brothers on Quinn McCullen's farm at Mount Savage. Because the Spirit of God said that I could trust him. Preacher Chet said the same, but I like God's voice to confirm in the wilderness.

Chas packed for Texas: Coffee, bacon, deer jerky, razors, bullets, revolvers, and two rifles, one handed down to him the last day he saw his Pa ride off to the great Civil War. Chas was too young to fight, or he would have been beside his father, reloaded, and fired. There was little need for a musket rifle after Winchester made the Henry "Yellow" Boy in 1866. Preacher Chet knew the day would come for him to pack for a long journey.

My lazy time had ended in late March when an owl woke my eyes to the drums of death, and I became a better scout, a good, noble scout for Chas Bellew.

It was dark as a coal mines.

"Bellew Boy!" shouted a man on horseback. "Come out, stand your ground, get your punishment for your sins, boy. It's time to meet your Maker, Chas!"

The hound barked.

The stranger fired.

The dog whimpered.

I saw a cold-blooded killer, but he was not my kill. And I felt sad for the hound, for that matter. The old owl, our friend, flew to the banister of the cabin, sharp talons dug deep into the rounded rail of the Bellew house, and the owl stared into the red eyes of Pistol Miller-Smith. He yelled and pulled the trigger on the owl.

"POW!"

"Over here, Pistol Miller-Smith!" said Chas, who stood in the dark beside a lantern that sat on the ground near the barn.

Nothing spooked the owl, and, in shock, the head of Pistol Miller-Smith rotated toward the voice of Chas Bellew.

"Ho-Ho-Ho," said Chas. "Ho-Ho-Ho."

The stranger missed the owl with his revolver several times. The glass broke on the lantern, and fire spread quickly when Pistol Miller-Smith hit the lantern. Chas ran to the edge of the black woods and scanned his enemy.

"No, over here, over here!" said another voice shouted behind the barn. "I am not over there, but over here, Pistol Miller-Smith."

"That sounds like Jackie Ray," said Chas, smiling, voice low.

In a circle, Pistol Miller-Smith reined his horse, and men he had never known were all around him. I saw him shoot the barn, the house, and again, he pulled on the old owl. His revolver clicked.

"Empty," I told myself. My heart was to shoot him, but I did not.

Then, Pistol Miller-Smith cracked the tree bark in front of the face of Chas, and a second revolver was emptied. Pistol Miller-Smith climbed down to reload behind his horse.

"Over here," a voice echoed behind the outhouse. "You missed again," said Chas. "Look into the woods."

That was my signal to fight.

"No, it's me!" said Jackie Ray, and smiled. "Look this way, Pistol Miller-Smith."

Pistol Miller-Smith turned around in circles, a bit dizzy, and could not find a figure to kill. The Lord had covered us with fog.

"Show yourself, you coward!" said Pistol Miller-Smith, striking a torch. The man tossed the stick of fire onto the wet snow. "I will burn this farm to the ground!"

My stomach and eyes laughed as his fiery flames died inside the depth of the pearl snow. No one knew that I was hidden behind the bark of the trees, deep inside the woods. I stayed low, just in case Chas and Jackie Ray needed the strong arm of a Cherokee to fight their battle for them. But it was the fight of Chas. Something deep that every man needs to settle for himself is the confidence of the unknown moment. Chas had moved swiftly and kicked Pistol Miller-Smith in the head. I saw the long-legged man, bear skin wrapped around his shoulders, and he was not bulletproof. He was shocked and alone. The man who was released from the Union Army fell flat on his back, moaning and groaning, blood on his face, and stunned.

Pistol Miller-Smith rolled to his knees in the thick snow, knife waving, left to right, and stood, and said, "You don't have the guts to fire that big hog, Bellew!" Mouth was loud, laughing. "Dog stopped barking, didn't he, Chas Bellew?"

"What do you want, old timer?" said Chas, who held a bead on his head. "This shot will kill you. No one will come huntin' for you, old man!"

"Pop!"

My Cherokee eyes witnessed a snowball being used as a weapon. He cleaned his eyes of thick snow and staggered, legs stubby. Chas heard my laugh from the woods, and he knew I was his scout for the long journey headed West.

Gun pointed at him; Chas closed one eye.

"Pistol Miller-Smith!" yelled Chas, who walked out from the darkness. "I have a hole in the ground with your name on it, and flames burn from the earth."

Pistol Miller-Smith held his knife at Chas and Jackie Ray.

"Don't hurt me, boys," pleaded Pistol Miller-Smith.

It was funny what happened to him. He ran into the woods and whistled for his horse. We never laughed so hard in our lives.

Later, we met at the Bellew log cabin.

"Surprised when I heard your hillbilly voice by the barn, Jackie Ray," said Chas in a truthful voice. Chas handed him some coffee and bread.

"Well, well," leaning back in his chair, "I heard from Kate that Pistol Miller-Smith was hunting you down. I knew you might need an extra gunslinger by your side tomorrow before you blast the Wild West like a stick of good dynamite in a coal mine."

Chas squinted his eyes and said, "I wished a gunslinger would have shown up to save me the trouble of throwing that snowball in the outlaw's ugly face."

"Hey, shut up!" said Jackie Ray. "Let's make this point straight and know that I was the one who distracted him before you lost your head in a gunfight and snowball shootout."

"Did you stop to wish us good luck on the trip to Texas, Jackie Ray?" I said, smiling.

"Heck, No," said Jackie Ray, a man who had filled his pockets at the poker table in Tennessee." He took his hat and stood. "I aimed to ride with you, like Frank and Jesse James and Atohi."

"Good news, cousin!" said Chas. "Knew you could not pass up a once-in-a-lifetime trip like this one."

"Proud to ride with you, Jackie Ray!"

He hugged us and slapped our backs.

Chas picked up his hat and kneeled by the fire, hands out.

"What do you think about Texas, Atohi?" said Jackie Ray, who poured three drinks.

"Well, Texas, huh? I said and chewed my food. "That is not the best land for a Cherokee brave."

"Jackie Ray?" said Chas, who joined us at the table with three drinks. "What about your love for Alice?"

"She might be with child when we return," I said, arms crossed.

The guys laughed.

"She's one fine woman," said Jackie Ray, "who will make a good wife. Thought I had better ride with you, get you back to Kate, 'fore the lilies bloom and before she sacks that outlaw Burly Bill."

"So, you two good men are going to Texas," said Chas, who turned and looked his friends in the eye. "No lying, huh? Did your horse talk you into going on a journey, Jackie Ray?"

In his country accent, "Heck, Chas," said Jackie Ray," holding a cup. "My horse and God hadn't never listened to me much. What makes you think God or my horse cares about me?"

"God will be with us. Got your pack and rifle ready?" asked Chas, turning from the fire to his friend.

"Heck, yes, bud," said Jackie Ray, chuckling. "Pistol, rifle, and a change of underwear."

I had never laughed so hard in my life, and we toasted cups.

"Chas," said Jackie Ray, "two beautiful ladies will be waiting for us in Denton when we return."

"Don't count on it, bud!" I said and knew women well.

The drinks helped us bunk down for the night. The owl flew away and hooted on the windmill, and the night was short, too short, and the sun was strong.

At Sunup, our horses were saddled.

"Hated to see him run off," Chas mounted. "But one of us had to be the hero with a snowball."

"Just another man who didn't get green-broke by his father," I said. "He will not bother us again. Let's turn these horses toward the Wild West, Sons of War."

Chapter 4
Horses Pointed West

Cold snow fell, and howling winds turned Kentucky into a tundra overnight; days were no better than nights with a storm so cold the "Sons of War" begged for the sky to open with a blaze of sunshine on our backs. Days later, we crossed into Louisville, Kentucky, headed to St. Louis, Missouri. A large rustic stablemate fed our horses on the first night in Louisville. We refilled packs with more supplies and found food, hungry as bears.

"Louisville!" I said, hands and face wet and cold. "Thank the Lord for Louisville."

"Where are you boys headed?" said the proprietor, who fed the horses, a heavy man twice the size of Chas and round as a small mule, who worked the stable. Firearm on his side for business and reasoning, he said. His boots were so tight, his toes wanted to climb out, and it must've taken two people to draw his leather boots, toe-to-heel on his feet.

"How many days is St. Louis from Louisville, my friend? How far?" said Chas, stretching his legs.

"Five long days. The weather may not be as good out by the Mississippi River as it is here in Louisville," said the proprietor. He stopped what he was doing. "One more thing," the man waved his hand, "you boys watch your backs on the rest of your journey."

"Why is that, old timer?" said Jackie Ray, who walked toward the man.

"That world ain't peaceful west of Kentucky, boys," said the proprietor. "That's all. Find a hot bath and some soap yonder way. The saloon is at the end of town. Ladies will gladly take money for a good circus act. Know what I mean, gents?"

"Can you fatten the horses by daybreak?" said Chas, who leaned on a post.

"That's my job. Yeah," said the proprietor, tugging on his pocket. "And if you're late, any bit of tardy, it'll cost ten dollars more for making me get up before the rooster crows. I like my sleep as good as the next man."

"Might have one eye asleep," said Jackie Ray, chuckling. "We'll be here, bud, sir."

"You better be here," said the proprietor. "I know you're not afraid. Beware, boys," tipping his hat. "Pleasant stay in Louisville. Good chatting with you men."

"Yessir," said Jackie Ray, who grinned. "We will find the circus act when we get froggy."

Ten paces from the stable, Chas looked back over his shoulder at the proprietor, and then he looked at Jackie Ray's goofy face. He was a man who knew horses and told us about the bad places in town and who to watch out for at the saloon, but he didn't say why.

"That man is serious," said Chas, staring at his friend. "Don't get him irate after working a long day with good horses and stubborn men. He'll kill all three of us and eat our horses for breakfast."

"A man that works with horses for a living," I said, pacing beside Chas and Jackie Ray, "puts up with a lot of crap, boys."

"Look!" said Chas, stopping on the edge of the dusty road. "Occasionally, we can find some good people in this world and a vacant room with ladies to talk to about a circus act."

"I knew you couldn't keep your promise to Kate, Chas!" I said, as large smile lifted about my mug.

"How did you about that promise?" said Chas.

"I was scouting," I said, "up in the barn. I kept my promise to Preacher Chet, watch you back. Can you keep your promise to Kate?"

"What promise?" said Jackie Ray, hand on his hat.

"No circus acts with women," I said.

"Time will tell, scout," Chas told us.

Jackie Ray turned to Chas and said, "My grandpappy said, 'Don't dance with the devil and you won't wake up with her in your bed, sounds just like him, don't it?"

"Yeah. All I'm interested in is a room and a hot bath," said Chas, who stepped inside a hotel. "Ridin' a horse for five days has bruised my tailbone."

"Chas," said Jackie Ray, "trade that leather wallet you call a saddle for one with some paddin' and comfort like President Grant has under his Blue Yankee butt, bud."

"My tail feels like it's been smoked and rolled by a herd of cattle," said Chas, who rubbed his butt.

We all three grabbed our belts when he told a joke, walking like we had ridden logs down the Guyandotte River for a week. My friend tugged his belt, laughed, and walked inside the hotel. Chas leaned on the counter. The noise in the street turned our heads to a large crowd who was in a pushing match. We stood and held the swinging doors at sundown.

"Madam?" said Jackie Ray.

"I have a name, young man, and it's Sherri," said the owner. She walked toward us. "If you call me by any other name, you'll sleep with your horses in the stable, and I'll whip you all the way there."

"Well, Miss Sherri," I said, "why is the black man protesting the acts of the white trolley driver?"

The thin woman walked over to the doorway, stood with a curious face, padded the shoulder of Jackie Ray, and listened to the argument for a moment on Portland Avenue. She ran into the street. We followed her to see if justice was about to be served.

"Well," said Sherri, "I'll put a stop to this bickering." She stepped into the faces of two large men, hands pressed against their chests, and shouted, "Guys, break it up, now!"

They pushed each other some more.

"I remember the tracks were built by white men and black men not long ago. Both black and white folks will ride the street trolley, seated shoulder to shoulder, just like you fought together during the Civil War. If I see any objection, I mean it, from either party, I'll personally free the mules, and you'll pull the trolley. Answer to me." She slapped the sweet pea gun on her leg, tucked away for rare occasions that made her blood boil.

"I believe you could part the river in Louisville, Sherri," said Chas, eyes sincere.

"She's a bad woman, men. Don't give her any trouble!" I yelled and opened the door for Sherri.

"This has been going on since last fall," said Sherri, who had poured some water at the counter. "I'm sick of it. This will stop. If I must take over as Sheriff of Louisville, I'll keep the peace in this town."

Chas leaned on the counter.

"If you have the money," said Chas, nodding, "anyone with the proper number of coins should be able to ride the trolley. Red, black, white, green, or unsure of color, should be able to mount the trolley and ride the same as the Mayor. They fought on the same ground at Gettysburg, two Battles at Bull Run, Chickamauga, and a hundred other places, and good men died for no good reason."

"Everyone fought the Cherokee," said Sherri. "That was the worst of the wrongs."

"Yeah, it was. And no one ever checked the mule. See what he thinks," said Jackie Ray, and he stepped inside the doorway.

"That's not funny," said Sherri, "one mule is white, and one is black, pulling the same street trolley. There's no arguments among the mules. Do you think the Black community and the White community will ever share something in common?"

"We all have enemies, few friends," I said. "God colored our skin all different, and one skin thinks they're better than the rest, and it's usually the side with the most votes and ammo at election time."

"Can you believe this crowd?" said Sherri, who managed one full-line hotel. She worked as an Innkeeper after her father was killed in the Civil War. "They're throwing rocks and mud at the trolley driver, acting like little children. Hey, just seven years ago, they fought together in the Civil War, huh? There's always a war."

"Every town is far from civil," I said, found a seat. "And every town has their war and rumors of wars, says the Good Book." I turned and watched the hostile crowd, white against black, and no one cried for the Cherokee man.

"We're still fighting over petty seats on a street trolley," said Jackie Ray, who stood on the front porch and leaned against the post of the Inn. Chas was beside Sherri, eyes on each other.

"Think you will keep that promise, Chas?" I said.

Chas grinned, head shaking, and he walked away. Guilty.

"I'm furious," said Sherri. "We serve whoever has the money to ride the trolley in this place, guys!"

For the next few minutes, Sherri and Chas talked about where they were from, where they were headed, and how she managed two properties and served food and drinks. She told how she welcomed visitors and found what they needed in each room, from sheets to pillows and the smallest items, such as soap. Jackie Ray spent most of the evening handling mugs of beer and shared stories about his time in Huntington, West Virginia, and two nights spent in Chattanooga, Tennessee.

Sherri spoke of her time managing the staff and remained behind the counter, talking and bartending, fixing her hair in a long mirror. Even when her back was turned, she knew what happened in her place of business. No one shifted, ducked out, or swindled her.

"What's your business in Louisville, Chas?" said Sherri, following him with curiosity.

"Just passing by," said Chas. "We'd like three rooms for the night, please."

Her green eyes caught the attention of Chas, and he finally found a seat. "Could you mark us down for a shave each, please, Sherri?"

"Are you men going to be in the theater?" said Sherri, holding up a poster.

"Not us," said Chas, who gazed at her, and she did the same. "Not yet, anyway."

"A face like yours ought to be in front of people," said Sherri, breaking a smile for the first time and grabbing the cheeks of Chas. "That handsome grin should be on stage, Chas."

"Don't encourage, please," I said, eyes covered.

Not answering her question, Chas lifted his mug and accepted her friendly attention.

"Nice place you got here," said Jackie Ray, spinning on his bar stool. "Each table has a flower. More flowers on every wall than I have ever seen in one place."

"Daddy built this place ten years before the big Civil War," said Sherri, hands feeling the wallpaper. "My mother passed away of a broken heart not long after the War." She pointed at the hand-painted picture of her folks on the wall and talked about the grand-scale windows and fancy doors. She made people, the ones who treated her fairly, the same as family. People saw the Inn from wagons, horseback, and trolleys, and some stood and just gazed, caught in amazement. "You three gents smell like firewood and smoke. Need some soap, huh?"

"I told you we smelled like polecats, guys," said Jackie Ray. "We'd like the best soap money could buy, a warm bath, and we'll see you back here in an hour, Miss Sherri."

Chas stopped messing with his hat in the mirror and spoke up.

"Three good bars of soap, three bottles of anything behind you, and whatever you got handy to eat tonight. Thank you, Sherri," said Chas, eyes winked, and hands waved. "And I'll see you later."

"Beef pot roast, cornbread, pound cake, and coffee in town," said Sherri, tapping the hand of Chas when she delivered the items and took his money.

Through the tall window frame, a small crowd had gathered on the tracks, and two men pulled a black man off the street trolley again. Chas rushed to his side and pulled the man to his feet.

"Let him ride, Mister!" said Chas, with a deep voice that silenced the angry crowd. "Take him wherever he needs to go, and I'll pay his way there if he has no money."

"I got money, sir," said the gray-haired black man, who climbed back on the street trolley, and the trolley pulled away. "Thank you, young man. You need to be President of this dang country."

Chas waved at the man and watched the street trolley smoothly make its way across Louisville, stopping for patrons and loading up more riders. It was common to see locals, well-dressed, some visitors, and some who rode alongside doctors and lawyers and ladies with beautiful dresses and anyone else who wanted to ride that evening.

"Don't give that old man any trouble!" said Chas. "Or you'll be in the mud, you hear me, driver?"

"Money can make a street trolley driver see all colors as the same," yelled the man operating the horses, tipping his hat and commanding the horses down the track.

"Much obliged," said the grey-haired black man.

"Good day!" said Chas, who walked back inside the Inn, where Sherri poured him a free drink of Kentucky bourbon for his justice served.

"Always got to pick a fight, don't ya, Chas?" said Jackie Ray, drink in his hands, speech slurred. "Shoot and ask questions later, cousin." He toasted the men from Denton with his mug.

"You gentlemen stay two nights on me. It's free," said Sherri. "That was a brave act, and it seems we have to provoke the street trolley workers to do what's right and fair in Louisville. Money spends all the same no matter what hand it changes to."

"One night will be plenty, ma'am," said Chas, who tipped his hat and paid the tab. "The next time we are in town, this is where we'll stay and eat, though."

"Well, hmmm, you better, yellow-head," said Sherri, watching Chas walk away. "Chas, have you ever considered running for Sheriff of Louisville?"

The Lord had blessed Chas, heart pure: His hair was light.

"Nope," said Chas.

Chas took his saddle bags and guns up the steps. Jackie Ray followed him and stopped midway when someone bumped into the piano and made a loud noise.

"I think she would like to see you around this town," said Jackie Ray, pulling his shirt. "Well, at least for a few more days, Chas. Until you make her mad."

"Chas could be the town marshal in a few days," I said, pushing his back.

"If I need a place to settle down," said Chas, sliding up the rail slowly and looking down at Sherri. "Might be Louisville, Kentucky, boys."

"Chas," I said, "maybe she's found what she's looking for in the Life and Times of Chas Bellew?" I stood and scouted Chas and Sherri as they admired each other from across the room.

"Keep your eyes on Texas, Chas," said Jackie Ray. "I'll watch the ladies for you, bud."

Sherri and her crew of workers had watched us ascend the steps to our rooms. I am sure we smelled better the next time we were on the lower level.

Jackie mumbled to Chas in the hallway and said, "Ain't nothing wrong with collecting a few memories along the journey, cousin."

"Keep your hands in your pockets, Monroe," said Chas, eyes pointed downstairs. "I better keep my eyes on Kate."

"I'll wake you up before supper," said Jackie Ray, waving, as he looked over the long banister and saw Sherri, who adjusted her glasses and watched Chas enter his room.

My room was a connector with my friend.

"Chas," I said, arms crossed, "she has her eyes on you, cowboy."

"Stop it. Get some rest and wash up, Atohi," said Chas, who waved at the ladies. "Pretty as a picture. Never seen such a sight."

After a soak in the tub, we heard good entertainment in the tavern lobby, which connected to the Inn, and through the windows, beautiful ladies visited Louisville. Sherri sent up new clothes and requested Jackie Ray play the piano, give it a go, as if he were on tour. Jackie Ray was grateful and had traveled more than Chas and myself. I had been to a few places, so we gazed at the attractions and the grand scale city life of fancy people, streets packed, and a few businesses boomed.

People gathered in a place where morality and religion had regular hours, and so did mischief and general tolerance, which had some exceptions. Both men and women took the same liberties as their ancestors did and traveled, made memories, and saw places, accessed what the world was like in bigger and faster places.

Rooms were $2 a night at the Inn, 25 cents for a shave and a cup of hot coffee, the same price as a smooth, relaxing shave by a lady. Freedom of activity and personal liberties had a price, and good company, with untied girdles, had a higher cost, more than most tavern drinks did, for the pursuit of happiness and freedom. Jackie Ray celebrated almost anything for his country, and happiness and satisfaction became no different to him in Louisville or any other town.

Louisville was the only town Chas had visited outside Huntington, West Virginia, and the ground he stood on was far more than a trading post in Grayson. The liveliness of downtown, even dusty and dry in places, mixed with people from the Midwest, fit people who treated themselves along their journey. Our stay was our first adventure toward many other places in the Great South. It was the first good-sized city along our journey, and, for sure, Chas and Jackie Ray were impressed: Men hungry before they'd stayed the first night in town. Thoughts crossed my mind, "Would they spend all their money on the first evening?" I thought. Only time would tell that answer.

The town was named for Louis XVI of France; two rivers collided, the Allegheny and the Monongahela, flowing into the mighty Mississippi. Splashed in a heavy fragrance from Paris, and in front of the wall mirror, Jackie Ray Monroe, Chas Bellew, and I smiled and stood dressed in white shirts, and the best black vests money could buy in Louisville, Kentucky. My outfit was bulky, with a big belt tight and a vest draped, and it was more like a tablecloth than a shirt. However, I shined my shoes and felt proud to be in Louisville.

Deep admiration was given to the new manners adopted by the leadership on the street trolley system. Riverboats and tall buildings were major attractions. Churches of each denomination stood under heaven and existed before God alongside the hustle and bustle of taverns and honky-tonks, guided by law, some order, and driven by post-war commerce and new money. The first experience of how the

Wild West moved toward civility was a good one, and both Louisville and Lexington competed for people and businesses.

***

In college, I knew the world existed beyond Denton, Kentucky, but my contentment was more personal, and satisfaction didn't come without a cost or sacrifice. These things I prepared Chas for, but Jackie Ray, that man was a rolling wagon on fire, especially when he visited taverns. And the evening got interesting when women called Jackie Ray "Handsome" and "Darling" on weekends.

At supper, Chas and Jackie Ray found a table by the window. I joined them.

"I could live here," said Jackie Ray. "This may be the place for me to spend my days, grow old, spread my wings, and settle down along the Ohio River."

"Don't get too comfortable," said Chas. "Imagine what St. Louis looks like, my friend." Chas sat up tall, leaned on the edge of his seat, and watched people move throughout the lobby. They checked in and out, and others ordered whiskey, held mugs, dined, and spent their last dime on self-appreciation and vanity.

"Did you see two guys walk inside?" said Chas, hat low.

"Two round guys with the ladies," I said. "I do now."

"Yeah, there," said Jackie Ray, who tugged on his vest. "He flipped his hand and nodded. "Two outlaws dressed in black, wearing matching revolvers. I know them, part of the York Gang, live outside Grayson, Kentucky. Think their Bad guys."

"What about them?" I said, eyes heavy from too much whiskey. "Nothing like whiskey after dinner, boys. But this place is packed on Saturday night. I'm seeing double-rounded men and four ladies."

"Sherri," said Chas, "could you bring Atohi some water?"

"You better say please, Chas." Jackie Ray whispered.

"Be glad to sober up your friend, Chas," said Sherri.

Jackie Ray slapped his leg and said, "Double-rounded men, huh?"

"Whiskey barrel heads," I said.

"Those two outlaws robbed the trading post in Grayson last fall," said Chas, who leaned forward. "I remember their big eyes from a wanted poster. It's common for a man to cover his face with a dark beard and stay low until people forget names and faces. I won't forget the dirty deeds of two men and how they struck that couple at the trading post. Bruises and purple."

Jackie Ray's face sobered up, and he covered his words with his hand.

I sat up with my water, finished the glass, and said, "How much did they take from the nice lady?" I spoke. My eyes were on the outlaws.

"Heard they got 300 dollars from the store," said Jackie Ray, eyes like a hawk. "Not before old man Reese Johnson and his wife took a beating for giving up their life savings and their personal belongings."

"That's dirty business, Chas," I said, eyes and face red. "I think we ought to remind them that we're from Carter County. Reese Johnson is a good friend of ours."

"I'll grab us a couple of mugs," said Chas, tipping his hat to think about his approach and the man paced in confidence.

Walking right between the York Brothers, Chas eyed both men at close range. Paul York was broader and laughed all the time, a man known to draw a fight from a knock on the elbow or push of the shoulder and a stare down, intentional things that meant trouble to him. Any likely contact or smirk or frown meant hatred, and Chas Bellew had intentionally walked between two hungry lions, men on the prowl.

"Denton, Kentucky, duo of the unsung, huh?" said Chas, flashing his hand for two mugs. I saw my friend place his back to the bar, arms crossed, just to see what the York Brothers had about themselves, fighters without guns.

"Denton, huh?" said Duke York, who thumbed the scar on his chin and dropped one shoulder lower than the other, making eye contact with Chas to see what was itching his pants.

"Dang," said Chas, eyes watery, "you polecats need some soap and a bath. Kill that musky smell," fist ready to club the first man who aimed his hand in the wrong direction or seemed like he'd wanted to fight.

"Watch your mouth, boy!" said Duke, with a head jerk.

The York brothers balled their hands; guns were behind the counter with Bad Sherri; her right hand sat under the bar, and her eyes waited for Duke York to flinch, who tapped his vest for a weapon. He had nothing to pull against any man, so he slowly outstretched his hand, balled fist, relaxed, flat to the bar, and waited.

"There won't be any trouble, Yorky." Sherri eyed them both. "Or anytime, gentlemen, you hear me? Settle it inside your hearts, Mr. York, and get out and find a hole through your heart. Chas, friend, we just met, but no fighting in my bar, bud. Drop that fever. "

He nodded, eyes in agreement.

"Hillbillies will pay, Paul, in time, very, very soon," said Duke, laughing, who stood tall and right in the face of Chas Bellew. "It gets dark every night in Louisville, boy."

"You threatening me, York?" said Chas. "You lookin' for trouble, mister? Say it."

"Your ears work, don't they, boy?" said Duke, who stepped in front of Chas, nose to nose.

"Bad idea, York. My friend has a "fool's fungus" on his nose that's contagious to only fools; that is, if you get close enough, try it, huh?" I said and walked beside him. "My long hair can whip you both. This knuckle took out a man twice your size in Harlan, Kentucky, doubled a man down in Corbin, and this right hand has a good scar, Duke."

"Ain't no scar on that right hand," Duke said and had a funny face.

I rubbed the knuckles on my right hand and said, "Right hand, it waits on your face, thief. Is your mouth open for business, York?"

"No fightin' in here!" said Sherri. "Go, Chas, now!" She flapped her hand and held a Billy Club. "I can shoot and gut you both. Dirty deeds don't matter to the Innkeeper. I need you over here, Atohi."

Each man went their own way. Sherri told how she wanted fun and peace, and fun brought plenty of business. Rowdy places were empty. That night, I worked for Bad Sherri. And Chas walked backward to his table, mug in his hand. He smiled at the York Brothers. Jackie Ray was gone, left his seat, and played the piano against the wall. The sound from the upright piano was like professional keys in Chicago or an accomplished musician on stage in New York City. Jackie Ray was something special behind an upright piano.

In his Irish accent, Jackie Ray played and sang and entertained the crowd into the night. They cheered and wanted more music. Chas, out of respect, had plenty of admiration for Sherri, the owner, and his new friend did not fight. Chas tapped his foot and listened with courtesy, too. I kept him under control, but the ale made him ill and brave again. For one night, and because Sherri was so beautiful, Chas enjoyed a good establishment. No tables or teeth, nor mirrors were broken.

Jackie Ray played everyone's favorite song that year and had their attention. And on his head, you guessed it, the silly gambler's hat. "Bartender Sherri!" he yelled, "Could I have some water, please?"

His fingers raced across the keys, feet pounded the golden upright pedals, and he faced Sherri for her answer, part of his showmanship.

Sherri led the crowd and responded loudly, "Jackie Ray, we only serve whiskey here, sir."

"Bartender Sherri," said Jackie Ray, winking at her. "I need a glass of water, honeypie."

He played the same keys, over and over, full of smiles, and entertained the crowd, folks who had not seen anyone like him play in Louisville before or anywhere else for that matter. The crowd responded, "Jackie Ray, we only serve whiskey here."

His hands flew across the keys, and he stomped the floor several more times and pressed the pedals.

"Bartender, I need a shot of whiskey. Bartender, I need a shot of whiskey."

The crowd responded, "Bartender, give Jackie Ray some whiskey, dear."

Sherri ran over to Jackie Ray and slowly poured a shot. Jackie Ray downed the drink between breaths and never missed a beat, playing with rhythm and a rare skillset few in the country could match.

Chas smiled and yelled, "Bartender, that's dang good whiskey."

The crowd responded, "Jackie Ray, that's all we've got."

"Bartender, need another round. The sun's going down, dear."

"The crowd responded, "But, Jackie Ray, that's all we've got."

"Sherri, lady Sherri," sang Jackie Ray, "thank you for the last shot."

The large crowd stood. We stood amid wonderment. Jackie Ray rose to the occasion, honored by the large crowd, and for what he'd done, the man deserved an award. The tangible man helped draw more people into her tavern than she'd ever seen; folks celebrated and cheered him on, more songs sounded, and rounds were served. They had never been more smiles and singing than when Jackie Ray Monroe played for a packed house at Sherri's Tavern Inn. His apparent style of fun kept down fighting and disagreements by singing and dancing until shortly after midnight. To watch Jackie Ray play was a dream come true, and to see him at his very best, voice full of songs, ceaselessly bent and swaying and turning cold hearts into warm faces, became a true pleasure of mine. I was there and saw firsthand his talent, and it was real; the place was lively, pleasant, and memorable that night. No war. No fights. And no one knew he could play with such power, style, and class. Talent observed. He did it. Jackie Ray played among the rich and poor and labored his hands for the wealthy and sane, the same fire and entertainment known in Boston and San Francisco. In a celebratory manner, Sherri was humbled and honored to be the host, and a full tip jar overflowed. Waving it off, Jackie Ray accepted none of the money and handed it to Sherri in front of everyone.

Jackie Ray was the King of Kindness on that evening.

Somewhere in the middle of his "Whiskey Song," the York brothers collected their guns from Sherri, left the tavern, and made their way to their horses. The crowd cheered for another song, and Jackie Ray played several tunes, too, rip-roaring, upbeat songs, hands and feet in rapid motion, and couples danced and sang on a hardwood floor. Sherri sold out of Kentucky's Best Bourbon, and two hundred mugs of beer were consumed. Her tavern became famous in Louisville. In his most celebrated moment, Jackie Ray Monroe became a desirable and popular man, well-liked.

Chas Bellew was surprised to see an elegant lady step inside the room and put her hands on Jackie Ray's empty seat. Being near the door, Chas stood when he saw the lady, hair dark and pinned up, eyes blue and lonely, and she found him to be relaxed and polished. She was dressed in a floral blue outfit and was very attractive.

"Can I join you?" she said. "My name is Elizabeth Tate from Lexington."

"I've been waiting on you all night," said Chas, who was a gentleman, even in silence.

"Promise forgotten," I reminded him. I rolled my eyes and said, "Well, trouble needs a seat; take two."

"I'm no trouble, sir," she replied with elegance.

I was rarely called sir. I loved her for it. Chas laughed and knew what I meant.

"Louisville had too much lady trouble and good bourbon," I said, and we smelled like royalty from the markets of France.

My friend held out his hand and said, "Charles "Chas" Bellew from Denton, Kentucky, delighted. This man is my good friend, Atohi, Chief of the Cherokee Nation of the Village of Denton, deep in the mountains."

We were introduced, and she spent more time with my friend than he deserved to have.

"Hope we might dance," said Elizabeth, moving close to Chas when she spoke.

"Why?" said Chas.

"I've been watching you and your brother," said Elizabeth, whispering into his ear, and she spoke privately to Chas. "He's good with the piano."

"We're cousins, ridin' out to Texas," said Chas, whispering to her.

"What's your business in Texas, Chas?" said Elizabeth after she'd ordered a drink.

"The prospect of my uncle's ranch," said Chas. "I've never met him."

I watched them take the floor and dance amid two other couples.

"Are you looking for work?" said Elizabeth, who held his shoulders while they danced. "I own plenty of horses in Fayette County. We are looking for a good man, and your friends could join you."

"I can work horses," said Chas, spinning with her slowly, "blacksmith, shoe, tack, and make saddles. I do a few other things very well."

"Other things, Chas?" said Elizabeth, eyes wide, face tilted against his cheek. "Other things, huh?" smiling and whispering, "What other things might you do?"

"It depends," said Chas, laughing. "Professional things, that is."

"Of course."

The room lit up when he spun her around, and so did Elizabeth. In some amusement, whether it was the banging of the piano, dancing, or Chas in general, she held him tight and purposefully. Her head rested on his shoulder. When the song slowed, under his face, she was close enough to kiss him, but the song stopped.

"Back to my racehorses, Chas, "said Elizabeth, walking back to her seat. "As I was saying, a great position is available on our horse farm, and a new Tate Family racetrack is being built," smiling at him. "That is if you ever see yourself doing "other things" in Lexington. Mark this as my personal, and I mean very, very professional and personal invitation."

"We must go, Elizabeth," said an older man who stepped inside the tavern.

"My father is at the door," said Elizabeth. "It was wonderful meeting you, Charles "Chas" Bellew, from Denton, Kentucky. Find me at the Tate Racetrack in Lexington, and anyone in town can lead you in my direction."

"Elizabeth," said the older man, sounding stern.

"Great meeting you as well, Ms. Elizabeth Tate," said Chas, who held her hand and, most of all, more than her attention.

Her father had no interest in meeting anyone in a tavern. He was well-dressed, hands clutched to her shoulder, nudging and waving to his daughter, clung to the exit.

"Chas?" said Elizabeth. "Remember, we could use a good man who has traveled and can work racehorses. My invitation will stand for a year; the racing of horses is popular now." She held his hand a little longer the second time, and I saw her thumb make circles on his palm. Finally, her eyes let go of him, and she stood between Chas and her father.

"I'll stop at the Tate Farm in Lexington later," said Chas. "Might be a year, though. I'll send a letter before I arrive, plan a visit to see your horses, see how "other things" operate in Lexington, Elizabeth."

"They operate well. I'll be building you a guest room. Name on the door, Chas." said Elizabeth, face lit up as if they were engaged.

"Great to know you, and it was my pleasure," said Chas, eyes determined. "We will meet again."

Her sky-blue eyes could have found the soul of a blind man, a thin frame, a lady starving for a man's attention. Chas must have forgotten about Jackie Ray's singing and the sound of the piano, far from his preoccupied mind.

"I am very much looking forward to knowing the other things you do well," said Elizabeth, looking at his polished boots, head lifting slightly until she was pulled away by her father, caught stealing glances of Chas as she left. He'd made another friend, a lady friend.

The best evening we could remember in a long while was at Sherri's Louisville Tavern and Inn. Jackie Ray turned a dull night into one of the most memorable and pleasant evenings of my life. His professional performance on the piano kept us out of jail and out of the graveyard. That was certain.

Chas and Jackie Ray didn't speak much at breakfast: gravy, biscuits, eggs, and bacon. I predicted their heads pounded like Cherokee drums on a pow-wow, spent from a night of whiskey and ale. I guarded both men and the door, paid by Sherri, who highly respected my size and native reputation or at least my long Cherokee hair and features that most men questioned.

The sunrise was warm on my face, and the stable manager had the horses fed, watered, and saddled for Chas and Jackie Ray. I saddled my own dang horse, and the horse preferred my hands, anyway. The wealth of such a tack room, organized with harnesses, martingales, saddles, stirrups, reins, halters, breastplates, bridles, bits, and new rifles. Two shelves stood solitary behind the counter, full of shells and cartridges and lined with pistols, some of pearl and others were Remington Army pistols.

Breakfast sobered Jackie Ray up, eyes opened, at least enough to chat with Chas, who had downed his hat from the sunburst and spent the morning talking about Elizabeth and Kate and Sherri, his three lady friends. That boy had more trouble brewing in hearts he barely knew, and in counties he had never known existed. Silver dew was on the tall grass when we filled our canteens and rode out of dusty Louisville, Kentucky, the city we'd befriended in only one evening.

Jackie Ray's face warmed up about midday when the horses were fed, and just outside Corydon, Indiana, where a clearing of green grass dotted the meadows, cedars staggered and lined the creek, and deer ran from the lush fields into the woodlands. Hundreds of pheasants and doves broke free across the blue sky and entertained the smaller foul. Between two fields was a shaded area, and an abandoned building stood alone, a frame of a house, one left behind by the Civil War or maybe it was a father who didn't come home, and a house full of memories became too much to recall, so the family moved to higher ground.

"I saved your hide from the York Brothers last night," said Jackie Ray, grinning and pouncing Chas on the shoulder, resting the horses under a hanging oak.

"You saved us from jail and a big fight," I said, grinning. "They were scared men."

"Who was that sweet cookie you had beside you while I was singing, Chas?" said Jackie Ray, who rested on his back.

"Elizabeth Tate," said Chas, who rested across from him.

"The horse race queen, Elizabeth Tate," I said. "That's what Sherri said."

"Yeah," said Chas, water in his hand. "Her family has a big spread in Lexington."

"Horses, huh?" said Jackie Ray. "Pretty country, I bet."

"Lots of racehorses and a new track," I said, eyes closed against a tree, resting.

Jackie Ray filled his hat full of water from a bubbling spring, poured it over his head, and leaned against a creek boulder.

"Melted snow tastes like heaven when you're thirsty," said Jackie Ray, water about his face. "Caught my breath, and now I'll smoke one. You have plans to see the Tate Farm, Chas."

"I don't know," said Chas. "Bud, that's a heck of a family. Hundreds of horses for sale and more fence posts than a man can dig in a lifetime, and a track wrapped around that farm, big as Carter County, I bet."

"Let's get going," I said. "Burning daylight. We can ride a few more miles until sundown."

We mounted our horses and fed the animals and ourselves. We rode for ten more miles or so and saw one wagon train full of supplies. Husband and wife, girl asleep in the back of the wagon, and the boy was mounted on a sack of grain acting like he was shooting Jackie Ray with his long finger.

Jackie Ray grabbed his chest, stuck out his tongue at the young kid, eight or so, and laughed. His father yelled at him for not shooting his tongue off.

"Look! Up ahead," said Jackie Ray, who stopped his horse. He tilted his head, and he watched two men caught in conversation. "Do you see them?"

"Yeah, I see two men," said Chas, reaching for his saddlebags.

"Two men on horseback," I said. "Half a mile away or so."

"Outlaws, you called it?" said Jackie Ray, rotating his revolver. "Might be our first big shootout, boys."

"They disappeared behind that hill turned to the right," I said and pointed. "Down that creek."

"Let's eat and bed down. Let the horses rest," said Chas, who kept his eye out for outlaws and animals walking around the campfire. "The sun is about to fall behind the hills, anyways. Get some rest and shuteye. I'll cook up something."

Two hours into the night, the sky rumbled and was as dark as a mountain cellar with the door closed. The moon and stars were the only things out that night. Coyotes howled, and my friend, the barn owl, was back and spooked our horses, too. Two rattlesnakes were nearby, and with enough moonlight for Jackie Ray, two shots killed 'em both. He cut the rattlers off and blew smoke out his gun. He was proud of his kill.

I stepped into the woods to water the grass.

"Here's a good rabbit," said Jackie Ray. "I need a bite or two. You can have the rest and finish that coffee."

"You sure?" said Chas, seated on the ground.

Twigs snapped, and a pistol clicked, "Yeah, yeah, for sure," said a loud voice. "He's sure to rest in peace when I pop this Smith & Wesson on his head for what was said in Louisville."

"Duke York?" said Chas. "Didn't know we'd have company, or I'd tied on my blue Sunday suit and made some Barringer stew for you and your brother."

"Looks like we have some unfinished business from back at Bad Sherri's Tavern, don't we, Carter County boys?" said Duke York.

"We don't want trouble," said Chas. "But…if you need reconciliation with the Lord, there ought to be a church in these parts for sinners and saints."

"Too late, boys," said Paul York. "Way too dang late for negotiations or running in your Sunday dresses back to town."

I heard them taunting Jackie Ray and Chas through the brush.

"I don't believe the world would miss either one of these boys, do you, Duke," said Paul York.

"You bring the rope?" said Duke. "It's time to hang two boys."

"I ain't got no rope, brother."

"How are we goin' hang these polecats without a rope?" said Duke, face shaking. Walking around the fire, and said, "How can we drag them behind a horse without a dang rope?"

"Whoa. Whoa. Whoa." said Chas, who raised his hands. "Why don't you two good men talk this out, huh? We'll just finish our food and ride out."

"Yeah," said Jackie Ray, who moved toward the horses. "We need to ride to Carl Bellew's ranch in Texas. Get out of here?"

The two outlaws stopped talking and slowly turned around.

"Did you say Carl Bellew?" said Duke. "Bad Carl Bellew?"

"He said Carl Bellew, Duke," said Paul, who repeated what he said.

"You boys know Bad Carl Bellew?" said Duke, dropping his pistol to his belt.

Coyotes howled in the dark of night and had enough voice to raise the hair on Jackie Ray's neck. Chas turned when he heard them. Paul York suddenly holstered his weapon.

"Heard Bad Carl Bellew was in the cattle business in St. Louis three years ago," said Paul York, walking up beside Jackie Ray to warm his hands at the fire. "He killed seven outlaws before they could blink their eyes and gunned 'em down by himself."

Jackie Ray stepped into the light of the fire and adjusted his hat, face lit up, and smiled with a curious grin, looking at Chas and seeing me in the brush. I nodded.

"Revolver has only six bullets, old man," said Jackie Ray, who knew he was a liar.

"He killed the last man with one punch," said Duke York, who mounted his horse and yelled. "See you boys in St. Louis or hell, whichever comes first."

Chas held the reins of Duke York's horse and yelled, "Bad Carl Bellew is my uncle."

"I'm right behind you, Duke!" said Paul York.

My revolver was empty when they rode off. They must've been scared because I did not see them again that night. Big Paul York mounted his black horse and reared him in an open field about sunup and rode off, pale-faced. Sunrise was burning through the tall cedars, and the smell of dust and earth mixed with the damp fog lingered, and cool air smelled like a fresh start of hope. We saddled our horses and talked about seeing Saint Louis.

For the second time, a good blessing, Jackie Ray and Chas dodged death with Paul York and Duke York and gathered up their bedroll and belongings. I put out the fire, and they crushed a handful of Kentucky soil inside their hands. Something their fathers had taught them to do each time they left the good Kentucky earth behind.

"I bet Carl's the fastest gun in the West," said Jackie Ray. "Must be a bounty on his head, though, if he's an outlaw, huh?"

"Yeah. We're burning daylight again," said Chas, who mounted his horse and kicked the side of the horse with his spurs on his boots.

I am not sure why he needed spurs. Black Sam was a good horse.

"Bad Carl Bellew has become a famous gunslinger, Chas," said Jackie Ray. "I wonder what it's like to ride the range with him."

"It's five days to St. Louis, Missouri," I said. "Need to get the horses some grain and point them to the Wild West."

The old owl flew overhead again, and we left Kentucky together.

Chapter 5
Prosperity

Saint Louis, Missouri, was an alluring town of trappers and traders, a towering place of industry, and undoubtedly, it was the amazement center of the Midwest. More food and drinks were served in Saint Louis than in all the counties in Kentucky combined. We stood in paradise. Our horses halted and mounted; we had learned to clap our hands to the grandeur of expansion and prosperity. It was a personal affront not to tip the hat at business owners stationed at doorways and, for a trio of seasoned blacksmiths, life as we knew it meant the prospect of labor and wealth. Hundreds of new stables and oversized corrals were built for stout horses, adventurous men, stubborn men, and good mules.

Outstanding leather shops and raw hides stood, and a round man with specs on his face shouted for business.

"Barber and trim for a few coins, men."

Several shops sold used revolvers, collections by the hundreds, listed by Smith & Wesson, Roat, Joslyn Remington, Colt, and Navy. Ammo stores handled rifles in large rooms, where firearms hung on the wall. Glass cases were tagged with merchandise. Additional rifles were on backorder, along with thousands of cartridges and leather belts, handmade holsters. We saw a line of specialty shops.

Strong men stacked bricks high off the ground, three milling lumber yards handled most of the materials, draft horses pulled steel, and crane-like structures meant more expansion was expected. Plans for a giant two-mile bridge that would cross the mighty Mississippi River became the talk of the town, but, of course, many of the good folks thought they'd never live to see such a grand structure.

Thousands of people each month moved to "Mound City," and the town expanded; homes, businesses, and group conventions were being held. And the pride of the Chickasaw Nation, Illini Tribe, Osage Nation, Otoe-Missouria Tribe, Ioway Tribe, Quapaw Nation, and others, those who had roamed, no longer ruled the land. Their names were written in the pages of regional history. Riverbanks and woodlands had been claimed, but the unstoppable stride of prosperity caught on in Saint Louis, where the industry banner waved, not the hides of indigenous people. No town existed like Saint Louis. They said the town was formed by Pierre Laclede and Auguste Chouteau and established as a place of trade, settlers, and pioneers. They knew stores and mercantiles would soon follow, erected near large Indian mounds, Mound City, the place, a flame to the cold.

Wagon trains headed west, and folks hoped to strike it rich in California and Utah. Some felt cotton and beer, some crawled behind the railroad, "King of the Land." We had no choice but to stop before we crossed the Mississippi River, by the mud turtle-like movement of a steady ferry system that trailed and turned south to Louisiana; still, people had to cross the river in a westward turn, which had no guarantee of safe trade or travel from bands of thieves that hid along wagon trails and trade routes, who hoped to kill and steal.

Jackie Ray feared water, and so was his frightened horse. We saw for the first time the awful devastation of what a tornado had done as we volunteered to pick up the broken pieces of Saint Louis in the late days of March 1871. We worked for days helping Presbyterian church members recover after a merciless storm ripped the town apart; built amid the Civil War, less than seven years old and destined to be an enormous river city town of prosperity and American commerce.

Tied our horses outside a saloon, and Jackie Ray and Chas walked inside for a drink when we'd finished our shift as volunteers.

"Welcome to Mound City, boys," said the bald bartender. "Known as newly built Saint Louis, Missouri to visitors. That paint is still dry on the door, so don't mess it up with dirty horse hands, or I'll have to shoot you, got it?"

"Yeah, we got it," I said, hands of sweat and dirt.

He smiled behind a snow-white beard, and his gray eyes, sharp and alert, the color of a shifting sky, lifted to movements, especially sudden motions from unknown men..

"Name's Russell Lightfoot, men, raised on the fork of the Missouri, two miles north of here. I've lived on the river forever and know pretty much everyone in town except for the three wandering fellas before me."

"Here's Jackie Ray Monroe, and I'm Chas Bellew. This serious face, Atohi, Chief of the Cherokee Nation, a good man from Kentucky."

Russell looked outside at the horses and turned, head cocked, and the horses were as tired as we were from pulling broken beams and trees all day, and we were the same.

"Rode in from Denton, Kentucky, just a few days ago, helping out with the storm," said Chas. "Don't mind good work when we see it in the mountains or otherwise."

The horse-keeping bartender poured three shots of whiskey, pushed the glasses under our noses, and waved off our hands when we went for the pockets for coins.

"Fine men for this town," said Russell, who steadied his old eyes. "Ain't no lazy bones ride that far without something on your mind, boys. First round, it's on me. Second, my hand is open."

The man drew a line on the bar top with two fingers, tapped the wood, waved his hands, and spoke of a dozen names of businesses that had closed because of the big storm.

"A giant tornado struck us a few days ago, and I saw the path of the twister. One eye is made of good glass, and the other, God gave me. The storm turned for five miles or so. Then, it twisted through the Indian mounds, turned out into the woods, and faded away. You can see the path, and if you like, hire a guide to show you around, huh, boys?"

"No thanks," said Jackie Ray, removing his gambler hat. "We've seen it. Nice town, though." Jackie Ray finished his drink. "Where's the women that run this town? Louisville had a good woman who ran that town."

"You'll find Madman McClain's girl, Renee McClain; she walks not far from here. The lady was here once. Handles a pistol like a champ, one on each hip." The old man nodded and poured himself a glass. "She runs Saint Louis, points and vents, vetting folks, does what she wants, and keeps the people in line."

"Beautiful Irish lady, I guess," said Chas.

In each town, Chas knew the women before he met them, and he connected with folks, felt comfortable, and talked to traders and trappers and anyone else who had knowledge. Our time on the trail was to learn from others, not just remain artless.

"Two old Frenchmen built this town in the spring of 1864 before the Civil War had ended," said Russell, one elbow on the bar. "For the purpose of a central trade route in mid-America. They plan to build a bridge from my saloon to the other side of the river. Men, the same as you folks, tired travelers, stop at my saloon from Chicago and Evansville and some places I'd never heard of before, like Hanover and Johnny Cake Mountain."

"Curious pioneers and mountaineers," said Jackie Ray. "Folks who want to open the door to the Wild West. Mister, watch for sodbusters."

"Explorers and surveyors," said Russell, "standing on the riverbank, making beer and building bridges over troubled water."

"Sounds like post-War industrial progress, don't it? Is it good to remove indigenous people and call it home, Russ?" I said.

"I am not sure what he just asked, boys." said the bartender, who polished his countertops until he had a fine finish.

"He knows what I mean," I told Chas.

"I see folks only once. Most of them just keep traveling, some for the hope of work, some for the hope of God. Others will leave here, some will live here, and all will eventually die. Three fine boys like yourselves are lookin' to break your backs in labor, I bet?"

"Not us, Russ," said Chas. "Just passing through, and you might see us again on the way back from Texas. But for now, I'm looking for my Aunt Ruby Bellew, half-sister to my Pa, they say. Wrote to her once, told her we'd visit in late March 1871." He opened his letter. "Maybe you know where 20th Street is located, right?"

"Mrs. Ruby Bellew," said Russell, who stood motionless. "You won't find her there on 20th Street, though," the old man turned toward him.

"Did she leave town?" said Chas, hat removed.

"Sort of, Ruby died of Cholera," said Russell, brushing his thin hair.

"Go on," I said.

"Dang epidemic broke out on us all, and if it didn't kill 'em, the typhoid fever killed 3500 people in Saint Louis, and it wasn't long ago. I am truly sorry. Tornadoes, typhoid, Cholera. It's the Lord letting us know that beer and bridges are signs of growth and sin. Whiskey is my remedy for a bad day, boys. Good Book says beer is for brawlers, though."

"What does the Good Book say about whiskey, Russell?" I asked him.

He leaned in close, laughing, and said, "Drunk on wine and whiskey, huh?" Russell brought his hands together and said, "The Good Book says with a cup of whiskey, you can't find your way home."

He slapped the polished counter and laughed, "That's the loss of the sauce, boys. Ha-ha-ha."

"Sad times for this young town, gettin' lost on the sauce," said Jackie Ray, who belted out and laughed in his country accent.

"Talk about railroad shipments of cotton going to Texas," said Russell. "I'll be dead and gone 'fore I can ride a train to Fort Worth Stockyards. So, I'll just get lost on my way home, Saint Louis style, wait on the big bridge, and load beer to Boulder and Bakersfield."

"Where can we find three rooms?" said Jackie Ray, who paid the man for his drinks and time. "Need a good hotel, Mr. Lightfoot."

We stood at the door.

"Anywhere but the Wagon Wheel, lads," said Russell, eyes steady.

"And you don't want the Wagon Wheel, gents," said an old drunken man, head and hat raised from the next room, huddled in the corner.

"The Wagon Wheel?" said Chas, hands spun.

"Yeah, for sure," said Russell. "Beware of the Wagon Wheel, boys. I can help you out of any trouble with the sheriff, but if you get turned around in the Wagon Wheel, well, hum, you'll be on your own. I'll say I didn't know you boys. You've been warned, and goodly warned."

I wasn't sure what "goodly warned" meant, but it wasn't "goodly news" for men unbeknownst to the town.

Russell's face changed, hand over his heart, and he said, "That's out of my element, boys. I'll swear by the Good Book, sober and everything, words of the truth."

"Thank you, Lightfoot and old man, the one in the corner,." said Jackie Ray, who tipped his hat. "Best be on our way. Stay the night."

"I believe gold would help me get you out the Wagon Wheel, not a dang dollar," said Russell, pocket open on his shirt.

"Appreciate the advice, Russell Lightfoot," said Chas. "We'll be on our way, be back for our horses soon."

We found a man who tended to horses beside Lightfoot, so they rested up, and we admired the churches and other buildings. Later, food met our bellies, and like Louisville, our tails needed soap of any kind! The dry evening sun had dusted workers. Our time was spent in the streets amid amusement. We found cheap rooms beside the Wagon Wheel, and despite their reputation, seemed to be a decent hotel.

"Look! Chas, Chas, Chas, o' boy," said Jackie Ray, a smile ran across his face. "Most beautiful women I've ever seen in my dang life just walked over at the Wagon Wheel. One lady with red hair just waved to me, bud. I like this big city life. That's a nice hotel."

"Remember what Russell Lightfoot said," I told them, "stay out of the Wagon Wheel, boys."

"Honeybees at the Wagon Wheel, boys." Three ladies waved. "Sweet honeybees at the Wagon Wheel," sounded one lady who stood at the door of the hotel.

"Sweet, glamorous ladies of delight, and I know while they call it Mound City, boys," said Jackie Ray, eyes popping. "Honey has been my favorite since I was born. She has beauty from her head to her nectar."

"First beer is on the house, boys." A lady spun around on the porch.

Brave women walked across the street, buzzed around Chas and Jackie Ray, and lifted hats, hands, and hair. Smiled, laughed, and felt our muscles. My friends were surrounded by hands of kindness and a soft fragrance that spun in the wind. I knew better than to put my foot in a trap, the Wagon Wheel; it was a big ole trap. I smelled trouble.

"I'm not sharing!" said one lady to the next. "This Cherokee man, darling, you are all mine."

"She's trouble, Chas," I said. "Don't take beer from honeybees, Jackie Ray. You've been warned."

"I won't sting him," said the red-haired lady.

"Do we look like trouble to you, huh?" said a lady, gambler's on her chest, who pulled Jackie Ray to the door of the Wagon Wheel Hotel. "He's a handsome Indian man, isn't he, Audrey?"

"He's the most handsome man in Saint Louis, and I want him," said the lady holding my arm.

"One drink, Atohi," said Jackie Ray, forehead of sweat. "Won't hurt, will it, Atohi? Just one mug from this shack to help these hard-working women survive in the friendly city, huh, bud?"

"Nope." I was uncertain. "Maybe."

Jackie Ray was under the spell, laughing, arm-in-arm, and a lovely lady escorted him to a private table. He shrugged his shoulders as the sun lost to the darkness of life, and what timing? Saint Louis was no longer visible; figures and buildings faded as if they were absent from the landscape.

"Three ole boys from Kentucky can relax," said Chas. "Just have some fun for a song or two, Atohi. Couple mugs, good food, and great friends to talk to, right?"

"Worse than the Trail of Tears, Sons of War!" I declared.

"You're in good hands, young man," said the madam, kissing the cheeks of Chas. Red lipstick highlighted his face. "Honey, you'll never forget the Wagon Wheel. I'll write it on a postcard for ya, honey," brushing her hand across his face.

An attractive, well-defined lady walked out from the back of the room wearing tight clothes and shoes of blue and did a cartwheel on the stage. She bowed and smiled and cheered. We all cheered, surrounded in happiness, as we watched women tumble and turn.

"One more Wagon Wheel," shouted the ladies. "One more Wagon Wheel, more for these good men."

"That's Bonnie Rose," said the madam. "That's why they call us the Wagon Wheel, honey. Bonnie made us famous on the river. Even the governor has been here."

All the ladies danced, and two ladies played the piano and sang, and more ladies did cartwheels and spun around and tumbled.

"It's against my better judgment," said Chas, who leaned over to Jackie Ray. "But I don't think it's a good idea to be inside the Wagon Wheel, gazing at so much glorious temptation."

Jackie Ray slapped an empty chair and accepted a beer.

"I am staying," said Jackie Ray, feet on the floor.

"Dang it!" I said, "Foot in the trap."

Chas joined him at the table. One man left. We were the only guys inside the parlor, and the night was young. Jackie Ray put his arm around the lady. He downed two beers. Chas relaxed, face bobbed, like he was sleepy, lost in the arms of comfort, resting good judgment.

"You can't touch the ladies!" said an older lady, finger high, meanness in her voice. "Unless, gents, they ask you for help untieing something secret or special."

"I need help!" One lady said, a table away. She was a fine woman with golden hair long down her back and paced slowly to our table. All of them smelled like a garden of flowers from Saint Louis.

Seven songs into the night, the guitar player stopped and rested. Ladies massaged our shoulders and danced and even played instruments, plucking strings and banging tambourines, all in unison. The arrangement was delightful and well-prepared, while a wonderful rhythm of saintly ladies adored our faces.

The performance happened as if they'd practiced for ages or even traveled cross country, even abroad. The bar and tables were in no particular order. Tables were split, curtains untied, partially hiding a large stage of pale ladies, who spun and kicked in colorful dresses and danced.

Stairs led to the second and third floors. More ladies were draped over railings, and during the show, dancers slid down banisters, one, then the other followed. They held smiles, teeth of pearl, and sang along in outfits of red, white, and blue. All of them were beautiful women, and not one was more radiant than the other. They swayed to the beat of the music, Irish songs, from the third and second floors, old amid young. Women, mostly in their twenties, redheads, blondes, and brunettes with long hair flowing and bouncing, held the bar. One lady had no hair at all. Three ladies had painted faces.

Part of the stage opened to the elements of spring, and snow blew in when the doors swung open. Performers changed into their evening wear of glamorous and yet wide dresses. The music slowed down, and more men gathered around inside, and so did more women. Our ears heard that it was the best sinful entertainment in the world and far from being Saint Louis.

The room overflowed with patrons, and tables were occupied. Meals were prepared by expert chefs and served by the ladies who had changed from professional entertainers to a staff of waitresses and stood with dignity and cared for hospitality. Ladies of culture and of style nurtured customers, too. No one asked the price of the meals, and no one asked the rate of pay for the entertainment, as if they'd been served before. Ladies were well-educated, and most spoke a second language: French and Spanish, and one lady spoke Cherokee. She sat to my right, and we became the best of friends. Others knew how to operate a restaurant and tended to the needs of customers, spinning in a wave of devotion and passion.

Madam LaBelle, the owner, spoke often and directed the entertainment for gratis and handled it well. The proprietor drew a large crowd on weekends to her establishment where more money exchanged hands, not for companionship, but for desire and showmanship, for the lure of attraction, and for the sake of curiosity.

Chas overheard a conversation at the table next to us, how the place was a school of ladies, women who wanted the finer things in life. Each morning, Madam LaBelle taught the ladies how to become proprietors and ladies of business and stand on their own two feet in a male-dominated society, such as the commercial industry of Saint Louis and

Chicago. She ran the place with a sense of discipline and ownership. She paid better than any business along the Mississippi River, to educate the practice of independence and freedom from men, especially those who held less manners and culture than women did.

A flashy middle-aged woman, draped in pearls with hair of brown, paraded around called Madam LaBelle, who checked our table several times per hour. But there was no time for a clock on the wall at the Wagon Wheel and barely enough light to grow a baby plant.

"Do you men need anything," said Madam LaBelle, "anything at all?" She spoke softly, face tight, and tapped a cane at men distracted by private conversations. She loathed men who lost vision and thought more of themselves than the cultured ladies who performed before the eyes.

"Fine as a frog hair split three ways," said Chas, who spoke for us all. He tried to collect his thoughts and had forgotten about his newfound salvation weeks earlier.

"If you decide differently, men," said Madam Labelle, who held her shoulders back, "raise your hand, bat an eye, or just say "help" and we'll serve you more than you can handle."

Upright, the cane was draped over her left forearm; her hand was filled with tips for entertainment. First-timers, less educated about the fashion of generosity, stood out and found a working system of persuasion soon followed the cane.

"What happened to men who held their money?" I said with my head cocked.

Always one among the crowd, less concentrated circles, I thought to myself. One man held his coins at tip time.

"You don't deserve to be seated in the Wagon Wheel!" yelled Madam LaBelle. "Twenty lashed and …" catching her breath, "into the dang river, the cold river covers the greed of selfish man!"

Women whistled and chanted, "River! River! River!"

Large men pushed the greedy man to an open door on stage, and he begged and pleaded; his hide slid into the mighty Mississippi River.

"Russell Lightfoot was wrong about this place," said Chas, eyes relaxed. "The Wagon Wheel is an excellent place of business, not a houseful of harlots, like he thought. The greedy man should have handed over his money. These ladies are angels."

"Off his rocker to think this place was a Dove House of Harlots," said Jackie Ray.

Must have been a hundred ladies stopped and stared at Jackie Ray's pale face when he finished his statement.

"Sir? Gentlemen?" said Madam LaBelle, tapping on Jackie Ray's shoulders. Chas was next.

"Yeah, what lady?" said Jackie Ray, half drunk, leaning back at her.

"Well, sir," said Madam LaBelle, first smile, eyes batted, and lashes bounced. "Kind sir, do you remember the name of the man who called this place a Dove House of Harlots?"

"Nope," said Chas, who knew something was astray.

"Why, Chas Bellew, buddy?" said Jackie Ray, "Sure you remember Russell Lightfoot's name, don't ya, bud? That man knows everything about this hotel."

"Russell Lightfoot?" said Madam LaBelle, cane raised, and she whistled, loud as a train. "That lowdown, dirty snake in the grass carpetbagger, son of a barber. Kill him, Duke!"

She nodded, eyes toward two burly men, who ran from behind a long "wall of eyes" when they heard her whistle. They'd been paid to eye the place through holes, I predicted. There were lots of holes and open places, and more men watched; the whites of their eyes unfolded, and lust ran across their faces alongside a parlor of women. Chas saw men exit the building from a hidden room. Madam LaBelle paced toward the two men, handed cash, and pulled money from her cleavage, more from her hips.

"Bring Lightfoot to me!" yelled Madam LaBelle, arms stretched in a rage, and handfuls of money flew across the rooms.

"The York brothers," said Chas, who stood. "Same men we saw in Louisville, days ago, at our campfire."

"Should have killed 'em days ago," I said, arms on Chas and Jackie Ray.

"I remember them," said Jackie Ray, staggering. "Didn't like 'em that night, like 'em even less tonight." He leaned toward Chas, speech slurred. "Now, what do we do?"

"Need two scars on my hand," I replied. "One for each varmint."

"Madam LaBelle told the York Brothers to kill Russell Lightfoot," said Chas, covering his mouth when he spoke about the York brothers.

A beautiful lady, one who had not performed, saw the whole thing and heard what Madam LaBelle said to the burly York brothers. Her eyes were blue as the ocean, and tears rolled down her face.

"I don't have time to go to the room with you, little lady," said Jackie Ray.

Everyone ran when Madam LaBelle roared.

"No. Help me!" the girl said. "I need your help." The lady leaned between Chas and Jackie Ray. "Please."

"What's wrong?" said Chas.

"Those men will kill my father."

"Your father is Russell Lightfoot?" said Jackie Ray. "Need to find him, or he's a dead man."

She wiped her wet face and held Chas, pulling him behind her.

"Please do something fast." She told Chas, hand in hand.

We ran outside into a pitch-black world, and snow fell.

"Follow me," said Lady Lightfoot. "I have an idea."

We followed the York brothers to a dark alley, and they knew where Russell Lightfoot was located, working his small bar and card table with men he trusted with his time.

"Is she serious about killing him?" said Jackie Ray.

"Most of the people in this town did not die of cholera," said the young Lightfoot lady. "She killed them. Sold their things to build a so-called School of Women."

"What do we need to do?" said Chas.

"I need to get out of this town with my father to New Orleans. We must go before they kill us both. Madam LaBelle will kill you since you know my father."

"I'll track the York brothers!" said Jackie Ray, running.

"Will you need some help?" said Chas, who stood close to her and watched the York brothers enter the stable where their horses were kept, and Russell's small bar was close to the horses. We found out from his daughter that he'd planned it that way to warn men about the Wagon Wheel. The first thing men needed was a drink when they arrived in Saint Louis, and Russell knew it.

"I'll get the York brothers, Chas," said Jackie Ray, who ran down the alley.

Chas stood close to the lady. I scouted for the York brothers behind Jackie Ray.

"We'll go with you to New Orleans," said Chas. "We're on a journey ourselves."

"Okay," said the lady, face worried. "I'm Liz Lightfoot." She hugged Chas.

"I'm Chas Bellew. The men helping your father are Jackie Ray Monroe and Atohi, two of the best men I know, all from Kentucky. They'll get the York brothers before they get to your father."

"Chas, listen," said Liz Lightfoot. "Surprise the York brothers before they kill your friends. Do what you must to save my father. We need to wait in the boat. My father will bring Jackie Ray and Atohi to the boat. We have a plan to leave."

The last thing Chas said was, "Two shots, two kills. Don't miss."

Snow fell when Jackie Ray slipped and tripped as he ran. I pulled him up and didn't know how we would find the York brothers, not being from the town. Liz led Chas down a dark alley, ducked out of sight, and found the boat. He placed his coat around her and walked her to the riverbank.

"Thank you, Chas," said Liz. "But will your friends meet us here?"

"I'd bet my life on it," said Chas. "Your father will bring them here when it's over."

Chas and Liz huddled in the boat, the vessel being filled. Time went slowly, and more snow fell.

"Jackie Ray," I said, "You had too much beer to scout. Go back to the river."

"I'm fine and dandy, Andy," said Jackie Ray, sick to his stomach, bent over in the dark alleyway.

"Brave friends, Chas," said Liz, pulling him close.

"All we can do is wait and see," said Chas. "They're pretty drunk."

She closed her eyes and stomped the boat.

"You sent two drunks to save my father, huh?" said Liz, holding her cold face.

"There was not a wide selection of men who volunteered to help you, now were they?" said Chas. "They're good men, Liz, sometimes better, but Atohi will find your father."

They sat in silence and watched the snow fall for a long while.

"My father is as good as dead, and it's all your fault, Chas."

"My fault?" said Chas, removing his hat. "How the heck is it my fault?"

"You and Jackie Ray told Madam LaBelle about my father calling the Wagon Wheel a Dove House of Harlots. I work there, by the way."

"Yeah, well, I didn't know that earlier," said Chas. "Jackie Ray did mention your father's name, didn't he? So did I?"

"My father is going to die," said Liz.

"Pow!" The shot echoed through the pouring snow. "Pow!"

Liz stood in the boat. Then fainted. Chas held her before she slammed into the oars. He covered her. Footprints slowly faded, the once dusty road had changed to mud, and snow left no good trail in a town that size.

"Elizabeth?" said Chas, touching her face.

"Is she dead?" a man's voice shouted from the riverbank.

"Russell Lightfoot?" said Chas "No. Heard shots. Fainted."

Chas helped him aboard, and he held his daughter close. He knew Jackie Ray ran behind my shadow, still in the dark alley, scouting.

"Pow!" Another shot echoed from the stables.

"Russell," said Chas, "have you seen my friends?"

"Yessir," he nodded, holding his daughter. "They were chasing two men. York brothers."

She moved her arm, head tilted.

"Daddy?" said Liz, head on his shoulder.

"I'm here, sweety," said Russell, holding her snow-covered head softly against his body. "Are you okay?"

"Yes," said Liz, raising her arm to Chas. "I'm fine. This man helped me."

Chas walked the boards to the riverbank and started up the hill.

"Mr. Chas Bellew?" said Russell. "Jackie Ray said he'll meet you at the riverboat. We're headed to New Orleans. Is that true, Liz?"

"Yes," said Liz, "it's true." She walked to the edge of the boat. "Madam LaBelle is a witch, Daddy. She'll kill us, so we must leave Saint Louis at sunup."

"Let's go now, Liz," said Russell, pulling on the ropes.

"Daddy!" yelled Liz. "We're not leaving without these men who saved us."

"Wait!" said Chas, turning and waving his revolver. "Whoa! Whoa!" Chas stepped toward the boat. "Our deal was to go together when your father arrived at the boat. He's here, so you two must wait on Atohi and Jackie Ray!"

"Chas Bellew," said Russell. "I saw your friends at the barn. Go!"

"Atohi!" said Chas, who stood. "Get in the boat, come on."

"You have ten minutes, and we're gone!" said Russell, checking his pocket watch. "Only ten minutes before the big riverboat docks at Saint Louis."

"Where's our horses, Mr. Lightfoot, huh?" said Chas.

"I meant to tell you," Russell said, pressing his hands together as he was about to pray. "Well, some Cherokee lady said she'd keep the horses with her. Said Atohi, and the Great Spirit sent her."

"Our horses are in good hands, Chas," I replied.

Chas took off his hat.

"What kind of crazy town is this?" said Chas, yelling. "Where's Jackie Ray, Atohi?"

"We don't have long, boys," said Russell Lightfoot, who held his shivering daughter.

"Jesus, need some help," said Chas, shaking his head. "I'll be back in ten minutes. Atohi, don't let them leave until I return, got it?"

"We'll wait," said Atohi. "Won't we, Russell?"

My face was as serious as two men fighting in the Civil War.

"Ten minutes, Chas," said Liz. "Hurry!" Did the Cherokee lady from the Wagon Wheel steal your horses, Atohi?"

"No," I said. "Horses are in Cherokee hands, though. I hope. The Great Spirit sent a horse keeper, a friend."

"I swear on your mother's grave," said Russell Lightfoot, lifting his head, hands up. "The Cherokee lady took 'em and never fired a shot."

"She is my old friend," I said. "I will not blame you if our horses disappear, Russell."

"Don't kill us, Atohi!" shouted Russell, face in a panic, shivering. "Please. We'll wait on your friends."

I went for my knife and walked over to Russell; the man's eyes were closed. In my pocket was an apple. I cut the fruit in half and held it.

"Apple, Russell?" I said, laughing. "Take both pieces, please. I'm not hungry, Liz, Russ."

Chas disappeared into the falling snow, walked down back alleys, and called for Jackie Ray. No one had spoken to him or had seen a man that resembled Jackie Ray Monroe. Chas checked the stable and two more corrals. Nothing. The stable was empty. No horses. No saddles or tack equipment. Pack mules were absent from the barn or at the small bar. The grain was gone, and four wagons were taken.

Chas saw the empty place.

"Russell has sold out, lock, stock, and barrel," said Chas to himself. "He has planned a trip to New Orleans for a long time with his daughter. We're the pawns down the river."

He checked every stall and looked for Jackie Ray. His friend was nowhere to be found. Chas walked back to the boat, thinking he may have missed him, ducking in and out of alleyways and taverns and passing a dozen buildings. No Jackie Ray Monroe. He was gone.

"Jackie Ray Monroe!" yelled Chas. "Jackie Ray!"

No sign of the York brothers, either. The streets of Saint Louis were packed with sinners, saints, and drunks.

He looked inside brothels and saloons and headed back to the boat. Between the swinging doors, Chas stood and was invited into an establishment by beautiful women, but he kept his boots moving toward the riverbank. Amid the fallen snow, he ran to the dark end of town and the wind blew, and he looked over the riverbank at Liz and Russell.

I stood.

"Did you find him?" said Russell.

"No," said Chas, who walked to the edge of the boat. "He's gone."

"Get in the boat, now," said Liz, who held the rope. "Jump! Someone is coming."

"I can't leave him behind," said Chas.

I stepped out beside Chas.

"Go on to New Orleans," said Chas.

Jackie Ray ran past Chas, down the longboards, jumping from bank to boat like a circus act. If he would have turned a Wagon Wheeler, it would have been fine with us. I remember a warm reception.

"Get in the boat, Chas and Atohi!" said Jackie Ray. "Let's go, bud, what are you waiting for, Christmas?"

Everyone was aboard. I pushed off with a long pole used to navigate shallow water. Five relieved passengers sat in silence; the horses were gone, and we floated slowly into deeper water. We heard a woman, Madam LaBelle, who had no cane on her arm, all a fake for the show. She used words heard by men and made her way to the riverbank.

"Unless you can walk on water, Madam LaBelle?" yelled Liz, "Goodbye, you hag!"

"Pow! Pow! Pow! Click."

Madam LaBelle fired and said, "No one escapes the Wagon Wheel alive, Miss Elizabeth Lightfoot!"

Paul York fired six rounds and hit nothing and said, "This ain't over yet!" Paul's voice echoed across the river, and the warmth of morning slowly offered a glow over Saint Louis.

Our small boat floated, snow blew, fog rolled, and the towering Town of Saint Louis disappeared behind us. I found a lantern under the bench. Russell handed out matches, and we had warmth.

"I didn't have the heart to burn my business, Liz," said Russell, who struck a torch in his hand. "We lied to you good men."

"I saw you sold everything, emptied the bar and barn," said Chas, rubbing his cold face.

"Don't do it again," I replied, took the torch from his clenched hands, and handed the lantern to Jackie Ray, who shivered.

"Thank you, Atohi," she said. "No more deception."

Russell Lightfoot walked to the front of the boat as the snow ceased; still, we drifted further downstream, headed to New Orleans, as Russell Lightfoot wept in guilt. The morning sky opened with enough light to reflect off the water in a sunburst of color that warmed hands and faces. Jackie Ray was frozen like a statue in the belly of the boat. Russell stood on the front and attempted to fall into the icy waters.

"Where do you think you are going, Russell?" I said, grabbed him, and sat him inside the boat. "If God would've wanted you dead, he'd had the York brothers kill you, so you have more days left."

"Daddy, it's going to be alright," said Liz. "These are good men, sent by the Lord. Atohi is right. More good days are ahead of us."

"Yeah," said her father, face tearful. "You are right, Liz. "We'll be in good company at Sonny Churchill's farm, just down the river." The old man smiled and cried.

I untied Russell before we landed.

"Live or die, Russell," I said, throwing the ropes inside the boat, "it's not up to me anymore."

Mr. Lightfoot leaned forward until he spotted a sandbar and recognized the spot. Blackbirds flew across the riverbank when Jackie Ray and Russell Lightfoot tied the boat to a weeping willow tree. Chas helped Liz; she kissed him for his good deed.

Chas was blessed with affection and many kisses. Lucky.

"Thank you, Chas Bellew," said Liz, who pulled him up the riverbank.

"Jackie Ray," said Russell Lightfoot, smiling. "Are you okay, young man?"

He nodded and shivered, eyes half closed, teeth chattering.

"Sonny Churchill's farm is this way," said Liz. "He's the red-headed stranger I have been telling you about. We deliver supplies to him once a week."

The voice of a howling owl startled everyone.

"Don't shoot my owl, Russell!" I yelled, both arms up.

"Pow!" Russell Lightfoot fired. "I missed the owl."

I knocked the daylight out of Russell Lightfoot. Then I picked him up, eye black.

"Don't shoot the dang owl, Russell!" yelled Chas. "He's our friend."

"The owl is a heck of a friend, mister," said Jackie Ray, who recognized the barn owl from Denton, Kentucky, the night Stan Brooks shot Preacher Chet Bellew.

"An owl means - it means death to the Cherokee," said Russell Lightfoot.

"Not this owl," said Chas, watching the owl soar across the sky. "He's been with us since Kentucky. The owl warns us of evil and sends friends when we need help."

"That's bull crap, boys!" said Russell Lightfoot, laughing and rubbing his eyes.

I shook my fist to warn him when he tapped his pistol again.

We jumped out of our skin when the eerie coyote howled behind a Hickory tree, and the only one not strapped with a gun was Liz, I guessed.

"Pow!" Liz fired, and the coyote was asleep forever.

"We all have weapons, huh?" I said.

She shrugged her shoulders and tucked her pistol away in a special place of disguise, squinted her eyes, and carried the coyote on her shoulder.

"I like Sonny Churchill," said Liz, who wrapped the coyote around Jackie Ray to keep him warm. "I introduced him to his wife, Mabel Lynn, two years ago. He owes me a favor, anyway."

The trail turned and twisted behind evergreens and loblolly pines, soft in places, clumps of heavy pine needles and briars, which were left to slow down intruders for almost a mile. The land was cleared with the steel blade of a scythe, operating from dusk 'till dawn, to make such a place a home.

"Down this way," said Russell Lightfoot. "Jackie Ray and Chas can check on the boat this afternoon."

"Covered the boat in pine needles and branches," I said. "Out of sight from trappers and hunters. Best if we didn't leave it by the sandbar, though. Let's fill our bellies with beans and warm our hands by the fire. Smoke and eat."

"Yessir," said Chas. "We made it."

"You saved us back there, Chas," said Russell Lightfoot, who slapped his shoulder.

"Think I earned my keep," said Jackie Ray. "I shot a wanted man, Duke York."

"Gentlemen," said Russell Lightfoot. "That's a brave thing in this world, and I owe you both. We'll take you as far as New Orleans, part ways, call it even, right?"

"Yeah," I said. "That's a deal. Sorry about the eye, Mr. Lightfoot."

"Sorry about taking a shot at the owl, my friend," said Russell.

Jackie Ray nodded his frigid face and appreciated what he'd said and done; still, he shivered and slowly paced behind the others. He couldn't wait to warm his body by the fireplace and clean his plate. The two-story house stood tall and wide in the distance, the only dwelling in that part of the country, a log-built house and barn, and the homestead was surrounded by a wilderness of game, a hidden paradise known by few people. Russell Lightfoot was his best friend and traded saddles and horses with Sonny Churchill when he was short on cash.

"We made it, Chas," said Russell Lightfoot. "This is the prettiest place in Missouri, boys."

All five of us stood tired and muddy and hungry. The sun burst through the dense clouds and warmed our red faces. We caught our breath and watched the sun reflect off a field of thin snow. Fog rolled across the creek by the house, and Liz raised her dress to cross the farmland. Patches of clumpy snow and ice filled the trenches, more than the rest of the land, relieved, running the last few steps on solid ground. Jackie Ray shivered, eyes closed and body cold, blue in color on his hands and face.

"Wake that man up," said Russell Lightfoot. "We don't have much time for him to sleep. His body temperature will drop, and he'll die. Get him by the fireplace!"

I saw something beautiful in the distance.

The Cherokee lady who had our horses sat bareback at the end of a golden field, sent by the Great One, a proper guardian for us. She waited until we arrived at the home of Sonny Churchill to make herself know only me. I held my eyes on the long feathers in her dark hair and walked toward her. She was dressed in buckskin and moccasins, still dry, and the tan horse she rode was mine.

Others thought I was crazy, and I walked toward her and raised my hand to her. She did the same for me. The second time I saw her, she had mounted, and no pack followed her. I walked across the meadow, fell in the mud once, and she laughed. We spoke softly and respectfully, carried on in our native tongue. Then I talked to the horse in English because the horse knew my voice, anyway, but he was a dumb horse. The horse favored her commands after that moment.

"You are a fine Cherokee lady," I said. She lifted her hand to the heavens. "O' Great Spirit, make for her a home at my home and keep her safe from the eyes of the outlaws." I kissed and hugged Meli.

The following day, I held open the second-story window of the home, saw the Cherokee lady three more times that day, and our horses trailed behind her. She disappeared from my life. It was as if we had unfinished business together, and more needed to be said.

"Our horses are in a safe place until we return," I said to Chas. "The Cherokee lady, Meli, will feed and keep them until we need them again."

"Let's go get our horses back," said Chas, pointing at the field.

"The world of the Cherokee does not work that way," I said, holding him back. "Our horses will be fine with Meli. The Cherokee need our animals for some reason." I told him plainly, but he did not understand my reasoning about women or horses.

"So, you gave our horses away to Meli, the lady you don't know, huh?" said Chas, walking away. "Black Sam is gone forever."

"I didn't know you, but I accepted you, didn't I?"

"Atohi?" said Chas, turning around. "How will we travel to Texas without horses and supplies? I'm not walking to Waco."

"The Great Spirit will provide," I said. "Where's your faith, anyways, saved man?"

"My faith was in our horses, the ones God provided," said Chas.

The young man did not understand what I knew about the Great One, Jesus Christ, and I was a believer, out of line sometimes, but I believed. The sermons of Preacher Chet still walked in my head, sermons of faith, provision, and words of the Sheperd. Timeless messages, small voice, even for men of Cherokee blood, and even for stubborn horses.

CHURCHILL FARM

Jackie Ray had recovered inside the white two-story west of the Mississippi River. At high noon, Chas slipped on his boots, and I followed him, and suddenly, birds stopped chirping, being flushed from a thicket. Our faces turned to the forest, motionless, and we listened for danger and knew we'd soon be in a battle. We left the field in a rush; trees stood to our right, and a man appeared who pulled a long rifle from his saddle.

"Who's back at the farmhouse?" said Chas.

"Jackie Ray and Liz," I whispered.

The man disappeared and fired into the farmhouse. Jackie Ray walked down the stairs to the bottom floor. Liz was in the kitchen and ran to Jackie Ray after the gun was fired.

"Take cover," said Jackie Ray. He smoked, squatted low down on the wide front porch, and scanned the field for the one who fired his gun.

"Between the trees," I said to Chas.

"In the pine thicket," said my friend, whispering. "That looks like Big York," Chas spoke and fired. "Missed him."

"I've got you pinned down, Chas Bellew," yelled Paul York. "You killed my brother."

"Should've killed you at the campfire, Paul," I said and gritted my teeth.

Chas slipped from the side of the house, crossed a split rail fence, and ran across the meadows, where deer and a raccoon made tracks the night before.

"Your brother wanted to die!" yelled Chas, chin up. "Any man who hits an old lady deserves a headstone." Chas hid behind a tree.

Paul York fired four rounds with his revolver and emptied his rifle. The man was alone. He adjusted his glasses and hit trees, and mud splattered beneath my feet. He was a poor shot or blind. Chas positioned himself uphill behind a fallen tree and watched Paul York move behind thick pines. Minutes later, the big man squatted low.

"Pow!" Chas fired.

Paul York fell to the ground, blood on his shoulder. I grabbed his head and held a knife to his neck. Chas saw my knife close the eyes of

Paul York. He died when he clutched his chest. Two crows flew down to the feet, and the danger of the forest birds settled the rest.

"Leave him for the turkey buzzards and crows," I said.

"Let's check the house," said Chas, who rushed through the woods, rifle in hand.

Russell, Jackie Ray, and Liz were alive. We spent the better part of a week at Sonny's Churchill's farmhouse. Without horses, the riverboat was our only way out. Meli broke my heart, and I thought it was love, but it must've been with another brave.

Not seeing our favorite horses again became a terrible loss for the Sons of War. Chas reminded my heart of giving away his good horse, Black Sam, while at breakfast. The slight grin on Jackie Ray's face meant the Great One hadn't provided new horses yet, so we walked and kept the faith that the Lord would deliver.

Chapter 6
Red-headed Strangers

Welcomed to the farm by a man toting a pistol, a good friend of Russell Lightfoot, the redheaded stranger, Sonny Churchill, who arrived to find his house occupied. We'd hoped he would show up. But until he arrived, provisions were made for the long trip to New Orleans. I was the brave who scouted at night with the eyes of a Skyhawk and the lurk of the red fox, but I circled the homestead like an animal on the hunt for more thieves and bandits. It was a time of little sleep under the silver moon, and I had no horses of my own to feed.

Chas and Jackie Ray sat on the front porch of the big house and collected feathers from fresh chickens at midday, smoking long cigars from Sonny Churchill. Our conversations leaned on what was expected in the next town. He had a not-so-beautiful wife, Lilly, and Bonnie, the daughter, was the same age as Jackie Ray and Chas Bellew. She was given an exceptional voice and good beauty - but from a long distance away. Inside the house was a second floor held for the women. Rifles and revolvers were kept with the men downstairs. Sonny spoke many nights about the horror of the Civil War and the Word of God and how wounded and evil men visited Saint Louis.

The Sons of War, Chas and Jackie Ray, were blessed with good company and gifted by the Great One with more food and warm clothes. My feet felt the bitter cold bite of an April frost, and snow blew wildly for seven moons into the barn, and I slept among an angry wind on most days. I had chosen to be alone early in life.

The Churchill daughter, Bonnie, stood, hair of soft red, eyes of green, and better features than her father and mother, and had a nice smile. She stayed near Jackie Ray and Chas, a woman accepting of most men and had no morals, the worst kind of person. Liz was jealous of Bonnie, like a rabbit who snatched spring grass from the field of the groundhog, the same for pretty women, I guess. All I could do was watch the redheaded Churchill lady, Bonnie, dance and sing like a circus parade around the young men, flirting.

Preacher Chet Bellew would have had her voice in the choir of singers, but not her dancing. To see her dance was painful for a man with good vision to watch, but we watched anyway. There were no horses to feed, and Meli was longer riding across the meadows.

"How long will you men be staying with us?" said Bonnie Churchill.

"Not sure," said Chas.

"The river runs to Fort Defiance," said Liz. "Next, New Orleans and all its wonder."

Her voice was soft, as warm as summer rain, and my Cherokee ears had never heard a voice that could speak to the animals the way she did in her low English language. My head heard many voices of the Great One while in Missouri. No voice was as sweet as hers, and Bonnie made the dogs bark and fish jump, they said. My eyes saw no fish jump, but the hounds made an awful racket when she sang the song about angels.

"The difficult task," said Sonny, sipping mudding water, "is dipping from a good water source, and you would think being close to the river that a man could find good water, but we can't."

"Mr. Churchill, sir," said Chas, nodding. "Follow me beyond the thicket of trees, and let's take the trail westerly. I have found something you want to see." He stood, eyes wide. "Bring the canteens and a bucket when you get ready."

Chas, Jackie Ray, Russell, and Sonny stood at the doors with their rifles and pistols, and we all hiked to the spring. My red face was among the white men taking the trail through the woods, and our feet became soft as spring hay in the water. To my amazement, Chas discovered five bubbling springs, and clearwater flowed from the streams to the muddy 'uweyvi' (river) of the Mississippi. Each man drank from his own canteen, and snow melted, and fresh water covered the muddy land. We celebrated the blessing of water.

"Ama Gvnida," I said to Chas.

"What did he say?" said Russell Lightfoot, who held his ear.

"That man needs to speak English," said Sonny, who leaned on a tree, water on his lips.

"Water is life," said Chas, nodding. "Water is life."

"It is a long hike from the farmhouse to the spring," said Sonny, who carried the wooden bucket. "But in time, this heavenly water, gentlemen, will supply my children and grandchildren for many years because of what you found, Chas."

My firm hand covered the mouth of Sonny Churchill from talking, and Chas Bellew knew to stop all conversations, knew the Cherokee ways, and something was wrong nearby. I heard two loud men yell in the direction of the farmhouse. I ran through the woods, and Chas followed.

"What's wrong, Atohi?" said Chas.

"The women are in trouble!" I yelled. "Renegades!"

"What's going on with that crazy Cherokee man, Jackie Ray?" said Sonny. He stretched out his arm, face in a panic, voice low to a whisper.

"Follow that brave Cherokee and take his counsel to heart," said Jackie Ray. "Shut up! Run and run now, men!"

Shots splintered the front door of the farmhouse; the wooden doors blew into several pieces. More shots downed the back door, and the ladies screamed when they saw blood on the dress of Mrs. Lilly Churchill. Renegades stepped over her wounded body and opened drawers and cabinets.

"Help me," said Mrs. Churchill, eyes closed, voice lost. "Please, Sonny."

His voice had faded away.

"What the hell do they want with my family?" said Sonny, dropping the water bucket. "I'll find them all."

"You cover the back," said Chas, standing at the edge of the woods. "I'll cover the front of the farmhouse."

We split up and meant to defend the farm.

"Are you going listen to this crazy Cherokee?" said Russell, hobbling alongside Jackie Ray.

"He tells no lies," Jackie Ray said, who rushed the men along and stood in the distance. "Draw your weapon for battle, men. Someone will die, and don't let it be you."

Back at the farmhouse, four men dismounted their horses, two big men slow to walk, and two smaller men. One yelled, "Bad Carl Bellew, come out and get your justice!"

"They think Chas is Bad Carl Bellew," said Jackie Ray to Sonny and Russell.

One renegade blew a hole in the front window, and the short man fired his revolver into the kitchen. Then, another man fired and shattered a wall mirror with his shotgun. Two more shots were fired, and the small men checked the entire house for gold and goods.

"There's no one here but an old lady," said one of the renegades.

"Let's go," said the leader of the renegades. "Get the horses."

Chas saw that I was inside the parlor, as I was with Mrs. Churchill during her last moment of life.

"She's dead," I said, towel over her eyes.

"Did they take the young ladies?" I said as I ran up the stairs.

Russell and Sonny walked through the front door and could not find the ladies. Jackie Ray slowly entered the back door.

"Find the men who killed Lilly, Atohi!" said Sonny, who held his wife and wept.

"I'll find the killers," I said, running back downstairs. "I'll bring back the horses of many men by sunup."

One horse had wandered to the barn, a gift from the Lord. We had no idea how it found the Churchill farm. I mounted an unknown horse.

Each man held up his rifle and stood at the barn: Sonny Churchill, Chas Bellew, Jackie Ray Monroe, and Russell Lightfoot watched. My lungs released a war cry, and it was my time to scout renegades.

"Atlesidi!" I yelled.

"What did the Cherokee say?" said Russell Lightfoot. "I can't understand a dang word that brave says," pacing with his cane.

My tracks disappeared into the cedars.

"Atlesidi, it means revenge," said Chas.

"He speaks of revenge," said Jackie Ray, who found a good place to bury Mrs. Lilly Churchill.

It was said Sonny held his wife until dark covered the day. Jackie Ray played somber music on the piano while Bonnie and Liz sang "God of the Valley" and sobbed. Bonnie walked downstairs when she heard her Pa screaming through the night and collapsed and fainted in the arms of her father, still broken late into the night.

Sonny Churchill, a God-fearing man, woke up, clutched his chest, and thought his daughter was dead. He gasped and fell over dead. Jackie Ray stayed behind with Russell Lightfoot to dig graves for Lilly and Sonny. Bonnie became crazy-eyed and in shock after she heard the news of her Pa and Ma; the best part of her life was gone. The following day came slowly.

"Bonnie, breakfast?" said Liz, who had cooked a small meal.

"Where is that girl?" said Chas, who climbed the stairs. "Jackie Ray, you gotta see this, but Liz, please do not come up here!"

"Bonnie cut her own throat," said Jackie Ray, who wiped his eyes. "She could not hold the pain inside her heart. This place has become a graveyard."

Three days in a row, men dug graves. Liz and Jackie Ray sang until their voices only made a whisper. Sadly, under dark thunder clouds that stretched across the damp plains of Missouri and, when they stopped, Liz prayed aloud, and the red-haired strangers were buried.

"Russell, you think a man can go to hell for defending his land and his family?" said Jackie Ray, resting on the front porch.

Russell shrugged his shoulders. "I believe God knows the difference between evil and good," said Russell, nodding. "And the Lord pardons his sin based on his heart and not what he had to do in a gunfight against renegades who committed murder and caused a family to break apart."

"Yeah, true," said Jackie Ray. "Would hell be a place a young man needs to worry about if he's not born again?" Jackie Ray held his coffee and smoked nervously, looking down the hill where three grave markers stood.

"I expect a man, young or old, might know his own heart well enough to plan his own eternity," said Russell.

Russell held his pose and said, "I'm sure it's not the first time a man has pondered whether he needs to be pardoned by God or not."

Russell Lightfoot pulled Jackie Ray's arm with his cane.

Chas walked seven miles, borrowed a horse, and followed my cold tracks.

"Let's walk down to the graves and witness what death looks like," said Russell Lightfoot, headed down, humming, and pacing.

Both men groaned and moaned from digging graves, and the wind whipped through the budding trees and the sky was dark, and the day was broken.

"I suspect, well, if..." said Russell, hands atop the Bible, "if you know of a man who needs to confess his sins to the Lord, I would not want to be in a gunfight to decide where I wanted to spend eternity? The wise way, settle it, be sure of it now, Jackie Ray."

Crows flew across the dark sky, the changing wind caused small birds to be flushed from their nesting places, and in the cold stillness of the evening, they said Jackie Ray did not confess his sins. I am sure death and what Russell spoke of… and more crossed his mind.

"Let's place more rocks around the Churchill family," said Russell Lightfoot. "Say a prayer or two over the bodies, and call it a night, what do you say, Jackie Ray?"

"Yeah, sounds good," said Jackie Ray, face long. "I wonder what is keeping Atohi and Chas hunting down some renegades."

The third grave was covered in rocks, headstones placed and marked, and no songs sounded among the men, like at most burials, just prayers of hope. They ended with the Lord's Prayer.

"I bet Liz has a kettle of beans and some cornbread by now," said Russell Lightfoot, who crawled up from his knees, stood between the graves, and his body began to chill, and his teeth chattered.

Over the next two days, they spoke the Word to each other and gathered water by the bubbling brook for meals. To calm Liz's nerves, they found paper at the end of a book and balled horsehair to make a paintbrush. Pictures were painted with wet coffee grounds, a style Liz had learned in Saint Louis. Her time was spent on meals and paintings for Jackie Ray. Three days had slicked by, and Chas and I had not returned. Russell had begged and pleaded, but Jackie Ray had yet to confess his sins. He played the piano while Liz sang and painted and spoke little after losing her friends.

***

Black wavy smoke and a big fire could have been scouted by a blind Cherokee brave, and I doubled back and found Chas, who knew my tracks, flat on our bellies. We scouted the rolling hills, counted four horses, and handled the horses while the renegades slept and the fire still burned at the camp. Chas had slowly walked the horses to a flat area, far from the camp of the renegades, and tied each animal to a tree.

"These are our horses now," I said, nodding and painting my face with the earth. "They will not leave this campfire alive." I turned my knife and readied my hatchet and pistol.

"What has the Great Lord said to you about these four men?" said Chas, who did not paint his face.

"Evil men must die a fast death," I said. "They have seen their last sunset if they shot at us."

"They have already shot at us," said Chas, "back at the Churchill farm."

"Men asleep cannot fight," flipping my knife. "Mrs. Churchill will get her revenge through us tonight. This Cherokee brave is ready for war."

"Let's pour it on them, Atohi."

We moved swiftly through the woods, and then, it was time to separate. Chas took the east side of the fire. I stayed west, positioned for a surprise attack on the renegades. Killing one, Chas raised three fingers; three men left. My voice was of a coyote, and then I scouted for weapons, and one man stood to water a tree. He watered no more trees.

I sounded like an old owl and moved closer to the two men asleep. Chas knew that he had spotted the third man. He watched as the man, round and slick-faced, was surprised to find a knife in his chest and fell to the ground. One finger was raised by Chas.

My friend had proved himself and wounded the last man with long black hair. Shot him a second time. The renegade stood and laughed, chest bleeding and shocked.

"Get up, brother!" yelled the last renegade; his gun fired into a tree not far from the head of Chas. He did not realize the rest of his friends had fallen asleep forever.

"Your friends are dead," said Chas, hidden.

The last man had no idea where Chas was, low to the ground, protected in the depths of the woods. Chas smelled his unclean body.

"There's a dozen men on your tail," I said, covered by the pine thicket; I fired my revolver to scare the last man.

"O' God, don't kill me!" screamed the man. "Please don't kill me," the man said. "Got a wife and a young boy at home."

The man fired at Chas and then fired into the pine thicket and once into the brush. He reloaded one bullet, fled to a Hickory tree, and fired again. The renegade knew our position.

"You killed a woman at the river just three days ago," said Chas, moving from tree to tree. He ducked and stayed low to the ground when the renegade pleaded.

I saw Chas aim true at the man. He missed.

"That shot was meant for Sonny Churchill and Bad Carl Bellew," yelled a tall man, squatting down behind a log.

"That was a house full of women, and you knew it!" said Chas. "Carl and Sonny were not in the farmhouse. The old lady was the one you killed."

Chas moved closer for a better shot at the man. Fired. He moaned when the bullet ripped his side, and he rolled over for cover.

"I shot her and thought she was a man," said the renegade in a rattled voice. "You don't know who you got in front of you, boy."

"What should I write on your tombstone, outlaw?" said Chas, who disappeared into the darkness of the forest.

I watched Chas slide his pistol down the bark of a tree and pull the trigger.

"Rolla Renegades! More men are riding for blood on Churchill and Bellew!" sounded the man.

I ran behind the outlaw, hooked his arm, and stabbed him. I took no scalp. I was not a savage but a writer. The Rolla Renegades were all shot in the chest by Chas Bellew to make sure none of them walked out of the woods again for what they had done to an innocent woman.

The last renegade was still alive.

"What do you want with Bad Carl Bellew?" said Chas, who lowered his frame to the ground for a clear look at the man, who clutched his bloody chest.

The man never answered.

I had not seen Chas Bellew fight with such determination and grit since he was a young man. He heard the leaves break from the wind that had moved the trees and exposed the moon through the tall cedars, and Chas fired at the silver April moon. We took their horses in exchange for the life of Lilly Churchill. We rode three days back to where Liz, Jackie Ray, and Russell Lightfoot had taken up a homestead at the Churchill farm. Chas spoke very few words on the trip back. What I remembered the most about him was that Chas had cold eyes.

"Atohi," said Chas, "I did not intend to take any prisoners, bud."

"Agreed, bud," I said, and we laughed for the first time since we left the Wagon Wheel. "Some men live too long, Chas."

"What did he need with Bad Carl Bellew, Atohi?" said Chas, turning the horse.

"Whatever Carl did," I said, "they aimed to kill him and Sonny."

"I hope the coyotes and bears fight over them."

My eyes were sincere, and we were two tired men.

"Maybe Russell knows why they were hunting Bad Carl Bellew," I said.

Chas walked inside the house and was greeted with hugs and kisses from Liz.

"We have been certainly worried sick," said Liz, who led him to the fireplace, handed him beans, and poured him black coffee.

"Hey, Atohi," said Jackie Ray.

No one greeted my face or hands as if I had Cholera or rabies. I got no hugs or special greetings and did not get a kiss from Liz.

"I fought 33 men with a butter knife," I said, making my own black coffee and beans.

"Oh, God, Chas," said Liz, "tell us what happened, please."

"Yeah, Chas," I said, seated at the table. "Russell, the horses are yours, I reckon. Put them in the barn all by myself. One horse kicked my chest. I died."

No one listened.

"Are you alright, Chas?" said Jackie Ray, taking a seat beside the table.

"I am fine now, bud," said Chas, drinking his coffee.

"Can I warm your coffee, Chas?" said Liz, who stood beside him.

"The boy already has a full cup of hot coffee," I said. "I could use some more coffee, Liz, right?." I raised my cup.

"Help yourself, Atohi," Liz said. "Coffee is in the kitchen."

"We were gone for six days. I am hungry as a winter grizzly."

"Liz just made a pie, Atohi," said Russell Lightfoot. "Help yourself, scout."

"Oh boy," I said, walking to the stove. "Think I will feed the horses and jump off a cliff." No ears heard my voice.

"Be careful on the cliff and don't spook the horses," said Jackie Ray, turning to Chas. "I'll be right out after Chas tells his story and rests his feet."

"I may not be back," I said, standing at the stove. "I will just jump out of the barn instead." Hands full of pie.

"Hope your back feels better, Atohi," said Jackie Ray, who threw up his hand and listened to what Chas talked about in his gunfight.

Russell Lightfoot walked outside to see the new horses. We were the only two in the barn and held my pie and coffee.

"What do you know about Bad Carl Bellew, Russell?"

"Carl stayed at Sonny's farm a few weeks ago."

"You know more than that, huh?"

"Yeah," he said. "They were good friends. Took gold from folks in Colorado."

"That man is the uncle of Chas Bellew." I feed the horses pie.

"His uncle is a wanted man. Robber, huh?"

"What is he wanted for?" I brushed the horses and opened a sack of grain.

Russell carried buckets of water, spilled the beans on Bad Carl Bellew, and we talked about New Orleans.

"They say he and Sonny killed a man for gold last fall in the Rockies," said Russell Lightfoot. He sat the bucket down to rest. "His men ate all the food at Sonny's farmhouse but paid in gold nuggets, so the Rolla Renegades tracked him here, and I guess they thought Chas Bellew was Bad Carl Bellew. They killed Lilly by accident. I am not sure why."

That night, Russell told Chas the same story.

"I miss Sonny, Lilly, and Bonnie," said Chas.

"We have dead friends in heaven," said Jackie Ray.

Jackie Ray recalled the horrible events when we left the farmhouse. In a sad turn of events, I stood beside Chas and paid our respects to Sonny, Lilly, and Bonnie.

Few words were spoken at the Churchill farm. We chewed on brown beans and pork. The owl hooted in a nearby tree as if the bird befriended Chas and followed him from Denton, Kentucky, to the Mississippi River. The owl called like it was time to leave. Even owls did not listen to my voice that week, and it was a bloody week.

"Tomorrow," said Chas, excitedly, standing up in front of the fireplace, "we will leave for New Orleans on the boat."

"I appreciate your invitation for Liz and myself to join you on the river to New Orleans," placing his fork on the table, "but we have decided to stay here on Cousin Sonny's farm," said Russell, who cleared his throat, " just take care of the horses and make this place a home, boys, will ya?"

"No. We must leave. You mean, you settling here?" said Chas.

"Yeah," said Liz. "This is home."

"Good farm," said Chas, who saw the tired faces of Russell and Liz. "Churchill loved you very much. I think it's a good place to live and makes a good home."

"I can paint and tend to the horses," said Liz, smiling. "You found the water supply, and it will be a good home for us." Liz rubbed the leg of Jackie Ray, head on his shoulder.

"Jackie Ray, you can stay with Liz until the frostbite is better," I declared.

"Yeah, yeah," said Russell Lightfoot. "Oh, that is a grand idea, my boy."

In a low voice, Jackie Ray said, "I am sorry, but I'm headed to Texas, boys. Like we planned from the start of this dang ride, back in Kentucky. Frostbite or no frostbite, my tail rides the next boat to New Orleans."

Everyone laughed and smiled.

"You must be drinking Fire Water again, Jackie Ray," I said, talkin' with a Kentucky accent. "No more whiskey from him, Russell."

"Well, good," said Chas. "You have a home, and I am glad we found water," smiling. "We will leave for New Orleans in the morning, Atohi and Jackie Ray. Be ready."

"Do you want the horses?" said Russell Lightfoot, holding the hands of Liz atop the table.

"Or will you take the boat?" asked Liz.

"Keep the horses," I said, and my mind read his selfish face. "They are your animals, and they like it here."

"We will sail to Orleans," said Jackie Ray.

Liz sat in her favorite chair and wept. She painted pictures, brushed out coffee grounds, and spent the day on a picture of a man, Jackie Ray Monroe, playing the piano. The picture was painted with a masterful touch. Russell Lightfoot had grown partial to Jackie Ray, taking care of him for several days. Out of respect, Russell Lightfoot removed his straw hat and hugged each one of us, and we walked down the long golden field. The same field where I last saw Meli days earlier, the Cherokee lady mounted on horseback. Liz did wake up to see us off. Fog rolled over the water, the riverbank muddy and wet, and at the top of the riverbank, Liz ran to the edge where Russell Lightfoot stood at the top, and lanterns were lit up. Their tearful eyes faded into the distance, and they walked away. Two wonderful people, folks we had grown to love very much, had made themselves a home.

Chapter 7
Broken Mirror

When I was a young brave, life was very different, all too much different, but I had learned how to survive on what I had and prayed for what was needed. Living in the mountains for twelve winters with game was plain and simple, yet broken, like pieces of an old mirror I had found in the mountains of North Carolina, left behind by pioneers. The Chieftain of the Cherokee tribe was my wise father, up in years, like the rings of a tree. I called him "Broken Mirror," and one day, he placed a glass mirror into my palms, and blood ran between our hands. His blood was my blood, and our blood was Cherokee blood. A person cannot change where they come from, but they are known for how they give of themselves or not.

By 1850, the brokenness of the Eastern Band of the Cherokee had started. The unfair displacement of my family made blood run, and the tribe lost too many braves that year and years that followed. Memories of my family bathing in high mountain waterfalls could not wash away what had happened. Arrows, spears, and bones covered the hillside mounds and were all that was left of the Cherokee Nation in North Carolina by the time of the Civil War. That was our mountains, a good land that became like broken pieces of an old mirror inside our hands. The mountains are still there waiting for our return, and we will return, one day as a nation, whole again, the Cherokee Nation.

The last time I saw my father was in the fall of 1850. I was twelve winters old: the same age as my dog, Waya, meaning Wolf. That year was a broken time for my people; they shed blood, and many deaths came at a high cost for the Cherokee and all people with skin red as the color of the earth. From 1830 to 1850, the horrible act of ethnic cleansing happened. President Andrew Jackson and his Army of Blue Union soldiers marched thousands of my people from North Carolina to Oklahoma. My people lost more than the "Trail of Tears." How was that an act of Christian love by a Presbyterian president?

Only one man escaped, the son of Wohali, which means Wolf in Cherokee, who was a brave writer, now from Kentucky. I called my father "Broken Mirror," and under the sunburst of the West, my eyes will see him smile again someday. I was not the only son of Broken Mirror, but I was the last one still walking on the earth with the Great Spirit of the Cherokee.

"My life will be Cherokee," I said sternly. "Nothing but Cherokee."

"I want you to be my Cherokee son," said Preacher Chet. "Nothing but my son."

He took me as his own bloodline before my thirteenth winter and raised me like his own son. The name Atohi means "Woods," and I lived in the woods, running fast into the darkness of the forest. I was the only young brave to escape the "Trail of Tears" from North Carolina while my family marched onward toward Oklahoma. If it were possible, my name would rebuild the Eastern Band of the Cherokee, and one day, the Great One will provide a Cherokee wife, and we will sing and begin again.

On days when the sky bands are filled with blowing snow, I think of my father, who gave me the broken mirror, and my mother, Tayanita, meaning Young Beaver, who screamed out when blood ran from our hands onto the Cherokee land and into the swift streams. With bloody hands, I ran into the woods. I was not discovered until the Holy Spirit sent Preacher Chet Bellew from Kentucky to North Carolina to my hideout at Mingo Falls.

The Great Spirit told me I would meet a friendly man with hair and beard gray in color near Mingo Falls. Three days later, Chet Bellew walked with his horse and drank water from the falls, where I was hidden. He was God's man, and I was saved. I heard his voice, deep and loud, echoing across the mountains.

"Atohi!" he yelled. "Atohi!" said the man, who cupped his hands, and his horse stood in one position. I stood where he saw my face, open and plain in the light of day.

I was not afraid of him, and the pistol he carried did not raise fear.

"The Great One sent you to me," I said boldly.

"The Holy Spirit of God sent me to find a brave young man who goes by Atohi," said Preacher Chet, nodding. "He is a brave hidden deep in the woods."

"You have found him." I ran to where the man stood. "Any Great One that sends a man to find me," walking toward him as I did, worn moccasins and wrapped in the hide of deerskin, "I will protect you and your family."

"I knew you would be among the woods," said Preacher Chet.

"Where are we going?" I said, following him.

"Kentucky," and he smiled.

"I hope you lived closer, but good," I said, laughing. "As long as it is not Oklahoma."

"Denton, Kentucky," said Chet. We met with open hands. "It is your new land, and maybe you can call it home soon."

"Let's go home," I told him.

"I should have bought you a horse," the preacher said with guilt.

"That would have been nice for my feet, Chet."

That is how I came to live with the Bellew family. When the snow flew from the cotton fields, I remembered the days that passed and recalled my journey to Kentucky. I gripped the hands of Preacher Chet Bellew, and he handed me the reins of his horse. The good man walked from the high mountains of North Carolina to his home in Denton, Kentucky, and because of his walk, I knew Preacher Chet was sent from God.

No Army found me in the woods, and no broken glass was inside my hand. The piece of broken glass, the one I carry to shave my head and reflect the sun, is hidden inside my moccasins. Sometimes, the past is my only path to the Cherokee Nation, still living in a white man's world, a broken world. My changing face in the broken mirror is a gentle reminder wherever I am, even amid the mountains or floating on the Mississippi River.

Atop the boat on the Mississippi River, I feel the cold wind on my face at night, and the Great One planned it before the Sun of Happiness that I will see Tayanita and Wohali again. In months to come, it will be written in the sky on this big journey with Chas Bellew and Jackie Ray or on another journey. Even Jackie Ray, a man sometimes slow as a little child in his mind, will be of some help. I promised Preacher Chet Bellew my protection over Chas Bellew as a scout, but not for Bad Carl Bellew; His face on a wanted poster burned an image in my dreams. I could not sleep for his face.

We drifted down the river of the Mississippi, which ran swift and wide, edged in a snow drift on the riverbanks, and at daybreak, the sunburst through the silvery clouds and brought hope for the journey by mid-April 1871.

Early on a rainy, disagreeable day blanketed the dark sky, evidence of rain clouds and a good prospect for the farmer, three days south of Saint. Louis, protecting Chas and Jackie Ray.

I shaved my head by the righted candlelight amid a storm the night before and, with some objection, developed a new image for myself, a look of the white man, and saw my face in a large broken mirror, one where my eyes caught the image of the Thunderbird fly across the depth of the broken mirror. The Thunderbird made one flight and soared high in the broken mirror, crossing a Sky Band, leading to great happiness and more prosperity. I had to tell Chas what had been revealed from the Thunderbird.

The following day, I leaned on the rail, the hat of a dead outlaw scratched my head, and a long pheasant tailfeather waved, one I found in Saint Louis, was tied atop my head. I overlooked the land from atop the steamboat we climbed aboard. Land of running deer and screaming eagles, and my eyes saw the same Thunderbird again across the Sky Band, but this time, it was not in the depth of a broken mirror, but in the air. My eyes were filled with a Spirit of Happiness from the Thunderbird. I might be the blood of a crazy red skin, or it was just another flight of the black bird, perhaps. I stood stupid in a round hat of an outlaw that made the Thunderbird appear. I am not sure, anyway.

Each of us wore a black vest and an overcoat from the wardrobe of Sonny Churchill, being his wife was a good hand at making clothes. His chifforobe robe was filled with used material and good shirts, well-fitted for slim men. Chas Bellew and Jackie Ray Monroe felt Sonny was a selfish man, but the time had passed to ask for his permission, so we wore his clothes anyway. I remembered no objection was granted from Russell Lightfoot, a man who shrugged his shoulders and was too fat to wear them and had no opinion about the clothes we picked for the journey.

Days later, I was the first to step on the earth after the ship docked at Camp Defiance on the 10th day of April, a former Army military camp, still occupied, and later became a strategic Army fort after the Civil War, where boats transferred supplies, and passengers spent the night resting between the Ohio River and the Mississippi River, the southernmost point of Illinois. Everyone had horses and dogs, and too many dogs barked.

We walked the land, and Jackie Ray was hungry like the Great Bear.

Good place for a meal," said Jackie Ray. "I feel safe among the Army soldiers marching around, making me want to join up."

"I am not excited," I said, walking close to my friends.

Jackie Ray smiled with a funny face. Beer was bad for some men.

No one has the nose of a Cherokee brave like me, and the Trail of Tears will prove my point. I was the only Cherokee, and no one watched my back with an old broken mirror. "I do not feel safe. No good for a Cherokee brave. Bad spirit. Cherokee killers walk around with long rifles and Colt pistols." Head down, tugged my hat into the wind and squinted my eyes at Chas and Jackie Ray, who had never seen an Army fort like the one that made them "Sons of War" and had never been on a large boat of that size.

"Many years ago," said Chas, nodding, "Lewis and Clark stayed here for five days and packed their gear to follow the rivers west. No different, Lewis and Clark sat for a meal just like us and were hungry like the Great Bear inside of Jackie Ray."

One day," said Jackie Ray, lifting his coffee cup, steam waving from the fresh brew, "someone might say they saw us here in April of 1871. Three handsome men from Kentucky who made a trail into the wilderness of the Great West, chasing Bad Carl Bellew."

A man in a crushed leather hat and brown clothes made of deerskin stopped walking and boldly took a chair beside Chas Bellew. He had the teeth of an opossum. He removed his hat and leaned in close and smelled like a goat.

"Pardon me," said the man. "Are you good folks chasing Bad Carl Bellew?" The man rubbed his hair and grinned, hands dirty and clothes stained, long stringy hair, and eyes the color of a dark cigar. His eyes blinked and widened with his face bent in curiosity. And without a doubt, he was the ugliest man I had ever seen.

"Yeah," said Chas. "What about him?"

I slid my hand under the table and gripped the handle of my knife. My face and eyes were on the stranger, turning toward him in my own defense. Jackie Ray continued to eat and did not know the whole story about Carl Bellew yet, being a known gunslinger and a man who was chased for striking gold and killing an unarmed man in Colorado.

Like a fox looks for a turkey," I said. "We are looking for Bad Carl Bellew."

Being the only Cherokee in the room, I saw the long-haired man seated beside Chas, and my ears leaned into his face. No man was more curious than his ears, and greed and jealousy were painted across his dark eyes. Death spoke from his cynical voice, like cold water in January that ran across my face.

"They say he stayed in the room with the broken mirror for three days," said the strange man. "Carl Bellew left yesterday before sunup." The man crushed his hat and shaped it again, as a look of nervousness and pride turned a nasty smile on his face.

My dreams saw his face in a broken mirror. I told myself as I eyed the face of a devil man and saw Warding Arrows in the sand. No peace pipe was in his hands. No words of goodness were spoken to mend the past. I knew the Path's Crossing was a bad day for a bad spirit. I was there to change things.

The face of a stranger formed an evil scar on his forehead as if Chas Bellew knew more than he told, but he did not and kept words to himself if he could, just like I would have done. But I had too much to drink, and my mouth was loose like a spring songbird.

"Our hunt is for Bad Carl Bellew," I said, tapping my knife. "Yes, we intend to catch up with him and meet him in Texas."

"We aim to buy horses in New Orleans and ride to Texas," said Jackie Ray. "We will find him, but most cowboys think he's a ghost."

"And Cherokee, we know he lives!" I said gladly. My hand was raised to represent the Cherokee Nation.

The curious man reached inside his jacket pocket. Jackie Ray and Chas pulled out their firearms, and the pistol of Chas shaved his nose.

"Whoa!" said the stranger, who untucked an artistic rendering of Bad Carl Bellew. "You boys got fast trigger fingers, huh? You want to take down an innocent man like me, right?"

"We will protect ourselves," I said.

I leaned backward against the wall and laughed under my breath. The night before, that picture of Bad Carl Bellew was in my mind. I felt the hair on my neck raise because the Great One was sending us to Carl Bellew.

"Something wrong, Cherokee man?" said the stranger, lips smirking, and he held the position.

"Yeah," I said, chuckling. "Big something wrong. I heard the words you had not yet said." Beer covered my breath. "Next time your nose wants your butt to take a seat, keep walking."

"Hey, hey," said Chas. "Let me see the paper of Bad Carl Bellew," holding out his hand to the strange man, who was up to no good from the time he made himself comfortable in his chair and flushed his cheeks red.

Chas saw features in the drawing that resembled Preacher Chet Bellew and his father's face, too. They were brothers a few short years apart and were on their own mission in life. Chas and Carl were the last of the Bellew family known to be alive.

"Might be the man we are looking for in Texas," I said to Chas.

"Heard he is on his way to New Orleans," said the man who wiped beer from his mouth. "And my men aim to find him, see if he has any gold left in his pockets for poker."

I looked at his long, red face and said, "You mean you and your husband plan to kill him, huh?"

All the men laughed at my joke. The stranger did not see it as a good joke, and when he stood, I kicked his chair across the floor.

"You might need to keep this drunken Cherokee's mouth shut," said the man with a scar on his face, who waved his hand at each man.

Chas tucked the sketched picture of his uncle under the table. Then he folded the paper inside his chest pocket and stood. The men walked away.

"Jackie Ray and Atohi," said Chas, nodding. "Let's go back to the boat cabin, make a plan and stay shoulder-to-shoulder, and ride this boat south, boys. What do you say?"

"Heck, yeah. Gentlemen," said Jackie Ray, who stood and smiled, "My stomach is ready to see a saloon in Louisiana and walk Bourbon Street. You think that town could use three more handsome men from Kentucky down there in the Big Easy, huh?"

"I'm not sure all of us are qualified," I said.

The stranger stood bowlegged in the dark shadows and watched our every move. His arms were crossed, and a dirty smile ran across his face. Two more men joined him and smoked cigarettes under the porch of an Army building.

One man spoke low to the strange man and said, "They know where Carl Bellew hides out. They will lead us to the gold nuggets soon."

The men spoke for a while.

"Yeah. I bet they'd lead us right to the gold treasure. Knock the daylight out of Carl Bellew and drop these three rats in the river."

One man said nothing, turned his mustache, and laughed. Then he finally spoke: "He will learn to fire us from a dig for no good reason," said the long-haired stranger, the man who picked the chair up and spoke with a disrespectful tone.

"Alligators will love the Cherokee brave, brother," said another man, yanking his arm back when he walked in my direction with a Bowie knife. "We could finish all three of them before they got on the boat, dump them boys in the Mississippi River. Everyone would think they missed the boat and stayed in Fort Defiance."

Both his brothers pulled his arm back, and one said, "Wait! They will be a better time to cut and kill a Cherokee than tonight. Plus, too many witnesses walking around the fort," said the tall man. "Let them stupid guys take us to the gold, make our jobs easier since they are runnin' after Bad Carl Bellew, anyways."

"That is exactly why you are the good leader of this outfit," said the round man, hand in his thick hair.

"Then once they find him," said the tall one, "they'll be gone. Drop them in with the gators, see if they can swim the swamp."

"Pitch them in the water like an old pork belly," said the long-haired stranger, who had spoken with us at the table earlier that night, "Take care of them, Bobby Redman style."

"No one messes with the Redman Gang and lives to talk about it," said the tall man. "No Cherokee insults me."

The Redman Gang followed Chas and Jackie Ray to the boat, and they eyed them like a hawk. I felt the Great One turn my eyes to the three men, and it was not surprising to scout and stay alive, so I ducked behind the steps of the steamboat on deck and waited for the coyotes to reveal themselves.

They could not find my Cherokee tracks on the boat. I was a ghost and became their shadow. The first night, they made no moves to attack. During the day, they watched every move I made because the Great Spirit warned about the eyes of evil men. They were ugly men, too. Three men trailed us on the boat, turned drunk and ill as demons talked to them, and some men listened to the wrong voice of the Wolf. I could sense the eagerness to kill in the way they carried their guns, hands on the wooden grip, and eyes on Jackie Ray and Chas.

Chapter 8
Riverboat Ride

In the bottom deck of the steamboat, Chas and Jackie Ray slept.

No sleep came to my dark eyes. We were being followed and scouted by three evil men of names I did not know, and the night turned blue cold, and the wind whipped in April, and snow spat until after midnight. The weather was no better from Natchez to New Orleans.

A man stood elbows on the rails of the boat and spat tobacco.

"Warms the blood, Cherokee?" said the old man, bottle in his hand.

I felt compelled and stood beside the friendly white man.

"Why not?" I said and nodded at the bottle.

"We will be in New Orleans at sunrise," said the old man, rubbing his gray beard. "My name is Blind Sammy Summers. I feel a very warm wind on my face." The man said. "Rare to hear any Cherokee voices when I travel. What is your Indian name?"

"Atohi."

The man worked his hands down the rail to a cabin where people who could not sleep stood.

"Few folks at night are friendly, Atohi."

"The night is for thinkers and prayer warriors."

"Bad men are on this boat drinking and gambling," said Sammy, hand on his chin. "Men trying to remedy their troubles and wash away demons. Evil lurks as much during the day as at night."

The bottle seemed to work for him. Sammy was the first friendly man I had spoken to other than Jackie Ray and Chas on the boat since we left Saint Louis.

"Well, um, Atohi," said Sammy, waving his hand, "let me tell you about a find healer in New Orleans. She healed my troubles three years ago. Marie Laveau has more patrons and customers than the Army. She will fix your hair and cure your illness in a matter of days. I overheard talk about how three men, men of the Redman Gang, out to kill her. And Bad Carl Bellew."

"What does she do for the Cherokee?" I said, leaning on the rail.

He told of her expertise in reaching the Spirit World. Sammy spoke about her music and dancing, how her healing powers were believed to be equal with God, and how her popularity made her notable as the "Queen of Spirituality" in her way as a healer. He told how she was the most respected person in New Orleans.

"Sammy, where can we meet her in New Orleans?"

"Why would you want to meet her?" said Sammy, head turned in my direction.

I clutched my hand, looked out across the water, and said. "My friends are searching for Bad Carl Bellew. We need your help, sir."

"I know of the man," said Sammy, face white like the color of ground corn. "He will kill you if he finds out you are hunting him. I am blind, but….. I can see things, real things, in my head."

"What kind of thing?" I said and held up my hands when the sun broke free from the night. "My friend, Chas Bellew, is Carl's nephew."

"The young man they call Chas, right?" asked Sammy. "The one who is fast with a revolver. Heard mention of the name."

"Yeah," I said and saw eyes that did not work. I turned up the bottle for another drink and thanked God for my sight. "Carl is his uncle, but he is a wealthy man with horses and plenty of land."

Sammy interrupted and said, "Two things make a man rich, Atohi. Gold and being a thief."

"He is known for cattle," I said. "Not sure if he is a good man, though."

"You know the truth, Atohi," said Sammy, eyes round and cloudy. "Carl is no good. No good man has a hundred outlaws beside him unless he is a thief, stealing something for each one of his men. Women or gold, perhaps, huh?"

"Perhaps. Sammy. But can you help us find this lady Marie Laveau in New Orleans? She can call on her Great Spirits while we are in New Orleans."

"Now, Cherokee," said Sammy. He finished the bottle and threw the glass into the Mississippi River. "You are about to get yourself killed, messing with Voodoo and Carl Bellew, my friend."

"Sammy Summers, how can we find Marie Laveau?" I asked him again.

The ancient face of a man pulled dark glasses from his black coat, the palms of his hands met, and his spirit spoke of a tall church in the distance. The boat shifted, and he knew better than I did about when it would stop. The warm air in our lungs meant we were in New Orleans.

"Home," said Sammy, moaning and humming. "My great vision says, well, I see mounted riders. Many riders will ride dark horses, seven wise men will cross the streets on St. Ann and the Upper Boundary, and a large crowd will surround Marie Laveau expecting her to heal them, but she does not speak of healing everyone who asks on that day."

"How can we speak to her about finding Carl Bellew?" I asked as the boat docked, and I knew my time was short with Sammy Summers.

"You cannot speak to her for several months, Atohi."

I pounded the rail.

"We cannot stay in New Orleans for months, Sammy!"

"You listen to me, Cherokee!" said Sammy, up close enough to smell the drink on his breath. "We will speak to her when she returns to town for the Day of the Seven Wise Men Parade in July." His blue eyes were cloudy in the moonlight, and his body stood tall, and without hesitation, he spoke: "I cannot take you to her right now," he said. "She is on her own healing journey."

"We can ride to her," I said. "But we need horses."

His hand rested on my shoulder, and then he firmly gripped my arms.

"The Voodoo lady knows that I will take you to her," said Sammy Summers, eyes closed. "I will find you when the time is right, by lantern and horseback, and we will meet her. Spirits are with her, and her Catholic Voodoo works when she feels ready, not when you think you need something. You are a selfish man, full of vanity."

His hand rested on my shoulder as a teacher to his student. No man had touched my shoulder but Preacher Chet. His eyes were Crossed Arrows, and I felt the Morning Star of friendship. He would be a great help, I thought.

"My bones and common sense tell me she has many burdens," said Sammy, who spoke with compassion. "She has troubled souls who surround her in the evening. Her body is tired now, and her beauty and the beauty of others make them proud to call her healer and friend. Marie will speak to no one else now. She has many people to heal and some to kill, but… Atohi, she needs your trust and help from the Redman Gang. Also, Atohi, she will help you with your father."

I was afraid to find out about my father. The boat slammed into the dock.

"Thank you, Sammy. We will find her and protect her."

"She is living around a lake, Atohi, and mixes Roman Catholic Saints with the spirits of the Cherokee. You would be good for her. She will be expecting you and your friends from Kentucky."

We stood for a moment and admired the river.

"I must go, Atohi. And you should leave now. Go fast."

"We will meet again."

"You need to find your friends. I will be the first man off the boat; it has always been that way. Bring your friends to Lafitte's Blacksmith Shop, and you will find work. But don't be a friend to everyone."

"If we need work, I will find you."

"I must go," he said. He edged down the boat rails with no help and made his way to dry land again. "Atohi, go help your friends right now!" shouted Sammy Summers. "They are in big trouble."

"Trouble?" I said, running to the bottom deck.

Sammy Summers walked off the boat and down the ramp, paced behind a row of willows along the water's edge, and met another man for assistance. He left in a nice horse and buggy. The morning sun glowed on the church steeples, something that had made New Orleans famous, the orange glow of early morning.

I hid behind a dark staircase between floors of the boat, and only the people on the top deck knew sunlight had busted through the trees, and Sammy Summers, like all the other passengers, felt the warmth of the April sun. The dying chill of night had faded away. I heard chains and voices below deck.

"Move your feet, I said!" said a man from the Redman gang, who had Chas and Jackie Ray cuffed and tied, marching them from the bottom to the top deck as if they were prisoners.

"You got the wrong guys," mumbled Jackie Ray, mouth tied.

"We don't know Carl Bellew!" Chas said, feet chained.

"Once we get off this boat," said the skinny Redman, "you might be traded to the whaling captain or shot in the back for stealing from us. This might be your last boat ride, boys."

"We didn't take anything from you, mister," said Jackie Ray, pleading his case.

"You can plead your lies to the gators," said the round Redman brother.

"Shut up!" said the skinny man, pushing Jackie Ray, a man ready to fight. "Keep your mouth shut," bumping him with a pistol in the backbone.

"Where are you taking us?" said Jackie Ray, head turned to the man.

My eyes saw Jackie Ray, but he never looked in my direction. Chas Bellew made eye contact in the shadows of the boat, just as Sammy Summers said would happen in his vision. I followed Chas and Jackie Ray, pressed in the back with guns in the early morning light. They left the boat ramp, and the Redman gang turned my friends down a dark alleyway, and I lost them in the morning crowd.

New Orleans was different from Louisville and Saint Louis in the early morning. A new church stood in the middle of town, streets were dusty, and a fresh rain had fallen on the cobblestone pathways between the alleys. I saw our friend, the owl, fly low to a nearby basement. The owl was right. Five men beat Chas and Jackie Ray like two sacks of potatoes until their eyes ran red. They pulled burlap sacks over their heads and left them in chairs. I ran to the nearest person with a handful of coins, but no man believed a Cherokee brave. I remembered the blind man.

"Do you know where Lafitte's Blacksmith Shop is located?" I asked.

Men and women were dressed and refused to help. One old man pointed in the direction and said, "Down that road. They will be working day and night, Cherokee."

"What is the street name?" I said, listening closely.

"Follow the smoke."

I ran the entire way and knocked on the shop door.

"Anyone home?" I yelled. "Sammy Summers?"

Three black men walked out, and each man had dark eyes, wrapped in leather, and held steel clamps and steel fencing in their gloves. Four more men of the same color followed them with angry faces and stood at the side of the building. Nothing was said until a smaller French man walked outside, the leader, I guessed.

"Where is your horse, scout?" shouted the big man.

"Kill him and burn him," said another man, who crossed his arms, flexing muscles the size of apples and gripping steel clamps with both hands. Ready to fight.

"The world may not miss him," said the small black man.

"Sammy Summers is my friend," I said, standing with my hands open. "We met on the riverboat."

"Sammy has been dead for five years," said the man at the door.

"He stands alive!" I shouted. "Sammy was on the boat this morning from Saint Louis."

The men walked closer and closed the gap, pacing face to face, eyes red from work. Then, a man's whistle stopped them in their tracks, and their faces froze, looking down at my right hand. Two men pointed steel grips, and one man stepped back inside the shop and spoke to an older man and talked of their intentions. Noon struck on the church clock.

A dog walked beside my leg while I waited in the street for Sammy.

"Where'd you get that dog, scout?" one man shouted.

"That's Danny Boy," said the big man in the back. "Here, boy. He has been lost for five years."

That's when a familiar face pushed his way to the front of the pack; still, Sammy Summers was blind in the daylight, the same as he was after midnight, and told good stories. He saw them differently than others, with his heart.

"This brown dog has followed me around since sunup, Sammy. He's a good dog, sir. We had breakfast at Café Du Monde." I said, petting the dog.

The dog yapped when he saw Sammy's sweet face.

"Come here, Danny Boy," said Sammy Summers. The hound leaped into his arms, and they fell to the ground. "I have called this dog for years."He took the dog in his arms, and tears flooded the face of the blind man. "Guys, this is my Cherokee friend, the one only, Atohi, from the Cherokee Nation of North Carolina. Greet him as one of your own brothers."

"But I hate my big brother," said one man.

"That's not the Christian manner I taught you," said Sammy.

The big man smiled, relieved, stepping forward to shake my hand. Others followed his lead, and the small black guy assisted Sammy Summers with his walk back inside. He sat on a bench and fed his dog some bacon with both hands. More bacon was fed, and the dog loved meat.

"Get us all a drink and some food, Robert," said Sammy, waving his hand. Sammy made his way to a barrel of water and washed his hands. "Wash up, gents. We will talk to Atohi to see how we can help him."

"I see he is without his friends. Bless the lunch, Pierre can tell when a Cherokee fighter is out of his element and needs some big guys in Nawlins to knock heads for him," said Robert, who handed each man a sandwich and lemon water.

"Yessir, boss man," said the smaller man. "We will help in any way possible. What do we need to do for this Cherokee man?"

"Sammy has a reward for his dog," said Robert, who poured the drinks and spoke up.

"Reward?" I said curiously. "Friendship is the best reward."

"I did have a reward," said Sammy Summers. "Now I have a friend to repay with good deeds, don't I?"

Sammy Summers untucked a coin from his chest pocket and flipped it high and the coin landed in my hand. The men laughed and chewed their food.

"Good catch," said Sammy Summers.

"How did you know I caught the coin? So, you can see some?" I asked.

"No sir," said Sammy." He flipped his ears. "Coins make a noise when they hit the floor and a soft noise when they hit the hand of a good friend."

Sammy and his friends held their lemon drinks and laughed.

"Sammy has been telling us about the boat and a Cherokee man who seeks labor, right? Any man who finds his dog works with us, Atohi," said Robert. "He has been expecting you, scout."

"Good to have friends," I said.

"If you take this Cherokee on, it's trouble, sir!" said a man with leather gloves and a tight hat. "Boss, do not take this feathers-man on and bring trouble to our shop. He might get us all killed. Talk to Queen Laveau, I beg you, sir."

"Shut up, Pierre!" said Sammy, raising both hands. "Would you just shut up for a minute, huh? Let me think."

"I can solve my own problems," I said.

"We will find a way to help our friend. Share a bottle of rum with this Cherokee man," said Sammy, who handled his drink, head canted, and his good ear turned in my direction.

"Got some beans and rice for this man, Sammy," said Robert. "I got spices, too."

"Humbled," I said and walked behind him to the bar. "Sammy Summers is a wise man to help a new friend. Women loved him on the boat."

Sammy walked beside Robert and held his arm.

"Not everyone in this town will be your friend, Atohi," said Sammy, petting his dog. "Danny Boy, here, he is a good judge of men. I like that about my dog, and he likes you, Atohi."

"He took up with me at sunup," I said. "Danny Boy followed me through the French Quarter. I kneeled to the stone floor and fed the hound, and we became friends."

"Atohi, do not go to the French Quarter tonight," said Pierre, with eyes of trust, and he warned with his face, a face of honesty.

"Avoid the streets tonight," said Sammy, elbows on his knees. "Stay in this place, Atohi. We will go another time, a time that is much safer." He held the dog with both hands.

The men continued to laugh at Sammy's good stories. They spoke of women Sammy Summers knew from town to town and how they loved him very much.

"Why do women love you, Sammy Summers?" I said, hand on my chin.

Everyone laughed. Robert was big enough to hug a bear, and that day, he was the first man to hug me other than my mother and father, naturally.

"They love Sammy Summers because they see beauty in their hearts and hear kindness in their voice. Then he sleeps with them," said Robert, who spoke for Sammy when he had the chance.

Robert was the man who met Sammy when the riverboat docked. He was likable, much like Preacher Chet, and a bit humorous and cheerful. Some people were that way, and he was one of them.

But his lively friends slapped their legs, tapped on steel, and laughed most of the day.

"Well, it is true," said Sammy Summers. "I am blind as a bat and ladies love me the way God made me, right here, born blind and happy in New Orleans."

They spoke of traveling with Sammy to California and Chicago, Illinois, and even told how friends bought Sammy beignets at the new Café Du Monde Coffee stand in New Orleans. When they needed horseshoes and steel, Sammy was the one who had never turned down a job.

Lafitte's Blacksmith Shop smelled of coal and smoke, and I saw more places that clouded the city just the same as Louisville and Saint Louis. I walked by smaller shops of iron and steel at Fort Defiance. New Orleans made men sweat, and working men smelled worse than forged steel.

Green covered the trees at Sammy's home, and the air was dusty and dry on the corner of Bourbon Street and St. Philip's Street when I first arrived for advice. In all the hospitality, I had not forgotten about my friends. The only sounds were horses and wagons, and people made their way to the city, and, in good time, I knew the way around. Colorful birds sang in the high trees and made nests along the stone walls where they walked by for church services.

He had trusted my character, and Sammy had a plan.

"Okay, gents," said Sammy. "Men get back to work. I have business to discuss with Atohi."

"Yeah," I said. "Business. Let's not forget why I am here. My friends, Chas and Jackie Ray, two men beaten like wild animals. I could use your men, and I would be indebted to you, Sammy."

"Let's find a private table under the trees." Sammy knew the way and lent his nose to the outdoors.

Sammy Summers toted a cane in one hand and a bottle of rum in the other. To speak privately meant a table behind the shop. Sweat ran down under his hat, and the hound, Danny Boy, was home again and remained close to Sammy. I was prepared to speak once he was settled and collected his thoughts. All the men hammered and pounded steel behind the hot wall, pitching coal on the flames, and were back to work for their boss man. The dog stayed with Sammy, and for the first time in years, Danny Boy fell asleep on his feet.

"I know who has your friends locked up, but we may need the power of Queen Marie Laveau to break this curse and find out how many men we are dealing with in this attack on Chas and Jackie Ray and what they want with your friends."

"Some men need no reason to harm others, Sammy."

"Marie Laveau is the best doctor of médicine in the Great South, and sets Voodoo over the life of people." He said, face hopeful. "You may need her sooner than you think."

"I believe in Jesus for my grace. I thought she was a Catholic, huh?

"Yeah. You guessed it, brother, for politics!" said Sammy Summers, who stopped to smoke, and his pockets were packed with plugs of tobacco. "I don't care what anybody says," whispering, "Marie Laveau runs this dang town. Her power is because people love her. I am one of them, Atohi."

"How old is she?" I asked.

Sammy Summers rubbed his head and said, "We were both born in 1801. That makes her seventy, I guess, the same number of years that I have on me. And she has done much better in her years than I have in mine."

"If the Queen will help me, I'll pay," I said and reached in my pockets. I put the money on the table, more than he expected.

"Well, you have called on the right person, Atohi, but keep your money in your pockets and hide it."

"Money stands to play, Sammy. I need Chas and Jackie Ray released, so we can work for you. They are good men. We need to find his Uncle Bad Carl Bellew. Rumor is, Carl Bellew has many friends in New Orleans."

Sammy Summers shoved a drink into my hands, and we spoke of retaliation.

"This's no rumor. Bad Carl Bellew was here last week, Atohi, and his men attacked Robert and Pierre." He turned and spat tobacco and coughed. "He stays down the street. Robert said two heavily armed men ride with him on black horses. They are planning to ride to Waco, Texas."

Most of the men from the blacksmith shop had passed out drunk each night for a week while I scouted New Orleans. Sammy Summers had a plan and a good plan, and it kept us up late at night. Gamblers and hopeful men played cards, and others listened to card readers and told ghost stories. They spoke of crazy stories about Marie Laveau, whose power and control were led by the Spirit. Strong firewater seemed to heal my worries late at night, and I never got used to the taste of absinthe made of wormwood.

My time was spent without sleep. Instead, I listened to the stories of Sammy Summers, who told the truth about the "Queen of Voodoo," a lady so powerful the law feared her in the French Quarter. Sammy told how Marie Laveau helped Indigenous people, Islanders, French patrons, the Irish, Scotsman, the Chinese, and men from lands unknown to my ears. I had never heard of Cuba, Puerto Rico, and Honduras until that night. My friend spoke of women he knew who needed favors and had high regard for strangers and good men, men like myself, but I kept to myself. Sammy told how Marie Laveau spoke directly to the Great Spirit. He spoke of the heart of herbs and roots to heal men and women, rich and poor, good and bad, and even some that desired beauty and love. While the Great Spirit was strong on the night of the full moon, Sammy kept my attention when he heard "questions from the owl" that were told. He understood the power of having a friend like the owl. I remained in the open for most of the night and sat at the table when Sammy Summers was frightened by uncertainty. He felt Chas Bellew and Jackie Ray Monroe, men he was eager to hear, lived in great danger.

Later, the horizon of a great city landscape glowed, and the coolness of night faded with the disappearing moon, and the voice of the barn owl became silent. The eagle cawed and circled the gray house as the sun climbed from the east and blazed the dusty streets of New Orleans. I wondered how my friends were doing, being locked up.

All the men had left the blacksmith shop, and Sammy Summers became silent and petted his dog and sipped his coffee. I sat across from him and poured more coffee, and we talked.

"Two men are going kill Marie Laveau," said Sammy, head down, and wept in his flat hat.

"Redman Gang?" I said, and held my hat to my chin.

"Get up, scout! The owl is back," said Sammy as he held the chair.

"The Great Owl," I said, "he will lead us to Chas Bellew and Jackie Ray."

"They have been moved out of the town. My men have found their hideout, Atohi," said Sammy Summers, making his way to the door.

At that time, the prayers of Preacher Chet would have been honored.

"God is with us," I said. "We need more prayers and guns, though."

Sammy Summers stood, held his cane in both hands, face tight as leather, and leaned inside the doorway and hesitated.

"Atohi, we must go," said Sammy Summers, leaning against the building. "You can see Marie Laveau, my boy. It all worked out."

"I'd like to drive the horse and buggy," said Sammy.

"You are a man without sight," I said, grinning.

"I know that," said the blind man. "But I have always wanted to drive a horse and buggy, Atohi."

"I'd be honored if you drove us into town, old friend," I said, laughing and holding him up. We had the time of our lives on Bourbon Street. The horse loved it as much as we did.

That evening, Marie Laveau was nowhere to be found. The two men had moved Jackie Ray and Chas again to another secret location. I checked the bloody basement and a dozen other buildings, but no one knew them.

Days had slipped by; Sammy Summers and the barn owl did not think it was murder. I disagreed and chewed my sandwich.

Chapter 9
The Favor

Weeks had slipped by in the summer, like a slow turtle climbing a steep hill in the mountains of Kentucky, resting for a long time before the turtle continued climbing. The sun baked the town on the 1st day of July 1871. To pass the time, my hands turned steel and hammered out horseshoes, and at night, we scouted, along with Sammy Summers and his men, who had unexpectedly become my close friends and even brothers. At sundown, we raided houses and abandoned buildings, searched old barns, busted down doors, and harmed no one. Our aim was to locate Chas and Jackie Ray, whom I had yet to see since the boat landed in the Big Easy, a hard city beyond reason.

Nothing came easy in that town, but I was determined to not leave until I found them. So, I labored hard, working for months for Sammy Summers and did what he requested in New Orleans and worked for nearly three months until the day of the secret meeting was planned. The rest of the blacksmiths had gone home when the old, wrinkled man made the announcement to me only. He took off his hat, brushed his gray hair, and felt the warm sun on his face, turned up a bottle of rum and shared it, as he often did, and we prayed.

"Tonight," said Sammy, "is the parade of the Seven Wise Men on Canal Street, sponsored by Carl Bellew." In July 1871, my friend walked across the room, and I taught him how to drive a horse and buggy that morning for the second when no one was on the street. He did what I expected and wrecked the buggy, but I told him he was an outstanding driver. In heartfelt compassion for his loss of sight, I wrecked the buggy just to make him feel better. We lapped the city and laughed at each other.

His hunger brought us back to the shop.

"What's going on?" I stood at the window.

"We unknowingly were working for Carl Bellew, the devil himself; a friend of a friend hired us," said Sammy, and his face rested inside his hands for a short moment. "We made hundreds of shoes for horses, fixed wagon wheels, and made steel bars and chains. It was a deal we could not turn down on Bourbon Street."

"We made steel for the enemy, huh?. The good news is we have enough good men and weapons to fight him tonight, though," I said, sliding into my chair. I put my hat on my head and waited until he cleared his face.

"Yeah. We can fight him and die," said Sammy. "Every man and woman will be at the parade tonight. My men are watching the shop until sunup. Someone must watch the money Carl Bellew paid us today. So, Atohi, we are staying here." The old man sat upright, and he wanted me on top of the building after dark. "I need a favor from you."

"How can I help?" I said and faced him and brushed my long hair. "Sammy, what is the favor about?" He talked more than any man I knew, but, at the moment, few words were said. He poured a glass of water and wiped his lips and mouth a few times.

"My men said Bourbon Street is crowded," said Sammy, listening to Robert brief his men, ear to the door. "Men in black suits and top hats sided with Carl Bellew. Killers. Fast guns."

I stood and walked over to the window, pulled the curtain, and saw men who leaned against the tall stone wall in front of the shop and one smoked. Several people walked toward downtown New Orleans, some on horses, some in wagons, and some stagged and shouted because I was different, Cherokee different. A steady stream of people, those interested in seeing the town, well-dressed and hungry, paced into town for dinner and drinks and to see the elite of New Orleans perform. Some only wanted to see the late-night crowds and celebrate anything on weekends.

"I will have my men double-check around town for Chas and Jackie Ray," said Sammy. "I have something for you to do while my men hunt for your friends, Atohi. Something that must be done and done tonight, outside of town." His hands found his cane, and he tapped the hardwood floor several times.

"Might be dangerous, scout," said Sammy, who pointed his cane in my face.

"You know I will do it, considering all you have done for me. We are being watched." I held the curtain, and a man across the street crushed his cigarette underfoot. Lit another one, puffed smoke, and walked away.

"Life in New Orleans ain't safe no more," said Sammy Summers, and sniffed fresh air at the window. "Kinda spooky on the river, even in church on Sunday, and you would think on the Lord's Day that people would be at peace."

He held the mouth of his dog from barking at the man, eyes closed, and he huddled with the dog on the floor.

"Not even safe for an old timer my age. I was born in the French Quarter. A man without eyes hears things he should not be hearing, Atohi, but I heard it. My eyes abandoned my face at birth. I cannot see a thing, but I hear the ghostly parts of this town, and my skin crawls. Hey, what am I going on about? You are not afraid of a favor, are you?"

"Scared, Sammy?" I said, leaning back. "Nope."

"Seven wise men and six bullets scare me," said Sammy, who unsnapped his tie and laughed.

"What makes a man like Bad Carl Bellew tick for evil, Sammy?" He was asked in an honest voice. I wasn't sure if I wanted to know the answer. "Why does he kill and kill again and take from others, push settlers into the dust of the ground, sir?"

"The same reason a minister tries to get you saved above the dust and into heaven," said Sammy. "Drink, Atohi?"

I sat with him at the kitchen table, thoughts rolled, and we talked.

"Nope," I said. "Too early for me. What reason do you know, Sammy?"

"The reason, huh?" said Sammy, taking a deep breath. "The reason is for the glory of it, for assurance of that glory comes from knowing King Jesus Christ. But to kill, for Bad Carl Bellew, the reason comes from being glorified, like a king. That's the real reason he kills and kills again and again, for kingship. Men follow the story of a man of glory."

"Glory, huh?" I said, wondering. "For the glory of it, being a legend and a king becomes a legend. Prince Edward in a can. Napoleon Bonaparte. Stonewall Jackson. Legends, right?"

"One day," said Sammy, waving his hand, "they will be a Jackson a lot more famous than Stonewall. New leaders and more idols will come."

I agreed.

"Atohi, your reputation precedes you," Sammy replied. "That is the talk of a legend, and a legend never dies," taking another drink. "But, Cherokee, to be a legend, you must be renowned and magnificent at what you do. Preacher Chet Bellew was a renowned minister, a saint, and perhaps, a man who walked with the Lord Jesus Christ. When his preaching landed his name in the newspaper, and people demanded the Chet Bellew fellowship to evangelize, that's when I noticed Carl Bellew became a villain in society. That is the truth. I see nothing but jealousy, envy, and death."

"How do you know so much?"

"Robert reads aloud. Good ears add knowledge, my friend."

I heard horses and lots of horses in town.

"Outside the window," I said, "the town sheriff, marshal, and twenty-five deputies rode by as if President Grant was in town from Washington."

The old man coughed and hacked.

"It might be a good day to die. I hear lots of horses, shoes I have made myself," said Sammy Summers, listening to the horses. "Hang up my cane at the Pearly Gates and get my heavenly eyes ready to see Jesus. Tell me, Atohi, what does the town look like?"

I will never forget what I saw: tears and a weeping man. He was the most honest man I have ever met. He never saw my tears, though, but he knew I had them in my heart.

"The town is decorated with flags of many colors for the Seven Wise Men Parade," I said and stood, dusty curtains in both hands. "Marches are planned, top hats, and many mounted riders are here. Rooms are booked, and many of these men need to be behind bars."

"Well, is the town dangerous, Atohi?"

"Yeah."

"Well, let's get you busy on that favor of mine. It's time for you to see the Medicine Man." He stood over his cane and arched his back. "I need some medicine to help my aching back. Bones ache. My head is clouded. The time is here for my favor."

"The Medicine Man, huh?" I said and clutched my arm.

"Address is on the paper. Robert left it for you, Atohi," said Sammy, who emptied the bottle and felt for his medicine. "I would read it to you myself, but I lost my good glasses." He laughed and wept. "I am in awful pain, Atohi. Can you do this favor for me? I would have Robert do it, but I know you would appreciate meeting the Medicine Man more than Robert would."

"Yeah. Yeah," I said. "I will find the Medicine Man in New Orleans." I raised both hands.

He hugged my neck.

"Good news, and Amen! Go clean up. Wear that new Shellum Splash Cologne; it's good for the ladies when you walk down Bourbon Street."

I stood tall and proud, washed away the day from my face and hands, and shaved. I did spell like Paris on a Saturday night.

"What about raiding another barn tonight with your men?" I said and filled my canteen with water.

"Yeah, but they know you are looking for your friends from Kentucky. My men will hunt them down. Months have passed, and tonight, no one will be guarding them. This ends tonight."

"Talk that over with the Medicine Man when you get my medicine, Atohi. Hurry up, son," said Sammy Summers, "and prepare yourself for the long road."

With each passing day, the city had grown, the food tasted better, clothes of style appeared in shops, and I had money. Parades and marches were new to my eyes in New Orleans. I had not forgotten my purpose and needed to find my friends before someone thought I was a white man and lost my will to scout as a Cherokee brave.

"What color clothes do you have on today?" asked Sammy, who felt the material at the door. "Dang, son, you sure used the whole bottle of Shellum Cologne, didn't ya?"

"No. No," I said. "I left some for you," chuckling and laughing. "Sammy, I am standing in front of a perfect mirror wearing your brother's black suit, black shoes and tophat, and his watch is in my pocket."

"Vanity! Vanity! It's all vanity! Frank would call you a white man in the mirror, Atohi." He laughed and untucked his paper. "Keep the address of the Medicine Man in your pocket. See you on the other side, Atohi."

"See you on the other side of the breakfast table in the morning."

He waved and wrapped both hands around my hands and offered a stern, manly hug. "This is my big favor, son."

He held himself up in the doorway and wept. I knew his back was in awful pain. My friend had fallen three times that week: once down the stairs, once over the dog, and one time more, but he did not see where he landed.

"Don't stop for anything. Do not stop until you reach the Medicine Man."

"See you tonight, Sammy," I said and gave a big wave. I felt stupid; he could not see me. "Get some rest, Sammy."

***

The smell of food lingered beyond the kitchens and cafes of New Orleans, and people crowded the streets, bumping shoulders and tipping hats to the ladies in big dresses. Many people stood socially connected in a fraternal order of "educated fools and political rats" of the city, which was what Sammy Summers said would happen. Life was much different than in Kentucky. Streets and walkways turned dusty, live oak trees became the scenery for finding shade from the sun, and candles were lit at businesses for light.

I was educated by Preacher Chet Bellew, sent to study at the University of Kentucky, and felt I needed to refrain from self-appointed wise men – "Seven Wise Men Parade" and the chance of being shot to death by Bad Carl Bellew and his men, but, more importantly, I had promised a favor to Sammy Summers.

It became difficult to determine the seven wise men among the hundreds of fools, but they were self-proclaimed men who were eating as much as they could in one setting. Then, in the long distance, roads narrowed, and the city turned into country trails, with whistling birds and deer and streams with big fish. To the East, the land was filled with squirrels and rabbits. Suddenly, a home place and a yard filled with young women chasing each other appeared in my sight. Some talked while others celebrated.

Two hours of walking under sunbaked heat caused a man to lose perspective and beg for good directions. I stood in the hanging shade of mossy oaks and looked down an endless dusty road, black tie loosened, shirt opened, and thirsty.

"Hello, young man," said a lady in a yellow summer dress.

"Hello," I said, tie in my hand.

"We have fancy lemon water!" The lady walked out of the woods and smiled. "Good to see someone on this road since the big parade is in town."

"Atohi."

"I'm Millie."

She had laughing eyes, eyes still swimming in ale, half drunk. I nodded and started down a narrow pathway toward her.

"I am very thirsty, Millie," I said. "Didn't know that it was this far out of New Orleans."

"Ten miles to Bourbon Street from here," said Millie, taking a few steps.

"You live with your family," I said and stood beside her.

"Yeah," said Millie, "sort of, a family of women." She stopped and turned right behind a row of mossy oaks. "My friends make the best lemon juice and water."

"Four, five, six, seven beautiful women," I counted. "I like this town," I said, watching women play some type of game in the yard. "Are these women your sisters, Millie?"

"No, silly," she said and flapped my shoulder several times. "They are your friends and my friends."

"Everyone could use another good friend," I said and wiped my head.

We watched women at work, doing chores, some with laundry, one stirred lemon juice, one painted, and another played music in a honey-yellow dress.

"Are you a Cherokee man?"

She twirled her long dark hair, earrings swaying, and then she adjusted her jewelry and had a big drink.

"Yeah. I am the best kind, full-blooded."

"Full-blooded!" she said, holding herself up with my arm.

"What is a "full-blooded" man doing in Louisiana?"

"I did not care for the sailors on the Mayflower," I said, grinning.

"Oh, you are funny-good man, Atohi," said Millie, burping. "A really good-looking funny man." She wiped her lips and stumbled.

"I left North Carolina for Kentucky as a young brave. I am on a long journey."

Our heads touched as the gentle wind turned toward the house, the smell of candy waved in the wind like something sweet lingering in the evening breeze, and the ladies labored on and on without a care in the world. Millie just flirted. We walked up a natural pathway, stepping ever so close to the lilies and butterfly garden, where red hummingbirds took flight from flower to flower in what was left of the last moment of sunshine.

"I need to find the Medicine Man," I said, arm out. "He lives on this road, out this way, right?"

"No! We have no Medicine Man house on this road."

She ran to the house, and I was not invited.

"I'll get you something for that thirst."

A whistle sounded. I stood and turned and walked to the edge of a long field of dark grass that turned lighter in color, and then another garden was planted. The grass waved and righted and bent, and I knew the waving field was called Tico Sunrise. Plants appeared in the distance, and before the large house were more plants and bright flowers. I thought of Sammy Summers, who felt tree bark and smelled flowers, and, for the first time, I cared about natural things amid a secret garden, where blooms came alive from buckets of water and the ground was moist and tender, soft in places, as if it had just rained.

No birds sounded like a whistle. It happened again.

The evening became still, and suddenly, a flush of bluebirds filled the sky, like coffee grounds on the pages of a painting. Birds became spots on a pearl canvas, wings stretched, and legs retreated as if something intentional and unnatural had stirred the fliers to rise higher. Then a third whistle sounded, one a bit louder. I stood still and scouted, caught in curiosity, the roundness of cobblestones beneath my foot, and I leaned and snapped branches.

With two glasses of lemon juice, Millie stopped and said: "What are you doing over there, Atohi?" She smiled and marched to my side, and we walked to a bench and sipped amid a large garden in bloom. "Make yourself at home, I won't bite. Finish your glass, and I will introduce you to the ladies, bayou ladies."

I remember being very hungry and somewhat sick. The chicken for lunch was gone.

"Would you happen to have some food to buy?"

"Inez is fixing gumbo," said Millie. "Do you like the taste of gumbo?"

"Yeah. One of my favorites, Miss Millie. "Gumbo! To Gumbo! To the Gumbo God of Louisiana!" I shouted and had no idea why.

She toasted. "To the Gumbo God!"

We shouted it again and again.

We emptied our glasses, and she poured more from a large pitcher on a table in the woods.

"Let's go meet your new friends," said Millie, who stood. "Eat some gumbo. To the Gumbo God. March with me."

That was the day the sun fell out of the sky, and I was dizzy.

"To new friends!" I yelled. "Good drink. Can't stay long, though."

"Men on this road, they just love our lemon juice," said Millie, laughing, snorting when she laughed. "Have another glass, Atohi."

Her face was close, and the smell of fruit was soft on her skin.

"Where are you headed, anyways?" asked another red-haired lady.

"Need to find the Medicine Man. I heard a whistle."

Two ladies stood, ladies dressed in yellow.

"There's no Medicine Man 'round here. My friends whistle for supper," said Millie, grinning. "We have lots of calling birds, too, but beware of.."

"Beware of what?" I said and leaned toward her.

They caught my arm.

"Beware of the beautiful ladies, Atohi," said Millie, voice soft, who ran and jumped around the yard. "I mean, they are beautiful creatures. Look! Ladybugs." She reached for my shoulder. Crawling was a black and orange ladybug, wings wide across Frank's black suit jacket. The ladybug failed to fly and walked across the long, pale fingers of Millie and suddenly took flight. "How many ladybugs do you see, Atohi?"

"Four," I said.

"Four? I count one bug," said Millie. "Need to get you inside, sir. The heat has baked your mind. It's the July sun." Her Cajun accent was heavy, and her voice was sweet to my ears. "These ladies have prepared a bowl of gumbo and corn just for little ole you, Atohi."

The whistle happened again. My head spun. Millie used her hand and whistled back and smiled.

***

My memory faded back to when I was a young brave in the Cherokee Mountains of North Carolina. When I spoke or whistled too loud, deer ran beyond the shot of the bow and arrow, out of sight. Young, long-faced, and saddened, I thought of the warrior and Chieftain, my father, a great hunter and one with nature; still, the image became fresh and clear in the woods when the deer ran deeper into the bayou and how startling creatures cost the Cherokee tribe meat in the winter months.

I had been taught by my father, as a boy of ten winters, to paint my face for war and be slow like the turtle and aware of my surroundings. My father said I was a good hunter, and I heard his voice as if we were together again.

"Eyes and ears will save your life, my son."

Listen with the long ears of a rabbit and hear the rushed foot, and that is how I became a scout. Sounds of nature and that small voice of the Great One, Jesus, who guided my steps softly and, most of all, helped locate outlaws and hungry bears.

"Men that hide are evil, like the fangs of a snake," said my father. "Listen and use the eyes of an eagle." It was our last hunt together at Mingo Falls. We smoked pipes, and he taught me more about humanity and nature than anyone I had ever known. I missed my father.

***

Thoughts filled my swimming head, and lovely women sang hymns softly in the distance after two glasses, when suddenly my steps became short and unstable. Likely, the first steps of a toddler were no different, the same as the wobble of a chick or the mush of a man in wet sand, and I felt slow underfoot. A tree held my body upward, leaning from tree to tree, catching my tilts and falls. I had been drunk three times that year, and that was the fourth. Resting and with blurred vision, my steps became slower, and the porch railing was tall under my grip; still, my eyes watered in dizziness.

Millie held my arm and laughed. Other ladies had on summer shades and colors, spun and bent and howled and gaffed at a stranger who wobbled under a cloud of a mixed lemon drink. I was better than the parade and caused great amusement when I swayed. First, one step up, and then another until the top seemed like a mountain hike, and I saw clouds through a windmill, tall and cottony in the orange and purple sky.

Holding my belt and arm, said Millie, "Your eyes are dancing, Atohi. You must like my secret pulp and lemon juice." The drink made me dizzy. "Keep your feet steady, steady, boy. Step to the right, rest your weary bones in the parlor. Sit down, Atohi."

"Who is this man, Millie?" said Inez.

"My friend, Atohi," said Millie. "He is searching for the Medicine Man."

Ladies danced, leaned, and cheered.

"The Medicine Man!" said a lady with dark hair. "No man out here has medicine."

Alongside them, the only lady I knew, Millie, danced in a circle and sang. I was dizzy on my back, shirt loosened, eyes crossed, less amused, and women found my condition to be the evening parody.

***

The hum of a long-winded sermon echoed in my head.

"Preacher Chet Bellew, sir," I said, humming in guilt and conviction, down in the big parlor room.

Preacher Bellew just held my right hand.

"Where have you been?" I said, all smiles. "Where did you go, Chet?"

"I am always with you, my son," said the preacher, hands held.

My eyes failed to open, and his face was missed. I was unable to turn upright. The trance and state of my condition was certain. I was duped. Ladies took turns slapping my face, "loud and clear," the preacher sounded in my head: "I said, walk the narrow road, not take the road to Harlotville!"

I heard another voice.

"Atohi. Atohi!"

"Sammy Summers?"

"Stop for nothing, Atohi? Where's my medicine, Cherokee?"

Thoughts of disappointment rolled like a landslide, and the room spun inside the parlor. I became curious as to where Millie was headed with my suit, and the world was soft. The room was a blur, and people laughed and danced. The parlor was my bed. My nose was marked by vanilla perfume, soft hands, well-dressed ladies, and beautiful ladies who had a big party at my expense. Stern voices of Sammy Summers and Chet Bellew echoed, sermon and advice, and my mind hummed a new song.

"Stay down, Atohi," said a lady with red hair. "Rest your tired feet." Shoes pulled off.

"You will have to stay the night," yelled a thin blonde, who spun from the porch to the parlor. "He's stern as a mule, a keeper." She washed my feet and cleaned my toes.

Seven women surrounded the sofa, feet propped atop new flowery pillows, and I could not object. My face was dampened with a cloth, and the tapping of tiny hands from a lady with long red hair was soft as fur. I soaked up the world, a world that I was unable to escape. My shirt was open, and my flanks became sweaty. Three ladies fanned my wet face and chest, flapping with pages from old hymn books.

I blurted out and said, "Does the Medicine Man live here?"

"Go to sleep, honey," said the soft voice of a lady. "No Medicine Man is here, baby. Only the Voodoo Queen."

"Marie Laveau," said Millie. "We live here. All of us live with Marie."

"You will be fine, sugar."

I was kissed by Marie and fell into a deep sleep.

Chapter 10
Old Friends

Sometime the next day, I woke up, half-naked, half asleep, arms extended, flat on my back, down in a dark and dusty room, neck arched; still, bobbing my head, eye lids batted from being laced with roots, herbs, and other alchemy ingredients. No sign of the Medicine Man, but from the beautiful Queen of Voodoo, Marie Laveau, who called upon my native ancestors through smoke and spirits late into the night, I was pleased. Ladies danced and drank, drew spells, and chanted over a Cherokee doll, one that resembled my face. Long feathers and some were cut in half, and beside it rested the foot from a game rooster.

Marie Laveau had added to her Voodoo altar the bottle and glass I drank from when I first arrived, one ladybug, several broken pieces of a vanity mirror, folded money from her bosom, my hat, and the gold watch from the house of Sammy Summers. All were placed on the table, the unloaded Colt pistol from my side, and some ammo. Marie Laveau's talent and witchcraft, known as a Louisiana Voodoo practitioner, typically tended to the sickness and untimeliness of her followers. But for the likes of a Cherokee man, the first and only brave she had known and cast a spell over fell into a moment of melancholy.

She chanted victory over my friends and defeat for my enemies, along with the ancient witch doctor, Sammy Summers, who felt she had crossed the line of their friendship at the Parade of the Seven Wise Men. Sammy became friends with several of her wealthiest seekers, all living in the Big Easy.

"Well, well, well, Chas," said Jackie Ray, sawdust flew when he kicked my feet, "look who has decided to join the dusty party." My friends were still locked in handcuffs and chains. "Welcome to the lost Louisiana Paradise, deep in this rock dungeon. It's dang good to see your face, Atohi."

"I'm alive, Chas."

SUNDAY RAIN

"Saw them bring someone down late last night," said Jackie Ray, a voice I missed. "But I thought it was some rich cologne patron."

"I am cuffed, Kentucky Boys," I said, "or I would hug your necks."

"Boy, it is been a long time," said Chas. "How the heck did you get in here, Atohi? Last time we saw you, it was on the boat months ago."

In a deep, slow voice, I said, "I was walking down this road, offered a drink from a beautiful lady, and knocked into a world that spun. Not long after the lemon juice, I had no clothes on my body, feet washed, and was surrounded by beautiful ladies."

"She drugged you, Atohi," said Chas Bellew, reaching to greet my hand. "They mix a lemon drink, some magical combination, makes you crazy and happy, but you sleep for a long, long time."

"What is that drink?" I asked, back flat against the wall.

"Herbs. Roots. Some magical voodoo medicine that makes you forget your name and lose your clothes" said Chas, who turned toward the light. "They have rites and rituals upstairs with dancing and chanting, and dust covers our heads when they party."

"Then, thank God, they sleep all night and wake up at noon," said Jackie Ray. "Crazy drunken life."

"Hundreds of people have been here buying and trading and drinking with this Haitian lady," Chas said. "The ladies left late last night, down the road. They grow roots and medicine in these woods."

"I heard a whistle, Chas," I said. "The second whistle sounded like a cat in season or a little girl whistling."

"That was me!" said Jackie Ray. "I am cuffed and couldn't get my hands held right, Atohi."

Chas grabbed his belly and bent over, laughing at Jackie Ray, trying to whistle again without his hands on his lips, the same broken whistle that failed.

"We have been hearing about these dang parties, drinking and smoking tobacco for months now," said Jackie Ray, who yanked his chains, hooked to the wall. "Marie Laveau tells the ladies to tie our mouths shut and serve us lemon juice. That's when the ladies get knocked out on herbs and roots."

"Spirits in the food and drinks, huh?" I said. My head bobbed and yanked on my chains, and my strength was not to escape. "How can we get free?"

"Can't," said Chas. "Locked up. Where's everyone?" Chas looked through the cracks in the floor for someone to help us.

"Don't know," I said and saw no birds or people.

I didn't know what the owl could do for us, men locked in chains, but we needed him and some good riding horses.

"Left early this morning," said Jackie Ray. "Marie Laveau took the horse and buggy and rode out to New Orleans, I guess."

The front door creaked and opened slowly, and the sun blazed through the thin floor. Someone stood on the threshold for a moment, and the breeze blew dust from the front door across the house, and our heads felt dirt and dust. Each man cleaned his own face, and suddenly, Jackie Ray coughed and hacked.

"Hey, anybody home?" sniffing loudly. "Witch?" said the man. "Marie Laveau, I aim to kill you and your dirty witches sent by Bad Carl Bellew. Put a stop to the witchcraft and Voodoo dolls you keep selling in town. Everyone knows about your underhandedness and trading tricks with the wealthy merchants cut into our territory. Hey, Marie, you hear me?"

A big dirty grin turned across the man's bearded face, and he chuckled, stepping easy, checking each room. He peered through the dusty windows to the back of the property where flowers and herbs were planted. Blackbirds flew by the window. One bird shattered the window and spooked him.

"Send blackbirds, lady, all you want, Marie!" said the man. "No deals. No trades."

The man stood in the center of the parlor, the room where the ladies danced and met with seekers and spirits, and his hands trembled with curiosity and fear. Beneath a painted picture of the Virgin Mary, seventeen candles burned, soft pillows, pins, chicken feathers, blue bottles, strange concoctions, and dried flowers. Bottles wrapped in strings and worn ribbons and rose petals sat between idols, and layered inside of bowls were dry flowers. Dolls painted with red polka dots sat against figures of the Virgin Mary, fashionable jewelry hung loosely, and red jewels were on a gold crown. Dark-painted faces hung. Some cried, and other dolls laughed. Less than blissful eyes were stoned, full of anguish and pain, and amid the smoky room were dragon brooches, bent hair pins, buckles of brass, and seven golden stars. My pocket watch was looped atop a broken arrow and tied to my long knife.

The big man handled dried bones in his fingers, crushed bones placed in a wooden bowl like powder. Suddenly, a black crow slammed into the window and fell dead, and blood ran from the bird's eyes. A swift breeze cut through an open window, the curtain rope loosened, and the rod fell to the floor. The outlaw's heart raced, feet rolled, and his eyes became unsettled, crushing dried bones inside his hands as his body shook and fell to the floor. He rose carefully and feet unsteady; still, he shuffled his legs, keys jingled, and curtains waved. Pages of books flew without a gust of wind or press of hand, feathers swept high into the air and spun around the room. The man stumbled wildly and caught himself inside the threshold like he'd been pushed by an unknown force or someone intentionally nudged him, but there was no one in the room.

Beneath the floor, dust fell on Jackie Ray's head and caused him to sneeze and cough again.

"Who's down there?" said the man.

The big man eased across the floor that led down a long flight of stairs to where Jackie Ray and Chas were chained to my left. The first light of day shone through the cracks of the basement, and the aged timber held overhead swayed under his heavy weight. The outlaw leaned down and made his way to the stairwell.

I saw the danger spoken of by Sammy Summers. Eyes bugged and faces turned upward, and we waited in the mud and dirt, half-naked, hidden in the shadows of the room. Chained men in trouble and no one to call for a favor.

"Dang dust," said Jackie Ray, voice low.

"Bad spirit," I said. "Bad time, too."

"Hush," said Chas, who readied himself low to the floor.

"You better speak up and live!" said the man in the stairwell.

The man took short strides forward, bent down, face shone, and stood amid the stairs. He struck a match against the rock wall and lit a wall candle. His revolver angled down the high staircase into the cold and hungry face of Jackie Ray.

"Boo!" said Jackie Ray, grinning.

The man jumped and slid down the stairs.

"Who do we have here, wrapped in shackles and chains?" said the man, head nodding on wide shoulders. "Two dang youngsters, huh? Voodoo prisoners. One Cherokee man, who was with Sammy Summers at the blacksmith shop just yesterday."

I realized he was the man who smoked in front of the blacksmith shop the evening I left to track down the Medicine Man.

We sat in a world of disagreement.

"You are the friend of blind Sammy Summers, who begged for his life yesterday when Marie Laveau put him down with his mutt dog!" said the outlaw as he spat.

"You're a damn liar!" I said, yanking on the chains. "Sammy lives!"

"Nope. Gone." said the outlaw. "He's as good as dead, and the undertaker saw that he stopped smiling. Rumor has it Sammy Summers and his blacksmith brothers died late last night in a bloody gunfight right in front of the blacksmith shop. Rain washed away the blood like it never happened, boys."

The outlaw sat on the bottom step and asked questions. No one answered him.

"Shut your mouth!" I said, neck red and flushed.

"Another word and you die, Cherokee!" yelled the outlaw.

I jerked the chains and said, "Fat mule, cut me loose and get your revenge with me outside, huh?"

"Oh, that's right," said the outlaw, who covered his chest with his hat, "You gotta funeral to attend, right, scout?" A smile ran away from his face, and he stood, aiming his gun at my face. "You need to die with the rest of his blacksmith men, Cherokee!"

"No," I said. "I will live forever."

The man hiked up his leg and kicked my face.

"Pow! Pow!" He fired beside each of my ears. I fell over and cupped my ears. I moaned and groaned, head in a panic.

"Leave him alone!" said Jackie Ray.

The big man fired two more rounds behind the head of Jackie Ray and busted his lip, popping him with the heel of his pistol. He stood and sniffed and hit him a second time.

"Outlaw, you are a fool," said Chas. "Fools die a hard death."

"You want my boot, boy?" said the outlaw, who bit his lip and kicked Chas. "Pow! Pow!" He fired behind the ears of Chas. Laughed and watched us bleed and moan.

"Who is in my house?"

"Marie Laveau!" said Chas.

The outlaw turned and looked upstairs. Jackie Ray wiped blood from his face and pounded dirt and mud, eyes in a rage. Jackie Ray yelled.

"Look! Fat man!" I said, throwing mud in his face. "You will die today!"

SUNDAY RAIN

He busted my lips with his knuckles. I gasped for air when the outlaw choked my neck. Jackie Ray kicked his legs out from under him. And Chas locked his head with the length of the heavy chain.

"Who's down there?" said Marie Laveau, who descended the stairs.

"You're gonna die!" said Chas, hands tight to the chains.

I watched the man struggle and release his hands, limp as a wet leather rope. His body was shocked and flattened in the dirt, and Chas kicked him away, out of breath. I chanted a war cry and beat the wall, like a big drum, and my friend, Jackie Ray sat frozen.

Marie Laveau pulled the keys from the dead man's hands and touched my head with her soft, aged hands, and then she did the same with Jackie Ray. No words were spoken, only eyes that acknowledged bravery and courage, eyes that honored ours for the first time in a long time. The Voodoo Queen unlocked our legs. Then, our hands were freed. Chas met her face-to-face. She cried and cupped his dirty face into her peerless hands and kissed his pale face.

"He came to kill me, young man," said Marie. "You saved my life."

"I had no choice but to kill him, Ms. Laveau!" said Chas.

She unlocked Jackie Ray.

"God be with you, Marie," said Jackie Ray. "You are a true saint."

"You two are free to leave, and I owe you my life, Chas," said Marie, who held out her hands to all of us in deep appreciation.

"I hoped you would return," I told her.

Chas and Jackie Ray ran upstairs.

She kissed and hugged my face. Not romantic, but in adoration.

"I am sorry, Atohi, that I put you here."

She held my face.

"I hold no grudge, but I'm thirsty."

"I have some good lemon juice for you, Atohi," said Marie.

Her words halted my pace.

We laughed, and Marie pulled on my arm until we reached the first floor, and the seven ladies who had lived there had gone to town.

"No lemon juice," I said. "For me, Indian pale ale, please." I grinned. "My friends love lemon juice, though."

She whispered in my ear.

I whispered back and said, "We did?"

I saw Jackie Ray check his hair in the broken mirror, slip on his boots, and prepare himself to travel somewhere, anywhere. Chas tugged on his hat, eyebrows raised in my direction, with a big smile hitting my arm. Marie Laveau pulled my arms and adjusted my clothing in the oval wall mirror. We walked together over to her parlor and returned my belongings. She knew I had to leave, and she cried.

"Smoke and wine again tonight, Atohi?" said Marie Laveau.

"No," I said, face red. "I might see you again when I get back from Texas. You are a lovely lady, and if times were different…we would join hands and have a village of scouts. But I cannot take advantage of our love again tonight, dear."

"Age, right?" said Marie. "I have tomahawk fever, Atohi."

"Take something."

"There's no cure for it." She laughed. "I would "never" cast a spell or lock you up again. I don't make promises, though."

Jackie Ray and Chas walked outside and waited.

"I need one thing… though," I said. "Just one for the road."

"What? Anything," said Marie Laveau, who whispered.

"We need your favor for three horses, sweetness," I said with all seriousness. "We must get to Texas," I told her goodbye and gave her a final wave.

"Do you think they are making little Cherokee braves?" said Jackie Ray.

Chas grinned and said, "Atohi, you ready, lover?"

"One moment, please!" I said.

Marie Laveau wrote something on the inside of my right arm with her long fingernail. We walked across her property, and I adjusted my dusty two-piece suit and never caught eye contact with Jackie Ray and Chas until I was close to them. I paced slowly down the road in silence.

"Well, well, scout," said Chas, grinning, "you two were inside the room for a long, long time."

"We talked," I said. I kept pacing, hands in my pockets.

"He has dang red lipstick on his neck," said Jackie Ray.

"All I know is," I said, "I got three horses and some saddles waiting for us in New Orleans. I served Kentucky well, gentlemen."

"Well, um," said Chas, "where have you hidden these Voodoo horses and saddles, medicine man?" He tried to catch my fast pace. "Slow down, talk, Atohi."

"When do we ride them-there horses?" said Jackie Ray, who nudged my arm. "Where's your watch, scout?"

I went ten more steps and checked my pockets, blinked my eyes, and said, "Traded it. She had my pistol in one hand and the time-ticker in the other, I bet."

"Preacher Chet told how there's a time to live and a time to love," said Chas, putting his arm around my neck. "Did you trade your dignity for leather and lace, bread maker?"

I lifted his hat and said, "Don't kiss and tell, Chas, until I see ale in my hands on Bourbon Street. I tell no tales about tails until I see ale, gentlemen."

"Where's your pistol, Crazy Horse?" said Jackie Ray. The man slapped my hips and tapped my belt, walking on my left side, and said, "Lost something, shooter?"

"Did she take your Colt and your dignity, Atohi?" said Chas, grinning and walking to my right side. "She has a great spell on men, I have heard it said."

We walked down a long and dusty road, joking and questioning about the events, but we were back together again. They had their own predictions, most accurate, about beautiful Marie Laveau and chasing the dropping sun. At the same time, I took significant strides toward New Orleans, tightening my belt and lips.

Twilight fell. I said, "Pastor Chet Bellew taught me to confess my sins to someone with a locked jaw. What can I say? I lost my dignity with the Queen of Voodoo. What would you do with that Voodoo, Kentucky Boys?"

Bowlegged Jackie Ray approached my shoulder and said, "You got me, Atohi." He covered his lips, smoked a fat cigar, and replied, "Why isn't Marie riding with us to Texas?"

"She will be under every moon and star," I said. "Watching us ride."

We talked about all the places we had been, close calls, good men and bad women, boats, and bourbon, and made it to New Orleans by lunchtime. I bought three mugs of ale on Bourbon Street and found out the ancient blind man, Sammy Summers, my best friend and boss, was indeed dead, alongside Robert, Pierre, and all his men had lost their lives in a good gunfight. Sammy Summers knew more than he said when he sent me on a wild goose chase after the Medicine Man, which was the long road to Marie Laveau's house, just down the road a piece.

Sammy Summers mentioned the gunfight to the sheriff, but nothing was done.

He spoke to the sheriff three days before it happened, so he sent me to find Marie Laveau for him and to keep me from being shot to death in the gunfight with Bad Carl Bellew and his men.

Marie Laveau never shot Sammy Summers. Danny Boy lived.

"The last thing Sammy said was, "It is a good day to die, Atohi."

The night Sammy Summers and his crew from the blacksmith shop were buried in New Orleans, Jackie Ray sang barefoot, grass over his feet. I never asked him why and knew he dealt with death and drinking differently than most men. Chas bought horses from a beautiful friend of Marie Laveau's at a saloon. He stayed late into the night talking about New Orleans.

I sat in the doorway of the blacksmith shop, faced St. Philip Street, a cup of coffee in hand, and felt compelled to confess my night with Marie Laveau. Taking the advice of Preacher Chet Bellew, I found someone I could trust with my love story, and he listened without a dozen questions and never judged my actions with the lady.

Under a silver moon, I said, "That was the way it happened, Danny Boy." I petted the dog at Café Du Monde.

Chapter 11
The Other Side

To handle a blacksmith shop in New Orleans took skilled tradesmen and a good eye for the craft, men willing to work long hours and start in the cool morning before sunup, turning iron and steel for good citizens. Two months had passed since the death of Sammy Summers, and it was September of 1871. In the memory of our great friend, the nearness of the dog, Danny Boy, was imprinted on their hearts, and we spoke to him as if Sammy was beside him and held him close.

Jackie Ray and Chas were hired at the blacksmith shop and were the best men for the job, so the business continued after we left Bourbon Street. In the fall of 1871, Lafitte's Blacksmith Shop, better known as the legendary landmark of blind man Sammy Summers, kept the fire and steel hot in the Big Easy. In remembrance, and for the sake of the blind man who smoked and favored tobacco in the black alley of Bourbon Street, we toasted and poured a drink over his grave and remembered the man that way.

"To Sammy Summers," I said. "Chas and Jackie Ray, I wish you could have known this blind man, heart of gold, born to help others, and he saw the soul of each man he met."

"To Sammy," said Chas. "I will see him on the side."

"To Sammy Summers, a man with perfect vision now," said Jackie Ray. "He saw the world with eyes, the eyes within a man's heart."

"We will see him on the other side, men," I said, lifting my hand. "He was a good man."

We returned to work.

With fire waist high, we branded hides of cattle and horses, alongside settling the balance with unruly citizens, and at night, the two men from Kentucky and myself were commissioned to settle what the sheriff and marshal failed to handle during the day inside the Big Easy. We were known as the "Iron Rifles" and became noble citizens of the town, rented land, and gained a good reputation for blacksmithing and justification.

Deep inside Chas, the grand vision of Texas burned; still, he spoke of his dream to see Texas at mealtime, and finding Bad Carl Bellew never left his thoughts. He had more justice on his mind for the havoc Carl had caused from Saint Louis to New Orleans, and finding him would be a true pleasure.

On the last day of September 1871, the old French provincial Louis XV blacksmith shop was handed over to the nephew of Sammy Summers, Little Sam. In a matter of pride and friendship, we parted ways on favorable terms.

We paid our lease on St. Philips Street and dined together each evening and hoped to finish what we had started months earlier. More than thoughts, provisions were needed, and we had bought good horses for the journey to the Wild West of Waco.

We met again at the Café Du Monde and held prayer at the Saint Louis Cathedral.

"Men," said Chas, "we are headed West, and it's good to be together again. We have good friends in New Orleans now," eating beignets at the table, "and made some money, branded cattle, turned steel and it is time to see leather on the other side of Texas."

"What do you mean, Chas," said Jackie Ray, chewing his bread, and he leaned back. "I was beginning like this place since we have been freed."

"He means," I said, "we continue to march to Texas. We are not homesteaders," hands clasped on my chest. "We are on the hunt for Bad Carl Bellew. He has killed too many of our friends in Saint Louis and New Orleans and taunted every good thing we have built and believed in along the way. He has tested us."

"What we needed was money, and we have made it fair and square," said Chas. "We have worked in New Orleans for months, just like Sammy Summers asked Atohi to do. It's time to move on now."

"You have my blessing, I'm in!" I said.

Chas pressed his mustache and said, "God did not bless us to guard brothels and eat beignets in New Orleans, gentlemen. We must ride before the winter snow covers the cactus in Texas."

"The Great Wind will bring heavy snow," I said, raising my coffee cup. "The mean winter will bring down those without a good harvest.

So, we must saddle up now while the Great One speaks to our souls and ride to Waco."

"You seemed a little dazed, Atohi," said Jackie Ray, drinking his milk.

"What do you mean, cowboy?" I said and stopped eating.

"He means," said Chas, "your heart is broken over Marie Laveau, huh? Would you like to talk about your love life, Cherokee?"

"Nope. Not as long as I am alive," I said, head down. "Danny Boy, the good dog, will tell you anything you need to know about my love life; just ask him and see."

We spent the next few hours packing our gear and handing over the blacksmith shop to the family of Sammy Summers. We told the sheriff and marshal where we could be found if he ever needed the Iron Rifles from Kentucky again. Three horses were loaded, and a pack mule was loaded with enough supplies to ride to Lafayette. The wind blew in September, and the dog knew something was wrong when the smell of horses slapped our clothes, and he sniffed. He laid face down in front of the blacksmith shop and pouted and whined until he fell asleep.

"Men, we are three weeks from Lufkin, Texas," said Chas, who shoved his rifle into his long holster and filled canteens with water.

Jackie Ray mounted his horse and said, "The wind is fierce, Atohi. Can you make this wind settle down?"

My hat blew off my head and rolled down Bourbon Street.

When someone tapped my shoulder, the wind stopped blowing, and the sky turned from dark to light, she said, "Stopping the wind is easier than making you stay with me in New Orleans, Atohi."

"Marie Laveau," I said, as my eyes grinned. "I hoped you would show up."

"I knew you would not let me say goodbye last night," I said, holding her hand.

"I made an obligation a long time ago," said Marie. "One that leads me beyond the love I have for you." I held her close, and she cried.

"I will return for you someday. I will buy the drinks this time. No lemon juice for me, lady."

"You have not gotten over me mixing a special drink for you, have you?" said Marie.

"I was knocked out on lemon water," I said, laughing.

She held Danny Boy, and we all three held each other.

"You did some crazy things under my spell, Atohi," said Marie, letting go of the dog.

In her hands, she offered back my Colt, long knife, watch, and the money she had taken from me, and she handed me extra coins.

"I knew you were a good woman, Marie," I said and collected memories along with my things.

"I saw trouble in your future," said Marie. "Long before you arrived, but I wanted to meet you."

When my horse walked up to my side, Marie placed my hat and stuck something in my saddle bags, and I turned to her and said, "One last kiss, and I gotta go, lady."

"Yeah, it is a spellbound kiss for you to return soon," she said. "I will always be waiting for you, Atohi."

"Hope to see you again soon, Marie."

Chas and Jackie Ray circled around the block and back to the blacksmith shop to let me have a private moment with the Voodoo Queen. Danny Boy sat at her feet.

"Take care of those ladies for me," said Jackie Ray, waving in the distance.

"Great meeting you," said Chas.

Seven ladies in floral dresses offered kisses and hugs, saying their goodbyes for Jackie Ray and Chas. The dog followed the ladies to where Marie stood on Bourbon Street and cried.

"You are a beauty," said Chas. "How do you stay so young?"

"Lemon juice and love," said Marie Laveau. She petted the dog and said, "Take care of my Cherokee brave, Chas Bellew."

"Do my best, Marie Laveau," Chas told her.

Marie Laveau and her lady friends spoke highly of the men from Denton, Kentucky, and wished for a safe journey across Texas and back. They cast a blessing over our heads with chicken feathers and touched the star-faced horses before we turned toward a Texas sundown.

The face of Marie Laveau was thin, her eyes brown, her hair pulled up, and her age could not fully be known in how she danced and laughed her way through life and friends were her life. Most people paid top dollar for her secrets and blessings, too. Her dress was red and black in color on that morning, long, thin arms of mocha, covered in fashionable jewelry, and rings of silver and gold wrapped around each finger. She had the benefit of wealthy friends. I heard her sweet words in the wind as she whispered and nodded.

"You walk protected, Atohi," said Marie Laveau.

Her nails touched my face, and orisons were spoken into my ears. And when she was finished, sighing and plucking her thin shirt until a sweet aroma opened my eyes, I was in love.

"We will meet again soon, wonderful lady," I said.

Her hands unfolded, and a white dove flew above the Saint Louis Catholic church, and it was amazing watching the bird in flight.

"Open this leather pouch when you get to Texas, Atohi," said Marie, cupping my hands in hers. "Burn the mixture on your first night."

Deep in my pocket, I looked into her dark eyes and handed her a Bible.

"I knew you would be here this morning," I said and covered her eyes. From another pocket, I handed her something."Here's a gift for you?"

"What is it?" said Marie.

"Something to remember me by."

Jackie Ray, Chas, and the ladies surrounded us and waited. She unwrapped the gift.

"A lemon?" said Marie, and she laughed until she cried.

Millie hugged my neck, still laughing and apologizing for what she had done when we first met. We all hugged each other one last time. Good men. Good women. The best of friends, made in front of Sammy Summers' Blacksmith Shop, caught in conversation on Bourbon Street, where we promised to meet again.

We rode out of town.

Something struck my soul and ran cold across my skin, like when an old whitetail deer was pressed from the fields deep into the forest, made to hide and survive from hunters. It was a cold chill, like mountain ice. Seven dark horses mounted with rough men in black vests who rode under the sign that hung "Town of New Orleans." I remember it was on the same morning we rode outside of the Big Easy. The time we passed them on the dusty road was like the cry of the Golden Eagle against the Thunderbird and how talons grabbed the soul of a man in a strange way, unresolved, and my ears rattled with uncertainty.

My horse stopped cold in his tracks.

I didn't command the animal beneath my hide to follow Chas any longer and go differently. My eyes went beyond the dark sky. I felt thunder and lightning, shivering with the reins in my hands. Unnatural thoughts burst inside my head that September morning. Then, my mind found the answer and became apparent as the streams in the mountains of Kentucky, pure and cool, a sense of nature, as my grandfather taught before the hunt how to read the sky. More than anything, I understood how evil horses carried evil men to battle and how good horses carried good men.

Chas and Jackie Ray wheeled their horses and heard my war cry.

"What has gotten into that crazy man, Chas?" said Jackie Ray.

Jackie Ray crossed his arms on the horn of his saddle, trotted, and watched in amazement and appreciation, and I danced. My heels hit the earth in rhythm and song, in movement and grace, shifting to the sounds of beating drums, a sound no man could hear but a Cherokee brave. Dance and war cries continued unattested in the early morning streets, where no voices were heard but the echo of a timeless spirit of adoration from the Great One.

"Wey ya Ho ya hey! Wey ya Ho ya hey!" I cried out and sang and danced. My body was in full motion and in rhythm. I stepped forward for battle. "Wey ya Ho ya hey!"

My Paint horse reared and landed toward the West. And I slowly painted something of blue color across the horse's face. I waved my hands over the rope and feathers tied to the halter, and the animal snorted, and my handprint was red and blue across the body of the horse.

When the dance had ended, I walked the horse into the shadows of the street. I met Chas and Jackie Ray, who had dismounted their horse and stood in reverence. It was no different when Preacher Chet finished his Sunday sermon. I danced in front of the horses, found my day with the Spirit Force, and prepared for battle.

"To speak," I said, "to think like an animal is something special and rare among mankind, and the cry of nature is the same as church bells in our world."

"Even the horse felt the evil from the seven riders, a rare thing in this world," said Chas, who whispered to Jackie Ray and explained what had happened, and then he nodded and understood.

"He is one heck of a brave fighter!" said Jackie Ray.

SUNDAY RAIN

"Not every man has the same nature to grasp evil before a big raid, and there is a window to the true soul of Atohi and his horse," said Chas. "They say a horse has the same smarts as his rider."

"My horse is as dumb as a turnip, Chas," said Jackie Ray. "You know that much, bud."

Chas looked at his friend, eyes wide, and nodded.

"Well," said Chas, "I reckon it must be a true saying."

"Yeah, it is, bud," said Jackie Ray. "It is the truth. Look! A Golden Eagle is flying over the shop of Sammy Summers."

"Well," said Chas, who removed his hat, "guess one more night in New Orleans with the Golden Eagle would not kill us, huh?" He held the reins of his horse.

"No!" I said, looking at my friends. "This battle is mind. You travel on to Baton Rouge, and I will find your fire burning one night and join you again, Chas and Jackie Ray."

"Heck, no!" shouted Jackie Ray, face tight and serious. "You cannot fight seven men on your own."

"Atohi," said Chas, in disagreement, adjusting his legs, "we fight together."

"He has lost his head with Marie Laveau, Chas," said Jackie Ray, who kicked the dirt and slammed his hat against a tree. "These men will kill you, Atohi!"

"Wrong," I said, hand in the face of Jackie Ray. "The Great Spirit spoke to my horse, who has more sense than you. I must fight this battle alone. No one can fight but me!"

"You picked a hot day to find your Great Death, Atohi," said Jackie Ray. The man walked away. "I will be someplace else when they bury you. I warned you, brother."

I grabbed Jackie Ray's throat and grunted.

"Stop. Stop it!" said Chas. "Broke it up! "Jackie Ray Monroe, go and leave him to his own death. The Great Spirit has called his number."

"What if he is wrong?" said Jackie Ray. "We need him in Texas, Chas. These men will burn a Cherokee brave."

"Wey ya Ho ya Hey," I shouted and cried out and danced. I spun and stepped and circled.

"Ambush," said Jackie Ray. "See if I care," adjusting his shirt. Jackie Ray mounted his horse, low in the saddle, and rode ahead.

Chas grabbed my arm to the elbow and wished a great victory into my hands.

"We will see you in three days, Atohi," said Chas. "And be careful. Wish we could fight together."

"This is my battle, Chas," I said with certainty. "My horse snorted and was ready for war. "No man can fight the war of another man. Three days from now, Chas, I will see you in Baton Raton. Tell Jackie Ray to relax and suck a lemon."

" I will, Atohi," laughing, "just to see his goofy look."

"Burn what Marie Laveau gave us, and I will find the smoke."

Chas and Jackie Ray left New Orleans.

"If he loses, Chas, they will feed that Cherokee to the gators," said Jackie Ray, picking up the pace. "We may never see his face again, Chas Bellew."

"If he is not in Baton Rouge in three days," said Chas, "then we must ride to Texas without him. All we can do, bud."

"Would you leave him in New Orleans, wounded for the buzzards?" asked Jackie Ray, eyes wide under his gambler's hat.

"Never find him."

"Made his own dang choice, didn't he? Atohi always wants to settle the score, take down all the outlaws."

"Some folks live too long, Jackie Ray," said Chas calmly. "They live too long and make life hard for others, don't you think?"

"Yeah. I hope he makes it back alive," said Jackie Ray, drinking from his canteen. "I didn't mean to fight back there, Chas. My nature is like an animal sometimes. Born that way, I guess."

Jackie Ray started to cry.

"Settle down. He will be alright on his own."

"I best do some confessing to Danny Boy myself. I miss that dog. Do you think that dog liked me?"

"Sure. God help us," said Chas, and slapped his hat on his leg.

As the blazing orange twilight hung over the French Quarter Market, I followed the men to Cafe Du Monde and traveled behind them to two saloons that evening.

I walked my horse inside Saint Louis Cathedral downtown in New Orleans and baptized him in front of a packed congregation. The barn owl was on the railing beside us. After the patrons had hugged my horse, and that night, like a ghost, I rode into the darkness of a black alley. The sound of the horse echoed in silent places, places no man should travel alone. Seven horses were tied, whinnying and snorting with red evil eyes. I met the outlaws face-to-face, all seven of them.

Chapter 12
Broken Stones

Three days had passed when Chas and Jackie Ray reached Baton Rouge, a town they had drifted by at night, months earlier, as green riverboat travelers. They were asleep and did not remember much about their days on the Mississippi River, until they became cuffed prisoners. They worried over my whereabouts and wondered about the battle with the outlaws on Bourbon Street and if my horse was full of crap or knew eyes of evil horses and evil men were the same.

One treasured friend, the kindness of blind man Sammy Summers, taught men how to notice life unseen and how unlimited deception worked in the Great South, and to better understand lawlessness. Much was spoken about moral decay, and ethical compromise, subjects of which I studied in higher education, had lost value, not only in smaller towns, but bigger cities. The men that worked at the blacksmith shop knew the importance of the gift of grace and being hospitable, counting blessings, and lived life that way, long before I became their friends and they gave more to the church than most families did.

The dusty road from New Orleans to Baton Rouge was different for two Kentucky riders, who had managed to age and learn the ropes of big city life, without my expertise as a scout to guide them. Their faces needed a razor's edge and hair turned lighter by the day and beard darker by night; two men in need of a steady river, some soap, food, and a good night's sleep. The world was cruel and deadly beyond the Bluegrass State, and folks were not as friendly and welcoming as we had expected. Indeed, one town in the Great South was as broken and unsettled as the next, towns still smoking with anger and discontentment from the Battle of Baton Rouge and other battles served by men from East Baton Rouge Parish were wounded and remembered war.

In a land of broken stones and shallow graves, Chas shot two rabbits and a turkey as the sun was setting low in the western sky behind the Mississippi River. Smoke billowed and fire blazed into an open evening sky, a signal that food and a good camp was nearby.

"What are all these broken stones about, Chas?" said Jackie Ray, leaning back on his saddle and blanket, kicking his boots off to dry his smelly feet.

"Graves," said Chas, pulling his hat over eyes.

"Tombstones?" said Jackie Ray, who sat up tall.

"Yeah," said Chas, taking meat off the bone. "We have picked a graveyard as a camp for the night, huh?"

"Yeah," said Jackie Ray. "Back in Denton, they'd be a church or a farmhouse nearby, but the graveyard is a long way from the nearest plantation house in Baton Rouge."

"No house for a mile or so," said Chas, chewing. "Thought this would be a good place to sleep for the night." Chas tossed the bones into the fire and finished his meal. "Head into town in the morning for supplies, find a bath and settle back down here tomorrow."

"Have you decided to give Atohi a chance to catch up?" asked Jackie Ray, face dusty and eyes full of doubt and uncertainty.

Horses whinnied and snorted, picking grass in the graveyard.

"If he is not here by sunup," said Chas, looking down the road, "something bad took him down." Chas kicked back and crossed his legs. "Scouting was the kind of death Atohi wanted for himself, Jackie Ray."

"Dang it, Chas!" He slapped his saddle blanket. "I told you. I told you, something bad would happen to him. I know Atohi is crazy sometimes, and riding that crazy horse of his, but sometimes we need to step in, and when he has too much to drink, help him."

Chas sat up and faced his friend, eyes full of truth, and my friend knew my ways better than any man alive, and he said, "Atohi is not crazy like Mrs. Brooks and he was not drunk the morning he turned back to New Orleans."

"What was it then, love?" said Jackie Ray, tapping his heart, face flushed red. "I bet he said that story so he could see the Queen of Voodoo again, didn't he?"

"Nope," said Chas, closing his eyes, meal finished. "Preacher Chet took Atohi in when he was a tawny little kid, a starving teenager. He was twelve winters old. Uncle Chet saw something about him, far beyond the likes of other boys his age. He knew Atohi had a rare spirit about him, something holy, sent from God, even as a young man. He taught him how to fish and hunt and pray and listen for things."

"What things?" Jackie Ray sat up and listened.

"Atohi learned from his grandfather about the woodpecker and about how nature works in the woods."

"What the heck does the woodpecker have to do with anything, huh? asked Jackie Ray, who took a big drink of rum.

"Uncle Chet knew more than he said about Atohi," said Chas, "and he said Atohi would become a legend among his people, a fighter and a warrior, and he is a great scout."

"Legend, huh?" said Jackie Ray, bottle turned up.

Chas observed the night sky and smoke rolled from the campfire. He had burned whatever Marie Laveau had given him.

"Yeah," said Chas. "God did not make the woodpecker with great wings or a great singing voice like other birds. The woodpecker does his crafts with wood and hammering his beak. The Cherokee legend says the woodpecker makes flutes out of branches. He is the only bird in the woods who does this craft. When God sent Uncle Chet to find Atohi in the mountains of North Carolina, God told him to listen for the woodpecker, the only bird that does not sing, and the forest is filled with many singing birds. The woodpecker is a carpenter and a craftsman of musical instruments. That makes the woodpecker special, far more special than other birds."

Jackie Ray cleaned the meat from the rabbit and handled his rum. "Well, heck I never seen a woodpecker flute in the woods before."

"Keep looking, you will."

"How does a woodpecker keep Atohi safe in New Orleans?" Jackie Ray finished his bottle, eyes heavy.

"Animals keep themselves safe and they warn others of danger," said Chas, elbow on his saddle and blanket. "God taught Atohi and Uncle Chet about animals, sounds of nature, and the way they behave. This story is about animals and how God uses animals to keep us safe."

"The woodpecker can't make a flute, Chas."

"Rabbits and deer run when they hear a branch snap," said Chas, snapping a branch. "In fear, animals warn us." Chas rolled over on his side. "When you hear horses snorting and whining, something is wrong. Trouble. You need to listen to the animals; it might save your life."

"Are you saying, when Preacher Chet found Atohi in a cave at Mingo Falls, the woodpecker led him to the Cherokee boy, huh?" asked Jackie Ray, face hung in disbelief.

Chas nodded, pulling his gun and holster close to his side.

"Yeah," said Chas. "Animals tell us things. So, when Atohi's horse stopped dead in his tracks the other morning, something evil was nearby."

"You think God signaled the horse to get Atohi's attention, right?"

"Yeah. The same thing happened for Uncle Chet when the woodpecker hammered the tree, his horse stopped in his tracks, and he listened to animals around him, and nature took its course."

"Speaking of nature calling, I need to go," said Jackie, the man stood. "I need to water the grass before I fall asleep."

"I could use a walk around myself," said Chas, who stood. "See if I can spot Atohi."

"So, if he's not here at sunup," said Jackie Ray, "you swear we are going onto Texas without him, right?"

"Yeah," said Chas. "It was his time to die." Chas walked around the broken stones with his torch. "Scared of ghosts, Jackie Ray?" He read names and numbers on tombstones and placed the matching stones together at night. "Jackie Ray?" Chas walked to the edge of the big graveyard, edging along the wilderness, and turned to the entrance of the gravestones where the gate led to the road into Baton Rouge. Chas waited and fell asleep on his saddle.

"You awake, Chas Bellew?" a man spoke.

The tired eyes of Chas blinked, head canted, and he eyed a silhouette of a man who stood in front of the morning sun. He poured water on the low-burning fire and the ashes caused Chas to jump. Chas grabbed his pistol.

"Who stands in the sun?" said Chas.

"The Bread Maker."

"Atohi?" said Chas, smiling. "You are alive."

I made the bread for Communion at Chet's Presbyterian church. Sometimes, Chas called me the Bread Maker in Denton, and it was a name he knew. I pulled the mountain man to his feet, and the ground was cold beside Jackie's Ray saddle. The soil was loose without footprints.

"Jackie Ray did not sleep here last night, did he, Chas?"

"No. He went missing last night about midnight," said Chas, and he scanned the land. "I searched around the broken stones and walked out to the gate, but he was nowhere to be found."

"Did you hear that coyote?"

I walked toward the sound, still low to the ground and a heavy fog rolled across the land and lifted. "Sounds like a dog with a broken leg. Is that a baby crying? Listen!" I ran.

We dodged gravestones and old broken rocks and stood over a hole in the ground. The woodpecker sounded.

"What is this we have found?" said Chas, grinning.

"You won't roll out of bed that way!" I said.

"Atohi?" said Jackie Ray. "You live and breathe, Cherokee. Can you two men pull me out of this dang grave, please?"

"What are you doing sleeping in a grave, anyways?" said Chas, dropping to the earth.

"Ghosts?" I replied.

"Yeah," said Jackie Ray. "Big white ghost. I followed a ghost to this grave and fell inside, and I must have knocked myself out."

"No ghosts live in Broken Stones," said Chas, pulling him up from the grave.

"They say ghosts walk among the living," said Jackie Ray.

I lifted him up and hugged both of my friends.

"I am hungry as a pack of wolves," said Jackie Ray, slapping his clothes and adjusting his hat. "Let's make our way into Baton Rouge, see what we can get into this morning. Hope they got eggs and sausage on the stove. Dang it, Atohi, glad to see you."

"Good to be alive. My baptized horse saved me."

They wanted to know every detail about what happened.

On the winding road out of Broken Stones, a long line of people dressed in black, paced slowly two-by-two, heads dragging and voices in tune, and they walked to the cemetery. Some strolled the pace of a small child and others rode buggies and horses. An old man led the pack with a black wagon, loaded, inside was a casket, and he was the first to acknowledge our faces.

Chas removed his hat and nodded, face full of condolences and grief. Jackie Ray followed. I did the same, hat held against my chest and hand outstretched to the family. Our clothes were filthy rags from pulling Jackie Ray from the dirty grave.

"Men, thank you for digging the grave," said the old man in the black wagon.

Each man and woman held out their hands and thanked us for digging the hole in the ground, some offered money. Chas stopped his horse to let them pass along the narrow roadway.

"Please take these coins, sir, for your troubles," said a kind lady, who cried and reached out her hands to touch Chas and he held her hands.

"We cannot take credit," said Chas. "No coins. Rest in Peace."

Chas kept riding and waved, head down. Jackie Ray rode up beside Chas. I followed. The three of us were greeted with a great reception by the crowd, but we could not explain our stay to them, either.

"They think we're diggers," said Jackie Ray. "We are dirty."

"Better than grave robbers," I said, and whispered.

"Ride faster to Baton Rouge, men. When they figure it out, and how we are without shovels, we'll be buried right beside the old man."

Chas told and he was right.

With our mouths watering, we steadied ourselves to a small, trickling spring. Because watering holes were often scouted by robbers and bandits, I stood guard and scouted.

"Fill my canteen, Jackie Ray," I asked.

I scouted the land with a brass pocket telescope.

"This town is milk and honey, Chas," said Jackie Ray, who often voiced his thoughts. "I feel good about it. Big River."

"Hope it is better than the handcuffs that we felt in the last town," said Chas.

At the next hillside, the land opened, trees had fall colors, and I remembered the day well. It was a revelation for long riders, who found little rest and missed home. Our eyes rolled heavily and clothes brushed with dirt, face unshaven; still mounted, and restless, three adventurous men from Kentucky, craving conversations, and substance. Atop the hilltop was where I scouted westward, closing the gap on Baton Rouge, Louisiana.

"Keep your wits about you, Jackie Ray," said Chas. "Less rum keeps a man alive."

"I will take his part of the bottle," I said, and adjusted my hat. "Since he's known to drown on a shot of rum and chase ghosts."

"Drown?" said Jackie Ray, half asleep. "I can outdrink you, bud."

"We will put it to the test soon," I said, loud when I laughed.

"Okay," said Jackie Ray. "Put it to the test."

"We must see this town," said Chas, kicking his horse, "before my time in New Orleans loses hope for all places comparable in wealth and passion, painting a picture of unknown ladies."

From a distance, steamboats lined the riverbanks and more boats were anchored to the docks. Smaller vessels remained roped to the banks, headed north and south, and the Old Ferry Landing building was to the right of the docks. Two buildings stood out above the rest, Tunnard Carriage and Harness Factory, and a grand steeple was high above the town.

"Saint Joseph Cathedral." I said, reading the sign aloud. "Baptize your horse, Kentucky Boys."

"Might do it. How long are we in this town, Chas?" said Jackie Ray, dismounting his horse. "Something is dead wrong with the animals, foaming at the mouth. Look at our mule."

"Sick!" said Chas, who turned his horse around.

We rode up to a big plantation home and waited for the owner.

"Hey, strangers," said a lovely lady in a yellow dress. "Men, please do not go into town!"

"Plague!" said the lady. "Everyone in town has the plague or cholera and something is bad wrong with Baton Rouge."

I walked over to see the mule and opened his mouth, and checked out the mouth of the horses.

"Lots of animals getting sick and folks are dying." said the lady, seventeen or so.

Her hair was pinned up, and she covered her mouth.

"Are you sick?" I asked.

"No people sick at my house, sir. No plagues here. Nothing has crossed our path, thank God."

Taking off his hat, Chas looked at the plantation home, big porch, two chimneys, with a long walkway and a winding road that led back to a big barn behind the house. A lady stood in the doorway, and someone was on the front porch in a rocking chair and listened, and he played the banjo. Playing a flute harmonica, a boy tapped his leg atop the steps. Workers were in the orchard. To the left, a beautiful garden of yellow lilies trailed alongside the pathway from the wagon road to the barn. Ducks and chickens picked on the roadside. Horse stables and a new cellar stood out back and red was the color of a big barn.

"Does your Pa welcome strangers?" asked Chas, hat in his hand. "Hope you got some food and a few rooms for the night, lady."

"No," said the lady. "My daddy didn't return home from the war. Momma prayed away the sickness from our land. She doesn't mind strangers, though. This is, if you got good wits about yourselves and some money."

"We have money, but short on wits," said Chas, and he grinned. "Well, one of us might be questionable. Hope there might be an exception to your hospitality."

"Is the gambler questionable?" said the lady. "That one, huh?"

"Me?" said Jackie Ray. "Clever as a fox, young lady."

"I hate foxes!" said the lady, lips tight, eyes steady. "Foxes eat chickens. I hate foxes!"

The lady held her hips, looked inside her house, then back at Chas and scanned the face of Jackie Ray. He did not speak again. She walked up behind the boy playing the harmonica to see if anyone else was following us. She paced to the road where we were and stopped. There was no one behind us.

Petting his own horse, said Chas, "My manners are acceptable. I can be a perfect gentleman when I want to at the table."

She waved her hand at Chas. The woman trusted him, not foxy and her face was sour in my direction.

"Jackie Ray and Atohi," said Chas, pointing at us. "Wait at the road." He studied her small frame. "Name's Chas." He walked his horse beside her until they reached the steps of the plantation home.

"Anna," said the young lady. "This is the McIntosh Plantation. You will see orchards of Anna Apple Trees, far as the eyes can see. Help yourself."

"Beautiful place," said Chas, who spoke for us. "I do enjoy apples. You are a busy family."

"My family runs the Ferry System, too," said Anna, pointing. "Unless you can fly, you will need the ferry to cross the muddy Mississippi River. Travelers trade and pay, keeping this plantation in full operation. God knows we enjoy the distance, far from the political corruption and the plague of Baton Rouge."

Chas aimed his hat toward town, and said, "What is the dark smoke over the town?"

"Sir, we don't bury the dead. Bodies are burned at sundown, and they burn all night. We must terminate this plague, burn out evil. Pardon me, I have to see my mother. You stand here, Chas."

She spoke with her mother on the porch for a moment and they argued. Both ladies walked inside the foyer and back outside again.

"Everything all right, Anna?" said Chas, studying the movements of the ladies, and saw black smoke drifting high above the town, miles, and miles from town.

"The man with pale skin, like yours, foxy. That man can stay and eat," said Anna, hands behind her back. "You are welcome to apple cider and food. We like good Christian folks."Her voice got deeper; green eyes squinted at Chas.

"What about my Cherokee friend?" said Chas, both hands on his hat, cap on his chest.

"We feel in our hearts," said Anna, clearing her throat, "the savage can find his own dang food. He must leave the property, now, sir."

"Where I come from," said Chas, hat on his chest, "that is not very Christian like, put people out on the street. The Cherokee, Atohi, is my brother, raised in a Christian home, same as you good folks. His skin, the one God gave him, just a little darker than our arms, it makes no difference." Chas smiled and looked at her mother. "He knows the New Testament, Mrs. McIntosh, good as you do, I bet. Can you reconsider our stay?"

She brought the pistol forward and cocked the hammer.

I saw what happened.

"Jackie Ray, the old lady has a gun. Get behind the mule."

We could afford to spare a sick mule.

"Listen!" said the old lady. "Sonny," stepping closer, holding the banister, "I do not care if he's President Grant's long lost Cherokee son-in-law, home from the Indian Wars, I want you and your savage off my property." Hand raised. "I will fire my Colt, burn you with the rest of the plague!"

"Yeah, I hear you," said Chas, hand close to his Colt.

The boy on the porch crawled to the middle steps and he played the flute harmonica with passion and style as if he had been instructed to do so on many occasions, entertaining visitors for a dime or two.

"Could you tell me which road leads to the Ferry System, young fella?" asked Chas, hand above his head and he kept on playing. No words were spoken from the lad.

"North of town, sir," said the old woman, speaking with certainty. "Keep riding, boys!"

"Thank you for your nefarious hospitality, ladies," said Chas, walking backwards and pulling his horse.

"Have a safe journey with the Cherokee, young man," said the old lady, laughing and leaning on the porch, still armed.

Chas turned around to the old lady.

"What's he doing?" I thought.

"As a good Christian," said Chas, hat over his gun. "I am sure you know who carried the cross for Jesus the day he was crucified, right?"

"Of course," blurted the old lady. "Simon of Cyrene, young man."

"Right, right," said Chas, placing his hat on his head. "He was a black man, and black as West Virginia coal dust, I bet. You remember those who lift Jesus up as we carry, white, black, red, or brown. We are the same to God, no different, lifting as we carry the cross, Mrs. McIntosh." He tapped his hat. "Good day."

Black workers walked out from fields and orchards, amid the disagreement, favoring the words of Chas. They cheered, some clapped, and smiled, and a strong whistle was belted by a tall man.

Anna spat and said, "That savage is no better than a stray dog!" She grabbed her mothers' gun. "You better leave, leave now. Go!"

Mounting his horse, Chas turned the horse around, and rode to the front porch and faced Anna and Mrs. McIntosh. Anna raised the Colt, arm stretched, beaded down on the heart of Chas Bellew, aimed to harm him.

I stepped out from behind the mule and watched, hand on my rifle. Nervously, Anna steadied her eyes, cheeks red as polished apples and she stuttered.

"You come any closer, you'll bleed!" said Anna. "Your sermon is not needed in the South! We have our own thoughts and traditions, traditions that work for us, far and wide."

"Traditions, well, that don't make it right, Anna. I got one more thing to say, Mrs. McIntosh," said Chas. "And we'll part ways."

"Say it!" said the old woman, contemptuously. "How you and that savage haven't been shot, is far beyond my knowledge."

"Well, then, Christian lady," said Chas, remembering his Uncle Chet, "speaking of red skin, Sunday School taught you that 1st Samuel speaks of King David, and the man had a freckled face, red hair color and his skin was ruddy, all in the Good Book," pointing in my direction. "Same skin as that man, yonder."

"What's your point?" said Anna.

Chas held his vest, grinned, and said, "Remember this day, King David had "ruddy" red skin." He aimed two fingers at the women. "King David was a man after God's own heart. Let it be a lesson for you, Anna, and Mrs. McIntosh. Good day, ladies."

"King David could not stay warm and died!" shouted Mrs. McIntosh.

"Amen and Amen," said a black lady, huddled beside a young boy, and she had heard every word. "Boy," holding her young son, "I hope you grow up to be just like that man."

I heard everything he said while Jackie Ray hummed to himself and crunched apples. Chas Bellew rode to the end of the road where the apple trees started, and he stopped. He steadied his horse and watched Jackie Ray, who stood on his saddle and picked apples. Chas crossed his arms atop his saddle and watched the smoke roll over Baton Rouge.

"What's for supper, bud?" said Jackie Ray. "Apple pie?"

"No, sir!" said Chas. "Dirty ole red beets, speckled corn," said Chas, petting his horse, "and black-eyed peas, some mixed with brown Cajun rice. I knew you men would not stomach peas and beets on the same day."

I knew I had not heard those words.

"I'd eat a polecat about now, Chas." Jackie Ray crunched an apple.

"Ride, men," said Chas. "Find a better place soon. I found a way to cross the river, straight ahead, gents."

Some men became great by harming no one with their words. Chas kept the conversation to himself, the harsh words spoken between him and Mrs. McIntosh and Anna, kept in secret. He never spoke of it again. His intention, to ride and learn from the journey, ride with less distractions, limit judgements and stop prejudge. I never told Jackie Ray what happened, and Chas respected my silence, and knew the ears of a good scout heard them talking.

Chapter 13
Three Riders

Somewhere around midday, the sun baked our skin, a ring of sweat soaked our hats, and dust covered our faces. Chas and Jackie Ray reached the Old Ferry System in Baton Rouge ahead of my horse, a big and slow horse, anyway. We rode around the city and dodged the plague, riding beyond the Cholera outbreak, which affected the water supply of the town. Folks of East Baton Rouge Parish blamed the people in Fort Defiance for hundreds of deaths, and the sick Union Blue Army could not be pinned to such a particular outbreak, either.

French trappers, mostly men from Canada, stood in front of doctors and officials, being questioned, and were blamed as the main source of the illness; two men had already been accused and murdered for it. Dark smoke rolled from burning stations, and the landscape smelled like the world was on fire in the capital of Louisiana. From a long distance, dark faces of desperation stirred longingly at us. They continued to work the burning stations, bitter and grieving and wept for fallen family and friends. Wagons were heavily stacked with dead bodies, still clothed, and emotional havoc raged among the locals. The harsh smell could not be forgotten.

Travelers and pioneers were presumed to be laced with the disease and stirred prejudice in the minds of residents. Guns were fired in anger, and fights broke out; residents blamed outsiders. At midday, church bells sounded, names collected, and the dead were noted by the clergy. Men worked at night at burning stations while women documented the names and made meals for workers. The peaceful town had been deserted and deadly. Fewer and fewer remained each week. Outlaws and bandits picked from vacant houses and businesses. Not much was said or done by the sheriff before he died. Untimely curfews were posted, and warning signs were nailed up. Lurkers became suspects and felt the heat of ammo on their tails.

The man operating the McIntosh River Ferry System was a kind soul. His health was that of a young man, one who never mentioned the fact of the plague or questioned us about Cholera or anything else when we arrived to cross the water. We loaded our horses and tugged our way into deeper water, crossing the muddy Mississippi River yet again.

"Welcome aboard, men!" said the gray-haired man with a long smile. His feet and hands moved fast, holding the ropes. "Jacob McIntosh. Been on this ferry since I was born, and one day, I will walk away from it. I fought in the big War, Battle of Selma. If you had a mind to ask me."

"You were too young to support the South, I bet?" said Mr. McIntosh.

"You are right, sir," said Chas. "Ten years or so, too young."

"Lost my little brother at the Battle of Selma, Alabama," said Mr. McIntosh. "Took a shot in my right leg, too." Limping and aged, he maneuvered the ferry as best he could in the choppy, swift current that beat against the side, rocking the vessel worst at midstream. "The South," catching his breath and leaning against the side railing, "The South, with all of God's power, well, we were winning when I was wounded at Selma and left the Confederate Army."

"I am Chas Bellew, and this Cherokee, Atohi, and the man with the horses, Jackie Ray Monroe, the best two men I know."

The man tugged ropes, and talk was a respite.

"Where are you from, Bellew?" said Mr. McIntosh.

"Kentucky," said Chas, winding ropes in a circle on the flat top boat, which eased through rapids like a giant duck gliding across the water. "We are from the same town, Denton, Kentucky."

"Bet you my old leather boots, you are headed to strike gold," said Mr. McIntosh, grinning and pulling a plug of tobacco from his pocket. "Are you headed west to California, dig for gold, huh?"

"Nope. Headed to Texas," said Chas, working beside him.

The mighty river, wide and full, rocked the boat, and waves beat endlessly against the ferry system.

"More to the story, I bet, huh? What are you doing this far from Kentucky, boys?"

"Tracking a man by the name of Bad Carl Bellew," said Chas.

"Are you bounty hunters?" chuckled Mr. McIntosh, grinning.

"Nope," said Chas. "Family."

"Bad Carl Bellew rode this ferry nine months ago," said Mr. McIntosh, who rested and poured water atop his head. "You aim to kill him?"

"Nope."

"Family, huh?" said Mr. McIntosh.

"Uncle."

"A name not too common in these parts," replied Mr. McIntosh. His eyes scanned the features of Chas and tried to place his mind back to when exactly Bad Carl Bellew crossed the river with him. "You have an uncanny resemblance, my friend. What do you need with a ruthless fellow like Carl Bellew?"

"My father is dead," said Chas. "My late Uncle Chet and Carl are full brothers. Aim to tell him the bad news, see him in person."

"Did you think about a letter?"

Chas laughed, and Jackie Ray moved. Chas said, "Heard Carl is headed to Waco, Texas. We are on his tail."

"Hey, Cherokee, Atohi?" said Chas, fingers snapped. "Atohi, hey, wake up Jackie Ray. Got to ride."

"I was not asleep. I was scouting with my eyes closed."

"Let's scout to Texas, eyes open." Chas pushed my arm.

We walked the horses from the ferry to dry land and fed them handfuls of grain.

"Stop dreaming about New Orleans ladies, Jackie Ray," I said. "Time to ride, cowboy." Pressed his shoulder, and I said, "Grab your horse, pull the ugly mule."

"Guys," said Mr. McIntosh, "I need to warn you about a madman." He held his chin, "Crazy as hell, one eye, bad shot when he's sober. He will shoot anything that walks, crawls, or breathes on his property. You must cross the McIntosh land, land I was raised on... but he has the best Quarter Horses in the country."

"Well, sir," said Chas, mounting his horse, grunting, and climbing up, "what should we do to get by this fool?"

McIntosh walked up the riverbank, tied his ferry boat to a big tree at the dock, and dusted his hands. The man turned and looked back at East Baton Rouge Parish, burning, and sighed.

"Portend, gentlemen. Beware of Bert, portend, portend," said Mr. McIntosh, a handful of his things in his arms.

"What language is he speaking?" said Jackie Ray.

"I can get you past my brother, Bert," said Mr. Mcintosh, voice of certainty. "Suppose he might have forgotten about our feud the year Lincoln was shot."

"Your mule is sick. May I, Chas?" Jacob released the reigns.

The mule splashed into the river.

"Best thing for the ole mule," said Jackie Ray.

Jackie Ray mounted his horse, eyes still shuttering. I was second and scouted the countryside for movement and waved to my friends. The sun was full overhead, so I adjusted my hat and felt good in the gentle wind. Crossing his arms, Jackie Ray dropped his chin bone on his chest, half asleep in the saddle; his horse stepped and woke him from his slumber. The route forked in all directions after we exited the ferry. Chas and the ferry operator spoke of the best route to Texas. I walked a while with my horse and picked grass along the trail.

"How far is your brother?" said Chas, arms crossed.

"Five miles or so," said Mr. McIntosh. "Big white house on the right. If you men don't mind good company, just to keep the peace, I can walk for a spell until brother Bert McIntosh decides to be cordial to the public ... or apologize."

Two miles into the ride, Jackie Ray offered Jacob McIntosh his horse, but he preferred to walk. The old man sweated like a giant hog before the butcher called his name, walking rapidly.

"Do you expect your brother to be a problem?" said Chas, who offered to let the War Veteran ride his horse, but he refused to ride a horse without a comfortable saddle.

"I might have to teach him some manners," said Mr. McIntosh, who walked and scratched his ear.

"Take him out behind the woodshed!" shouted Jackie Ray.

"I am pleased to have company," said Jacob McIntosh.

The windy trail to Krotz Springs was a long ride, and the woods were much thicker. The path narrowed into brushy pines, where small swamps and wetlands dropped into the earth along the lower parts of the land, and downed trees from a storm were common features along the trail. We dodged hanging oaks and pines, and the trail was much more dangerous than McIntosh first explained. No safe place existed to bed down for the night amid snakes and other creatures. At a trading post in the middle of nowhere, the owner toasted whiskey and chased it with beer. That's when McIntosh became loose and told how he killed Yanks single-handedly, too, and carried a sword into battle, taking down men too scared to fight.

"Three days later, I was wounded at the Battle of Selma," said Mr. McIntosh. "Rode home. Ended it."

Mr. McIntosh paid no fee to cross the Atchafalaya River from Saint Martin Parish to Saint Landry Parish, with a simple nod from Jacob McIntosh and a handful of past favors from a lady who opposed President Grant. Chas tipped the man so no trouble would follow our horses for lack of coins. The next day, birds flew in the distance at Opelousas and reminded us of the serenity of home.

I saw movement in the brush when limbs cracked and snapped with the weight of a heavy man or many men, and then my horse stopped, the same as it did in New Orleans. My hand was raised to Chas when more birds were flushed from the golden grass beyond a wide, flat area where fine horses ran across rolling hills that faded, the forest became quiet, and trees were without game or foul.

A rifle was fired. Pine bark split and fell in front of my face. I dismounted my horse to scout low to the ground, waving to my friends. The man stayed low. The gunfight had started.

"One-eyed weasel!" I said to Jacob McIntosh. "He has a Henry rifle behind that tree, hundred yards away."

"He stole it from me. That's Bert, Atohi, yonder way!" yelled Jacob McIntosh. "Take cover, boys! Bourbon and Cajun boudin sausage got him spent. Time for battle!" Jacob McIntosh kicked his legs and took cover in fear of his foolish brother's evil ways.

"Where's this crazy man tucked his head, McIntosh?" said Jackie Ray.

"Lost him, Jackie Ray." Jabob stood to get his brother's attention.

I crawled between downed trees, hidden behind rocks and dirt, expecting a good shot from Bert. Chas tied the horses. Three shots were fired, one by one, and our horses fell to the ground.

"My baptized horse!" I said, hand covering his eyes.

"He killed our horses, Jacob!" said Chas, comforting the horses, and blood painted the earth.

"This man is a deadly savage!" yelled Jackie Ray, who fired three more shots.

"He's down," I told Jacob McIntosh. Bert moaned.

The Great Spirit led the way to the man, and I circled around his land and found wide trees where the green field folded and ended on the narrow road. I edged the road for an open shot. Bert McIntosh was known to rob travelers at the fork in the road at Opelousas. That was how Bert had stolen Quarter Horses and supplied himself, trading stolen goods from wagons over the years. Bert became popular among trappers and traders.

"In the bead of my rifle is my enemy," I told myself. Gun cocked. "I want him to fight for his life." I paced to the next tree until the last ray of light shined.

"Pow!"

Brother Bert McIntosh dropped his Henry rifle to his side. Red-colored clothes, pressing his rough hands over the wound that had ripped through his chest. Chas, Jackie Ray, and Jacob stood over him.

"Jacob," said Bert, voice low and slow, "you are no better for taking my life, brother."

"Brothers, huh? We have never been brothers."

Jacob squatted and eyed his older brother, lifting the patch on his left eye, where no eye had seen sunlight for a long while.

"I will take my father's land back while I'm here," said Jacob McIntosh.

"You'll take nothing while I'm alive!" said Bert.

Jacob grabbed his throat. "And these good men will need three Quarter Horses," shaking him, "since you murdered their animals."

Jacob stood in anger, face dry and wrinkled.

"May darkness cover his life!" shouted Jacob.

The owl swiftly came and landed on Bert's arm.

"The owl plucked his eye!" I said, caught in amazement.

Brother Bert screamed and rolled wildly in the dirt.

"Evil has been repaid, Bert!" shouted Jacob.

Chest soaked and eyes gone, Bert McIntosh dropped his arms to his side and rested, head back. Chas and Jackie Ray stood, arms crossed, dropping pistols by their side. I scouted for anyone else who might be lurking around the farm. I spoke the 23rd Psalm.

"An eye for an eye, my brother," said Jacob, smiling, "and for what you did to my wife and daughter, you get the same death." He laughed, and away from his brother, tears fell down his cheeks.

"Mr. McIntosh, sir, hey?" yelled Chas, and the shoulder of his friend was turned. "Let's leave this man to crawl and stumble, huh?"

"Yeah, to wander." replied Jacob, who stood dazed in front of Chas, back to his brother." I did my family a good justice," said Jacob, eyes full of tears.

The big arm of Bert slowly raised.

"Watch out, Jacob!" yelled Jackie Ray, who lunged for the hand of Bert, who had aimed a Dragoon revolver from under his coat. Bert kicked and fell dead.

"Sir, Jacob!" yelled Chas, who grabbed his friend before he fell against a tree. "Rest yourself."

"Bury me beside my wife and daughter, Chas. I'm taking the ferry home."

***

I remembered the rough, low voice of a good man, Jacob McIntosh, who laughed and smiled, a man full of life, and he enjoyed telling stories about boating the river as a kid. Of all the stories he told, the last one was about the Civil War. The old man spoke of troops who gave their lives for the cause and other troops who lived to tell about battles and wars and rumors of wars.

Hundreds of troops used the ferry to cross the river, men in blue and gray, young men, some teenagers, too, and older, the wounded, who kept the cause. Many were held as prisoners, prayed for victory, lived through battles, and had nightmares after the Civil War. Jacob befriended veterans and became educated about their reason for fighting the Union.

Old man Jacob McIntosh swatted big mosquitoes that buzzed his head and told of biting bugs that lived in hollow trees in Krotz Springs, Louisiana. He spoke of his evil brother, who lived between two rivers at a fork in the road. Bert settled on his family farm and was known to be a horse thief, stealing and selling livestock. The worst of his time was spent trading dogs to trappers for furs and coins.

"Good men of Kentucky," said Jacob McIntosh. The old man was red-eyed and wired and said, "We will ride into Opelousas with caution and guns loaded for bear. My brother is a one-eyed, cold-blooded killer and a good shot with a rifle."

Bert killed whoever walked the road in front of his land. Jacob told of all the men his brother had killed, rumors of hundreds of men and settlers buried, and some tied to trees in the swamps.

"Men of God, fed to the souls of alligators," said Jacob McIntosh. "The ugliest creatures the Lord has created," and he held his hat over his eyes as he walked. "This is my last chance. I'm truly sorry I lied to you good men about it being a short ride. I knew you were true to the Good Book."

"You lied to us!" said Chas.

"I did," said Jacob McIntosh.

The Cherokee in my blood questioned things: "I do not know what purpose God needed with an ugly alligator or men like Bert."

I remembered a sermon in Denton one Sunday that Preacher Chet Bellew spoke of many times. He said, "Some things have no good explanation or clarity on this earth. Other things we will assuredly find the answer to when we cross into heaven, and heaven will have all the answers, but, saints, by that time on our journey, we will have forgotten the smallness of earth and questions."

On a windy day, the gusty dawn swept big clouds from a giant blue sky, and it seemed leaves turned colors overnight in the Great South. The promise was settled between Jacob and Bert, buried, and two McIntosh brothers whom we'd known for less than a day, both perished before our very eyes. Out of high respect for Jacob McIntosh and his family, Chas and Jackie Ray hitched a wagon and loaded Bert and Jacob, back-to-back, heads covered, into a long wagon, and the brothers were pulled by Bert's Quarter Horses to the graveyard. The McIntosh brothers would have disliked being so close, distancing themselves in their youth, and felt the same as older men. I knew little about brotherhood other than Chas Bellew and I felt compassion for Jacob and wept for him, much more than Bert.

"Hey, Jackie Ray," said Chas, who stood with a shovel. "Just bury Bert as far as possible from Jacob."

"Leave no pathway between the graves, Chas," I said, hand aimed at the empty graves. I planned the greatest distance on that land, and we agreed it was best that way.

I spoke over their bodies and said, "And since there was no road they cared to travel between them in life, let there be no path today."

The sun fell, and the night was cold. Chas made soup from the meat of rabbits and a fat pheasant that he'd taken from the field. Many rabbits and birds called Opelousas home in the fall of 1871. We stayed at the McIntosh family homeplace without prior permission, but no one asked us to leave, either. On our journey, a trail of broken hearts existed.

"We could have finished much earlier if Atohi hadn't taken so many breaks to look around and act like he was scouting," said Jackie Ray, cleaning soup from his chin and chewing meat.

I threw better than most men, so my knife crossed the room and landed pretty close to the man with soup on his chin.

"Keep it up, Jackie Ray. Next time, I may not be so careful with my aim," I said, laughing.

Chas stacked a deck of cards on the table, grinned from across the table, and said, "The Cherokee was watching your back for bandits while you peacefully dug two graves. Maybe thank him from time to time."

I pulled my knife from the timber above the head of Jackie Ray, and it was the best I had thrown in years.

"Well, well, Atohi," said Jackie Ray, who sat further across the room peacefully at a window. "Next time, I'll scout, and you dig to China. But thanks for scouting, bud. We're alive."

I lifted the skinny man, feet dangling, and placed him on a wall hook meant for heavy coats and guns.

"Hey, hey, hey, guys," said Chas, "enough fighting today. Been a long day," and he collected his cards. "Time to call it a night. Put him on the floor."

I brushed the shoulders of Jackie Ray and said, "Sorry, I get a little excited when I haven't had any lemon juice in a while."

"Someone is at the door. Horses!" said Chas.

"I bet it's the three riders I invited over," I said and walked to the door. "While I was protecting Jackie Ray's butt from being shot down." I tucked my knife away and holstered my pistol.

"What three riders?" said Chas, who moved to the window and saw three horses. "Someone is on the porch."

"Grab your gun," said Jackie Ray, cocking his revolver, arms extended to the door.

The door was slapped three times.

"Are you going to get the door?" I said, flapping my hand toward Chas, who nodded and held his gun behind him.

"I think they are harmless," I said. "Or they would have taken our lives earlier today."

"Who is it?" said Chas, hands on the door.

"We are just being neighborly," said a lady with a sweet voice. "We brought some warm food and something for your thirst."

"If it's lemon juice or anything lemon," I said, head down, sharpening my knife and grinning, "we're not interested."

"Lemons?" said one of the ladies. "They're sour and we're sweet."

"I'll get the dang door, Chas," said Jackie Ray.

Jackie Ray walked up to the port hole in the door and shrugged his shoulders as if he was cautious about who was on the other side and why they knocked at night. One lady stood on the front porch while two more ladies stood behind her on the ground. Each lady had a basket of food. All three ladies had long hair and dark coats on their shoulders.

Curious as a hawk scouting a field mouse, Chas stepped in front of Jackie Ray, swung open the door, and said, "Welcome aboard," with a surprised voice. "Good to see smiling faces. Not many people live around these parts."

"I'm Betty." The lady walked inside the house and sat beside Jackie Ray, who holstered his gun and relaxed. "We've never been invited to this house before."

"Who invited you?" I said, laughing, eyes on the ladies.

Chas took their coats, and guns were kept on their hips.

"Who invited you to stay, feathers?" said the lady who walked past Chas and sat to my right, smiling. She slapped my leg.

"You don't scare me." I grinned. She felt my clothes.

"I'm Sary, not scary," said one of the twin sisters. "Yonder with the horses and gifts; she's my sister, Mary. We live on the next farm, end of the road." Smiling, "We live alone."

"We made ourselves at home," I told her. "No one asked us to leave, either. I saw three riders today, and you seemed friendly."

"Being women might not make us friendly," said Betty, legs crossed. "We knew where you were at noon and at sundown. We can scout better than you, Atohi," brushing back her dark hair.

"Yeah," said Mary. The lady walked inside and sat beside Chas, skin the same as the Cherokee Nation, and she looked my way. "Thank you for having us over."

"Our pleasure," said Chas, touching Mary's hand and scouting for other strangers outside.

"I forgot something," said Mary.

Mary walked to her horse and handed Chas a jug she'd brought him and smiled. The three riders were the same age as Chas and Jackie Ray. None were married or had visible rings about their hands; women of singularity, for pride of independence, for freedom. By the cute smiles and gentle eyes, they were harmless. But so were the ladies in New Orleans, ladies who worked for the Queen of Voodoo.

"Not much gets by these parts without us knowing it," said Mary. "We saw you kill Bert McIntosh today and bury him at the end of the settlement."

"Hold on!" said Chas, raising his hands. "But not after he shot his own brother in the back and aimed to kill us for riding across his property. Let's make sure you know how the gunfight started, and Jacob was the one who finished it."

"Bert McIntosh claimed all of this land was his," said Sary, head turned to the men. "But his property line is nowhere near the wagon trail or water," who poured each person a cup. "Our mother was a sister to Bert McIntosh and Jacob McIntosh."

"So, I guess you own this land," said Chas, handing Mary the keys. "Handed down through attrition, and I'd look to the Parish for an answer. Hope you have no trouble with the right to own your uncle's land."

The men stood in honor and respect. That night, I felt like saying something.

"To the three riders we just met," I said. "Saintly sisters."

"I'd like to make a toast to three sweet and beautiful ladies," said Chas, lifting his face with a giant smile, "who had scouted us all day and finally had the courage to offer their newfound friends some food."

"Courage?" said Mary. "We become friends with whoever we want and harm whoever we have a grievance against. We let you three live today."

"That's not courage," said Sary, "It's compassion."

The ladies touched their faces and laughed.

"To living a better life," said Chas, grinning. "I know we will become the best of friends."

Each one raised their cup. The women finished first, and we admired each other and grinned. We paired up and had private conversations together by the fireplace.

Morning broke into Opelousas, and a golden sunbeam brushed the town, the kind of burning light few had seen because of the smoke from Baton Rouge. Chas appreciated how God brought light to the world like a giant candle, and fog rolled off the stream by the barn. He found an old, dusty rocking chair and enjoyed a good cup of coffee. On that brilliant morning, our eyes saw fences that divided openness across the land, a land clouded with dust and broken light as far as the eye could see. Giant mossy oaks and southern pines waved in the morning breeze. The sun burst through Blue Beeches and Eastern Red Cedars and warmed our faces, and melting was peerless dew, and to Chas, the McIntosh farm soaked up the life of a real cowboy. Chas raised up and stood barefooted. I joined him. We heard the sound of horses, louder and closer, thundering across the foggy landscape, where golden meadows and rolling hills edged the forest, and, in the distance, dust rose above the landscape for a quarter mile away. The sun cast long shadows from where the barn and home trailed to the corral. Next, Jackie Ray walked up. In a short time, all three men from Kentucky stood, boots on the ground, and leaned against the corral, caught in adoration. Jackie Ray spilled coffee on his boots and cursed his eyes, head in a slumber.

The day started, born just as spiritual as a Sunday sermon, more physical than any we had ever seen. A day that began with hundreds of horses in stride, some wild and few broken by the crest of a whip, and all ran was unwonted. In the distance, horse faces appeared, dark eyes, countless faces, anticipation broken, shone true in illumination, faces with stars and bald faces of white, splotches of diamond and faint stars. More horses burst through the silvery white fog; still, they ran fast toward the corral. Dust covered thick bodies of chestnut and bay, red and roan, in motion, legs stretched, horses of smoky cream, some of buckskin and some of shiny dun, and few of golden champagne ran. The herd thundered toward the open gates. More horses raced in an allegiance than most men could count, fluid, lotted, packed, shoulder-to-shoulder, and the animals formed an endless unmounted line, randomly paired and blanketing the shadowy farm. What was once peaceful and serene became picturesque. The recollection of Jacob's story, the truth, appeared as a parade of horses filled that void with beautiful colors of cream and reds and shades of brown.

Without retreat, my heart was honored. In my own tradition, I danced and chanted and spun the way my ancestors did. In the wakening of my past, my mind was someplace else, lost in spirit and sound. Voices sang aloud to the Great One, and once again, the silence was broken in thankfulness, handed down from thousands of years of life with man and horses - forces swept beyond any man's control. I was grateful for the hand of God, lost in the light of an unexplainable morning with animals that needed to be handled.

Jackie Ray and Chas leaned on the fence, and we'd left behind simple words and felt less utterance, hats adjusted, belts high and tight. Our eyes reflected the harmony of thunderous horses. The herd paced and settled down, and the land was alive. They turned and circled slower, and all eyes watched in expectancy of who'd commanded them. Three horses panted, and each man found their favorite horses, and perhaps, the horses had found us.

Faces warm to the touch, one dun, one bay, and one sorrel, and all of them were Quarter Horses. We claimed, roped, and saddled the horses we wanted, a promise spoken of by Jacob and our lady friends.

My chant halted.

"Smoke," I said, pointing to the south. "Fire!"

"Look!" said Chas. "Horses have ashes on their legs."

"Mount up," said Jackie Ray. "Dark smoke."

"What will we do with the horses?" I said, mounted. "These are the horses Jacob McIntosh promised us. What about the rest?"

A whistle sounded in the distance, Chas and Jackie Ray, hands atop their pistols, and new trouble brewed. I did no different than my friends. The sound of a second voice lifted behind the barn, and the third voice, all female, echoed further from the woods.

"Here's your horses, Kentucky Boys," shouted Sary, adjusting her dusty hat and holding a bright smile.

For me, it was angel dust. I grinned at my friends and rode to where the women crossed a muddy stream and headed to the barn. We made our way to the corral again and dismounted, and Sary's dark eyes roped my heart. She kissed me. It seemed that my confidence, a natural part of my character, eyes touched, was reserved for that moment.

"Well, well," said Chas. "You brought a few more than three horses, ladies, so what do you aim to do with these animals?"

"These horses were stolen by that demon Bert McIntosh," said Mary, pulling her long brown hair over her shoulders and dipping water from the well. She washed dust from her long hair and rested. "Most of this herd are branded. Our aim is to find the brand and return the horses to their rightful owners. Those without a brand will join our herd across the spread, and some will be sold at the local stockyard. That's the way we live."

"You men are welcome to stay and help us run this place," said Betty, who turned her canteen up and brushed her long blonde hair.

"We would love to stay," said Jackie Ray. "But, well, we aim to be in other places, right Chas?."

"Yeah. What he meant to say," said Chas, slapping the shoulder of Jackie Ray. "We'd love to be here, but our journey takes us onto Texas. Might get back this way next year. Our mission is in Waco, Texas."

"Might finish our mission, get back this way soon," I said, shaking hands with Betty. "I love horses, though. This land would make a good horse ranch."

"Skip Texas!" said Betty, who walked between us. "Stay here." Her hand ran down each man's shoulder. "We're here. The nights get cold."

Raising her voice and lifting her hat, said Sary, "The invitation is open, cowboys. Lots of money in good horses since the big War ended, Chas. More farms need good horses than ever before in Louisiana and Texas, and folks love our trained Quarter Horses," waving her hat. "Good horses like these bring top dollar. What do you say, men?"

"We don't settle for rejection," said Mary, saddle in her hands. She was a lady full of laughter and smiled as she walked inside the barn.

Chas locked the corral and said, "We can send you a telegram from Waco, ladies," grinning. "If things go well in Texas, we'll have an answer for you by next spring. How about that?"

"I don't care for your answer," said Mary, who leaned forward to brush the dusty horse.

"We might be a little too tough and loud, Atohi," said Betty, hand on my face. "Most of our evenings are spent in the river bathing horses."

Strong images, happy ones, had crawled into my mind, and I kept them to myself. The ladies removed their vests and stood at the end of the barn in white and navy shirts and dusted their clothes. They waited, arms around each other, and drank water, faces wet and unsatisfied with our decision to leave.

"If you change your mind, Chas," said Sary. "Might be more than you bargained for on this farm, right?"

"Wouldn't want any less," said Chas, laughing.

Laughing and wetting their hair, Sary, Mary, and Betty, beautiful faces full of delight, had us pondering the need for an exodus. I had become mighty thirsty and joined them. The three of us shared a good lunch of potato soup and bread at their home. We held each other and said our goodbyes before midday.

To my recollection, we had trailed five miles on horseback before the first man spoke or hummed a song.

"Do you know why we left three beautiful ladies in Opelousas?" I asked each man.

Long faces, shoulders shrugged, and Jackie Ray cried again. We had no idea why we left that part of Louisiana. No one had an answer. For the first time, we spoke of becoming homesteaders and growing old as blacksmiths. Chas bit his lip and chewed beef, part of what Mary had packed for a long journey.

Chapter 14
French Trapper

Three days ride beyond Opelousas, back aching and burnt skin, low on food and thirsty again, tails sore, God had made that part of Louisiana a lush wilderness. We found endless virgin forests on both sides of the trail and narrow wagon tracks pointed in a westerly direction. My heart thumped with great expectations, and I imagined the pioneers before us, full of uncertainty and ambition and had deep desires to make a good life for themselves somewhere in the Wild West. For miles and miles, we trailed through rugged terrain, saw small vegetables, like speckled corn, tomatoes, and potatoes, and filled our stomachs. Most of what was spoken, wild horses, big cattle rides, and shootouts, was led by Chas and Jackie Ray. I had my own thoughts; days with Millie, Meli, and Marie, and all of it, was a mystery of love that tugged on my heart. Each man spoke of dreams and desires, some wholly, and some were memories and events.

The road forked.

"Twelve more miles to the Texas line," said Chas. "Wake up, men!" Arms crossed in the saddle, he said, "I can smell Texas from here, Sons of War."

I fell asleep, and Jackie Ray slipped something under my saddle when he leaned forward and backward, and the horse reared up, and I felt pine needles in my face.

"What the heck was that all about?" I yelled.

"Happy Birthday, Atohi," said Jackie Ray and Chas, standing and pulling my arm.

"Birthday?" I said, and thoughts of my father and mother rushed into my mind. "It's not my birthday. I was born at night. Birth night. My birth was in the dark of night."

"Birth night, I've never heard of such a thing!" said Jackie Ray.

"People born at daylight, it's birthday," I told the men. "A man born in the dark, it's a birth night. Everyone knows that."

"Ain't no such thing as a birth night," said Jackie Ray, climbing in his saddle.

My friends brushed earth and leaves from my back and hair.

"I will not celebrate until darkness falls." I meant what I said.

"He's a piss poor celebrater, Chas!" said Jackie Ray, eyes stern.

"No better way than to fall from a horse to remind you of your age," said Chas, laughing. "Birth night? Where does he come up with such, huh?"

"Hope you didn't go to no trouble for a gift, boys," I said, eyes curious.

"No gift!" said Jackie Ray. "To ride with us, it's gift enough, Crazy Horse."

"For me, I'd like to trade both of you selfish fools for a couple of Spanish angels and two umbrellas!" I said.

Our bodies bent and we laughed until we cried.

"Hey, men!" said Jackie Ray, horse halted. "Something has happened up ahead."

A broken wagon stood, two abandoned houses, the graveyard burned, and the landscape brought to mind a sermon about Hades. Chas dismounted first and kicked the old bones of horses and goats. I scouted for rifles stuck out of broken windows before we made a collective decision about what had happened on that small farm. It was an awful sight to see a family severed by bandits.

The Texas border, a passageway of rolling hills and the Great Southwest we'd eagerly yearned to see since March, was in our sightline. The sound of coyotes echoed in the shadowy valley. On top of a hill walked a big cat, one we did not shoot at because gunfire alerted strangers.

I was nervous on horseback being in the open. The further we rode, the more our horses snorted, the bigger the game grew, and the wilder the countryside appeared, a land that made men restless in the saddle.

Towns we'd heard of, mapped by Preacher Chet years earlier, were expected. On his first trip to Texas, Chet met old-time missionaries and baptized more people than he could count on Sundays, where he turned "Sinners into Saints," and we hoped to meet them.

"Hush!" said Chas. "Stop talking. There's a man walking in the river," who held his arms up like a military captain.

The man heard our voices and became friendly. His face was covered in a thick gray beard, and his head was bald as a Crenshaw watermelon.

"Boys, boys," said the man in a Cajun accent, an accent heard often in New Orleans. "Good to see a man in these parts. Sunshine Frenchie, that's my name, known to trap river beasts."

"Good to meet you," said Jackie Ray, who'd stopped his horse.

The trapper flattened his long gray beard to his chest and spoke rapidly, yet so fast it was hard to decipher.

"You're lookin' at a good ride straight into the gates of hell if you are headed to Texas, friends."

"You think Texas is that bad, Sunshine Frenchie?" I said and kept my eyes on him.

"They call the land 'The New Southwest,' and it's the truth," said Sunshine Frenchie. "The best part of the journey is in Jasper and Crockett. My brother once rode onto Waco, and he was killed," tears clouded his eyes. "His last ride took him to Texas. You don't speak much, do ya, kid?"

"Yeah. Sometimes," said Jackie Ray. "Sometimes."

Jackie Ray and Chas dismounted and introduced themselves and had a dozen questions for the river trapper. I had only one: "Why won't you cross the river to Texas, Sunshine Frenchie? Trappin' looks better along that side of the river, anyway."

"Sabine River Rats," said Sunshine Frenchie, washing his face. "And once you see one, you won't forget a muskrat that big, boys. Muskrats that stand big as draft horses. You better watch out."

We eyed each other and grinned and knew there was not much truth about this man. He stretched out his hands and widened his arms, sat on the riverbank. Sunshine Frenchie flipped his hand, checked traps, and pulled his horse behind him. He trailed a short distance and stopped his horse.

"Danger is along the way," said the river trapper. "Rivers, good roads, and bandits, and it makes no difference this close to Texas. I trap my game in Louisiana. These parts are as rough as Kentucky, I suppose. Kentucky is good trappin', I bet. Texans don't take kindly to squatters and thieves, especially Cajun people and men who speak like me. And another thing," he watered his mule and chewed tobacco. "Young men like yourself seem to wander around saloons and drift inside late-night holes in the wall."

"Keep to ourselves," said Chas, still mounted at the riverbank.

"Kind of places gave me messy blackeyes in Cajun country," said Sunshine Frenchie. "Had a dozen fights since 1849. Got shot twice in the back in '64." He laughed and said, "So, my best advice to you is to keep on your horses headed for good business." He washed his body. "What's your business, anyways?"

"Lookin' for my uncle Bad Carl Bellew," said Chas, pulling deer jerky from his saddlebags and passing it around.

"That's a popular man along the river," said Sunshine Frenchie, who scouted the riverbank, grunting and checking his traps while he found our conversation interesting.

"Lots of men after him, huh?" I asked, watching his hands and eyes.

"Yeah," said Sunshine Frenchie, hands kept working. "Folks say the name, mostly in vain, of course. He's an old outlaw. Found it to be a cruel profession myself. Don't worry about getting involved in gunfights. Just a good trapper for furs, and that's all I'll ever be in this life. Keep to myself and my traps."

"On a journey," I said. "We have seen a few wild places."

"Where are you headed, pilgrims?" said the trapper.

"Next town and maybe the next town," said Jackie Ray, who walked along the riverbank watching Sunshine Frenchie and helped him pull traps. "Then, out to Waco."

"Tip well to the Texas ladies," said the trapper, fanning his sweaty face. Sunshine Frenchie undressed himself for a bath in the cold river. "Look for the good church people to help you when you fall into trouble, pilgrims."

The man washed his beard and bottom.

Our next meal of fish at night was cooked by him, of course, clothes about his backside, and he told good stories.

"Appreciate the friendly advice," said Chas, halting his horse at a forked road.

He spoke few words in the early morning, but warned us again.

"Think of Old Sunshine Frenchie when you turn your first ale in Waco, friends, and our days together, as good as it has been, must end this morning at this Sabine River."

"You helped us more than any man, Sunshine Frenchie," said Chas, shaking hands with the trapper.

The man shared his morning catch with us from the river.

"Youngsters," said Sunshine Frenchie, leaning forward on his mule. "Keep your heads and manners about you." The trapper turned and spoke over his shoulder and rode away.

His mule trotted along the winding riverbank, headed North where the yellow road stayed along the path of the Louisiana State line. The road ahead of Chas forked, and the trail disappeared into shallow water. Less shoals ran, and flat rocks dotted the low gap into a deep river basin.

"Texas is across the Sabine River, Chas," said Sunshine Frenchie, pointing with his rifle. "And yonder way, the mightiest of all states, the Lone Star State of Texas, and life is rough, yonder way."

"By God's help, Chas and Atohi," said Jackie Ray, gambler's hat about his chest, "we will cross this river to Texas, and we've made it."

"No different than Kentucky, Chas!" I said, teeth shone.

"Some good men never come back," said Sunshine Frenchie, whose voice echoed across the low-cut river. "Riders get lost somewhere out West. You made it, boys," waving his hat one last time. "East Texas. Don't say anything to get yourselves killed!"

The man and the mule became smaller in the distance and soon out of sight. We celebrated at the Sabine River and made tracks in the fall of 1871.

***

By the fireside, on the night before we thanked Sunshine Frenchie, the burly trapper from Southern Louisiana who helped celebrate my birth night. Other than Sammy Summers, Sunshine Frenchie was the best man we had met, and both had spoken about old legends, curiosities in Scripture, past women, and panning for California gold. And in a short time together, Sunshine Frenchie told of the Great Flood of Noah and how God made it happen. Jackie Ray kicked back, half asleep, head bobbing, and his saddle held his neck, and he rested his eyes for my night birthday. Chas handled the fire and cooked apples and fish. From supplies, I prepared sweet potato coffee mixed with chicory coffee, camp bread, and beans. At the same time, we listened to Sunshine Frenchie recite tales of his life in Louisiana.

"Frenchie," I said in my deep, commanding voice. "Tell us about the bread you want to make in this Bossier City restaurant, huh, good man?"

"Have not mastered my thoughts on the bread yet, Atohi," said the trapper.

"Then tell us about your idea on the Great Flood," said Jackie Ray, who was seated across the fire from Sunshine Frenchie and saw the bottom of each man's warm boots and the honest eyes of the trapper.

Rubbing his hands together, the trapper said, "Boys, do you believe in the Great Flood of Noah?" spoken deep in a Cajun accent. "Do you believe Noah was the best trapper on earth, boys?"

"Noah was no trapper!" said Jackie Ray, chuckling. "What did Noah trap?"

Raising his hands, Sunshine Frenchie said, "Noah was the greatest trapper in the Bible. He baited two of each animal into his boat."

Chas stood, pistol in his hand, listening to a coyote bay.

"Not sure I believe animals were trapped and pulled into the belly of a big boat," said Chas. "Noah didn't trap animals and eat them, did he?"

"Preacher Chet Bellew said God commanded the animals," said Jackie Ray. "Animals walked by their own accord into a giant boat on dry land. It was couples night, two-by-two, like they were courtin' on weekends. That part of the world had never seen a drop of rain before. Clouds burst; storms covered the earth with water. Men, women, and children of heathens, like Cane's family, drowned. Life was started anew."

"Didn't know you listened in church, Jackie Ray," I said, eyes opened, head raised.

"Yeah. I listen to the sermons," said Jackie Ray. "My eyes are closed, but my big ears scout for good stories about animals and how they mate."

Everyone who heard his voice rolled in the dirt and grabbed at their guts, faces turning red, and men coughed until air left their lungs. I have laughed about that night for years.

"The Great One never flooded the earth," I said, eyes on the trapper. "Did he?"

"Boys, I can prove the earth was flooded, Atohi," said Sunshine Frenchie. "It's one thing Old Frenchie can prove."

"Prove it, French man!" said Jackie Ray. He adjusted his hat and laughed. "Prove it to my eyes and big ears. Let's see, Frenchie. I am awake and eager to see how this trapper proves it, boys."

"The evidence is in my saddle bags, bud," said Sunshine Frenchie. "Right here, and hold your horses, Doubting Thomas." Jackie Ray held a lantern, and Sunshine Frenchie's face glowed when he reached into his saddle bags, revisiting something of the past, and his palms held something

"What's that in your hands?" said Jackie Ray.

"He has some type of shells," said Chas. "Shells from the ocean."

Sunshine Frenchie had a leather satchel full of off-white seashells, and some were pinkish patterns. Shells of no general shape, pale and ridged, striped, turned by the sea, and worn by time and pressure.

Filling his hands with more seashells, Jackie Ray said, "Shells can't prove a dang thing about the Big Flood."

Sunshine Frenchie rubbed his hands over the spirals and flipped shells over and over inside his calloused palms. Then he poured the seashells into his hat and passed his cap around to each man for a good look-see. And the man with the big ear tried to hear the ocean.

"Where did you get these shells, Sunshine Frenchie," said Chas.

"Rivers and streams," said the trapper. "Days on the beach searching for shells and fishing. I found them one night working the coast of Alabama, held lousy Rum and a good woman."

Each one of us passed the seashells around the campfire, testing each man's knowledge of how the seashells were formed and how they washed up on the coast. Sunshine Frenchie told stories about his younger, less responsible days as a trapper and coastal fisherman in Biloxi and Mobile and how he fell in love with a lady in Gulfport, Mississippi.

"I fished for whale oil, boys," said Sunshine Frenchie. "The kind of fish Preacher Jonah was inside for three days."

"How can you trap a big whale?" said Jackie Ray, with eyes that carefully scouted a cap full of seashells.

We listened to our friends... with our hearts, just like Preacher Chet had taught us to do in church, and our faces were lit up by the glow of a man's face we barely knew. If he told the truth, it was on that night.

"Whales are as big as a barn," said Sunshine Frenchie. "The idea was, we'd surround the big whale with ten small boats and harpoon the dang whale and pull the animal to the larger boat." He jumped up and down and clapped his hands like he was on the boat again. "We trapped him! We trapped him!" shouted the trapper.

That was the first time Sunshine Frenchie sat by my side, and I slapped his friendly arm and trusted him.

"Today, men raise good horses and drive cattle for a living, it's true," Chas spoke up. "Are you saying men are dragging in whales for big money from the Gulf of Mexico?"

"Yeah, lantern oil brings big money, gentlemen!" said Sunshine Frenchie, warming his hands. "But the time I was in Gulfport was much different."

"Different, huh?" said Jackie Ray. "Did you fall in love, Sunshine Frenchie?" Jackie Ray handed a cap full of seashells back to the trapper. "Never pictured you as a lover of good women, sir."

Sunshine Frenchie clutched his hands and said slowly, "The French are the best kind of lovers. Ha-ha-ha. We invented love after love, boys."

"Listen to him, laughing," said Jackie Ray, eyes smiling. "Frenchmen don't know a dang thing about love."

"We are the world's best lovers," said Sunshine Frenchie. "There is no better lover than a Frenchman! We are good trappers. But better lovers."

Sunshine Frenchie told it that way, but he still had yet to prove how the Flood of Noah happened.

Jackie Ray spoke in a long country accent and said, "The man traps foxes and beavers and thinks he's the best lover in the business. I swear it, I heard it all, boys!"

"He speaks the truth," I said. "But women love a Cherokee man and his peace pipe. Only Atohi can draw smoke and make women dance before a pow-wow. Make them blow smoke out their ears, too, I bet."

I have never made men laugh so loud in my life.

"We are surrounded by Rustic Romeos and French lovers, Jackie Ray," said Chas, grinning.

"What did that lady look like, Sunshine Frenchie?" said Jackie Ray, pulling off his socks.

"She's a beauty of brown hair and eyes the same," said the trapper. "Full body, and not heavy like the weight of a coyote or beaver pelt. Her hair was soft like the fur of a mink."

"Why didn't you marry that beautiful lady?" I said, hands on my knees, legs crossed, Cherokee style.

"One small problem, though," said the trapper, who chuckled, tapping his finger. "The marriage she was in ..." His shoulders dropped low, and a tear fell down his cheek.

"Married, Frenchie? I am sorry," said Jackie Ray, whispering. "Where you stealing pelts from the trap of another lover?" laughing and slapping his leg.

"You trapped that lady?" I said, chanting, and fell back, slapping the leg of Sunshine Frenchie. "Way to go, Frenchman. Tell us the rest of the story, sir."

"Wait! Wait. Wait." said Chas, hands up. "Let him finish," grinning. "I gotta hear this love story all the way to the end. He has us hooked and trapped now."

Sunshine Frenchie stood up, dusted off his pants, and gathered his thoughts for a moment when his hand felt his long beard.

"Back to my love story, boys," said the trapper. "While the whale captain was out to sea, she was deeply in love with this crazy Frenchman. We were crawfish crazy in love. Night and day. The captain sailed out to sea for many, many months, to my advantage. One day, he came home and knocked unexpectedly."

"Did he catch your hands in the trap?" said Jackie Ray.

"Don't tell me, Sunshine Frenchie," said Chas. "You trapped the lady with Rum and fish, right?

"Nope. Well, heck of a fight, boys! Blackeye." said Sunshine Frenchie. "Two crazy men were fighting for her love."

The trapper pulled his pants to his ankles and showed his tail. "I must confess."

"He's been shot in the tail!" said Jackie Ray, coughing out a laugh and pointing.

"When he couldn't win, the whale licker shot me in the tail, boys. I limped away and found another lady who pulled the bullet from my French butt," shaking his hand. "That was the night I believed in the Great Flood, boys."

"How can you prove the Great Flood existed with love and a butt wound?" said Jackie Ray, flipping the last drops of coffee into the fire, and he sat upright and listened, elbows on his saddle.

"Prove it!" said Chas. "I'm curious for him to prove it."

"Look around you," said Sunshine Frenchie. "All you have to do is pick up the broken pieces left behind by our ancestors." He held seashells in our faces. "Look and see, it is all right here before your very eyes, boys."

"Bullets and butt wounds don't make a hill of beans of proof to a man without Jesus," said Jackie Ray, who threw dirt on his feet. "I cannot see it in the seashells, either. I won't see it!" He held the seashells close to the glowing fire, back and forth.

"Take these two seashells, push 'em together closer, Jackie Ray," said Sunshine Frenchie, walking around the campfire. Two seashells were inside the palms of the trapper, one in each hand.

"Broken seashells are no secret evidence to a Cherokee," I said. "Two broken seashells, that is all I see. Nothing more!"

"Yessir, Atohi," said the trapper. "It proves a lot to me if you know where the seashells came from. Where did I get them, Atohi?"

"Where?" I said.

"Where'd you get 'em?" said Chas, and he held seashells inside his palms and turned each one.

"Found one side of the shell on the beach of Gulfport," said the trapper. "Look closely! And ... I picked up the other half in the dunes of Biloxi, Mississippi, boys. That was the night I believed in the trapper Noah and the Great Flood. That was the night I believed in God. That was the time I accepted Jesus the King as my Lord and my personal Savior, boys."

"Simple," said Jackie Ray. "Two seashells washed up by the tide near each other." Each hand had a seashell. "Here, Chas. Look! These two shells are a perfect fit."

"Gulfport and Biloxi are twelve miles apart, boys," said Sunshine Frenchie. "I rest my case to tell you, God, the Father of Heaven, made a Great Flood happen. Thousands of years ago, halves were once a complete seashell. They were broken by the Great Flood. Together again. That proves it, Kentucky Boys."

"If that's the case, well," said Chas. "Oak trees that were broken during the Great Flood may have floated to two different locations, preserved in mud and muck, and could be reunited."

"The Great One can break our vanity and put us back together again. That's reconciliation!" I said. Convinced, "God flooded the world for forty days and forty nights. Sunshine Frenchie proved it on my birth night. These two halves matched up." I held the seashells up to the harvest moon. "It is just like grace and salvation. Broken sinners washed in the water and made whole again. Seashells touched, and I said, "Sinner into Saint, broken and made whole again, healed by God."

Each man believed Sunshine Frenchie had proved it.

"Mighty convincing love story and a good spiritual story, Sunshine Frenchie," said Jackie Ray, who lifted the pinkish shells and made them whole again. "Perfect pieces, boys."

Face pale as flour, said Sunshine Frenchie, "Yeah. We are broken and made whole, Atohi." He pointed in my direction. "I like it."

"Where is my midnight whiskey, Chas?" said the trapper. "You have me singing Amazing Grace, boys."

Jackie Ray cleaned and loaded his revolver.

"Watch out, Chas!" yelled Jackie Ray.

"Good shot. That's a dead mountain lion, boys!" said Sunshine Frenchie. "Chas, I saw Jackie Ray just save your life."

"Get this mountain lion off of me!" Chas yelled.

The body of the mountain lion landed atop Chas, eyes closed, wet tongue on his face. When the large head of the lion tilted, I fired. My dark eyes bulged, and my heart pounded at the sight of such a large animal. Chas was lucky that it wasn't a giant Sabine River Rat. My friend rolled out from under the large body of the mountain lion and caught his breath.

"He is a beauty. Oh, my goodness, look at the size of that cat!" said Sunshine Frenchie, rubbing his hands together and lifting the big head of the mountain lion. "That is a dandy kill, boys!"

"The cat is my kill, men," said Jackie Ray, eyes excited. "I will skin him out."

"Good shot," I said, stretching out the mountain lion. "My time to help and scout for Jackie Ray."

"Eat what you can tonight," said Sunshine Frenchie, pressing his hands against the paw of the big lion. "The smell of blood will draw in black bears, flies, and hungry coyotes."

I remember how we spent the night dressing the mountain lion and cooking the meat until sunup. Each man was covered in blood, bellies full, and we cooked the shoulders and legs over an open fire. Shifts were taken to scout for black bears and coyotes, the type of animals that smelled blood in the wind at night.

***

On the ride through Newton County, a small county of wilderness and rolling fields, the sky was pearl blue, and excitement stirred within the heart of each man.

"The telescope is a good tool," I said, taking my position at dawn on the edge of the woodlands.

"What do you see, Atohi?" said Jackie Ray, head turned.

"Far as I can see, more virgin timber," I said. "Tall thickets and abandoned cotton fields. I can feel the Great Spirit."

"Might be a bear in the big woods!" Jackie Ray sounded.

Jackie Ray and Chas rode out to the top of the hill where I stood with my horse, and we saw the great land that took six months to reach.

"Texas… is truly a secret land," said Chas, his eyes shined the size of a seashell. We scouted for another big cat, searching for movement, but nothing was visible. "Fertile land, richer than any I have seen since Kentucky. We could make a substantial living in this forest. Trees are lumber, boys."

"Where's the dang trail, Chas?" said Jackie Ray, restless atop his horse. "This is no better than a foot trail, heavy underbrush, and leaves as wide as a hymn book."

"We're not the first people to appreciate this land," said Chas. "Someone has been cutting timber, but they only started."

Chas mounted his horse and bravely led the way through the thicket. No clear way was defined in the dense gray trees, or they were off track, and no horse and wagon were safe, much less the horse. We watched for snakes and more mountain lions in an eerie land, a land barely suitable for the likes of Billy goats. In the mud were big cat prints and signs of wild boar. Deer and rabbits were as abundant as birds that crossed the big sky.

"Ideal land for bushwhackers and bandits," I said. "Just as we did ages ago to other tribes who tried to take our horses and land. Life is no different, red skin or white skin; it's only a matter of who says they want it more. Then, hundreds of men who carried gunpowder and ammo took what they wanted, and sadly, it's called freedom and milk and honey. Hard to believe, but that is the way it happened, still happening."

"Preacher Chet told us how a man should never underestimate the jealousy and greed but respect rage unlashed from another man," I said, scouting the land. "Those who may have more gunpowder and bullets and more friends to fight his battles with him will have more land. That is who rules Texas and other places that exist, just like Texas."

Jackie Ray steadied his horse slowly behind my sorrel horse, a horse stubborn and barely broken. Just a few miles from Jasper, we could see the shape of the town, smoke in the sky, and the land was fertile in the fall of the year.

"Night will overtake the day even if we get stuck in this endless forest, Chas," I told him and rode around Chas. Jackie Ray followed. We raced a Jackrabbit, one so fast that we did not try to shoot him out of respect for the animal.

"Guys, dang it!" said Chas, who kicked the horse for the first time and dropped his head behind the ears of the horse. We trotted two miles outside the wilderness, and the last glow of the day fell behind a strand of elm and maple trees, open country, and we felt sundown.

***

I remember Sunshine Frenchie spoke of Jasper, a small town with more guns and more death, a town no different than Newton. The sign read "Jasper, Texas, 5 Miles," and the land had opened where fields of dry grass leaned with the breeze. In the trunk of a hollow tree, our friend, the owl, hooted again, and large turkeys roasted atop a dead tree. I left the turkeys out of compassion for the Thunderbird in my narrow mind. I am not sure why we fasted until evening.

"Where did you put that chicory coffee, boys?" said Jackie Ray. "Sunshine Frenchie left us his coffee and some apples, huh?"

"Check your dang saddlebags for more food, boys," said Chas as he flipped open his leather bags. He confirmed and had more food in his hands than we had seen in a week. "Sunshine Frenchie packed our saddlebags for a long, long ride across Texas. Good man."

"Found big potatoes in my saddlebags," I said and held a handful of vegetables in both hands. "Indeed, Chas, that man Sunshine Frenchie was a true Christian. I have spoken wrong about him. It is best to give a man a chance to show himself approved."

"He left me all his dang seashells," said Jackie Ray, who held a cap full of white and pink seashells. "Here are the two shells broken by the Great Flood!"

We told stories, the ones we'd heard our Cajun friend tell days earlier.

***

Chas was exceptional with a flint rock. He started the fire and made good coffee, too. My time was spent sharpening knives and listening to the woods. With one shot from his pistol before sundown, out of the corner of a field, Chas took a pheasant in flight, a heck of a kill with a Colt. Other than the full moon, the warm flames of the campfire were the only light found in the hilly part of East Texas when I scouted. Forest to field, I saw no bushwhackers at night.

We camped under a blanket of stars in peace except when Jackie Ray woke, face wet, and yelled, "I'm in the belly of a whale, boys! I'm the belly of a whale!"

The camp had little conversation since Sunshine Frenchie had left our small group of Kentucky riders, for it was his day to find independence and trap. For his stories and the smile in his eyes, something told me he was headed to Gulfport for the lady he left behind to heal him and unite broken places. There is hope for the likes of a man made whole again. What was it like to be renewed, I thought, and slept little? I still think that way.

With pen and ink, Chas found enough light from the campfire to recall the journey on paper. His letter was the first envelope to Kate, a lady worth writing to in Kentucky, and he cared more about than he spoke of on the journey; she waited for him, or maybe not? Not all men had someone waiting for them at home. The couple were wonderful seashells, separated and meant to be together. However, those things were left up to the Great One, King Jesus, not me or the kindness of a good letter.

When Jackie Ray's eyes closed, that's when Chas wrote something down. No man could concentrate while Jackie Ray talked or snored. Chas finished the letter, eyes covered, and soon he was deep asleep inside his hat. The stars flickered. Some ran across the sky. Others kept the moon in good company and held perfect illumination for most of the night.

And for a while, I ignored his letter, the one by his side in a book. My short bout with temptation had ended when the breeze blew open the pages my friend had written, and a subtle curiosity began to move my eyes across the pages. Yeah, I read it, folks. For a short time, no guilt was felt in my eyes to read what he had written, such a reliable account of our amazing journey.

Newton County, Texas
Westside of the Sabine River
12 October 1871

Dearest Kate,

Through God's grace and divine intervention, by writing to you, we have crossed into Texas, as intended, a land abundant in trees and game, more beauty than I could imagine, and yet soon to be claimed by the likes of saws and rifles. I am not sure where to start with this letter, but to write and say my journey has been without killing a man in self-defense and withholding that part would be unfair to say in this letter. With certainty, I live without regret. Bushwhackers and bandits, some covet and live for evil, do exist, more beyond Kentucky than I had expected. Men and women kill for sport, a sort of game, to accept the fight or just try their best hand in a shootout. Some fools do it for the simple act of claiming the leather of another man's boots or to take his Henry Rifle because of the darkness of wood or the design of his leather vest.

I have been chased and poisoned, shot at and nearly killed. On the other hand, being employed as a blacksmith was where I prospered in New Orleans. I have sampled food from different cultures, some from Haitians, some Spanish, the Chinese, and one Frenchman, a true man of God, who was a good cook. Things I speak of will one day reach Denton. I expect expansion by train will someday reach the small world of where we are from; the land we know will be no different than Texas or Missouri. My favorite horse was lost somewhere in Saint Louis, in a land where few saints roam. We have crossed into Texas, and the hope of cattle is in our conversations. Jackie Ray and Atohi are faithful men; no finer can be found among men. Both have proven themselves more than once to be frontiersmen and soon-to-be cowhands in Texas.

Not all the countryside comes with brokenness, for beyond evil and chains, I have fought my way to Texas, handily in dignity and respect, for I have made a daily practice of what Uncle Chet taught in the Good Book, more of his sermons are remembered the further west I ride. By candlelight, my prayers were heard at Saint Louis Cathedral in New Orleans, one of the finest churches I have ever seen. Some goodness and character do exist, a fair amount, just as much in men as in women, but more godliness is needed beyond Kentucky, that I can assure you. I have found other religions people practice daily. Still, the world believes in other spirits, and they worship more than one God, just as holy, in their opinions, greater than Christ, but not to me. In times of peace, the sovereignty of God remains my only true Source of hope. I look for the Lord when I ride.

People are familiar with Carl Bellew, and lots of folks have heard of the messages of Preacher Chet Bellew, calling him "a fine missionary man" and a man with a big heart for people. Many folks have offered their condolences and prayers for both of our fathers.

How is your mother and sister? Days of simple living on a farm will be few and far between, as ports and trains stretch across the land, coast to coast, they say. If I lust, let it be for more chocolate and beignets in New Orleans, and I'll one day tell you the story in person about the taste of wonderful city food. However, the taste of an alligator still lingers in my stomach. We have come a great distance since the spring and have been educated, both by friends and foes. We hope to make Waco before the first snow falls in Central Texas. When you speak of me, speak well. I will write again.

Love Always,
Charles "Chas" Bellew

Chapter 15
Lone Star State

We rode into Jasper, Texas, mouths cotton-dry, faces tanned; still, the world was hot in late October; three men on horseback must have intimidated seven little girls, the first house in Jasper County. I was happy to meet Texans, people I found to be the same as others. Girls of different ages and sizes, some played, some ran, and others leaned on the fence and watched our horses; two small girls chased butterflies into a meadow of pumpkins. The sound of our horses caused the girls to stop their liberties and return home. They stood in amusement, surprised to see rough-looking men, men unshaven and tired, stomachs rumbling and turning like tumbleweeds over dry land.

"Is your daddy about, little girl?" said Chas.

"My daddy died at the Battle of Elkhorn Tavern," said the biggest one of the bunch, hair curled and flowing red to her shoulders. "Sir, I thought I told you that the last time you stopped here to water your horses, right?."

"No, little lady," said Chas. "Never been to Jasper, Texas before in my life. We are from Kentucky, just passing by."

"Kentucky!" shouted one of the girls. "Are you Daniel Boone?"

Chas adjusted his hat and kept his hands on the saddle horn.

"No. Ain't no Boone." Chas grinned.

"Hope this place is friendlier than the McIntosh Farm," I said.

Three more girls walked up to the fence and had on white dresses and turned smiles brighter than a paper moon and fed the hungry horses. We nodded. They walked slowly to the side of the horses, mane in hand. Their heads angled, and tiny arms opened the gate, and one girl with long arms fed each horse an apple. Blue dresses covered two more girls, and one paced with dozens of butterflies on her back. Small creatures, wings slowed and ticked, like the second hand on a wall clock. The butterflies did not walk but flew steps atop their soft hair, one after the other, and several took flight. For all of us, voices low, watching carefully not to disturb beautiful natural things, and we soaked up the amusement. A man who held creatures and long thoughts, I had to believe in a Creator.

Undeterred, one girl looked at Jackie Ray, face frowned, arms crossed, and her words could not be held.

"Are you outlaws, mister?" said one of the little girls in blue clothes, who had decided to walk outside to the fence to see horses.

"No," said Jackie Ray loudly. "We're not outlaws." He shook his head and held a friendly grin to make sure she knew he meant no harm to her or the butterflies. Jackie Ray slipped off his ugly gambler's hat. "Peaceful Presbyterians."

"Baptists say they ain't much difference between an outlaw and a Presbyterian," said the little girl and walked to the fence.

"That Baptist is wrong," I said and held my horse.

"Ms. Goodman said not to talk to outlaws." Face frowned, and she questioned, "Are you bank robbers?"

"Nope," I said, showing my happy smile. "I do not like black-tie bankers, girls."

"Black tie bankers," said a little girl, giggling, hand over her face.

"We can be friends then," said the tall girl, hands on her thin hips. "I will talk to the good horses for a minute, and we won't harm your animals, friends. No bother to your horses, and I promise to be easy. Don't you bother our butterflies, riders," she said, pointing, her face serious.

One girl became friends with Jackie Ray as soon as he tied his horse to the fence.

"Wanna hold my butterflies, mister?" said the girl, arms out.

"Yeah, sure would," said Jackie Ray, who had made a friend and held out his hand. "Little creatures, got to be careful."

Inside the white picket fence, the tall girl held a dipper above the bucket, signaled her approval, and said, "Water, mister? Got plenty of fresh well water for your pretty horses."

"Where's Ms. Goodman?" I said.

"Yonder!" One girl pointed toward the outhouse.

Chas dismounted and tied his horse to the post made for travelers and pilgrims, and out of respect, she held his hat while she handled the water bucket. He thanked her.

"Butterflies show up in Jasper County every October, mister," said one of the girls. "They stay around a while and then fly away again, go to somewhere in Mexico, they say."

The tall girl did most of the talking until the others felt we were friendly riders. And not outlaws or robbers. The word Presbyterian charmed her face a little bit.

"Monarch butterflies," said Chas, who held a butterfly on his arm.

The girl beside him held three butterflies in her hands, and they slowly crawled up her arm, and with her country accent, she reached and said, "Orange and black means they fly away and never come back, mister. White-spotted at the tips, no words from their lips." She held up her tiny arms. "Just look at these creatures; it proves there's a God. No man can create such beauty. I love these beautiful Monarch butterflies."

She walked inside the house and mumbled a prayer over the butterflies.

"Yeah. Beautiful wings," I said, still holding the creatures. I dropped low to the ground and said, "My father said butterflies bring you good luck, according to the Cherokee people."

"What's a Cherokee people?" said the girl.

I held ten butterflies on my arms and felt like a lucky man. In my mind, I heard the crafted flute of the woodpecker playing a song. We spent a short while talking about how the Cherokee tribe lived in the big mountains of North Carolina for many years until the great U.S. government drove them away to Oklahoma. She wanted to know when Monarchs flew to Mexico like the geese did in the fall. I told her where they lived. My mind faded back to when I was a young brave, hunting in the mountains with my father.

***

My father told many stories about lucky butterflies. I remembered a wide, flat river where trout jumped in the spring, and he gave me the name Atohi back in the mountains of North Carolina.

"It is the luck of the wilderness to hold a butterfly, Atohi. The next one that holds you, remember our time together." I told the little girl about my father and how he was long gone.

***

Two girls in dark dresses gathered around my horse as I walked and told how my father knew about the luck of butterflies, how he protected creatures, small and large, and how he loved animals.

"Never kill a butterfly, or your luck will die with the creature," I said, lifting a handful of butterflies. "This is until you find the next lucky butterfly, and then many years of luck will follow with you and your family."

"I don't have a father or a family, mister," said the girl, crying. "How is that lucky?"

I did not know what to say to her misfortune and had not spent time with little children, especially the ones with too many questions. I gave her a seashell, and my face was surprised with a hug and a kiss.

"Thank you. Our fathers are on a long journey together," I smiled. "They fish together every day."

She smiled and was convinced. Her tears stopped. About the time Jackie Ray danced with the girls, we all became friends.

"Do butterflies make butter, Jackie Ray?" said the little girl.

Jackie Ray scratched his head and pondered the thought. The girls laughed and pointed at her.

"People make butter from cow milk," said Jackie Ray. "Not butterflies."

"Where are your parents?" I asked.

"Is Ms. Goodman 'bout finished?" asked Chas.

"She might be asleep. We have no parents to tend to us, sir," said the tall girl. "Orphanage homeplace. Men from the State of Texas drop off orphans each month. Happened after the War ended. Lived here seven years, and later, sir, we get married off, they say."

Guns thundered in the distance, and four riders fired at anything that moved and caused the young girls to run inside the farmhouse. All but one girl ran. The talkative girl, who had a hundred questions, stood by my side, hands on her hips, unafraid of firearms even though the law was few and far between in Jasper County.

Dust clouds swept into the blue morning sky, and more shots were fired, targets unknown. Chas ran the horses into the barn and stood in front of the door, out of sight. Jackie Ray bent down behind the well and took his position. The Butterfly Farm was the only house for miles, they said, that had fresh water and food on the trail. I led the girls up the steps to the house and protected the orphan girls from the side of the home.

Goodman must be asleep, I thought.

"Atohi!" yelled Chas, watching the riders close the gap between him and the farmhouse. Butterflies stayed on his hands, and he had some luck. I heard men shooting from a distance but could not see the outlaws. "Get the last girl inside the house!"

Chas yelled at the tall girl to take cover, who tucked one butterfly inside her hand, grabbed her cat, and ran inside.

"Where is that Goodman lady?" said Jackie Ray.

"She took her pistol and newspaper inside the outhouse," said the tall girl through the open window. "She's not afraid."

The door suddenly swung open on the outhouse, and a lady ran out, red-faced, and yelled, "Get off my land, you are thieving outlaws! Hope you burn for stealing chickens from orphans."

From an easterly trail, four riders raced by where Ms. Goodman stood as if she was invisible. Men in dark clothes laughed and shot into the clouds, and never tipped their hats, and turned their horses toward Crockett, Texas.

"You damn chicken thieves!" yelled Goodman, waving her pistol, arms wide. "Get off my land!" She fired her pistol into the air several times but never pointed at the outlaws.

Chas tied our horses inside the barn, pistol in his hand. The girls watched from the big window inside the kitchen. One of the little girls with butterflies became my friend and said, whispering softly: "Come inside the farmhouse, Cherokee. You are gonna get yourself shot and dead, Chief Atohi."

I walked inside the farmhouse at her request and, from the front window, saw Jackie Ray had repositioned himself down on one knee in case the men wanted trouble with Lady Goodman, the caretaker. And she must have noticed we were good Presbyterian men or felt it in her heart because she offered no trouble or disagreements with us. She never raised her voice in our direction, not once.

One of the riders halted and turned his horse toward Lady Goodman while the other three outlaws kept riding on the westerly trail. The man dressed in black leaned forward and watched the other outlaws disappear behind a high thicket of tall pine trees. The lone rider gritted his teeth; one hand held the reins, and the other held his pistol on the saddle horn, eyes beamed at Lady Goodman. I suspect it was to teach her a lesson each time they rode by her farmhouse. The dog growled at the lone rider when he stopped and ran out from under the wagon, not frightened by the sound of guns but recognizing his face and voice.

"What did you say to me, Goodman?" He jumped off his horse, ran up to her face, and his hat fell to the ground. "You tighten that lip when I ride by your house, Goodman. Drop that weapon!"

"Nope!" she pulled it close, hands tight.

He took the gun.

"Get in the house, or I'll be glad to dust another dog." He sniffed and laughed.

"I'm not afraid of you."

I think she would have said those words even if we were far away. The outlaw fired a warning shot at her dog. She turned her back and whistled. The gray dog followed her toward the big white farmhouse, and she stood on the first steps.

"Inside, Buster." She told the dog.

The girls encouraged the dog to run to the door. Chas loved dogs as much as he loved horses.

The outlaw cocked his gun and yelled, "Got no compassion for a smelly dog and an angry woman, Goodman! Be glad for you to offer up an old friend some hot eggs and a good kiss. Whatta ya say, gal?"

Both wide doors of the barn swung open, and Chas walked outside. About ten paces to his left, the man was shocked and stopped talking to her. He stuffed Goodman's gun down inside his pants and smiled.

"I don't think Mrs. Goodman aims to cook for you today," said Chas. "She told you to leave, chicken man."

She walked to the big window and watched the standoff. The dark-haired man spun around, face of a Billy Goat, dark and sunken eyes, sweating down his flanks, and his shirt soaked where a man normally perspired.

Being inside her home, I asked Ms. Goodman if we could stay. She said yes. I thanked her.

We turned and watched Chas and the outlaw in a standoff.

"Got reason to stay now, sonny. Come out, meet me and your Maker, young man." said the outlaw.

In the Wild West, especially in Texas, a man called out another man for a standoff, and I speculated, "Was his style of gunfighting waist high or low on his leg? Would he fight regular, straight up, or reversed pistols?"

Though, Chas feared no one. I'd never seen him in standoff, but he'd practiced at forty paces. One man judged the other man and sized him up.

"Will your friend fight with double pistols?" asked Ms. Goodman.

"The way he handles his Colt, Ms. Goodman, the outlaw will have to be mighty fast to take down Chas Bellew."

Each man circled, taking a few steps right. The eyes and nostrils of Chas sensed when danger lurked. Indeed, once a man was called out, forces often brought them to square up, dead center. Many feuds had been fought and settled, white man or Indian or outlaw, things had to be settled. Not with small talk or poker, but revolvers settled it in the Wild West. One man would fall, I thought.

We walked around inside the house and introduced ourselves. The lady acknowledged I was sane and remained still. We stood in the window, and small girls were hidden under the table, eyes closed as if they knew something was about to happen. Someone was about to die. The tall girl, friendly and curious, whose name was not known in the early morning hours, had a big heart and understood the power of suffering and death. Goodman let her witness what she wanted and did not stop her. She was bold and eased outside, shrugged, and refused good advice.

Out of the corner of my eye, I saw the dog behind the legs of Lady Goodman; her soul was content with three unknown men protecting her orphaned girls. She'd nodded and spoke with her eyes and offered a big smile of appreciation for our timeliness.

Jackie Ray had taken a seat by the partially covered well, bent down, unshaven and unsettled by the fall of the year. He knew like I did, Chas was a rookie, and all we could do was watch and wait. Deep down, I knew the capability of Chas Bellew, but what I did not know was the ability of the man he faced, a threat to the lady and her orphans. Lady Goodman stood, eyes cautious, and her hands covered her face.

"You made my day with the hillbilly accent, son," said the outlaw.

"What's the name, old man?" asked Chas, stepping out of the shadows of the barn. His range was forty paces or so.

"Cassidy Coleman, kid," he said, hand about his lip. "Red sash of Bad Carl Bellew." The outlaw laughed and pulled on his mustache. "Why do you need my name, kid?"

Chas held steady eyes; the eyes of a hawk were no better.

"So, I can mark your grave, outlaw. Goodman does not appreciate you stealing chickens and eggs from her orphans. You afraid to trap your own dang food, coward?"

"Hope you can back that trap up, boy!" The man planted his heels into the earth.

The outlaw was spirited, tongue protruded, jaw rounded, stride was long and careless toward Chas, his top lip ticked, and his head slowly settled down. I watched for the other three outlaws, in fear of an ambush, men able to kill, reason or not.

"Best mosey on down the road," said Chas. "People will say they saw you steal your last chicken, Coleman."

"Don't think your head is straight, hillbilly," said Coleman. The man squared his shoulders for battle, face pointed at my good friend.

"My pistol is fine, though," said Chas, grinning. "Seen your last sunset, outlaw."

"Oh, you aim to make a name for himself, kid?" said Coleman.

Chas tilted his head and said, "Draw when ready, chicken man."

Tapping his belt, Coleman said, "Kid, bad mistake." The outlaw eased his hand alongside his hip, edging closer to his pistol. "Last mistake, though."

"Call it, outlaw," said Chas, eyes locked. "Times up."

I saw the concentration in the eyes of Chas, mind ready, hand steady. To ride out West with Jackie Ray, some days my heart ached, but to see Chas Bellew was something, a rare mountaineer in the midst of a battle. His father would have been proud.

The hand of the outlaw waved, ticking in the wind like the last leaf of fall. The battle was waged.

The lump inside my throat turned over as the hand of the outlaw slid onto the grip of the revolver. Then, Chas fired. The man gritted his teeth, face wrinkled when the bullet raced through Coleman, blood soaked his chest. Chas fired a second round and made a pair of eyes in the vest pocket of the heartless man. The outlaw stumbled and met the earth in a restless fall, twitching his arms. Out of the woods, in a sprint, God sent turkey buzzards, and three birds fought to finish him off. Coleman had seen his last sunset, and no more chickens were stolen from the orphans.

"Thank God!" I said to Goodman, hand clenched.

"God bless you, Atohi, and may the peace of Christ be with you and your friends." Lady Goodman said, arm resting on my shoulder.

"And also with you," I told her.

Ms. Goodman opened the farmhouse door, waved at Chas Bellew, and thanked the gunfighter. The swift wind picked up, and in the distance, three riders were headed to the orphanage farmhouse.

"Look! More riders, Chas!" I yelled and pointed. "Take cover!" "I'm hit, Atohi." Chas was soaked in blood.

With my fingers, a high whistle between friends, a signal that meant trouble. Chas knew three outlaws raged behind him, and my friend quickly found cover. After the first rider saw Coleman dead, he halted his horse.

Behind the broken wagon, I waited. Leading the pack, one man fired. Deep down, like blood brothers, I felt the pain of Chas. Next, what he did saved his life; the second outlaw was dead; a shot that was at a close distance landed after the man had fired and missed. Half had fallen. The third outlaw, a wise man, hid behind the barn, but he never realized Jackie Ray saw his feet ascend the ladder through the narrow slat boards. Jackie Ray hesitated; a bad mistake. He got away, but he reloaded and returned. The next man stayed low, and Jackie Ray killed him with his rifle from fifty hundred yards, which was a heck of a shot to the head.

Three men were dead before morning coffee. One man was left inside the barn. The wind blew dust from the Great South, a strong wind that could have been from Marie Laveau. Dark clouds hung over Jasper, and the wind stirred wildly across the farmland and blew dust through my hair. Chas was at the chicken house and waited alone.

I heard the voice of the Great One inside, the Lord of Hosts, not Marie Laveau. In my head, music, a flute made by the woodpecker, too, sounded. That dark morning gunfight in Jasper was yet unsettled, for the morning was marked in my memory and known too well in my life - forces happened, the eagle screamed. I witnessed white dust, the type that covered the land, and the broken sun was no longer warm but hidden. The day was no different than when the U.S. Blue Cavalry prodded my people from the mountains, whipped and beaten, pressing them to an unknown land. I was not to be oppressed anymore. Two dark days claimed my life and scared my heart. The outlaw saw my face, and for the first time, death crossed my mind. He knew I was not white but a Cherokee brave, and he did not take the shot to kill me. The big mistake happened.

"You're a dead Cherokee!" said the wiry-faced outlaw. The man was hidden and suddenly extended his arm with his Colt to send my body

SUNDAY RAIN

to the worms and cast my soul to the Great One in the sky. Hair raised on my neck when I heard him yell, "Too late for you, native!"

Then, the unexpected and wonderful happened. Butterflies flew between my stance and the position of the outlaw, a distraction from the Lord, which blocked his clear shot and distracted him. I heard the Lord, and God said, "You are saved again."

Orange and black Monarchs, a blanket of extraordinary fliers, soft and fragile, yet harmless creatures covered the Texas sky and flew to the Southwest. Little acts of God happened on our journey, and acts spoken of by Preacher Chet Bellew and words in his sermons happened in Jasper County, Texas. Things that could not be explained had happened.

"POW!"

I jumped out of my skin and felt my chest break open. Did God save me? The shot fired jolted the outlaw's chest, and he fell from the hayloft of the tall barn and hit the ground. In a moment of curiosity, I spun and wondered where the shot came from, and I was surprised to be alive.

"Who fired the rifle?" yelled Jackie Ray.

I rushed to check on wounded Chas Bellew. Ms. Goodman screamed. Jackie Ray turned, and a giant grin erupted. Leaning forward and sighing, he said, "Good for you, young lady."

The tall girl, the next to marry, maybe eighteen, who had spoken freely for the orphans, fired the fatal shot.

"I told him not to come back," said the girl, holding the rifle under her arm.

God handed us His grace, the Great One, who sent Monarch butterflies, orange and black fliers, creatures of all shapes and sizes, large and small, planted on her shoulders. And I saw other butterflies in flight land on her as she stepped off the porch of what we called Goodman's Butterfly Farmhouse. She was straight-legged and proud of herself; she had the shooter's eye, the eye still closed, still on her target, a face without tears. In that pivotal moment, the Henry Rifle that seemed out of place in the hands of a young lady now fit naturally inside her arms. The orphans danced in celebration and went unharmed for the first time in years.

"It was her," said Jackie Ray, who saluted her. "She pulled the trigger on the chicken thief. He's gone. Well done, little lady."

"Raised those hens myself," said the girl, barefooted and tall. "He won't steal from me again."

"He will be among the thieves in hell," said the littlest orphan, partially blind.

The orphans hugged her and laughed.

By evening, the broken wagon wheel was fixed. Jackie Ray held the reins, and four outlaws were transported to the Sheriff of Jasper County, who gave them to the undertaker. Four outlaws of the Bad Carl Bellew gang stood on public display for three days. We did not return to Ms. Goodman's Butterfly Farmhouse but stayed in Jasper. The bullet was carefully removed from Chas. My friend, still in pain, mounted his horse and rode to Jasper to find out some information. Chas sat and told about the attack from outlaws, the same way Jackie Ray and I had spoken to Sheriff Dunn. He accepted his story, and we walked free from the Jasper County jail.

Not before he had sent a telegram to Waco and Austin, and one request was made.

"This will send a message to other outlaws in the Republic of Texas," said Sheriff Dunn, who was seated at his desk. "And make them think twice about intimidating the good citizens of Texas, especially stealing chickens from an orphanage in Jasper County."

The good Sheriff of Jasper County, Elisha Dunn, spoke of his idea, and we became friends, and the request was that we signed on as Texas Rangers. The form was backed by a telegram of approval from Governor Davis of Austin, Texas.

"You are now full-time Texas Rangers," said Sheriff Dunn, and we had breakfast with him to celebrate.

"Texas Rangers!" said Chas, surprisingly.

"I like the idea." Jackie Ray told the men.

I have not made up my mind, I thought.

"What do we need to do?" said Chas, face shocked.

On the 18th day of October 1871, Sheriff Dunn had coffee with his new Texas Rangers, handed Chas a picture of the man he wanted, and said, "Take him dead or alive, Rangers. Bring him to me on a rope, on a horse, or in a wooden box. To me, it don't matter," slapping the table. "But I prefer to have him, right here, buried twelve foot deep in Jasper County."

"Dead or alive, huh?" I spoke.

Chas tucked the picture in his pocket.

"Does not matter, Rangers," said Sheriff Dunn. "No preference, and I'm depending on you to bring him to me."

Chapter 16
Like Kings

Texas. It was no different than any other town east of the Mississippi. Men were known to kill, and made famous for it, too, and harsh acts were taken with allowances. My eyes had seen too much death by the fall of that year.

The government felt the need to control my people, taking our land away, especially calling all tribes - "Indians and Injuns" and had little interest in knowing our Cherokee names or, later on, our Christian names, such as, and had a lack of respect for their own Christian culture. We found the offense of the white man to be different. To say "all Indians lived the same way became the wrong idea." It was no different than saying "all white men lived the same way" in towns, on farms, or hidden in the mountains. Hence, remarks were made to provoke war and cause offense, and parties became defensive because of what was said. Fewer freedoms and opportunities existed for Cherokee braves than most people realized, and without a wife or children, for me, the morning pinned as a Texas Ranger down in Jasper County was the first time I felt honored, even part of the 37 states across the land. Credibility and honor to the Cherokee Nation were not universally recognized, of which Preacher Chet Bellew would have been proud of our level of success in Texas. I wanted to write him, tell him, but it was too late.

When Preacher Chet Bellew came to my rescue inside the dusty rock cliff of Mingo Falls, he saved my life - forces spiritually bonded our friendship, a man sent by God, no less. Inside, I knew no one on earth knew the secret hiding places of my ancestors, only God and Chet Bellew, and he was a true miracle.

So, being pinned as a Texas Ranger was the second miracle from the Great One, handed down by Christ Jesus, above all kings, from the true Great One himself. The first evening as a Ranger was a revelation, and to celebrate, we had Texas beef stew in the only restaurant in Jasper County, a town of nearly 300 people. Three Rangers, Jackie Ray,

Chas, and myself celebrated. We agreed to make a tremendous difference for the Republic of Texas, and I will tell you what was spoken.

At dinner, we were close, more like brothers than Rangers, and we felt like kings, too.

"Just call me Jackie Ranger from here on out, boys," said Jackie Ray, the face of a proud man. "Might make a career out of my first job at 75 dollars a month." His eyes lifted, and he said, "Now that is good money, some for us all."

Chas smiled, but not that day. "We have our first assignment, Rangers."

"Chas, what is wrong with you, my friend?" I said and nudged him. "You seem down ever since we signed on as Texas Rangers."

Chas opened the sheet of paper; the one Sheriff Dunn handed him before breakfast.

"Here's our first job," said Chas, who stopped eating his bacon, "see the man on the paper, huh?"

I unfolded the paper while Jackie Ray chewed and savored his eggs and sausage.

"There must be some mistake," I said, looking at Chas.

"No!" Chas shouted. "He wants me to hunt down Carl."

Jackie Ray stopped chewing his food, and his eyes popped open.

"Carl is a wanted man, Chas," said Jackie Ray, who stopped eating long enough to talk business. "He's family, bud."

Chas studied our long faces and did not know what to do. The reality was Carl Bellew had killed people from Saint Louis to Texas. To catch him and bring him to Dunn was a difficult job for three Texas Rangers.

Later, we settled down for dinner, sitting at one of our favorite places.

"Cattle," said Chas, holding his bread. "Sheriff Dunn said Carl Bellew owns more cattle than the King Ranch, down in South Texas. Some people don't like it when they hold second place. I guess when they drive to the cattle conventions in Amarillo and Fort Worth, Carl Bellew, the man we want, is praised as the "Cattle King of Texas," good or bad. And some folks think the cattle outlaw of Texas is Carl, too, stealing longhorns from other ranchers. Three ranchers were killed just last week in San Saba."

"You mean," I said, "your uncle became wealthy in the gold rush like the indigenous people before him," hands clasped. "Had land, horses, and favor from the Great One, and with these things, thousands of my people perished, huh? Next, wealth and social order climbed, and then they wanted to kill him for it, whether he was a savage or a saint, right? Seems familiar, doesn't it, gentlemen?" I raised my knife at the table and said, "Government order, huh? Plus, Carl Bellew has taken many lives in the process, just to make himself a legend, and he has yet to be caught."

"What is that Cherokee doing to my table?" said the waitress.

"It's okay," said Chas, hand raised. "He's a Texas Ranger."

She walked away. We whispered something about Carl Bellew and the plan to catch him.

"Preacher Chet had a sermon on social order," said Jackie Ray, rubbing his shaved face. "Chet spoke of passing Jesus from King to King. Another act of social order, and the kings felt enraged about Jesus because followers called him Lord." Jackie Ray cleaned his plate.

The waitress walked up to our table again.

"Can I get you any more beef stew, Rangers?" said the young lady. "Never served a meal to three Texas Rangers before. Special day in Jasper, Texas, I guess. I reckon someone is on the loose and needs to be tied down, huh?"

"Yeah. I reckon that's why we're sittin' here," said Jackie Ray, tapping his Texas badge, face serious. "We are just passin' through, lady, on our way in the morning."

"We're ready to pay up, miss," said Chas. He crossed the fork and knife in his plate and said, "Excellent stew and cornbread." Teeth shone enough to know that he was sincere when he spoke.

"Glad you liked Pearl's Texas Beef stew," said the waitress, pointing to the kitchen. "President Grant's cook cannot beat her stew, finest cook in the country." She whispered to Chas, low on his shoulder, and said, "She doesn't care much for Grant, though, or Sheriff Dunn." Then walked away. "I will settle your tab shortly, Rangers."

"Best get some rest, Texas Rangers," I said, yawning. "Respect is a strange thing to have."

My friends never tried the apple pie, but I did. I walked outside to witness our last evening in Jasper while Chas and Jackie Ray took care of the bill at the restaurant. Mercantile. Saloon. Jailhouse. Feed store. It's not as big as New Orleans, but a fine town of people and a place

SUNDAY RAIN

of a million butterflies. The church was in the distance. Inside, I saw the pulpit Chet Bellew preached and held years earlier. He loved his time as a missionary. He was one of the great fathers of my life, and every man needed a great father like him.

My stance was in the dark shadows of the well-lit restaurant, hidden halfway in the alley. I stood as my father had taught, finding the shadow, and I tried to get used to the badge that picked my shirt and pressed my skin. While men smoked and talked, I overheard things. My eyes remembered the faces of pretty women, how they smiled when they saw my badge, and how men shook my hand in gratitude that evening. I was honored like a minister or a man of public office. I walked down the small streets of Jasper, and butterflies flew about the red evening sky, and fine horses were stabled at the end of town. The sun fell low beyond the evergreens, but not a word was spoken among the Rangers. My thoughts were about Chas Bellew and what he aimed to do about his uncle since the sheriff wanted him "Dead or Alive" on the poster. I heard the voices of two men.

"Trouble will happen when the sketch of Bad Carl Bellew gets into the hands of the public, true or not," said Chas, who stopped at the hotel lobby. "Bounty hunters and more Rangers will make their way across this country to get their hands on Carl Bellew for the bounty."

We walked into the lobby. Our eyes had never seen Carl commit a crime.

"It depends on whether the bounty is posted or not," I said, nodding. "Money will make men saddle and ride to kill someone and bring them to justice."

"How can we prevent this from hitting the wire before we can land him ourselves?" asked Jackie Ray, who took a seat in the hotel lobby, toothpick in hand.

"Sheriff Dunn has not sent out a telegram about Bad Carl Bellew yet," I said, brushing my face while I read a book in the lobby.

"How do you know that?" said Jackie Ray, head quickly turned.

"While you men were settling the beef stew bill, I heard a few things," I said, arms crossed, grinning, and leaned against the side of the bookcase. "I overheard Sheriff Dunn and his deputy, who stood in front of the restaurant, say how he gave the "Kentucky Boys" until Christmas before he went public with the announcement. After Christmas, Dunn plans to post Bad Carl Bellew's picture, draw in bounty hunters and more Texas Rangers, and see if we can catch him."

"Well, well, good ear, Ranger Atohi," said Chas, who walked over beside his best friend and smiled, shaking my hand. "I will stop by Sheriff Dunn's office," slapping my arm, "see him and make it known that the "Kentucky Boys" are on the case."

I chuckled. "I'm calling it a goodnight."

"Sounds like a plan," said Jackie Ray, who stood, stretching his legs and arms. "Yessir, heck of a good day in our lives. Chet Bellew is smiling down from heaven, eyes on us."

I thought of my father and what he would like about my time as a Texas Ranger, and I was unsure what he would say.

"Chet may not like us signing up to lock up his brother, either," I replied and walked upstairs behind Chas and Jackie Ray.

"Let's try and get some sleep tonight," said Chas, "and tackle this problem after some biscuits and white gravy." He handed each Ranger his own room key and menu. "No more sleeping in haylofts or on the back of wagons for the Kentucky Boys. Might make enough money to ride out to Tombstone and settle down for Cream of Fricassee Chicken and Asparagus Points, with a little English Plum Pudding. Sounds good, Rangers?"

Each man stood inside his own doorway and grinned.

"I'd like to try a plate of Columbia Rider Salmon, au Beurre Noir. I remember that dish Sherri spoke of in Louisville," said Jackie Ray, scratching his head. "What is au Beurre, anyway?"

"Oh boy," I said, watching my friends recite the menu. "I have a headache, trying to keep up with the dreams of Chas Bellew and Jackie Ray Monroe," tapping my badge. "I need some Kentucky Bourbon to wash away the thoughts of high-priced meals."

I closed the door.

"We'll make Crockett on Thursday," said Chas, smiling. "I will buy some Leg of Lamb, covered in wine sauce, and a side of grilled oysters, plated for each Ranger. Then I will have no money for the Wells Fargo Bank."

"Don't forget the ale, Chas," I spoke.

"No guns, no badge, no ale, Rangers," said Chas.

"Ale, yeah, Chas," said Jackie Ray. The man tapped his doorway. "Get some rest, Rangers."

In the hotel lobby, two men in dark jackets spoke to the hostess, Lucy, grinning when they watched Chas and Jackie Ray speak French.

SUNDAY RAIN

The bald man said, "Who are the new Rangers in town," said Wade Longworth. "Never seen 'em in Jasper before?"

"Rumor is," said Lucy, "Sheriff Dunn hired three fast guns to track down Bad Carl Bellew. They're staying upstairs for the night. Been here all day and got their horses full of grain, supposed to ride out in the morning for Crockett."

"I only saw two Rangers," said John Longworth.

"I can count to three," said Lucy as she cleaned the counter.

"I say we give the Rangers a little scare tomorrow night, John," said Wade. "The best riders cannot make Crockett in one day. You know what that means, don't ya, John?"

"I do, Wade," said John, and he slapped his hip. "Rangers will sleep on the ground, burn a campfire, and it's a bandit's best friend."

"Leave them alone, guys," said Lucy, elbows on the counter. "That's all you Longworth boys are good for is stealing cattle and scaring good folks out of their goods."

"John, when they build a campfire," said Wade, who snapped his fingers, "we'll not hesitate to take their supplies and own their good horses."

"Leave them Kentucky Boys alone, Wade," replied Lucy, who spoke with concern and pleaded, hands out.

The bald man, Wade Longworth, snatched Lucy by the neck and bit her shoulder. Fear raced across her face, and Wade said, "You tell the Rangers we're behind them, and you'll be dropped into a deep well, head first, Lucy."

"What did you eat for dinner Wade Longworth, huh? Dead muskrat?" The lady slapped his face. "You smell like the back side of a mule."

"Watch your mouth, Lucy," said Wade, who forced a kiss on her. He pushed her away and backed up to the door as if it were an accident.

"Get out of her!" yelled Lucy, who had found her gun.

"Loud voices," I said to myself and jumped out of bed. I knew something was wrong in the lobby. I stepped into the shadow of the dim hallway and watched Lucy cock the pistol. Blood ran down her shoulder, and her new blue dress was torn from her arms. The Longworth brothers stood inside the doorway and laughed. Then disappeared into a dark alley.

"Don't ever come back to Jasper!" yelled Lucy, face full of tears.

Having been trained as a young brave, I felt a chill on my neck and searched my surroundings. And most towns were just the same as the wilderness. I thought about how my father listened to sounds and voices. He taught braves how to read the face of a man, eyes first, hands second. That was his lesson of trust and deception. I could read a man by how he kept his eyes and hands when hard questions hit him.

From my window, I saw their horses and the direction they took out of Jasper. Jackie Ray snored, and he did not hear anything. Chas must have been asleep or in a hot bath. I walked down to the lobby to see Lucy, and the lady was the only one on duty that night. The tearful lady poured herself a drink, still crying, and pushed a second glass in my direction.

"Lucy?" I said, concerned. "I will buy you a new dress."

"It's nothing." She held her dress and took a drink.

"Where do those two men live," I asked sincerely, "the Longworth brothers, where are they staying?"

"Built a cabin two miles west of here," she said, face red. "Between Sandy Creek and Trotti Creek." She handed me a sandwich, some ammo, and a small map and pushed it all into my hands.

"Do not tell my friends where I am headed. Tell no one that you saw me. Here's money for new clothes," I said and held her hands.

She sniffed and held a grateful face, the kind of thoughtfulness my mother expected from kind people. I took the whiskey bottle, paid her triple for the ammo, and left with a bite of food. I did not tell her that I had no appetite for sin. My anger erupted when I saw her sad face and a dress that was ripped apart. Lucy was the only one who saw my exit from the hotel and knew I'd left Jasper. Even the stable hands were too busy at a big poker game to notice anything. I planned to have my horse back by the time they sobered up at sunup. The horse ran fast. Hope raced through my veins, and smoke rolled from a cabin in the distance. When I followed the two men by the harvest moon, one of their horses was in season, which caused my horse to desire romance. It was the time but not the place.

Two miles outside Jasper, built between Sandy Creek and Trotti Creek, I saw a small log cabin, and smoke billowed out of the chimney. I waited until they were settled in for the night, but Wade, the bald man, and he wanted to take a walk. The man's staggered steps had no line of balance, and a tree held him up. When he stood for his business, the man was within arm's reach of my pistol.

"Do not speak," I whispered. My eyes, big and round, hand tight on his neck.

"Who are you, mister?" said Wade, whimpering.

In a Cajun accent, my mind drifted to an old friend's voice, and I said, "I'm the man who made the dress you just ripped. And I am pissed, took me two weeks to design her dress. You made my friend cry, didn't you?."

"Hey, mister, please," he pleaded. "Please don't kill me."

"Walk backward until I say stop," I said.

"Okay, sir."

"Whoa! Let's practice to make sure you got it, pumpkin."

"I'm drunk, mister. Sorry about her dress."

His arms twitched, and tears left the corners of his eyes. Not many men liked to see a Cherokee brave after dark, and neither did he, evidently. I heard Jackie Ray's voice inside my head: I reckon you picked the wrong dressmaker, bud.

I could never get used to that word, and it's not a word found in the Cherokee language. My father did not use "reckon," and neither did I.

"Keep walking, varmint." He rubbed his face, and in his pockets was a silver flask. He had one sip. "I'm the "Ghost of the Dressmaker, outlaw."

I walked him to my horse.

"Ghosts tell me that you hit women, Longworth. You should never hit a lady, Wade."

"I will never touch another woman, sir," he pleaded. "I swear! I swear. Let me live, will ya?"

"Here's a cigarette. Smoke. Strike it."

"Tell Lucy I'm truly sorry about hitting her."

"So, you hit her, huh?" gun to his head. "Keep smoking, bud. Turn around."

"What should I do, Cherokee?" said Wade, voice broken.

"Puff and close your eyes, varmint."

I watched him take one more step near my horse and nursed a long puff. The horse did not want to talk to a man who had struck a woman. He puffed again. Later, I let my horse have his glory day with the young mare.

A sermon crossed my mind, and Preacher Chet said, "Let us recall, there's a time to mend, a time to speak, a time for war, and a time for peace."

The next morning I stood between Jackie Ray and Chas, belly full from a good breakfast, and we waited for Sheriff Dunn to walk inside his office. I wiped my dusty face from the short night of sleep, star on my chest, and rest flooded my eyes.

Sheriff Dunn walked inside, boots loud, mouth loud, and shook his head.

"Did you see a ghost, sir?" I said, one eye open, sleepy.

"No ghost," said the sheriff. "Good morning, Rangers." He fell back in his chair and sighed. "Two men, two bad men, men that I do not care for, were reported dead this morning. Gone."

"How did it happen?" said Chas, head tilted. "We could hunt down the suspects."

"I'll volunteer," said Jackie Ray, hand up. The man tapped his revolver and grinned happily. "The same goes for Chas, and I know our scout, Atohi, here," arm nudged, "he's ready to ride."

"Wade and John," said Sheriff Dunn, "the two Longworth brothers, found dead this morning. The undertaker cannot, for the life of him, well, explain how they had no bullet holes. No ammo was found at their log cabin, either. They had been kicked!"

"How did they die, Sheriff Dunn?" said Chas, arms crossed.

"Sad case. Horses? Makes no sense!" said the sheriff, head clutched in his hand. "It looked like horses broke the men, like smashed pumpkins. The animals kicked the daylight out of each man. Strange. No one to chase for an accident like that, gentlemen. Found cigarettes beside the dead men."

"Accidental, for sure," I spoke. "First rule of the barn, Sheriff Dunn, never smoke behind a horse."

Interrupted by Chas, hand out, who said, "Never walk behind a horse. It's not a pretty sight."

"My father," I said, clearing his voice, "said 'never smoke behind a horse. The animal thinks his butt is burning.' Longworth was smoking the wrong brand, sheriff, I reckon."

I knew what happened and how it happened, but I only confessed to Danny Boy, and I was too far from the Big Easy to talk to my dog about a horse.

SUNDAY RAIN

"The question is," said Sheriff Dunn, "can you Kentucky Boys bring in Carl Bellew? I want that desperado in my office by the first of the year. Then, we will celebrate your pay raise." Sheriff Dunn stood and rested his hands on his belt. "Well, I need you in Waco. I know he is your uncle, Chas, right? Justice, for sure, in Texas serves over blood, Jackie Ray and Atohi."

"He's family, sir," said Chas, hand on his belt.

"Friend. Family. No family! He'll face trial and hang!" yelled Sheriff Dunn. The man slapped his desk and explained how law and order worked over blood and water in Texas.

"Sir, we'll find Bad Carl Bellew," said Jackie Ray.

We shook hands with the good sheriff and knew our next mission and where we were headed: a land that had no peace for anyone, Waco, Texas.

Halfway to Crockett, few words were spoken by Chas, only facial expressions and generalities. Jackie Ray spoke of how he looked forward to seeing McLennan County, home of Waco, Texas, and asked a dozen questions about what it meant to be saved by grace.

When we stopped for lunch in the cool October air and walked into the thick forest of Houston County, we rested. Legs stretched. I knew Chas had something on his mind. He noticed how the leaves of Kentucky were the same color of red and golden brown as the giant forest of Houston County, Texas, and the land stood no different. It was a hard two-day ride from Jasper to Crockett, stopping to offer the horses grain from our saddlebags, which was a trick Chet Bellew taught if we ever took a notion to leave Carter County and see the world.

I remember peanuts being offered by Chas for lunch. When Jackie Ray watered a sapling off the beaten path from Crockett, I stood beside Chas, and my blood brother cleared his throat and became curious.

"O' friend," said Chas, "you wouldn't happen to know how the two Longworth brothers were killed, struck by the kick of your Sorrel Horse, would you, smoker?"

"I have never smoked in my life. And the horse knows more than I do." I said and held a handful of peanuts. "I don't smoke."

"Lucy sure had on a pretty new dress this morning," said Chas, eyes full of smiles, "and said it was made by a ghost."

We cracked peanuts and chewed and laughed. I said no more and didn't have to. Jackie Ray scratched his head and had no idea how a ghost made enough money to buy a woman's dress.

"That was a pretty clever trick you pulled, Atohi," said Chas.

"You should never smoke behind a horse, Chas," I told the men. "The worst part, the Longworth brothers were beating up on Lucy, the nice lady at the hotel. My horse wanted to talk to them, held in private, and mostly about tobacco."

Chas chewed peanuts and laughed.

"Wait!" said Chas. "You didn't sleep last night, huh?"

"Right," I said. "My horse had a date, and I had to buy a new dress. She loved it."

"The mare or Lucy? Good deed, Atohi," said Chas, dusting his hands of the peanuts. "Some men live too long and ruin the good lives of others."

"I love Lucy, sweet lady," I said, mouth full of peanuts. "She walked around minding her own business. I kept my promise, though, and brought her a dancing dress."

"I have seen it happen in a barn, the sudden kick of a stallion," said Chas, taking off his sweat-stained hat. "Boards flew across the barn, busted all to pieces, and my eyes popped out of my head when it happened. But Atohi, I had never seen it before used as justification and reasoning before."

"I had my reasons."

"Sorry I was gone so long," said Jackie Ray. "Lucy had on a find dress today, didn't she, gents?"

"One of a kind," I said, climbing on the horse.

We made our way to Crockett, Texas. Jackie Ray talked about all the pretty women he'd seen in the French Quarter of New Orleans, but he looked forward to seeing the beauty of a Spanish woman.

Chapter 17
Unknown Men

Somewhere between Texas and Kentucky, a letter was being carried, mailed prior to his time as a Ranger, so Chas could not predict if his letter would ever reach Kate in the autumn of 1871. The only letter Chas Bellew had mailed on the journey was from Newton County, Texas, weeks earlier. I had not seen the hand of Jackie Ray at work on a letter, but I did not see everything. I wasn't sure if he could even write. Having never written a letter to a lady, mailed a card, or even pressed a stamp, I became less communicative and withdrew from such tactics early in life. However, I pondered the thought and did more writing in later years, but this became the humbling story of my life.

I laughed and appreciated the stories of Chet Bellew and reread his valuable letters when he was a missionary in Texas and other places. On the other hand, Chas Bellew penned some fine letters - letters that were timeless and meaningful, read yet still today. He became a writer and an artist early on, developing a new style, one of self-conviction. Kate was a good woman for Chas, a lady who cared about education and worked her farmland as well as any man could have, laboring in the winter as much as in summer. Things had to be done during daylight hours, and everyone had a purpose and a role at night, too. By candlelight, Kate favored letters and the comfort of a man who penned well and added thoughtfulness as a wordsmith. I imagined the fall in Denton, a place that was no different than autumn in Texas, being golden yellow and red in color, and I was right. My mind was clouded as a Ranger, being armed, a star on my chest, riding beside Chas and Jackie Ray. We rode as unknown men and armed with guns and pages of a book as well.

I had no interest in coffee or candlelight writing at that time in my life, but bold respect was given to those who did, especially Chas. It was his time to cover blank pages. He honored himself in that manner, just as Chet Bellew did with sermons and notes whenever an idea tumbled inside his pastoral mind. Like fallen acorns on the forest floor became essential, so did nuggets of thought, jotted down, more valuable the more my hair turned gray, like the fur of a fox. Letters and telegrams shortened the distance between parties, just as if two people were seated in the same room, more personal and intentional. Inspired by my own stories, my hand formed letters later in life, and many stories were told. The hard year of 1871 was when Chas handled the pen, even when he was shot, more so than the rest of our winters.

***

For Kate, that fall was beautiful in Kentucky, with auburn trees and golden leaves, day framed the canopy and shut-in of mountains, fields rolled into the mountains, and waves of bright earth tones marked her memory, thoughts noted in her own letters. She held glimpses of how autumn mirrored atop motionless waters and how golden reflections could not be removed from conversations even when fish broke free from the surface or when whitetail deer soared across shallow streams. Not even the dust of valleys, the coolness of the air, or the hanging fog at dawn could erase how Kate yearned to hear from Chas, just a letter or a thought of concern. She spent the evenings laughing by the pond, and remembered jokes and stories he'd made when they were together at Misty Spring the summer prior. Whether it was the color of gold in the forest of Denton or the smell of fresh-cut cedar that sparked her desire for him, she pined for his return or even a hand-delivered letter. She was a talkative lady - a lady who collected a diary full of poems and pleasant thoughts, things she'd read. The small community missed seeing them, huddled in the high country and on horseback. Some women judged a man by his eyes, voice, and silhouette, touched by thoughts in a letter or the simplicity of a kind gesture.

Kate and Alice kept busy at harvest time, raking hay and chopping the winter wood. Alice missed Jackie Ray. Both sought the pen of a writer. Deep down, a letter from Texas, deservingly so, would bring another revelation of hope and inspiration.

The horse beneath my saddle and the Lone Star on my chest was far from Denton, Kentucky, but I missed home. We all did. Men were no longer under the hold of sermons, messages of good news, and ages of care from the missionary preaching of Chet Bellew, but we all felt his prayers from earlier years must have reached heaven. We had traveling mercies along the way, shared friendships, and labored for profit; more was needed. In some wild turn of events, an unsettling acceptance of a job had changed the stakes, far higher stakes, and through our strike as Rangers, we'd edged a bit closer in our friendship. Being Sons of War mattered, but not to Sheriff Dunn; for him, "Dead or Alive" was noted on paper, so we hunted.

The three of us spoke as much about God and Kentucky as anything else, but some folks in Texas were far from either. We rode toward Houston County. In hand, we carried a small map, fingerprinted by Jackie Ray, and I felt my stomach rumble, which forced a short break. Two-day-old jerky and dry biscuits bought from the restaurant in Jasper became lunch, ten miles east of Crockett, Texas.

"The deputy in Jasper said it was a thousand miles to El Paso, a hot land of beautiful Mexican women, Atohi, right?" said Jackie Ray. He leaned back under the shade and removed his hat, face, and flanks beaded of sweat, and his right hand fished in the depth of a small stream.

"Listen!" said Chas, raising his hand. "Get the horses out of the stream, pull 'em behind the hillside, Jackie Ray. I will edge closer, and you two follow behind when you can."

"I heard men talking," Jackie Ray said, eyes alerted to their unexpected company.

"I have the horses," I said, ducked low. "Follow me."

We made our way to a dense part of the woods, lined with cedars and hollies, where flatland rolled downhill and the small valley forked.

"Look, two men are roped to a tree," said Chas, head low behind trees. "Ropes around their necks, tried up."

"Why?" I said and whispered, hand on my pistol. "We are Texas Rangers. Outlaws need to answer a few questions, right? Let's go, guys."

"Why would two black men be mounted on horseback, Atohi?" said Chas. "Let's go investigate why these men are not in front of a jury, and where's the sheriff?"

"Pull pistols, gentlemen, if needed," said Chas, face serious, adjusting his coat.

We rode fast.

Each man could shoot the eyes out of a razorback hog at a hundred yards, and Jackie Ray had taken twelve black bears in three years and led no different life than Chas. When it came to skinning the hide from a deer, Jackie Ray was David Crockett and the best man to have close. We were as accurate with a Colt as any military commander who had marched with General Custer in the Civil War.

"I have a plan," said Chas. He stopped and turned in my direction. "I'm gonna walk in behind them, and one guy will go for his gun, and both will skin their Colts. We need to go fast. These men will have broken necks if they spook the horses."

"The men on horseback have bags on their heads," I said. "And little time to talk their way out of death. We must save them. Let me walk in first. I know they'll draw on me, and you'll have to defend yourselves."

We heard the two men asking them questions about stolen horses.

"Don't kill us, sir!" said one of the black men. "You got the wrong two men, mister." His arms were roped behind his back, and the horse was unsteady beneath him.

"Wait up! Wow!" I said, forty paces from the horses. "What do we have here?" I flipped my jacket to where the Texas Ranger badge was no different than a cinder of light after dark.

"We got ourselves two horse thieves, Ranger," said one of the men. His eyes widened to the man beside him, ready to turn their guns at the drop of a hat.

"Not us, Ranger! We didn't steal no horses!" said the broad black man nearest to my horse. "We told this man a dozen times, we rode with Bad Carl Bellew last week, and we drive cattle for a living, that is all. These are our horses."

One man did all the talking while the other man shivered his teeth, sang hymns, and mumbled the Lord's Prayer under his breath.

"Said they didn't do it," said Jackie Ray, who walked out from the woods, hand on his hip, pistol ready. "Heard him plain as day say it. They work cattle for Carl Bellew. We want Carl Bellew and his bad gang."

"Like I said," one outlaw waved his hand at Jackie Ray, "we got ourselves a couple of thieves and aim to hang both men 'til dead and gone. This is our business, Ranger. We don't need badges and some bad advice in our face."

"Where's your judge and jury?" said Chas, who paced. "And you don't have the sheriff to back up your word, do ya, outlaws?"

The two outlaws were dressed in black vests, hats crushed, and boots were dark and worn. Their black horses were tied to the bushes behind them. No one else was around to help them or verify their story. I scouted the hillside to see if other outlaws saw our trail.

"Do you believe Carl Bellew would hire two thieves to run his outfit?" said the black man, who had done all the talking.

Both outlaws stirred strangely at each other and laughed.

"That man has more pride and money than the King Ranch," said one outlaw. "Don't have the time or the patience to spend with redemption and confessions, Rangers."

"How about you three Rangers mount your horses and pretend we never saw each other today, huh?" said the tall outlaw with a dark beard. The outlaw walked over to Jackie Ray, sniffed and turned, and faced him with the hope of negotiating, money in hand.

"One more step and I will make your vest have eyes, outlaw?" said Jackie Ray, shoulders squared, face-to-face with the long-haired man, a man who had not seen a razor since Christmas.

"Don't believe you got the strike fire, young man," said the outlaw. He grinned slightly at his friend. "You, uh, old enough to own a gun, sonny?"

"You don't want to draw on him, outlaw!" Chas said, laughing. His hand tapped his belt, eyes on his enemy. "Best if you just ride on, keep riding on, and say this was something out of your element, kids. Only gonna warn you once, and I've said it."

I learned something that day, thoughts spoken, truth or not, did not always end well.

"Rangers, we ain't no Judas traders," said one black man. "We own these horses, raised and branded them in Crockett, not five miles from town."

The horses stood motionless, head tugging on the reigns. Each man nervously lifted out of the saddle and stood up, necks stretched, arms straight, and firmly roped. They had no chance without our help.

"We are not leaving, Rangers," said the tall outlaw, face tight, one eye closed. "Finish what I start 'til these two men are dead, down in the dirt for their dirty deeds."

"We will catch the rest of his gang next later on tonight," said the other round outlaw. "Soon as we find them, law dogs."

Only the horses moved about, legs shuffling, tails whipped, and the two men breathed heavily on horseback. Few words were spoken. One man continued to mumble, head toward the sky, less relaxed.

"My soul is prepared!" yelled the black man. "I am meeting my Savior. How about you, Alford Sandy?"

"I see a narrow door opening in the sky. Save my soul, Jesus!" yelled the other black man.

"You speak again, Alford," the outlaw warned him. "You'll see a fast bullet in your head."

"Shut up!" said the tall outlaw. "Heard enough talk!"

Chas and Jackie Ray talked and focused on the outlaws.

Both were taught by Chet Bellew how to handle a gun at close range. I know because I trained beside them. Yeah, even a man of the cloth needed help with a Smith & Wesson; still, for Chet, the Lord first, so he spent his days between sermons practicing the art of marksmanship and became better for it. He trained us to defend ourselves.

Jackie Ray was taught no different than Chas Bellew. In 1861, the boys were eight winters old when the first major Battle of Bull Run broke out, and not knowing how long the Civil War would last, Chet Bellew readied the boys each day for more War. In Kentucky, the Governor made it so that Kentuckians could volunteer but did not have to enlist. Some joined the fight and never returned. By 1864, fighting slowed down. However, by that summer, we knew as much about firearms as we did about Matthew, Mark, Luke, and John.

***

Near Crockett, seven years had passed since the Civil War had ended; still, the world was unsettled and wild back in Texas, filled with outlaws and bandits who had hoped to make their mark in a vast, unguarded land. I felt a lump in my throat, uneasy, and sweat ran into my eyes. My mind was no longer concerned about the eagle in flight or game on the hillside. It was the occasional twitch of the big shoulder that had my attention. The thought crossed my mind when guns were fired, horses jumped, and men of heavy weight would break their own necks, dangling. Silence fell over the rolling crest of the golden valley, good or bad, innocent or guilty; all men and horses were subject to death. Cherokee men were not exclusive and generally disliked, anyway.

Two outlaws backed up, standing ready and steady, less than forty paces away. Two black horses under the weight of the accused men neighed nervously and shifted. The accused saw daylight through a grid of loosened burlap stretched about their heads. Eagles screamed. Dark clouds slid by the burst of sunlight, and shadows blanketed the rolling valley beside the swift stream, and that was when hair raised about my neck. No one was safe at that moment. To guess a man's speed in a draw was like guessing where gold was hidden inside the rocks, unknown to me, until it was seen with the naked eye. Gunfighters loved to be tested. My heart raced, and I was about to be tested.

"Say when, Ranger," said the tall outlaw, one eye closed, the good one held for Jackie Ray.

He adjusted his hat, a subtle signal among gunfighters. Then, without warning, his left hand drew on Jackie Ray.

"Pow!"

The other man drew on Chas.

"Pow!"

The land echoed with gunpowder and lead. In seconds, five or six more shots were fired. Smoke clouded the flatland, and blood splattered onto the dusty earth. Horses under the weight of men bolted and ran a short distance. I shot the ropes under tension, one then the other. Two men fell to the ground; one gasped for air, and the larger man who had done all the talking, head down, was motionless. The outlaws were on the ground, shirts soaked in blotted amber, one bleeding more than the other, but asleep.

"I'll make that journey a peaceful slide into the flames of Hades!" said Jackie Ray, arm extended.

"Jackie Ray?"" I yelled and ran.

"Chas, you hit bad?" I crawled between my bloody friends and held their hands. "Jackie Ray, your leg is bleeding."

In a cheerful fashion of victory, Jackie Ray laughed and dropped his gun into the dirt.

"Burns like a cattle brand, Atohi," said Chas, flat on his back, five miles from a good doctor.

"The fool shot my dang leg, Chas," said Jackie Ray, blood on his hands, laughing. He pressed his own wounded leg and groaned. Then he grinned and held a handful of blood, laughing again, and said, "Still alive, bud. I'll kick until the end." Flat on his back, he rested and holstered his pistol. Jackie Ray stood up.

"Two men tougher than barbed wire," I said. Both men could go, I thought.

When I saw the faces of Jackie Ray and Chas, men barely alive, I cut ropes from the two black men and checked the neck of the heavy man, loosened and broken, a man on his way to the next life. His praying friend wiped his eyes, and because of his friend's death and a history of trouble, he jumped on his horse, rode away, and left without a word of thanks. Innocent or guilty, a moment passed without debate.

"Gotta find a doctor and fast," I said as I loaded Jackie Ray on his horse first and sent him on ahead to town. Chas followed him, head dragging and his shirt soaked in blood.

Filled with compassion, I wept deeply on the ride to Crockett, a time of pain and sorrow, as the horses ran smoothly. Chas still had not spoken.

"Rangers shot!" I yelled to the doctor. "Bloody Texas Rangers are shot up!" At dusk, Chas and Jackie Ray, deeply wounded, rested in Crockett, eyes closed, and passed out on the second level of a hotel. As for me, a Cherokee, I sat in jail yet again. Questioned about the shootout at Crockett Spring by the sheriff.

"Send a telegram to Sheriff Dunn!" I said and explained myself to a man who would not listen to good advice. "He knows us. Send him a dang a wire!" I pleaded.

Confined and outraged. No one was interested in the innocence of a Cherokee man caught amid a gunfight, and I was being held for no good reason. That is until I mentioned the name Bad Carl Bellew. The sheriff stood, head canted, and his new-found interest brought him to the jail bars, the one in my hands, and he shook the jail.

"Cherokee man," he said. His hands gripped the bars, face enraged with curiosity. "I am completely hammered about how you know Bad Carl Bellew of Waco, Texas, and you claim Kentucky as your home state, boy."

"The blonde Ranger upstairs, Chas Bellew," I said, "well, Carl Bellew... is his uncle. Blood uncle and not adopted orphan blood, either."

"My men will find Bad Carl Bellew until we sprout another plan," said the sheriff, the brim of his hat slammed against the bars.

"Find him!" I yelled. I was confident. "See for yourself and get word to Sheriff Dunn, now, for me, while you and your men play politics and kiss the public's butt, sheriff!" It was something I should not have said. Somehow, I was forgotten during mealtime for a few days for those words.

To this day, what was said inside the jail against the sheriff was something I regretted afterward.

And it was the day I began to write for the first time, and many stories followed. Someone had to pick up the pen and communicate about our time in Texas, so I did it.

Chapter 18
No Man's Land

The whipping winter wind swept through Kentucky, frigid and blue, in November 1871. Buckets of water were scooped through broken layers of ice in preparation for a plump turkey, the same with corn, potatoes, and squash as the year before. The pace of widow Brooks had slowed, heartbroken, hurtful, and she resented God from when her husband had passed in the early spring. However, she had no reason to prevent her daughters from having a proper Thanksgiving meal. Her cornbread had the same flavor and crust from past years, a coveted craft, a slight hope of survival. Naturally, to give thanks to the blessing of the harvest they had taken, spring to fall, even for only her daughters, Alice and Kate, and God seated at the table, and enough plates for the Trinity.

"The Lord desires His part," said Mrs. Brooks, "Head of the church. Head of the cabin. Head of this table."

The grieving mind of a widow woman was framed wildly with the loss of the husbandman, and traditional ways were honored with fall fruits and vegetables and toil. Providence was rarely overlooked at the table for Mrs. Brooks, and being the first year they had been without Stan Brooks at harvest time - forces dimmed the conversation, and few words were spoken outside of daily chores.

Alice missed her father and took his role as town Ferrier, hard at work, found game, and tended to fields of corn and pumpkins. Kate, on the other hand, mended dresses and made quilts in the small community, made ends meet and continued academics on her own time, such as science and liberal arts. She borrowed books from neighbors, hoped for college, had thoughts of relocation to Louisville or Lexington, and had the notion to help her mother find a better social life.

"Did you see the newspaper, Kate?" said Mrs. Brooks, eyes half closed. "One-sided!"

"No. I have not read it."

"Well, I read the article!" said her mother, voice loud and clear. "Our beloved President Grant said in the newspaper: "Bless the husbandman for the harvest is in his hands" and the family that we should be thankful because all nations are at peace. Lies. It's all a pack of lies. Men deceive us from Washington, D.C." She crushed the pages and tossed the paper into the fireplace. "Let it be known that because of evil men, coveting men, such as him, I mean our president, that jealousy and greed will prosper more than anything else," waving her hands, "leading far less of a Civil War than predicted and winning for his cause is an outrage. Now, the Commander and Chief, Mr. President Grant, we can expect no nation to be at peace in our lifetime!"

With a big smile, said Kate, "You should run for public office, mother."

"She could do a better job than what we have in Washington," said Alice. She sat with a glass in hand and toasted her mother, and that's when she wept.

"Ladies," said Mrs. Brooks, tears rolled down her flushed cheeks, "let us not forget this time and the months we have stood alone in the fields, laboring women in hardship because my loving husbandman, your father, a man who rode off to fight a senseless war and came back as a trained rouge and a lair. And far from a peaceful and civil man. Families suffered, and still more will suffer."

"When the husband dies at War, pain is felt, an endless pain," said Alice. She moved to the sofa and hugged her mother, sighing, and said, "War or no war, families are broken forever, shattered into the future for generations, and good stories will echo pain for decades."

"Because this is no man's land," said Kate, elbows on the table.

"We were made orphans and widows," said Mrs. Brooks, "and for what rightful cause. Does anyone know?" The widow remembered what she'd read and told, "So industry is rewarded in 1871, said our faithful President, the man who conquered the South and prospered his cabinet." She cried, and said, "Girls, I love you, but the war was more about land and money and disabling men of the Great South than anything else. That's what will be made of it years later. I see no other reason but to bring chaos and upheaval to the citizens of the Great South. How can we trust leadership in Washington?"

"I have read the same words," said Kate. "Before they announced the Civil War, trade between the North and South was peaceful, and people lived in contentment. Then, someone provoked the other side.

So, where is the peace on this blessed table of Thanksgiving? I do not see it at my table." After dinner, the house was warm, and Kate journaled the things her mother spoke of, and she fell asleep.

***

Back in Texas, Chas was wounded, face turned to the window, blood on his chest, and his eyes were closed. He was alive.

Kate saw Chas wounded in a bad dream. Three days had passed, and the wood supply was low, far from what the Brooks needed to make it in the cold mountains of Kentucky.

A smile ran across Alice's face as she brushed her hair, and she said, "I don't know about you, but the winters in Kentucky are harsh, and it would be nice to see some strong hands and smiling faces around here, don't you think, Kate?"

"Nope," said Kate, eyes open wide. Lips tight, head turned, and she knew her sister was the biggest flirt in Carter County. "This farm is off limits for men, Alice. This is no man's land. We have made it this far, haven't we?"

Three days into a cold December, the first snowflakes began to fall in the late evening. Kate and Alice felt they could no longer stay inside the cramped house, one that seemed without blessing and peace. Her mother fussed about the newspaper and what leaders in Washington had to say about the prevails of home life for the husbandman.

What to do? Kate wondered. Layered in her father's clothes and boots, Alice turned circles in the snow and made snow angels with her legs and arms. Both sisters sat atop the mountain. Kate was relaxed and danced among the spinning snowflakes. More adventurous and daring than Kate, Alice was not the prim and proper type. They laughed, padded snow atop old britches, and tucked their blue hands inside layers of clothes. They had not played and talked outdoors that way since they were young. Though, each lady tried to outdo the other one. Both had dissimilar ideas.

"I bet I can make my snowman a real man," said Alice. She relocated the carrot and fell into the snow, giggling.

"I cannot believe you!" said Kate, hands on her knees, and she fell in front of the snowman. Both amused.

"Men?" Alice shook her head. "I swear it's true, Kate, we are going be two old maids, sitting in Kentucky, losing our youth, if we wait for Chas and Jackie Ray to come home."

"Did a letter come in the mail from Chas?" said Kate, who stood and helped her sister up.

"Two letters came on Friday, Sis. Mother has them."

Kate pushed Alice down. Alice cleared the snow from her face.

"What!"

"There's a letter from Jackie Ray and Chas," said Alice, "it was a love letter from Jasper, Texas." She said nervously.

"I need to see Mother," said Kate, who stomped by her sister. "Secrets make me angry, Alice."

Her sister said, "Mother read them both, Sis."

Kate stomped her feet until she reached the fireplace, hands like ice, and waited until her voice had courage.

"Mother?" back to the fire.

"Yeah."

"Do you have a letter for Alice?"

"I do." She held her glasses.

"Do you have my letter, Mother?" hands on her hips, and she waited for the truth.

"The letter from Chas, huh?" said Mrs. Brooks. She gazed over her glasses. "It's in the fire."

"What?"

"Look in the drawer, Kate, postmarked from Texas, and it's unopened, Kate."

Kate ran across the room.

"You taught me to be honest, right?"

"I didn't want you to get hurt," said her mother, towel draped in her hand. "He could have found a Spanish lady, that's all. I try to protect my girls from heartache. I lost my brother in the Civil War, and now my husband is gone."

"Why would I be sad?" said Kate, eyes intrigued. "We are not engaged, mother."

"Love outlasts a wedding ring, Kate. You know your feelings are real, ring or not."

Her weary eyes focused on her daughter as she stood at the table.

"Last night," said her mother, "I dreamed Chas and Jackie Ray were shot to death, Kate. That is why I hid the letter. I'm sorry, dear."

Her mother spoke, but she could only hear the voice of Chas inside the letter. Not thinking of anything else, Kate imagined him writing the letter by a cold campfire, and she felt his voice through the words weeks earlier. She wept.

Alice sat beside Kate, held each other while they wept, as ice and snow blew against the wavy glass window, and they exchanged letters and spoke of what big city life was like.

Her mother sighed and opened her eyes.

"I've been depressed since your father died," said Mrs. Brooks. "You both have seen chills take over my sad body. It's not the winter chills. I will bid you that much." Her hands covered her face, and tears rolled down her flushed cheeks when she thought of being an old widow, like Naomi in the Book of Ruth. Legs kicked, and she rocked steadily, back and forth, until her eyes and head became motionless. And she fell asleep.

Alice jumped up and said, "We must sell this place and find us three good mountain men, start over, and move to West Virginia!"

"Yeah. I agree." said Mrs. Brooks. "We must!"

"No! I did not agree! We must keep our land!" said Kate, eyes alert.

"Our mother is right," said Alice, who stood, her voice loud and confident. "We could find men. Men with big, strong shoulders and a bit of money would hold, um?"

At the top of the stairs, back against the wall, widow Brooks faced her daughters and said, "This will be our last Christmas in the cabin, girls." Her eyes broke loose in tears. "I spoke to a friend about buying our farm."

"No! We are not talking to anyone!" said Kate, who walked to her mother, both in tears. "I will find a way to be here when Chas returns home, and we will make this farm work for all of us."

"Honey," said her mother. "As bad as the world is, Kate, he may not make it home."

"We need to go somewhere, just go." Alice held Kate and shivered.

"We don't have enough food for winter," said Mrs. Brooks, reaching for her daughters. "We need some help. I'm tired. The last choice is to sell the property. Since Kate is the oldest, she will have money for college," said widow Brooks. Alice, you can go to school in a few years if we can survive."

"Let's pray for men," said Alice, who smiled and climbed into bed with her mother.

By the fire, Kate read the letter a dozen more times before midnight. She prayed Chas would be able to find her if they moved and that the postman would forward her mail to wherever the Lord led her family to in the coming New Year, 1872.

Kate and Alice spent the next few days trying to think of a better way to afford to live in Denton, by working in Grayson, Kentucky or Huntington, West Virginia. She planned to send money back to her mother, who had worked herself into a state of worry and was unable to farm a place in the mountains. Too many questions were unanswered, and Kate prayed for her mother to reconsider leaving Denton, Kentucky. Still, her mind was set on parting with the farm, a place that would bring fair market value if sold.

Chapter 19
Wounded and Warned

His eyes eased open at the break of dawn; the vision of Chas was blurry. Like a big black bear awakened too early from hibernation or over-prescribed medication, the type that fogged his mind had lifted eyes. In a short time, half-conscious, warm, calloused hands folded and arose, slow at first, and then Chas rolled his head from translucent curtains, and his hat shielded the first light of day. Objects soon had clarity of shape, aroma filled his nose, and touch became normal again. The ascension of his nose met a whiff of freshly brewed coffee, paired with cooked apples, fried eggs, chunks of fall ham, and the reality of an early spread punched his nostrils. He thanked the Lord.

I remembered his eyes popping open brightly, Chas gasped for air, and my feet found motion, and I danced in the hallway. I felt as good as if I had breathed mountain air and stood in an icy Kentucky river. No random pivot suited my soul, but a purposeful celebration of arms and legs, my head bounced, and my feet anxiously tapped the hardwood floor. My heart had rhythm as my friend witnessed the arrangement and a decent attempt at tradition.

"My mouth is as dry as a desert floor, Atohi," said Chas, who smacked his lips.

For me, the dance had finished. I was a servant again.

"Your strong Kentucky voice is no longer hidden from the world," I said, elated. I propped my boot on the rung of the footboard. "Brought up some good Kentucky water for your soul," I told him. "Just for you, Chas Bellew."

"No better drink on earth," Chas declared, in good spirits.

The sheriff knocked and found a seat.

"Texas water is as pure as a heavenly stream," said the sheriff.

"I am back to life, good sheriff," said Chas, face afresh.

His lips smacked, finishing the water in one turn, and he burped. I stood and called from beyond the hallway railing and waited until the pretty lady, Rosa, had finished brushing her dark hair. She steadied her pose in the heart of an oval mirror and adjusted her dress when the placement of her hair flushed her cheeks. Skin of a Spanish princess, and she forged my eyes to her smile. When she walked through the foyer, my heart stopped. The removal of my felt hat caused a sensation; a feeling of being love-struck crossed my heart, and I saw her dance at a wedding, and I was available. The thought of being a happy groom was favorable. The Great One added many blessings of dance to my steps that weekend, particularly the way Rosa spun in my arms.

"My hat!" I said and watched the cap dart to the lower lever.

"I'll catch it," she said, and in midair, hands outreached, and she did. "Told you, Atohi, see, it's a perfect fit."

"Good hands, Rosa. Beautiful fit."

Placing the hat atop her head, she fitted her face in the mirror again and matched from head to toe. Thoughts ran across my eager mind to be married, wide and little braves, and when she placed her foot on the first step of the grand staircase, canted with the feel of a female matador, I stood in complete adoration. Unsure of her own grace, less confidence was shared; she cradled and clutched my new hat to her side, taking the stairs that led her to where I stood at the rail. She giggled, eyes tight, and did not realize her own acceptance into my lonely world, proposed friendship in Crockett. Unknowingly to me, Rosa spent her life as a laborer - she was a flower in the wilderness, lovely, a Spanish princess and sunshine among the poor and dark spirit of Texas.

"You can wear the hat," I said and met her at the crest.

She stopped at the platform amid the staircase, where another wide mirror hung, trimmed in gold. Her stance was steady and true, strikingly rare, and an uncommon moment lost in time to anyone else but this writer. Deep in my heart, vanity, vanity was felt, and I was provoked to retrieve the broken mirror from my pocket, now the size of a coin. The glass rested in the wrinkles of my palm, and somewhere in the past, that segment of mirror was meant for the radiance of a stylish woman, a lady like Rosa, and more than anything else, well, she desired it. The shame was her stance and reflection were without the snap of a photographic camera. I held the realization that the actions of pleasing moments, pretty faces, especially needed to be caught on paper. My wavy memory gathered such moments of glory, and I recalled the day more than once and held the story no differently than when it happened - and she was the understatement of elegance, such as the red feathers of a Cardinal, lost in a glorious flight on a snowy winter trail.

"How do I look?" said Rosa, glowing. She twisted and turned effortlessly, dress flaring and waving, a slower spin, arms to her waist, like a figure atop a wooden music box.

I knew my answer.

"Like the star on a Texas stage," I said, voice low, hand over my heart.

"Might keep this new felt hat, Atohi," said Rosa, who dropped the brim lower, eyes squinting into the bend of natural light. She was a treasure, a star, a cardinal, a lady, and even when she was reading and drinking coffee, the world saw an unforgettable face.

We spoke for a moment, close enough, whispering in private, and our weight was on the railing. I discovered she was from Laredo, deep in South Texas, and her Mexican hands were tan and soft. We spoke of North Carolina, and I told her my story. Her eyes were dark brown, the color of a roulette wheel, and her shyness had been left on the first floor. I also found out her name was Isabella Rosalina Ortiz, a beautiful name, and she preferred Rosa among friends.

"I will remember this day more than most, Atohi," said Rosa, head on my shoulder. Her words meant something, a testament of sincerity, and she whispered softly into my ear.

"Don't you ever forget our first conversation, either."

"I will hold it like gold," I replied, holding her sincere words.

Clearing his throat, Chas said, "A man under severe medication is alive in the next room, and my ears work perfectly." He rang a bell, an idea that I had regretted. "My state of endless thirst is calling again. I can hear whispering voices, conversations travel, as I perish in this Texas hotel."

"Might be your time to leave this dreadful world, Chas," said Jackie Ray, a voice echoed from down the hall. "But we will have a heck of a stampede parade in your honor, my friend."

We were united and lively again.

"Could I get a pitcher of your water for these Texas Rangers, Rosa?" I asked. After the moment we had shared, I remembered she was at work, not a guest on holiday from Laredo. She held my Cherokee jewelry with both hands and then stepped away in contentment. "These men have risen on the third day and interrupted our sincere talk, Rosa."

"We will talk over dinner."

Her happy face stuck in my memory years later, even today.

"Some folks eat early," I suggested and winked.

"Some folks have not eaten in three days," Chas said, ringing that dang bell. "How about some chicken on a stick, huh?"

"I know where I would like to stick that bell!" Jackie Ray yelled from down the hall and laughed for the first time in days.

Rosa took the bell and threw it out the second-floor window.

"Now! I'll be right back with some water for these men," said Rosa. She left for the downstairs kitchen and had a few customers check in, which delayed her return.

I saw Jackie Ray's face, sound asleep. Out cold by the time she had returned with the cold well water for him. She had sprayed an alluring fragrance of rose perfume on my hat, and we spent the evening and the night together.

The next morning, I made the coffee and breakfast. She said she enjoyed our time together, and we entertained each other for days.

The doctor spoke of Jackie Ray and Chas; the man was terrified about the spread of infection in their bloodstream.

"Infection?" I replied. "Dear Lord, it's time for the Medicine Man to drum up a mixture of lemon juice."

***

My devoted friends needed help from the Great One, Jesus. Darkness covered my eyes; the railing, yet high, was sturdy and held my weight. The place I came to ponder and pray was at the Presbyterian Church of Crockett. I bet Rosa was not to speak of their health conditions to anyone. Some doctors preferred it that way. Such secrets were held in private and on paper. And good doctors wanted to be the first to speak about illnesses to their patients. To keep medical secrets was the choice of the practitioner, I thought to myself: My two closest friends are being monitored daily – science can go far, but the Lord is the Great Practitioner. That year, such things crossed my mind and crossed prayerfully into the clouds, far above Crockett, and I called upon the Lord Jesus for help.

***

Very few times in my life had I ever felt the goodness of God and been humbled by my friendship with Rosa, a gentle light of surprise from the Great One. My most significant time of prayer was spent on the health of my friends, and the chance of infection weighed heavy on my heart.

On that morning, heavily influenced by Texas badges, the men we had killed came up again, determined as guilty men, up to no good. Of course, with the backing of the governor, I was elated by the current position we held in Texas. Being pinned as a Texas Ranger was my first employment, a good one, yet long overdue. As newly sworn in by Sheriff Dunn and being the novice class of Newton County, we had been the first to send men to the grave that autumn. However, Chas was not out of the woods yet; still, the man was wounded and weak, laced with opium and unsure about the infection, and being served because of his badge by fine ladies, who thrilled his overfertilized ego. I unexpectedly became a spectator of his recovery, and such elegance and beauty could not be hidden, even if the Spanish nurses did tend to him and Jackie Ray and no one else.

Chas had not spoken to anyone much and remained dazed and healed slowly the first week. The finger-sized holes in his body, still tender from a bullet, were a swift beacon of the hazards of being a Ranger. Scars were the reminder of the deadly shootout at Crockett Spring.

After breakfast, the sheriff left, and the doctor stopped by with more medication. Pacing up and down the stairs, I stood in his doorway with a cup of coffee. I had conversations with Rosa, the lead servant of the hotel, and we knew everything about each other by the end of the week. More than we both expected. A gentle breeze fluttered the curtains, and the smell of lunch crowded the hotel. Chas brushed his thin beard and relaxed his position in recovery.

"I declare the medicine has worked," said the doctor. "Jackie Ray Monroe does not have an infection, and Charles "Chas" Bellew is healthy enough to ride a horse or plow a field."

"You are alive, Ranger Bellew?" I said and sighed.

"Yeah," said Chas, head back on a pillow. "Good news, Doc. "I have a thousand good years left because of you."

White blankets covered his legs, and soft, long pillows made from the feathers of geese propped him up. I remember his meal was coffee, pears, a slice of pork, and three biscuits, or enough for a small army.

"Comfortable as a king, aren't you?" said Rosa, pulling on long hair inside her hand. "He's spoiled after a week, huh?"

"Yeah. Governor Ed Jack Davis would be jealous of this good service, I bet," said Chas, grinning.

"Yep," I said. "He might appoint you to a tail-kissing, high-paying cabinet position in Austin. Jackie Ray has not been cleared to ride by Doc Sheridan, Chas."

"That's bad news, Atohi. The beef and pork made me better," said Chas, who sat up. The man suddenly stood and latched his own belt.

The following day, the three of us stuffed our ribs with beef and cabbage, chunks of bread, and several large buttery potatoes. Our dinner conversations were about the two dozen cowboys who'd showed up in Crockett days earlier, and more men added trouble for the locals in a small town. We did not know their purpose around town, but they had made a mess of a few saloons.

"I had a good meal, Chas," I said, pulling up a chair beside the window. "No need to offer me any beef ribs, Ranger."

"Don't count on it," said Chas. He moaned and laughed, face suggested that he was in pain. "I am sure you were kept well fed and cleaned."

"Gained some weight for the winter since our time in Crockett," said Chas, slapping his belly. "Should have sent a telegram to Marie Laveau so she could've visited you, made lemon juice. Your body would have healed with two cups."

"No, no, no, lemons for me. Where did Jackie Ray go, Atohi?" said Chas. He stopped eating. "Thought he would have stopped in my room."

Head shook, and I said, "That man is worse off than you are, Chas?"

"Fever?" asked Chas.

I nodded, face long, hands clasped atop my head, and thoughts of death and disease clouded my mind about the screams and hardships of the Cherokee Nation. I imagined how Jackie Ray would have felt having to walk from North Carolina to Oklahoma with a fever or a leg wound. The window ledge was where the black crow landed. Rosa moved about between rooms, stood by the window, and pushed the crow until she persuaded the black bird into flight.

"That black crow will not shut up and keeps coming back for bread," said Rosa. The lady left to deliver a lunch of peaches and chicken to Jackie Ray.

Chas leaned forward and asked, "Is Jackie Ray going to make it, Atohi?"

"The doctor checks on him three times a day."

Rosa returned with a surprised look.

"I checked his temperature," said Rosa. "He is healthy as a horse," said the lady.

I paced from the window to the doorway, closed my eyes in the midday heat, and thanked God for his recovery. My time spent at the Presbyterian church had hope. In the meantime, more cowboys had arrived in Crockett, hundreds of them.

"Our friend is under the best care he can get," said Rosa.

The crow landed again.

"If someone cannot shut that crow up, I will!" said Rosa. The lady clutched a small revolver and pulled the trigger. The crow was warned and flew away.

I sat up tall myself in my usual chair and grinned at Chas, who laughed like he was again at the stage in New Orleans. With my legs crossed and the departure of the crow, conversations were without interruption. We gazed to the Northeast land across Blanchard's property; dust clouds revealed more cowboys and dark horses, and my mind became worried for the people of Crockett.

"Where's all the cowboys headed?" I said, window open.

"Industry or worse," said Rosa. The lady pulled the curtains and dusted the glass. "There's talk about the railroad splitting the town in half. Men surveyed last spring."

Her finger felt the scar where the bullet entered Chas. She made a Catholic cross with her hand and clutched his hands in prayer.

"Shipping out timber and lumber to sawmills all over Texas, I bet," said Chas. He handed plates to Rosa and thanked her. "With the railroad expansion, the town will triple in size before the next election. More men will ride long and hard for opportunities in Crockett, Texas."

"We need more Texas Rangers to keep law and order around here," I said, and in the doorway, I stood. "Peacekeepers. Good ones."

"Hotels are booked on weekends," said Rosa, fanning her face. "Packed with railroad men, land surveyors, and those dang cowboys.

They stay and bring trouble to this pleasant town." She held the plates, spoke something in Spanish against the Cowboys, and turned and walked away. "Chas, are you Rangers staying in Crockett for a long time?"

"No," said Chas, eyes steady. "Headed to Waco."

"Hotel owner Truman Vance claims that we'll need more town deputies, more Rangers, and a faster gun than Marshal Johnson. Slow as molasses, that man. My dead grandmother can fumble her hands over a dozen biscuits faster than Marshal Johnson can pull a pistol."

"Lots of thirsty cowboys in town," said Chas, leaning out the window.

"Our Marshal Johnson beats all," said Rosa, hands on her hips. "When trouble turns up at the card table, Marshal Johnson disappears, offers provisions and protection to the night ladies of Houston County down the street. They say he is a very generous soul with his money."

"More churches and good ministers are needed to correct such problems," I said. "It is a problem of the heart. Deep problems of sin."

"No, Rosa," said Chas, nodding. "We aimed to leave soon. Got business across Texas." The Ranger stretched his legs, knees bent under his own weight, and he counted men on horseback. Most of the men headed to the corral, found stable hands, and some paced to the Crockett Saloon. We were headed to Waco as soon as Jackie Ray feels up to the ride."

Moments later, Rosa returned from downstairs with soap and towels in her arms and said, "Take your clothes off, Chas."

"What?" said Chas, eyes large.

"Time for your sponge bath," said the lady. "Rapido!"

"What?" I yelled.

Rosa stood in the doorway, towel in hand, and waited. "But if he's of sound mind and good health, he can wash your own dang backside, Rosa," I told the lady.

"Oh dear," said Chas, and crawled back into bed. "A bath would suffice, the perfect remedy for my latent condition. My shoulders and feet are tender." He grinned, winked in my direction, and did not know she was my woman. "Better get in the tub, ready my feet."

"Leaving for the stables," I said.

"I am unable to do certain things, Atohi!" yelled Chas, lowering himself inside the tub.

"It's okay to drown him, Rosa."

I shut the door.

Later, the sun dropped, and seated between Chas and the wavy window was Sheriff Arden Ellis, who had questioned why we passed through Crockett, Texas. My arms were crossed. I did not remind him again why we needed to be in Waco. Among his questions, the sheriff tried to find a reason to lock me up again because of my part in what happened with the two outlaws. Three men were dead. No truth and no witnesses stepped forward to verify my story at Crockett Spring. Speaking to Chas, his answers matched my good story, and Sheriff Ellis left us alone for a while.

Talking out of his head with spiked medicine inside his Kentucky veins, Jackie Ray was in the next room, a makeshift hospital bed, where he faded in and out of sleep. After a good supper, Jackie Ray spoke for a while and shared his side of the story with Sheriff Ellis the day before I was released from jail. He continued with the same questions when his mind was without clouds. No one knew why a black man was dead, two white men were dead, or for what real reason he was atop a horse. We all three offered the same testimony. Marshal Johnson found our words to be truthful, faith that he was hesitant to accept at first.

The undertaker verified his broken neck. No one knew the name of the black men, the outlaws, or the whereabouts of the man who rode away. All three men were buried in unmarked graves, located on the south sector of Glenwood Cemetery, third, fourth, and fifth graves; atop was a fresh spread soil and stones with numbers, died in 1871. Other than the date, they had not written or even speculated about names.

The next morning, Jackie Ray woke up, mind clear and voice rested, and beside him, bacon and eggs. Sheriff Ellis, a man of many questions, sat at the window. Chas stood and spoke with liberty and confidence and was recognized for his diligence as a Texas Ranger. The good doctor walked into the room before he got to my recognition, which was a quick nod to any Cherokee. I am sure it was sent from Washington, D.C., and autographed by President Grant.

"Here, young man," said the good doctor, hand opened.

"Is this the bullet that nearly killed me?" said Chas.

"Two inches from your heart," said Doc Sheridan.

Chas dropped the bullet in his shirt pocket.

"Enjoyed having you men in Crockett, Texas," said the doctor. He brushed his slick head, smooth as a Crenshaw melon. "You are free to leave today. My work here is done. They'll be more wounded men by morning. "

"Our work has yet to start," said Chas. He shook hands with the doctor who saved his life. "Heck of a sendoff committee. We wouldn't be walking out of this room if it were not for you, sir."

The doctor left the room. Sheriff Ellis nudged his chair close to the bed, elbow resting on his knees. His face was aged and wrinkled by the kiss of the sun and worrisome tilts of life.

"Chas? Chas. Bellew. Bellew," said the sheriff. "Something about that name that bothers me, boys." He mumbled to himself. "Now, where have I heard that name before, huh? The governor and the sheriff of Newton County," snapping his fingers, "that's where I've heard the name." He pointed. "Why would two white men and a Cherokee from Kentucky be named Rangers in Texas, tell me, huh?"

"Why?" said Chas, who tossed his clothes atop the bed. "For the same reason Crockett County, the first county in Texas," slipping his pants on, "was named after the frontiersman Davy Crockett, a man from North Carolina who fought in the Texas Revolution and The Alamo, by the way."

"There has to be more!" said Sheriff Ellis. Arms and legs crossed.

I stood by Chas and could normally answer questions for him, but his answer was why we'd traveled to Texas in the first place, to close the gap on family. Jackie Ray was downstairs flirting with ladies. Singing voices carried into the hallway, and he had a fever for women. Arms crossed, I stood in the doorway, the place where I spent much of my time while stuck in Crockett. Other than being seated on the front porch of the Crockett Hotel, eyes and ears were open to the fact that the men with red sashes and guns were rowdy and evil, a crowd of close men, Cowboys. In my spare time, Cowboys had stirred my mind in Houston County. Still, I was curious to witness Chas defend himself against Sheriff Ellis.

"To be King of the Frontier," said Chas and buttoned his shirt. "For the adventure of living and breathing in the wild, for the unusual experience of life, being a Ranger. I respect the farmer and rancher and lumberjack, but law and order beats farming for potatoes and cutting trees, sir."

"You rode from Kentucky to Texas just to feel the satisfaction of an adventure, Ranger Bellew?" said the sheriff, his face shocked.

"Yeah, why not?" said Chas, who parted his blonde hair, saw his reflection in the mirror and strapped his belt. "For the love of an adventure, and it's why men join the Army, hunt whales, trap river beasts, and pick a fight in the Civil War. They do it to make a difference, for the good of being daring and rare - to live and make a good life for people. The same reason pioneers drive wagons and travel out West, to experience the worst and best of what this world has to offer and find a new life – learn about faith and trust God."

"I hope they put that on a dollar bill, Chas!" I said.

Standing by the window after the spill he heard, Sheriff Ellis tapped his boots on the hardwood floors, rested his hands on his holster, and ran his finger freely to his buckle. His foot stopped the rapid movement, and he said, "I want to know the dang truth, Bellew. Is Bad Carl Bellew your father?"

The sheriff dropped down heavily into a chair and waited, grinning.

"Carl Bellew is my uncle, sir," said Chas. He pinned his Lone Star badge on his shirt.

"Good to know, son," said the sheriff. He looked at Chas. "Do you aim to take his side or defend the law and order of Texas?"

"I took an oath to defend Texas, sir," said Chas, straight-faced. "That's what we will do. Uncle or not, right, Atohi?"

"Yeah, to the end." I defended my friend. "Just because they share the same last name does not mean Ranger Chas Bellew, here, won't do the right thing when it comes time to take a stand for the law in Texas or anywhere else."

He grinned and chuckled, face in disbelief. His smile turned serious, his shoulders remained motionless, and his friendly smile disappeared. Chas closed the door to the room where he lost blood, rose with a fever, sweated uncontrollably, and then returned to normal in a short time. The three of us walked downstairs. No one spoke until Sheriff Ellis led us to his office, down the street from the hotel, and closed the door. We were under his advice. I reckon it was his town and his turn to let his words be known to outsiders. My mind felt that way, even as Texas Rangers, the sheriff aimed to chew our hides, I predicted.

"Men," said Sheriff Ellis, "sit down."

"What is this private talk about, Sheriff Ellis?" said Jackie Ray. "We are leaving your good town in the morning, and we don't have time for a father-son chat before we depart Crockett."

We all had a laugh because not only was his accent funny, but he was careless with his words, and he did not care to voice his opinion when something needed to be said.

"It would be best if you three got the hell out of here before sundown," said Sheriff Ellis. The man stood, stopped laughing, and smiled long enough to rub his nose.

"We kinda like Crockett," said Chas, face in confidence. "It has that adventurous, undone spirit about it. Jasper has butterflies and outlaws that never come back."

"Are you on opium, boy?" asked the sheriff.

"Yeah, it runs on my daddy's side, sir," said Jackie Ray, laughing. He was louder than a drunk man on election day.

"Is he feeling okay, Chas?" said the sheriff.

"Maybe."

"Are you men taking me seriously?" said Sheriff Ellis. He hung his hat on the rack. "You listen to me and listen good, gentlemen. You have been warned. Heed to my advice and get the hell out of town today while your heart still beats, boys."

"First, we are paid up until morning," I said. "Second, I see no reason to leave at sundown to bed down in the dirt, sir."

Chas whistled, interrupting my thoughts, and said, "Hey, we don't fear any man who walks the streets, rides a black horse, or pulls a rifle from his saddle, got it, Sheriff Ellis?"

That is when Chas surprised us and stood. Jackie Ray stood next. I followed. Slowly, the sheriff muscled himself up with the help of his oak desk and belted a deep sigh, face disappointed.

"Well, men from Kentucky, to carry good intentions is different than stupidity." said the sheriff, grinning. "As I stand here, you have been warned. Remember what I said."

"We'll take our chances, travel our own way," said Jackie Ray. He pushed his chair and stepped to the doorway before anyone, even the sheriff, was surprised.

"The men who ride in here …" The sheriff had trouble with his sentence while the church bells stopped. "Words out, the Cowboys have a large gang riding in tonight. You can help keep the peace or ride out peacefully. Hey, I wouldn't blame you men for being wise to the Rough Riders in Crockett. You are not from Texas," said Sheriff Ellis. "This is not your place to defend this town."

"Guys from Kentucky," said Chas, hand snapped to his belt buckle, "raise your hand if you would like to leave town, huh?"

No hands were raised.

"And if you aim to stand down with the good folks of Crockett and be here for Sheriff Ellis tonight, tip your hat, huh?" said Jackie Ray.

We grabbed our hats.

"What is that smell of perfume from?" said Jackie Ray, laughing. "Smell of roses or something strange, too strong for a man's body soap."

"Looks like you three men have more guts and guns and less brains than most Rangers in Texas. I have seen too many Rough Riders to count in Houston County."

"Let's see what happens tonight, huh?" said Chas. "We take warnings as a sign to load pistols and rifles for a long night of peacemaking and scouting."

Chas and Jackie Ray stood outside.

"There's no peace in Texas. Never will be," said Sheriff Ellis. The big man stood at the door. "Meet me back here at eight o'clock, Rangers. Be ready for blood."

"Pallaton!" I said.

"Means warrior," Chas told the sheriff.

"You will find a big war, Warrior Atohi," said the sheriff. "It's already here, boys. Be a long, long night."

A knot formed in the sheriff's throat, and the world became crowded at the end of 1871. That was the year pistols and rifles stopped hearts. The sheriff smeared sweat from his head and rubbed it deep into his palms.

Chapter 20
Two Wolves

Residents of Crockett, Texas, welcomed us to consider their small town in November 1871. That was the year history was made in Houston County. Crowded times were expected because the railroads and the harvest of virgin timber had not changed their hearts about our consideration. Two hundred men on horseback packed saloons and filled local businesses, satisfying owners.

The Cowboys rode into town around sundown atop stout horses, too, and pride ran across their ugly faces, handling high-dollar purebred animals. They unsaddled their horses and turned them into the corral, mostly well-fed geldings sporting shiny black coats, held at the end of town. I studied the brands, something I had learned as a young man, and kept in the last golden hour of the evening. Strange rumors were spoken about the Cowboys; the darker the horse, the more fire shot from the animal's nostril after dark. This was the first time anyone had seen such dark and ghostly horses of that caliber race through Houston County, and few folks searched for horses on fire after dark.

Rumors like that and others even more vile had crossed county lines, spoken about in Palestine and Nacogdoches and Centerville. I found it was a subtle way of intimidation. Proud raider outlaws and Rough Riders, heavily armed and dangerous, were said to be on the way. Big and fast shooters held red sashes and were loaded for battle; still, Cowboys had similar traits and were less friendly to folks in town. Hatred hung high from the saloon to the chapel bells and sunken eyes at night, and people watched from windows with bent curtains and studied their opponents. Tension was felt among the locals when outlaws and Cowboys arrived, especially when the law dogs jailed drunks for disorderly conduct and destruction of property on weekends.

Wagons and stagecoaches arrived in Crockett from parts unknown, loaded with happy faces, and expected to be catered to in a rare fashion. Seated inside red wagons were groups of traveling entertainers who faced their fears with Cowboys and befriended cattlemen and farmers with just the same tone. Beautiful and lean women were helped to the ground, dressed for showtime, such as actors, singers, and dancers. Their talent had raised hopes in Crockett; the flair and expertise for showmanship were on display, where tickets were sold on the streets. Twenty of the finest traveling theatrical performers arrived at sundown, halting painted wagons on the steps of the Grand Crockett Hotel; a wagon painted the red color of a fresh, sliced turnip seemed to draw a crowd of spectators to the streets.

Hotel rooms and inns were booked as soon as the entertainers could cross the street and sign papers. People of all sizes and shapes were welcomed into the small lumber town, and for more than an hour, the efforts of bulky men were witnessed, toting trunks filled with bright-colored outfits. Some sparkled, some with stylish, fashionable designs, and others suited no differently than for a king or queen. Women pranced around in custom-fitted fabric, tight-fitted outfits, and apparel draped and flared at the bottom of dresses.

Entertainers juggled. Others danced in the streets while men built anticipation and women spun in silver and white capes. At the same time, short men collected money for good tickets. Others were fitted in a flash of red fashion and sported carnival-style entertainment. In the cool night air, the strangest sight came from a man jailed inside a wagon, who rattled the bars under the moonlight and entertained folks when he howled, jumped, and played wolf. Fine folks of great talent and establishment were ushered into Crockett with cheers and respect by the town's people and all planned to spend the week being amused.

The prospect of trouble began to flood the hearts of performers when guns were fired overhead. Amid the crossfire of outlaws, folks sought protection from Texas Rangers and deputies. Men dressed in black paced slowly from the corral along Old San Antonio Road and paraded around the town for a large enough venue to sell tickets on 4th Street. However, the arsenal of men, eyes alert, carelessly walked from the corral, and some men were destined to be noticed, who shouted at the moon.

I was seated alongside Chas and Jackie Ray, perched on the tallest hotel in Crockett, the best crow's nest in town. Our eyes witnessed hundreds of men circling the small town by horseback and foot traffic, surveying the place from the sheriff's office, onto the bank, and down

SUNDAY RAIN

to the Crockett Presbyterian Church just east of downtown. Dark clothing and drunken men made folks nervous. Expecting the worst, most folks headed home, some left town for the weekend, others prayed inside churches, and some made warehouses and general stores bedrooms.

While Chas and Jackie Ray were in bed, rumors spread about the Cowboys overtaking the town, so Sheriff Ellis sent word by telegraph to neighboring towns for help days earlier.

"We need more deputies, trained men, good men with guns and rifles to help defend the first county in Texas," said Sheriff Ellis. "We need men sworn to handle law and order in Crockett. Send men ready to fight. STOP. No one had responded to the telegraph message in forty-eight hours.

From high above the town, I sat between Chas and Jackie Ray, and we witnessed a historical day in Houston County and made our own bets and plans.

"What strange moon made outlaws and entertainers find Crockett, Texas, Atohi?" said Chas. On small occasions, the man sought wisdom, which, in time, I felt called to render.

"There's an old Cherokee saying, Chas. There's a battle inside a man to win, told by my grandfather, and his deep voice lingers over me on nights like tonight. Even though the Cherokee Nation has been displaced and scattered about the land, a man must determine which side of the animal lives inside his heart and which wolf will win the fight."

Leaning back on his elbows, the roof still warm from the day's sunshine, and by the sour look on his face, Jackie Ray became a skeptic of my Cherokee story.

"What do you mean, Atohi?" said Jackie Ray. His hat tipped when he chuckled. "How does a wolf live inside a man's heart?"

"Inside of you," I replied, "there's two wolves: one has an ego, self-pride, greed, and jealousy, and a strong wolf battles to win the fight." I looked at Jackie Ray and Chas, faces blank and curious to listen to my grandfather's story. "The second wolf also lives inside of you." I nudged Jackie Ray's shoulder. "That wolf is truthful, faithful, kind, generous, and full of forgiveness, wrapped with the fur of love and peace. That wolf speaks with a good spirit and a gentle heart."

"Ain't no wolves inside of me, are they, Atohi?" said Jackie Ray. He filled his face with doubt and independent thoughts, and his head turned like a white canvas that needed colors of paint to make it useful again.

"Which wolf will win, Atohi?" said Chas. The man's eyes tightened as the last orange rays of sunlight glowed across the land. "Who wins the fight?"

"My grandfather said there's only one real answer, Brave Atohi: the wolf that wins, is the wolf that you feed your heart to, men."

"So, tonight," said Chas, face convinced, "it makes perfect sense that this night will prove if the Great Wolf story is true. Cowboys will feed the Evil Wolf, I predict. And ale and whiskey are being fed to the Rough Riders now. The good folks of Crockett, Texas, will see a war and not a wolf of peace. We'll find out which wolf they aim to feed tonight, my friend."

"My grandfather would agree with you, Chas," I said and spoke with great confidence.

"I believe your grandfather is right," said Chas. He stood and ducked his head, walking inside the hotel window. We followed him and found chairs and rested.

"How do we aim to defeat the Cowboys and fight the Rough Riders, Atohi?" said Jackie Ray. Back against the wall, head tilted and still curious about feeding a wolf.

"I noticed Cowboys didn't remove their saddles, and a brave Cherokee notices such things like that. Rough Riders did the same."

"Why do you think so?" said Jackie Ray.

"They don't plan to stay too long. Short timers," said Chas, arms crossed. "And they didn't book rooms when I checked with the hostess, I noticed. They just kept on walking; some men in the saloon, and others stood guard. Men are at the corral, too."

"Count your men," I said. "Count your men, just like Preacher Chet Bellew did on Sundays, counting each one. Know how many people you're dealing with and how many witnesses are around to keep tabs." I saw a curious look about my friends. "Who is absent from the bank? Who is watching the town? He always told me that much. When I was young, riding in the woods of North Carolina, men followed me. The good pastor Chet had to shoot a man off his horse, who trailed us. He knew there were three of them. That was the day he taught me to count my enemies and get to know my friends. Later, he shot the second man at long range, and the third was killed as fog drifted across the tall mountains."

Three men left for the buzzards and bears.

"Did you hear that owl?" said Jackie Ray, who stood at the window.

"The eagle, the owl, and the crow flew across Crockett," I said. "The owl is a Cherokee messenger. The eagle is for the battle and can be peaceful. The crow is a time to talk, a sacred bird, winged and full of wisdom. I'm still a warrior, boys."

They felt confident that my Cherokee stories had truth.

"Are we going to fight or have peace tonight?" said Chas. His fingers were clutched underneath his chin, and steady eyes meant deep thought.

"There'll be no peace, Chas," said Jackie Ray. "If you see hundreds of armed men in one place, the time of peace has passed, and the owl has sent his message of a Great War from the male Eagle. The battle will be tonight, and the crow has given us his best wisdom."

The wind blew the treetops a long way off, and twilight was peaceful as I had coffee with two men of courage and wisdom.

"You took the message from my Cherokee tongue," I said. My heart was satisfied with Jackie Ray, thoughts composed, and for the first time since his birth, he made sense. "How did you know all of that?"

"I just guessed," said Jackie Ray.

His shoulders lifted, and I lost my faith.

"Just an educated guess," said Jackie Ray. "Preacher Bellew told how young men needed to use their heads and put together the pieces of their surroundings. I prepare myself that way each day." He pressed his hands atop his britches and sighed.

"What surrounds us now," said Chas, "is men who wouldn't mind killing us if the Great Eagle calls us into battle." Chas nervously tapped his legs. "Now what, Atohi?"

"Why don't you keep guessing, huh?" I said, "Use that education Preacher Chet Bellew taught to find your answer?" I ducked my head outside and offered a short war cry from our window.

"You alright." Jackie Ray told us.

He held my arm because I was clumsy at night and fell.

"He's tough," said Chas. "I'll pull you up, old man."

"There's forty-nine women in the town and over three hundred men who rode in tonight," said Jackie Ray. Wiped his forehead. "I counted them at suppertime, not more than an hour ago."

"You just gave me an idea," I said. "Grab some paper, Chas."

Chas and Jackie Ray listened carefully to my plan. We knew where the fastest horses were saddled and mapped how far it was from one end of town to the other and how far it was from the saloon to the bank, and by practice, we knew the distance from the saloon to where women met men, too. Warm baths were located amid the township, and some interesting company was planned as soon as the Rough Riders and Cowboys' leaders were named. Dark taverns were filled, and Jackie Ray noticed, pivoting occasionally, and stayed in the alleyways. Walking down the dusty street, Chas felt the November wind chill his smooth face, and he stopped long enough to admire entertainers singing and dancing in the back of a saloon, a clad of endless laughter.

Across the street, The Houston Restaurant served slow-roasted beef and baked chicken with butternut squash and string beans. Dessert was a good portion of English Plum Pudding paired with dark coffee, steamy, and waving above white cups through the window.

We stayed off the roof, talked in the busy hotel lobby, and then decided to take a routine stroll down the loud, crowded streets of Crockett. Amid the strange people, peacekeepers from Jasper County showed up. I had the eyes of a hawk and ears for trouble and rage when the Rough Riders and Cowboys clashed. It was soon to strike like fire to dynamite. After one full circle of the town, each of us walked our own way and returned, and the plan was to meet at the creaky steps of the Crockett Inn.

"Multiple our steps," I said. "Like beating drums and covering this town as if we were on the hunt as Cherokee braves." My voice held low and confident, and we stood across from the sheriff's office. "We need to stick together, ducking our heads inside businesses until Sheriff Ellis assigns deputies and peacekeepers to streets and buildings. Then we'll make our own rounds and see what happens tonight. I'll find out who called this meeting in Crockett. I smell trouble."

"Yessir, Atohi," Jackie Ray said. "Trouble will come by way of the card table and taverns. I've seen a dozen fights on Bourbon Street, down in New Orleans, and it's no different in Crockett. Same type of Wolf lives here, and tempers will cut loose, and men will need to prove themselves."

"Let's meet every hour in front of the Crockett Presbyterian Church," said Chas. "Pass on what we find out to each other and how we might control this big mob of drunk outlaws." He watched the bustling town behind the post on as dark a night as we'd seen in Texas.

"Looks like about fifty riders just saddled up and left for Jasper," said a strange fellow who pointed his arm eastward. "They'll be sleepin' under the stars tonight. Wonder why the Cowboys are leaving town?" The man scratched his bald head and kept his pace.

"Someone will die," I said. "Town is packed. Restaurants have people lined up because of the performers and the strange acts that rode into town."

"Other than a few men pushing each other in the saloon, no trouble in this town," said Jackie Ray. He stood with Chas in front of the church. "Has to be a good reason why all these Rough Riders are in town."

Crossing his arms, Jackie Ray said, "I was walking by the feed store and overheard a few men talkin' about the San Antonio and Arkansas Railroad meetings in town and how lots of people are needed in Crockett next year for work. Tried to sign me up to work, too."

"I'm telling you," I said, nodding, "two wolves will reveal themselves tonight." I leaned against the porch. My hand held my forearm. "Someone will wear the face of the Evil Wolf by midnight."

"I heard Bad Carl Bellew was in town," said Chas, and he scouted the large crowd of people who passed by and crossed the street. "If that's the truth, he'll reveal himself just as people came to New Orleans to see Marie Laveau when folks needed a big favor from an outlaw and a queen."

"People like to say they've seen a legend in Texas," said Jackie Ray. His hand twitched before a big fight.

"I knew it was more than entertainers and railroad workers," said Chas, who seated himself on the steps of the Presbyterian church. "Fancy ladies draw a crowd, though."

He held his vest with pride, and Jackie Ray said, "Bet I can outplay any of them on the piano, right?" He had a contagious laugh. "Crockett might need a little excitement from a real musician. What do you think, men?"

"Wait until we see Carl Bellew's face, bud." Chas held his belt and rubbed his chin slowly. "Let's meet back here in a few. Aim to talk to the man at the corral, saddle our horses, just in case we need to ride out and catch some outlaws and Rough Riders."

"Watch yourself, Chas," I said. "Always keep an eye behind you. With that silver star on your chest, things change in Texas."

Chas walked with his hat pulled low, head down, paced to the end town, and stepped into the shadows while Jackie Ray waited for the saloon to unhinge or the poker table to be flipped against the wall.

"Can't believe you don't want me to sing, Atohi!" said Jackie Ray. The man unfolded his knife and sang low. "Hoped to gain a bit of approval from my Cherokee friend."

None was granted. Songs were not my cup of tea.

"You're a better Texas Ranger than you' are a singer," I said. "Not bad."

"Not sure I fully agree," said Jackie Ray. His smile never left him. "My voice needs practice and praise, that's all. Dang it!" He struck the post with the bottom of his fist. "Need to sing a few songs with a large crowd this size. Time to showcase my talent in front of these professional entertainers on the stage."

"Piano is fine," I said. And I scouted while he sang. I adjusted my coat, buttoned the dark flap, and stood in the cold. "But the singing sounds like a hound dog caught in a steel trap."

"No way!" said Jackie Ray. His head lifted in disagreement. "Folks say, 'Jackie Ray Monroe, you got a big voice that needs to be in San Francisco.'"

"Wish it was!" I said. My hat was full of wishes. "Hush!" head turned. "The Wolf! Gunshot, it's thatta way!"

We made our way into the dusty street, and the wind whipped, and we listened.

"Yeah, I heard the gunshot," said Jackie Ray. He folded his knife, and the young man jumped down from the porch into the dirt. "Gunshot came from where Chas was headed. The corral."

We ran as fast as two men could travel. The horses jumped.

"Not good when you hear just one shot," I said and eased my pistol from my side. "Someone is dead, Jackie Ray. Hair is standing on my neck."

The dark corral was ghostly, and the only light came from a rusty lantern, and in the dark shadows, my eyes drifted down to my friend and said, "Chas, my boy?" I spoke with a warm voice.

"The Evil Wolf revealed itself, Atohi," and Chas, who held the owner of the corral. Blood ran, and his long sleeves were soaked red.

SUNDAY RAIN

"Mr. Buck is dead," Chas said. "Shot the man who stabbed him, though."

"I'll get the sheriff," said Jackie Ray. "Report his death."

"Right behind you," the sheriff stepped up and held the hand of Mr. Buck. "He's never said a bad word to anyone. Best Presbyterian in this town. Who's the other man?"

"I saddled my horse," Chas said, "and the man jumped Mr. Buck, stabbed in the heart." Chas rolled the outlaw faceup. "The man went for his gun, and I shot him, sir."

"He has a handful of Mr. Buck's money," I said, squatting down between the two dead men. "Three days ago, Mr. Buck said, I've had enough of being robbed by Carl Bellew's Cowboys."

"I guess Mr. Buck defended himself," said Jackie Ray, who lifted the small man into an empty wagon. "More men defend themselves; men just like him have had enough of this sin."

"Do you know this outlaw, Sheriff Ellis?" I said as I lifted the wagon gate.

All of us stood by the wagon and saw the life of another good man lost to evil-doers and another family was shattered over money.

"Roscoe Millard," said Sheriff Ellis, the name rolled off his tongue like a menu item, and his face turned sour. "They say he used to ride with Carl Bellew but stopped. They must not let a man out." Held my rifle and prayed for his family.

"Sheriff Ellis," Jackie Ray asked, "is Carl Bellew in Crockett?"

All curious faces turned to the sheriff.

"Yeah," said Sheriff Ellis. "One man, Lonnie McKee, came to my office at sundown and said he saw Bad Carl Bellew ride into town with two other men. Three dark horses ride among us, men."

Chas drove the wagon to the undertaker.

"Can you trust that man's word?" said Jackie Ray. He kindly locked Mr. Buck's shop.

"Trust him with my life," said Sheriff Ellis.

I scouted to see if anyone else had heard the gunshot. No one else was on their way to that side of town. In the streets, people danced and sang, half drunk, and money was spent on beer, whiskey, and entertainment tickets.

"Mr. Buck is a good Presbyterian," said Sheriff Ellis. "Known him since the Cowboys killed his uncle and father three years ago, down at the Big Trinity River. He's hated Rough Riders and Cowboys ever since."

The sheriff rode with Chas to the undertaker's office.

"Where do Carl Bellew and his men stay in Crockett?" said Chas. He stopped the wagon three streets away, west of the corral, and waited to talk about what he knew. He hesitated.

His head turned, and a sour gaze ran across the sheriff's face because he knew more than what he said. Rumors were as much the truth in Crockett as they were deception. The sheriff was not an easy man to read, even for a Cherokee man.

He gripped his own vest gently, and Sheriff Ellis groaned and said, "West of here, a little place called Crockett's Tavern," waving his right hand. "Near Davy Crockett's Spring. They'll have guards atop houses, and seven or eight men will be inside the house beside the tavern, that is, if we make it that far."

I felt good and said, "We'll make it that far." I listened for the barn owl to send a message. "All of us need to make it in and out alive." The owner sounded, and my eyes smiled.

"Can we get past the guards, Sheriff Ellis?" said Jackie Ray.

The man with piano hands seated himself and jumped from the wagon. The undertaker was asleep. The sheriff pointed down the road to where Davy Crockett drank from the spring years before.

"Move slow, Clyde, step up," Chas said to the horse.

Sheriff Ellis handed Jackie Ray a folded message and tucked the note into his pocket. Jackie Ray handed it to the undertaker who came to the door at the telegraph office.

"I'll send word for Sheriff Dwyer and his men to join us," said Sheriff Ellis, who nodded in confidence, loading his guns. "He'll ride to Crockett Springs. We need 'em and every man who'll volunteer tonight."

We all unloaded the dead men and returned to the corral, where Sheriff Ellis and Chas mapped out a plan to get past the guards at Davy Crockett's Spring. All of us carried a Colt .44 pistol, and Sheriff Ellis held a Winchester rifle, as good with a gun as any man I'd seen in Texas. Once Jackie Ray had returned, the owl hooted a good message for us.

Inside the wagon's rear, loose, busted hay-soaked dried blood alongside a pitchfork and wrapped in a blue blanket was one more item of value. Feathers hung from the edge of the blanket. He applied the brakes. I walked up to the rear of the wagonette, wrapping both hands around the rail, and my teeth shone.

"Where did you get a bow and a dozen arrows, Jackie Ray?" I said, surprised.

"The undertaker said to give this to Atohi," said Jackie Ray, "and he'll know what to do with it. I grabbed them for you, my brother. And a good bow needs to be carried by a warrior."

"Yeah, for sure," I said, and I knew my own hands.

The feelings I had that day were no different than when I was handed my first bow in North Carolina in early autumn, and a deer was taken with the bow by sundown. Blood was on my hands, and every part of the animal was put to good use in the mountains of Cherokee. Many more deer were taken with the bow in the fall of 1851, and one bear was killed; part of the hide was on my mother's back the last time I saw her. My father proudly wore the necklace I made of dark claws, and I bet he'd never part with it.

"You bet," I said. "I owe the undertaker a chicken dinner at the Crockett Hotel, don't I?"

"He said you would say that," Jackie Ray said, slapping my shoulder. "And I know you will hit your enemy."

My heart felt it was time to move toward the spring Davy Crockett favored on his fateful journey to the Alamo in San Antonio, Texas; three months later, on 6 March 1836, he was among 188 men who were killed defending the Independence of Texas.

After two long, grueling hours, volunteers and deputies had yet to show up to stand with Crockett and pursue Bad Carl Bellew and the gang of outlaws and Rough Riders. No one volunteered to fight with us.

A short man stood in the street, held up both hands and said, "You'll die without me, amigos."

"Padre, Padre, mi amigo," said Chas.

Preacher Chet taught Chas how to speak the Spanish language.

Outnumbered. No one in our small posse had even seen Bad Carl Bellew, sober or drunk, but me, or any of his gang, for that matter. They were elusive, like mountain lions or ghosts. Not even the likes of Sheriff Ellis had seen Bad Carl Bellew, but many people wanted him dead. Only a sketch was in our hands, and we'd memorized his face for months, that is, if we saw him seated in decent light. Four men marched toward Davy Crockett's spring, Jackie Ray and Chas had been wounded in a shootout a week earlier; still healing, and Sheriff Ellis, was scared and had his reasons for wanting him dead. I knew his men set up the ambush on blind man Sammy Summers and his blacksmith crew. I knew Carl Bellew killed the Churchill family of Missouri and had sent a man to kill Marie Laveau. My eyes had witnessed enough killing by Carl Bellew and knew he'd hang for his dirty deeds, but first, I had to scout him and bypass his men.

Chapter 21
Hidden Away

The plan to raid the farm west of Crockett, where Bad Carl Bellew was stationed, became a good one. Though we had changed our minds several times, we agreed in the end. Just like the swift gray sky of fall that moved through Eastern Texas, nothing stayed the same in our conversations, and the clouds of the sky were no different than the opinions of wise men. Ideas seemed simple on paper. Guns changed Texas, but confidence was held within the ranks; just the four of us had borrowed an abandoned home.

Chickens perched high, and the coyote yip-howled and barked in the distance. My ears no longer listened to how to capture Bad Carl Bellew and his gang but seated by the open window, the sounds of nature were no different than the words of Scripture and notes of music, except when Jackie Ray used his voice.

By that time of night, the silver, ghostly moon had broken away from the gray cotton clouds, and an eerie fog rolled high through the treetops. The wind chilled my skin, or at least I thought it was the wind. I stepped outside to scout. Someone was hidden in the shadows of the cedars, lurking. I smelled smoke from a cigar before I saw his profile. My eyes caught him, and he knew it. He was not in a hurry.

Later, I slowly retreated to the dusty shack, a place recommended by the sheriff, and spoke to no one about the man with the cigar, waiting to see his purpose and if he wanted to talk. Again, my thumb found the rays of the moon over his head, and he was no longer hidden in the woods. He revealed himself when he saw my face and my gun pointed at his head.

"Man of peace," said the man, still smoking.

"Peace or pistol!" I said.

"I come in peace," said the man, wrapped in the robe of a man of God.

My heart felt calm when I saw that, indeed, he wore the clothes of the clergy. A small man with short hair, outfitted in a black robe, a square of white about his collar, stepped inside the abandoned shack. His worn hands were empty, and he waved carefully; defined in his face was more than age and concern, yet upright in his posture. The smile he shared felt sincere. Out of respect, hands shown, unarmed, he paced, and we were confident he had good intentions.

"Padre?" said Chas, closing the door behind him. "You'll meet your Maker, sneaking up behind a loaded gun, especially a Cherokee, who doesn't miss a shot."

He nodded apologetically. Candles were lit by his hand, and lanterns were pulled from hidden places like he knew the place and had done it many times before and would do it again for himself.

"Mi casa, amigos. My house of prayer and study." He gripped our hands and smiled. The smell of cigar smoke followed him around the room. "Stay as long as you like, but I already know why you are here."

"You live here?" said the sheriff. "I thought I knew everyone."

"Forgive us for entering your home," said Jackie Ray. "We're Texas Rangers."

"Sheriff Ellis." The Padre held out his hand again. "I know of you."

"I need to know you," said the sheriff.

"Yeah. This became my home after my wife disappeared in the spring, and my daughter and sons are gone," he said. "One year. The farm occupied by Bad Carl Bellew, it's mine. His gang converted the farm into his hideout. That's why you are here."

"The Great One sent us," I said.

"I am here because of no other reason." The Padre assured us.

His English seemed very poor; his eyes were sincere, though sitting at a long table meant family: wife, sons, and a daughter. Or, at least, I imagined the home that way, long ago.

"This shack is used for sessions of prayer. I followed you good men, men of the law, because God sent me to speak to you, all of you, and there will be no other time to do so than tonight," said the man, hands folded. "No other time. This is it." He stepped to the window and motioned his hand. He closed the windows.

Padre opened the door. We cocked our guns when someone approached. Jackie Ray stood beside him. He turned. Witnessed his face was pale, hands over his heart in the night.

"It's only a boy," said Jackie Ray, gun to his side.

"No guns, amigos, please. Meet my adopted son, Antonio."

I kept my pistol near until his words were proven true. Ten or eleven, the boy was young and held something. The items were covered, and the boy entered slowly.

"Pollo. Agua. Beans. Tortillas." The boy said and smiled happily. The boy sat the food atop the table and was told to leave by the Padre.

"Maybe you're just a dang spy for Carl, huh?" said Jackie Ray, hand in his chest. "Tryin' to get us killed?" He lifted the man off the ground and pulled a knife to his throat. "Tell me, Padre! Tell us all!"

"You loco!" said the clergyman. Hands lifted to fight. "I could knock you out with one punch."

"Hey, Jackie Ray," I said, rushing to his rescue. "Let him alone."

"He's a liar!" yelled Jackie Ray, close enough to see his teeth were stained from coffee.

"The man brought food," I said. "Get out of his face."

"Yessir, he can stay," said Chas. "Bless the food, Padre. We're hungry."

Jackie Ray never closed his eyes during the blessing of the meal, and Chas helped the man of God pass plates that came from an old, dusty cupboard. Each man stepped up, helped the man of the cloth, and thanked him by nodding while they held their food.

"I'm curious to know his purpose," said Sheriff Ellis, voice deep, chewing. Padre was seated in a corner, legs crossed and alone at a smaller table. "Move him beside the fire so he can talk and eat."

"I'm here to help." The man slowly stacked wood. "My name is Padre Orlando Manuel Ortiz."

We exchanged names and where we were from with him and spoke for a short moment. Padre Ortiz felt comfortable and pulled two bottles of wine, hidden and dusty but unopened, untucking the bottles from a crafted box underneath the floor. Each man took wine and chewed the chicken, watching the little man build a warm fire in his old home. The wood cracked and popped in a short while. No one spoke while he worked to keep us warm, closing the curtains, white material from a bygone time. The place was hardly a home as the wind whipped through the seams of old boards until it bent and swayed the fire. Padre Ortiz graciously split good food between five men; not a crumb was left, and no one else joined the room.

Padre Ortiz positioned his seat with his back to the glowing fire. We were attentive to his reserved way, in wait, watching him, legs crossed, and listening for why God sent him to the sheriff and a trio of Rangers.

"Death will greet you if you charge tonight," said the clergyman. "That is why God sent me. My words will save your life."

"We plan to raid and capture Bad Carl Bellew," said Jackie Ray. "We have the guns and men to do the job. We are not open to patience."

"You are stupid, and you do not listen to my words!" shouted Padre Ortiz. His voice was loud, face tight, and he stood over Jackie Ray at that moment, hands waving.

"You're starting to piss me off, old man," said Jackie Ray, rattling his chair.

"Why do you think we'll die, Padre?" said Chas, gun in hand, leaning forward.

"Carl begs for trouble. Loves to fight." Ortiz warmed his hands by the fire. "I have given you food, fire, and wine. I hope we will become friends tonight."

"We know Carl is a gunslinger. We're grateful for your help," said Chas. "You have not heard our plan yet, have you?"

"No," said Padre Ortiz, brown-black eyes cautious. "I know your plan, the wrong path, amigos. I am sent to save your lives. Take heed."

"What is your way of thinking?" I said, elbows on the table, hat in my hand. The room lit up with more firewood and candles and felt like a home again.

"My plan is to rest you here tonight and march you before first light." Padre Ortiz walked around the room, shoulders back, pacing as he must've done amid his Sunday sermons, hands behind his back, deep in thought. "I know the terrain better than anyone in town. I have few possessions. Carl must have thought my home was vacant, but my time has been spent here, in this shack, since my wife was taken in the spring. My heart is not good any longer."

"Do you travel between towns, Padre," said the sheriff.

He nodded.

"This man has been sent to save us." The sheriff relaxed.

His pacing reminded me of another man of God.

"What else do you know?" I asked him.

Ortiz was a good man of spirit and knowledge, settled down all at one table, and carefully warmed us up to his plan. The man spoke as if he was having a night of prayer and felt led by a Higher power.

"My thoughts, men, make your move before daybreak, Cherokee," said the clergyman, back seated, fireplace to his back, and hands opened.

"Maybe you're trying to expose our position, smoke and fire, huh, Ortiz?" said Jackie Ray, drinking, who hurried to the window and scouted for others, more men in the woods.

"What do you mean?" said Padre Ortiz, hands together.

"Smoke out a signal to some of your friends who rent the large farm. How'd they get that track of land of yours, and you hadn't come to Sheriff Ellis for help, huh?" said Jackie Ray, eyes beamed at Padre Ortiz. "I'm no lawyer, but how's Carl Bellew have control of your property, and you ain't reported it?"

"He's squatting on my land, sir," said Padre Ortiz. "Rumor is, Carl is headed to Jasper to see his new baby boy. Sheriff Dunn's daughter."

"What does that mean?" said Chas, hands clutched. "Does Sheriff Dunn of Jasper want Carl Bellew dead because his unmarried daughter had his child?"

"Yes, Chas. It makes sense to me," said Sheriff Ellis. "Does Sheriff Dunn have a warrant against Carl, some evidence of a crime, or has Sheriff Dunn made up this story to get us to bring Carl Bellew to Jasper just so he can kill a man for courting his daughter?"

"There's no warrant. I assure you of that. Are we sure Carl Bellew has committed a crime?" said Chas, unfolding the paper with his uncle's face sketched on the front page. "We need witnesses. All we have are rumors."

Jackie Ray snatched the page from the hand of Chas.

"Paper says, WANTED - DEAD or ALIVE," said Jackie Ray, walking over beside Padre Ortiz, eyes on the poster. "Sheriff Ellis, sir, how do we know this man who fed us is not feeding us a line of crap? I just ain't buying how he knows all this stuff, but he's not tryin' to kill Carl Bellew for himself and courting a man's daughter. That's what I'd like to know, right?"

"Wrong. His faith holds him back," said Sheriff Ellis. "Only time will tell, gentlemen," said the sheriff. "I'm not discounting his story…. But…" pointing at Padre Ortiz, "why do we need to attack in the morning if we have no witnesses to prove any of his story is true? Men, I have a wife at home. Until someone comes up with witnesses or murder charges against Bad Carl Bellew, my time here is done. Rumors aren't enough to chase anyone."

"I have to give a man of faith some credit. On second thought, maybe God did send Padre Ortiz to help us," said Jackie Ray, shaking hands with the man of the cloth. "But I'm not so sure of this raid myself. Padre, here, is our light in a dark world. I'll drink to that story and his plan."

The sheriff stood in the doorway.

"Whoa. Whoa. Stop!" I said, moving toward the door. "Where are you going, Sheriff Ellis?"

Door in his hands, he said, "I have no substantial charge against Carl Bellew. It's only hearsay and an angry grandfather in Jasper, Texas, who needs him." He laughed. "And I have a town of Rough Riders and Cowboys prowling, I bet, taking my town apart board by board. Was good meeting you men. Padre Ortiz, stop by my office on Monday for coffee and eggs. I'd like to add my family to your congregation."

"Please do. You bring food, I'll bring prayer," said Padre Ortiz, who smiled and closed the door.

"Do you mind if we stay here for the night, Ortiz?" said Chas.

"Please stay. I will be at my brother-in-law's home for the night," said Padre Ortiz. "As I said, stay as long as you need, Rangers. I'll check with you in the morning."

Padre Ortiz fired up his tobacco again and walked until the smell faded away down a long, narrow road east of Crockett, and the man disappeared into the night. Jackie Ray finished two bottles of wine and fell asleep. Chas, deep in thought, didn't say much and stayed awake, penning a letter, until the fire became loose embers. Then, I added more wood. Chas stumbled to his bedroom, tapping the wall as if words were held there and reserved for another time and place. Two cats ran from his room to where I was seated in the small parlor.

Something was on my mind, and no sleep met my eyes that night. The glow of the full moon turned my thoughts to what was spoken of by Padre Ortiz, his wife, and his daughter, and my time was spent in meditation. I asked the Great One for help to absorb the stories I'd heard. My grandfather taught me to sleep in my moccasins. Then, the coyote barked, and my feet met the ground and out the door, and I walked a new path until morning.

Chapter 22
No Other Way

Sadly, a former U.S. Army officer said that the life of a Cherokee was no different than the lowly, unwanted life of a wild, raggedy coyote. The battle raged inside my head to prove him different, and that was intolerance in my book. Pine needles and the scent of fresh cedars waved in the heavy air; I was restless. The glow of the striking moon lit the way, and a trail was outlined by the tree line. There was no other way out of Crockett until I saw Carl Bellew, just like the curious Thunderbird saw the plains of Texas and spread its wings across the glorious sky for the hunt. My eyes popped open each time the coyote yip-barked and circled the shack, scouting ahead and doing what Sheriff Dunn and the governor had hired us to do. I scouted. Many people feared Bad Carl Bellew and being grafted into the family, my destiny was awakened that night, and I wanted to take down the defiant man. The smoothness of my tanned face was painted, pressed in gray and black ashes from a forgotten fireplace, mixed with the good earth. The moon found the path I needed, a narrow passage, and I bent, bow in hand.

The farther I scouted from Kentucky, the more fragmented the broken mirror felt in my front shirt pocket. Dark hair striped with dark ashes, and I matched the fur of the barking coyote at the edge of the trench. Both animal and man were on the hunt, lurking the same, in the same world. The shack was amid the dusty farm and near Crockett Spring. I scouted the place at night, a land owned by Padre Orlando Manuel Ortiz; his voice told the story of how he missed his wife and family, known by amigos as Papa and Padre. Armed with arrows and a bow from the kindness of the undertaker, I followed the trail of the coyote, and the Great One warned of the dangers, echoing in my clouded head. I stopped, saw the Ortiz farm in the distance, and made my plan alone. Behind tall cedars and apple trees, the road ran west and stretched to a popular town called Buffalo, and beyond it, Waco.

"Someone is here," I told myself. "The good earth moves."

Sounds made by a man on horseback, body low and fast, face unknown in the distance, who rode from the east, crossed Crockett Spring, and down into the bedrock. I scouted the rider. My next step was into his pathway.

"Whoa. Whoa." I said, and my bow anchored.

The horse reared. The man's eyes were as big as bottles.

"Chas Bellew," I said, relieved. "Where are you headed, Ranger?"

"No rest for the law," he said. The horse settled down, and Chas dismounted. "Aim to hunt Carl Bellew down, Atohi. Same as you. I want to find him and settle this."

"Where's Jackie Ranger?"

"Drunk again."

I dropped my bow. "Why didn't we leave him in Kentucky, Chas?"

"I thought wrong. Knew where you were headed by the handprints on the door. No Cherokee snored in the next room. Your boots are too loud. I thought you were building a porch." He grinned and tied his horse.

"Blood brother," I said. The animal rested from the hard ride. "What's your plan, Atohi?" My friend scouted the farmhouse with my telescope and couldn't see anything at night.

"Don't have it yet."

"You can't ride into his camp, Chas, and expect to live."

"Nope," declared Chas. Touched his thin beard and said, "There's another way. Not sure what I was thinking, but we must get Carl. People in this town live in fear because of my uncle. I'll do something. Do you think he'll talk?"

"Nope. Should we offer beignets and coffee and a spot of tea?" He grinned.

"Get serious."

"Every rancher has a hound on the porch," Chas said, hidden behind the barn. "Look, the long-eared hound, an old black and tan, is in front of the door. I told you."

"Blackie is unlucky," I said. "God's not with us. The hound will bark. Listen?"

Our faces changed when the dog trailed something into the woods and never returned.

"Might be the luck we need," said Chas, low behind the fence. He suddenly released seven horses from the barn of Carl Bellew and his outlaws. Then, we carried a cut of alfalfa hay to an open field, and the horses made less noise, fed themselves, and wandered off.

"No guards are out tonight," said Chas, who made his way back to the fence.

I scouted the barn as Chas walked in my direction. No sign of the dog or the horses, open shot, free-range. The owl flew from the barn, roosted in an apple tree, and landed without a sound.

Pounding like a Cherokee drum before an attack, my heart thumped inside my chest. We watched seven muscular, dark horses vanish into the distance, making my heart covet the animal's freedom. They slowly slipped away into the golden dry fields, horse after horse, breathing in gestation, caught in the spirit of being released. My wish was to own them, scattering the animals in all directions, an uncivil act. We needed them far away from the outlaws. Three of them stayed on the path to the Town of Buffalo, two trotted to Gary Hill, and two horses hesitated and ran eastward toward the Town of Crockett. The battle was about to commence. There was no way out of either side of the house: a cliff, a high wall, with one way in and the same way out. Chas checked his pistol and saw my arrows and the rifle; still, all we had to defend ourselves …was in our hands. No swords. No cannons. No dynamite. No way out and not a friend in sight.

"I wish Jackie Ray was here with his guns," said Chas, hand on his face, humming. "Ready to fight."

Branches snapped under the feet of a man, and the smell of three-day-old clothes was nearby. His face was pale, closing the gap. The man cleared his throat and breathed heavily.

"Good men," said Jackie Ray. "Didn't think I'd let ya take all the credit for raiding the farm of Carl Bellew, did ya?"

"Well, I'll be. It's Dandy Wine," said Chas, grinning.

"Half sober, half-naked," I said. "The Great One told me we would battle together, chasing and fighting." A big smile ran across the face of each man. "Third gun makes it far better."

"Dang it. Didn't bring my pistol, Rangers," said Jackie Ray, lip bit. "The cat woke me up. I followed the cat straight to you."

"God help us," said Chas, whispering. "Might die now." He kicked the ground. "I'll tell you what, man. Take my horse, get your dang guns, Ranger." He removed his hat and said, "Don't need to be forward, bud. This is the day we live or die, huh?"

"Yeah. Where'd that cat go?" said Jackie Ray, toes wiggling at the end of his busted boots, and his smile missed a tooth.

"Forget the kitten, get ya guns." I grabbed his shirt.

"There goes the dang cat under the porch," said Chas. "Jesus, can you help us? He stomped on the ground. "Get out of here, Jackie Ray, go back to the shack." He pushed him. "You and your cat, gonna get us killed."

"I'll get my ammo, hold your horses," said Jackie Ray.

He limped his busted boot down the narrow way, where Chas slapped his horse on the tail. Jackie Ray mumbled and wobbled, trying to find his path back to the shack.

The Texas Star pinned to our chest was a daily reminder of law and order, and what we signed up for was not an easy job. We could not open fire, guns blazing, and shoot up the place without regard to our own safety. We were outmanned. Our message was one of respect and consideration. Somewhat. But we were being paid to track Carl Bellew, and Sheriff Dunn of Jasper County depended on our courage and boldness to get the man back to Jasper.

"Who the heck is out there?" yelled a man from the front porch.

"Carl," I said. "Your kin, not mine."

"That's his face," said Chas, body behind a tree. "Big man."

I spoke low to Chas, hidden in the shadows of the woods. Only God could see my face.

"I knew him once as a young man, Chas, "I said and remembered his abuse on my face. "Before you were born. He turned against me because of my skin. Carl disliked Preacher Chet for taking me into his home, feeding a Cherokee brave."

We no longer needed the WANTED poster. The man was broadsided, flesh and blood, and an easy target stood before us. Years had passed since I had seen Carl Bellew. Blind man Sammy Summers was right; Carl and men like Carl sought glory and fame and wanted to be feared and known. Carl was disgraceful and the worst one of three brothers. My teeth gritted. I wanted him locked up, and he left us no choice.

"We can take him," said Chas, whispering. "Same deep voice as my father, half-dressed and carelessly stood in a decent light, too. No question about it. Do not move, Atohi. Carl is looking this way."

"Sounds a lot like Chet," I said. "The hound is back, yonder."

The long-eared hound had returned from the hunt and chased the cat under the front porch. Then, the kitten, being faster, brought first blood to the ear of the hound and jumped inside the window. Texas was full of animals, wild and domestic, too many animals to count.

I favored the owl who had followed us from Carter County, Kentucky. The same owl had faithfully flown to New Orleans, and now, the closeness of his friendship was felt at Crockett Spring. More birds would have been a gift from the Great One, but God did not send more birds. I knew the face of the owl, dark painted eyes, and we trusted him. Chas disagreed, but I knew only one owl, our friend. He was not named, but I thought he may have known my name.

"Texas Rangers!" yelled Chas. My friend stood in the dark but was hidden and safe from the pistol of his enemy. "We got this place surrounded, Carl Bellew. You can turn yourself in, or we'll drag you out!"

"I'll die before I'd give up to a couple cowardly Rangers," Carl said, dropping down. He ran inside and yelled, "Get up! Rangers got us surrounded. Up, get your guns, outlaws. Move! It's time!"

Warm rays of sunshine burst through the fog in the early morning; the sash of Cowboys, guns firing, loud voices, and the world was no longer peaceful. Five rounds busted bark off the barn near our position. Chas had taken his post inside the barn, directly across from the outlaws. Pieces of wood fell at his feet. Chas fired and hit one man who fell dead from the second-story window. The longest shot Chas had ever taken with a pistol, a fatal hit, one that counted.

"Now what, Chas, wise guy?" I said it that way. "You just opened the door to Hades, didn't ya? Agreed to wait on Jackie Ray."

"Should have killed Carl when he opened the door," said Chas from behind the barn. "Long overdue, though," heavily breathing, guns aimed. Pistols in both hands, and the man unloaded each pistol on the outlaws. "Got a better plan than being held up behind this barn, Cherokee."

My eyes raised, and I said, "Yep." I nodded. "Gotta a good idea. Time to bring some fire."

"You aim to smoke a peace pipe with them, do ya, Sitting Bull?" said Chas. His confident eyes widened.

"Burn 'em out," I told him.

"It will look like fire fell from the sky, Chas," I said as I struck the flint, lit the first arrow, and drew the bow again.

"Pow!" A loud shot came from the farmhouse.

"You hit, Atohi?"

"Yeah! First time." I said. Down on the ground, dazed, in pain.

My head spun, eyes fogged, and blood ran down my left shoulder. Pain stung like a thousand summer hornets, and I was mad at myself for being in the open far too long. With all my strength, I released the arrow into the morning sky, and my mission was to burn them out. Less of a warrior than in my vision, my position was low, and I rested behind a wide oak tree, and nature blocked many rounds. From the darkness of the woods, more arrows were fired, and the Great One had supplied a valuable weapon from the undertaker. War paint and blood, and one thought crossed my mind: "I intended to keep my word and protect Chas against seven outlaws."

My friend ran to my rescue, but not before she shot the second man.

"How's the wound, Atohi?" said my friend. "Need some lemon water?"

"Wish I had a cup and Millie to pour it," I told him, coughing.

"Make it rain, Cherokee!"

"More arrows. More fire." I said and pulled back.

"Tell this story with fire and smoke, Atohi!" yelled Chas.

I saw my father's face in the morning clouds and had new strength from his smile, a father's smile, and hidden in a thicket of evergreen, Jackie Ray ran and took his stance; his face was sweaty. He tucked a pillowcase into my hands and knew I could bring fire.

"Hey, Jack wagon, do you think I can cut this cloth with one arm? Huh?"

"Use your knife, Cowboy," said the piano player. He laughed and adjusted his hat.

"Cowboy? Cowboy!" I yelled. "I should scalp your top, Jackie Ray."

That man knew how to strike a fire inside my veins. Then, I ran like a Cherokee, moving as I once did with younger legs, stronger arms, and better eyes. "Cowboy?" I wrapped the linen and fired it.

Then Jackie Ray held his grin and joined Chas behind the barn and scouted our enemies. I stood in amazement and watched two young men, close as brothers, raised from scrawny boys, become fighters and Texas Rangers, two of the best men I ever knew. A drop of water ran slowly down my cheek, or was it Sunday rain? To the north thunder and lightning struck in the distance, and I was certain clouds held rain, for sure. I was relieved, a short and definite reminder of Preacher Chet Bellew; the man said, "Like a bear lying in wait, like a lion in hiding, he dragged me from my path, mangled, and I drew my bow to defend what was mine." I loved the way he taught in his sermons. His words were my daily bread, but it was a bad time for raindrops or tears.

Gun belts loaded with ammo were wrapped around Jackie Ray's waist and shoulders; he prepared for war, shot after shot, and the man gave it all he had. Chas walked, chin up, eyes down, and carried himself into the gunfight with his favorite Winchester rifle, two Colt pistols, and more courage than a small army.

Jackie Ray stumbled, wine laced, tongue dry, and fired anyway. I did not claim that boy. Chas could not deny his shot was true and deadly, even as he stumbled.

"Couldn't wait on me, huh, Chas?" said Jackie Ray, who loaded his pistol again.

"No time to discuss drinking and catcalls, Jackie Ray," said Chas. "Pick a man, take him down."

"We are outmanned," said Jackie Ray, who pressed his back against the barn. "My eyes are salty with sweat, bud."

"I'll pick up the slack. I got more firepower for Carl," said Chas. He struck a cigar and puffed. "More courage, too."

Jackie Ray sobered up, eyes clear, checking his pants when a round hit between his knees.

"That fellow is a poor shot," said Jackie Ray. "Close one, though, Chas. Too dang close."

Chas dropped low, rifle in hand, hidden behind a feed trough, and fired, one eye closed, and missed his target. Five outlaws remained. Windows were broken from the farmhouse, and more men fired at the barn, where Chas and Jackie Ray were positioned. Stepping into a clearing, my bloody hands fired another arrow into the farmhouse, and curtains caught fire, and the old house was engulfed. Dark smoke filled the sky, flames ran about the farmhouse, and dust exploded inside the highest level of the home when the seventh arrow hit a lantern. The farmhouse burned, top to bottom, and five men were still inside. Hungry for death.

"I hit two men with my rifle," said Chas. He held his position. "Three more men. One man ran into the woods."

"Good," I said. "Saved his own life. Two outlaws then."

"How many men do you see?" said Jackie Ray, who fired. "I hit one. When he splashed into the water trough, my heart sobered up. I'll take a nap after this fight."

Two men knew our position. One had escaped.

"Atohi just killed a man with his arrow!" said Jackie Ray. He changed his position.

"Take Carl. Dead or Alive!" said Chas. No horses. No wagons. No way out.

The clothes I took from the line belonged to a lady. Chas saw the dress, too.

"Inside! A woman!" I yelled. Aiming at the house, I fired another flaming arrow into the window and hit the bedding and blankets. The farmhouse became an inferno.

My mind flashed back to when Preacher Chet Bellew counted his congregation and touched each shoulder: men, women, kids, and young babies. He blessed them on Sunday morning. So, he taught us to be no different, counting friends, enemies, and even horses. We took his advice as Rangers, counted boots and clothes, and noticed such things. Good advice. The Great One revealed that a woman, a brave woman who sought freedom, huddled inside a burning home.

"Two men are inside," I said, fingers up. "One is Carl. Who can breathe inside that fire?"

The door opened, and a man ran out, fire climbing his back.

"Pow!" a gun went off, and the burning man fell from the porch.

Carl stepped in the doorway and shot the man a second time.

"Coward!" Carl yelled.

He fell three feet from the water trough, a moment too late. Chas was to my left and witnessed the murder. I saw the face of Bad Carl Bellew, laughing after he fired on his own man. His hair was gray by that time in his life, and his jawline was the same as his brother, Chet.

Eyes of hesitation, Chas could have killed Bad Carl Bellew, blindfolded at that distance. He did not take the spur-booted man down. Though I trained Chas to hunt and fish the rivers of Kentucky as a young man, to take the life of Carl Bellew was not the killing of Jackie Ray or the Cherokee who tells this story, but for Chas. It was much different when blood fought blood, like the time of the Civil War. Times that redefined such days, I suppose.

It appeared Carl knew he was being followed, and word spread fast to East Texas, and he rode from Waco to Crockett to find out for himself who chased him. Uncle and nephew, outlaw and Ranger, stood respectfully and saw each other for the first time, face-to-face, forty paces from each other, faces red with revenge. Neither man was the same since he'd left Kentucky, and life became hard. The world became cold and changed men with time. The War hardened Carl and carved him into a killer, the way certain men defended themselves to stay alive. I needed Chas alive; my bow was aimed and ready. My eyes saw Jackie Ray positioned to my right, and the two men, eyes locked in admiration, caught between the seeds of law and order, sin and evil.

Who would win? Crazy thoughts ran across the faces of fighters and felt no different for a Christian.

"Spanish lady," I said. "I was right, Jackie Ray. Inside!"

"Ayuda!" she cried and held the kitten. "Ayuda! Ayuda!" she screamed, face filled with fear and anguish, and the tail of her dress lifted in flames.

I covered Jackie Ray as he ran to aid the lady. Carl cocked his gun and aimed at the lady or Jackie Ray, but he did not fire his pistol. He had another plan.

"Mrs. Ortiz?" yelled Jackie Ray. Dazed. He remembered her pretty face and long dark hair from the picture held by Padre Ortiz at the dinner table the night before.

"My wife!" yelled Padre Orlando Manuel Ortiz, arms extended.

I knew Padre Ortiz witnessed the gunfight. Mrs. Ortiz had been taken from her home a year earlier by Carl Bellew, who traveled through Crockett for God knows what reason. Carl knew Chas Bellew had found him, and he waited.

"Pow!" One man fell when Chas fired, and the man who had escaped returned to protect Carl. He had something to prove and now was dead.

"Click." Carl aimed at Chas a second time. "Click."

Chas walked up to his face and said, "No ammo, Carl, but I have a message from Denton, Kentucky."

"What message, boy?"

Chas drew back and rang his bell. "Touch another woman!"

"Everyone is gone, Carl," said Jackie Ray.

"The Great One did not show me that punch," I said to Chas.

Jackie Ray had a blank face. I knew Carl Bellew would not surrender or admit defeat in front of anyone. By that time, members of the

Catholic Church had followed Padre Ortiz and cheered for Chas when he struck Carl.

The battered woman fell into the arms of her husband, feet no longer on the ground, eyes rushing with tears, and she was happy.

"I love you, Maria," said Padre Ortiz, heart satisfied.

Arms around his shoulders, she said, "I love you, Orlando."

Her smile was genuine and endless. The man held Maria's wet face while she rested. In all my life, I had never seen two faces with more happiness than what I witnessed in the Spanish couple. Their daughter was still out there, whereabouts unknown. Sixteen was a tender age to be alone. She had also vanished. Someone knew her whereabouts.

Jackie Ray stood close to my bloody shoulder, guns cocked. The moment was intense. Suddenly, the scream of the eagle cried over the fiery farmhouse. The lonesome Thunderbird sounded across the black sky, and I knew the Lord was with us. Like the sound of a thousand horses, more rain fell across the land, soft and wet faces. Ashes floated to the heavens and fell back to earth, where the trail of black smoke faded and drifted for miles, dark and wavy in the cool breeze. Families gathered from the church to welcome home sweet Maria Ortiz. Faces had broken open into tears, arms opened gently, and the scars of hearts were healed. Prayers answered, even from folks far from the reverence of the Lord Jesus Christ.

"Well, well, Cherokee Atohi, baby Bellew," said Carl, face holding a mirk. "You rode a long way to get whipped again."

"Carl, you ain't that bad," I said. "He's no boxer like John Heenan."

Walking up beside Chas, Mr. Ortiz said, "One favor. Fight Carl like the bare-knuckle champ John Heenan and Tom King did years ago in Wyoming?"

"My eyes have journeyed a long road, Carl, to see you beaten," I said, and held my bloody arm and paced toward him. "No cheating, and it's a fight until death." My face flushed, slapping my bloody shoulder that held a bullet. "Try me again, Carl. I am no Thomas King."

Carl took a swing at my head, and he missed.

"I can match you up, Cherokee," said Carl.

Arms wide, Chas stepped between us.

"No. No, brother Atohi," said Chas. "This fight is mind."

SUNDAY RAIN

Chas turned, and the sky opened over Crockett; a slight grin rose on his face, and draped over my shoulder was my bow. Chas rolled his long-sleeved shirt to his elbow and smiled.

Jackie Ray checked the necks and chests of fallen men. All gone.

He carted the grave-bound men to the wagon.

More Catholics crowded. No one objected to the fight, an eye for an eye, and I held Bad Carl at gunpoint inside the church until Sunday Mass was over. Carl refused to take confession and said only a few words to Padre Ortiz, words I cannot repeat. His face was slapped by yours truly for speaking that way in front of women and God.

"Hey, Chas," said Jackie Ray, walking under the oaks. "You are not gonna fight this man, are you, buddy? Twice your size."

After Sunday Mass, even more people had gathered: more outlaws, more Catholics, young boys, and folks from the Town of Crockett collected and made bets on the fight.

"Si, Jackie Ray, he will fight the pig," whispered Maria Ortiz inside the back of the small Catholic church. "If you don't, I will."

We all walked outside.

Maria Ortiz walked behind Chas, pushed his shoulder, and said, "Cut off his reason to live."

"You wanna dance, Carl?" said Chas, arms loose, head canted, and he waited. "Time has come, high noon."

"Dance to the death, Chas," said Carl.

"Hold up! Chas has changed his mind!" said Padre Ortiz. "We fight at sundown, amigos."

Jackie Ray walked his friend beside the church.

"Chas, people will call you chicken to delay," Jackie told him.

Chas ran after Jackie Ray and choked his friend.

"No one will call me anything!" yelled Chas. He held his throat as tight as he could. "The man of God said sundown."

"Let him go! Stop this bickering, now!" I said and divided two men about to kill each other.

"Padre Ortiz said sundown, and that's when it will be!" said Chas, hands up, and he walked away.

Chapter 23
All or Nothing at All

Shortly after midday on Sunday, the 17th day of December 1871, Padre Ortiz had graciously finished his long-winded sermon, having milked out every word in Hebrew and the Greek language associated with hardships and hopes Jeremiah had penned in the Book of Lamentations. Since his time in Crockett, Padre Ortiz had never been marked absent from worship, and that day, he shared his dedication. The faithful, dark-eyed minister was not about to disappoint his church members because his wife had been lost for a year, and the Lord was his Source of recovery. His streaming eyes provided such relief and rich happiness, telling the story the way it matched the Good Book before his eyes.

"Today, congregation," said Padre Ortiz, handkerchief in hand, "might you pardon my tears," eyes pressed. "But on a day like this, this happy day, I am delighted to cry out my gladness when I found my loving wife, Maria, alive and well. I anticipate many mornings of warm coffee together. God is good, church," hands raised. "But before it can be complete and prayers answered, my hope rests on the three amigos, Chas, Jackie Ray, and Atohi, to fulfill their promise. These outstanding Rangers ride for the good sake of Texas. Mostly, they ride for the Lord. They have promised to find my daughter, Isa; she is so lovely, and one day, she will join us in a fiesta and walk free again."

Word spread about the bare-knuckle fight between the Texas Ranger and Bad Carl Bellew. More people came from the countryside for church services, dinner, and amusement. More paraded in for the fight than predicted. Two fighters were no different than a famed bullfighter from Spain or Mexico, drawn to power, anticipation, and action. Like predator and prey, racing to Crockett for a rare event, for meals, and for drinks, even if the fight was held on a Sunday night. The fight was a drawing card, a series of bets from the largest crowd to ever assimilate in the Town of Crockett, the first of any kind, which redefined the town in business and entertainment.

After the benediction, the minister spoke of the goodness of God and said, "Lord, let Chas be the victor over the devil man, Carl. Amen and Amen."

The Padre spoke of "The Soul Objective of Life" and how each man and woman would be remembered for their walk on earth and how they conducted themselves with the brethren and among sinners. Padre Ortiz decided to preach his first sermon in English, so the message would not be lost in translation or forgotten for lack of understanding. The same sermon followed in the evening service, yet spoken with zeal in his native tongue.

"In the gracious words of the Weeping Prophet Jeremiah, I remember my afflictions and wandering, the bitterness and the gall, I will remember them, and my soul is downcast within me, yes, I call to mind." His voice softly raised, "therefore I have hope. Friends, that is the soul objective. Take this hope forward today and every day, and again, I say, "Therefore, we have hope.""

He invited the town's people in attention, the largest crowd he had ever seen at his Catholic church, pressed each hand and counted 174. Jackie Ray could not be found. Chas and I sat behind Carl Bellew, the man made to attend, being persuaded at gunpoint. The murderer was locked in chains and cuffs with the help of Sheriff Ellis and Marshal Johnson, and Carl sat between the smirking faces of law and order.

Three hours before the fight, more people gathered at taverns, people booked rooms and talked on the streets about the upcoming fight. Patrons swung the doors of saloons to see what would become of the town, known for the railroad and bare-knuckle fighters. Outside of town, Padre Ortiz found Chas and talked about what was to happen in the match, just as he had seen in other places as a professional referee and boxer in Mexico.

"Please don't request a dismissal of the fight," said Chas, face tight and serious. "Turn around if forgiveness is your request."

His Spanish accent was well-defined around his church family and at home. Still, he had his own opinion, aside from his sermon on Sunday or anywhere else. He knew how to speak the best English and offer counsel as well.

"Chas. May I take a seat, amigo?"

"I hoped we might talk before the fight," said Chas, who brushed the ground.

"Son, I like you," said Padre Ortiz, legs crossed and a hand cupped each knee. "If I had my son back, my hope is that he would be brave, just like you."

"Me loco, Padre!" said Chas, bent in laughter.

They leaned back, and the two men were filled with joy.

"Chas," said Padre Ortiz, with his contagious and grand smile. "Brother in Christ, my thoughts are simple words." Hands held his knees, and he followed, "I hope you kill Carl with your bare hands for the way he treated my wife, taking her away to Waco for a year."

"Is this a sermon on reconciliation and forgiveness?"

"No, Chas. Carl's act is punishable," said the Padre, eyes stern. "Unforgivable. And who knows where my daughter is now. I believe he has sold her or traded her to banditos, and her life swapped for gold or who knows what. My life is smaller without her in it." He sniffed, and tears rolled down his face. "But he knows something, and God knows it all. I pray my daughter is safe, Chas."

"My heart is broken for you," Chas said. Strength and certainty rose in his eyes, and his face held a firm profile. "Here, drink." Chas handed him a canteen. "I will fight. Then we will find her." He held his friend's shoulder. "I have promised you the luchar and your daughter."

"Justice will be served, Chas," said Padre Ortiz, head raised and he gripped his fist. "Hard justice will be served, and if not today, then tomorrow, or the next day, and every day that follows. Carl Bellew will see the pain he has planted inside of others. No man has come forward to say he took my daughter. Isa is my life, and Carl has caused brokenness."

"He will stand for his crimes in Texas," answered Chas. "And other places."

"I will not talk to that man while he sits in jail," replied Padre Ortiz. Their hands shook. "I will not see the face of that man either, for my broken heart will do something outside law and order." He stood. "The road a man walks, he walks on his own accord, on roses, through the depth of turmoil, he swims, and in his walk of pride, he walks on the sharpness of jagged thorns. That is my philosophy of good and evil; one brings goodness to the Lord, and the other brings death and sorrow."

"A rivalry lives inside each man, all men," said Chas. He scouted the land. "The conscience of a man decides his own fate."

"My good friend, you sound like Preacher Chet Bellew," said the Padre with a smile. "The man taught you well, didn't he?"

"Indeed, he did."

He stood alongside his friend.

Padre Ortiz looked down a long point of land. Rocks divided the property, a land filled with cedars, oaks, and young mesquite trees that grew low to the earth, and the sounds of trickling streams ran unprotested. The air was cool and brisk by evening. They drank water from the bubbling Crockett Spring, and his wife had packed two sandwiches, cut lengthwise, wrapped in cloth, and Chas spoke first and blessed the meal.

"What sandwich is this, Padre?" He felt the crunch of bread, and his eyes closed because of his deep hunger.

"Bocato!" The minister held his smile with thankfulness.

"I taste pork and onions."

"My Maria has the heart of a chef," said the Padre, head tilted. "She makes this sandwich for her favorite people."

"Me?"

"It is me today, mi amigo," said Padre Ortiz, who held the bread and pork.

He looked at his Spanish friend again and nodded out of respect.

"She is a great woman, rare indeed, Padre."

In a sincere voice, said the clergyman, "I was ready to give up on my wife. My prayers and the many friends I have made in this good town had fed me spiritually, especially on her birthday and our anniversary when weakness covered my body. No es bueno. No es bueno, amigo."

"I got a lady back in Kentucky waiting on me, I guess," said Chas. The boy stopped eating to talk. "I will see her in the spring. That is my promise to her."

Turning his face, he asked, "What is her name?"

"Kate. I hope she still has her maiden name when I get back home."

"What does your Pa say about you getting married?"

His lips became tight, and he sighed, hands together, and rocked his legs.

"My Pa died at the Battle of Chickamauga. I was twelve. Jackie Ray has no father, either. Both died in the Civil War."

"You are the true Sons of War," said Padre Ortiz, who found a seat on a rock. "Your father would be proud of you, having the courage to step in the ring with Carl Bellew."

"I think he would be against it, Padre."

"Why do you say so that, Chas?"

"Carl Bellew is my uncle." Chas stood when he said it. "He is my father's full brother."

"I cannot lie to you, Chas," the clergyman rubbed his face. "I knew Chet and Charles. Knew them well before the big war, but there is no matter of blood now or your family anymore."

"What do you mean?" Chas leaned back.

"Knew he was your uncle," said Padre, who paced when he spoke. "Hate to hear of your father's death. It was long before you ever arrived in Texas, amigo. They were here once together, in Waco, and sat in my church, too. We had a meal one year before the Civil War. Chet spoke of his nephew, Charles Bellew. I was the one who called you Chas. My teeth chattered in the cold Texas wind, and it was funny the way I said your name to your father, Charles."

"You were?"

"Yeah. Your father liked the way I said Charles sounded like Chas Bellew to him. He called you Chas from that day on. You were named Chas Bellew in Waco, Texas. You were big as a Chihuahua pup, I bet," said the Padre, laughing. "I know that you almost died at birth. You've always been an underdog." He hit his hand. "To me, that is the best kind of dog; an underdog ... is a winner."

"How do you know such a thing?"

"You are an underdog, amigo, and you were in my dream," the Padre's dark eyes became bright. "I saw the blood of two men. I believe in my heart that your uncle and father knew you would be a winner. You have chased Carl through Missouri and now Texas. Carl is a very bad man. God is here to stop the chase. Your father would be proud of you for standing against a man so evil, El Diablo."

Chas held his cheeks.

"You think my father would want me to chase down his brother, fight him, harm him," said Chas, who faced the Padre. "See him hanged."

"Chas," said Padre Ortiz, shoulders upright, "God allowed this day to happen. All of this is not because of you and your trials or your tough road in life. It is because you see a resolution, the resolve of which is for the greater good of mankind. You are here not by some long mistake, by a stumbling stride, or because your horse was taken or some voodoo lady in New Orleans," he chuckled. "Eyes made of truth," he said. "You are what is left of your father and uncle. Your blood, the good kind, is for Texas, my wife, and Kate, and all of us are happy to see you here. This may be your new home."

Chas stood, folded his arms, and said, "Never planned to harm any man, be it is my road or destiny or whatever God has on my back. I do believe the good of God is far more important than the deeds of an evil man."

"You are here to allow good folks to prosper and bury the bad ones," said the Padre, full of sincerity. "That is God's promise down your road. At the end of my dream, a man stood on a long road, and that man was you, Charles Bellew, and the place was here, in Crockett. It's my home."

I was curious and learned a lot that day. A lesson that good had to be written, so I did my part. From a distance, I walked close enough to hear their conversation. I was not always proud of my ability to scout and hear the good voice of Padre Ortiz and others; it was the way I learned, though. The usefulness of some men could not be denied, and the value of compassion for the service of a fellow man was led by God. It was how Cherokee people learned and passed on knowledge to others. With guns, I backed up. With good advice, I leaned forward and listened.

"Big question, Padre," said Chas. "With fighting, do you think I have a snowball's chance in Hades?" Chas smiled. "Come on. How did you bet your money on the fight?"

"Look at the time. The time has come!" the good Padre flipped open his pocket watch. "Here," he picked up his sandwich. "Eat the rest of my meal. More strength is needed, Chas."

"How did you bet?" replied Chas, hands lifted with his sandwich.

Padre Ortiz walked beside Chas, hands behind his back, and said, "You know the part in the Old Testament where David beats Goliath and becomes King of Israel, right?"

"Yeah," said Chas. "He used a slingshot and killed him."

"On this foggy day," said the Padre, head dropped, "you do not do slingshots, just bare knuckles and blood, bud."

I watched Padre Ortiz, who walked away, whistled, and sang in his native tongue for a long while until he met his wife, and they went inside the shack with two cats.

"Chas, Chas," I said. "The Sheriff said the fight starts in two hours. He wants you to be early for your funeral, so hurry along."

He nodded and prepared his knuckles. Later, I walked beside Chas at Crockett Spring to where the crowd was lined on both sides, and people supported the fighting Texas Ranger. Fans slapped his back, and Chas kissed the babies. Some folks wanted him for public office. People genuinely liked Chas Bellew.

"What do you think, Atohi," asked Chas. "Do you think I can beat Carl?"

He faced my direction. A good-sized sandwich was placed inside my hands, four bites, and I rubbed my belly.

"My strong grandfather was the Chieftain of the Cherokee," I said. "He would say: Do not talk with your mouth full, Atohi. So, I chewed. Walk with me, though, to the corral, Chas. Tell the sheriff your hand was hurt in a fight with an ugly bear, so they will put up more wagers, and the odds against you will go up even higher. I could stand to win a lot of money on you."

Chas stopped at the barn door.

"You did bet on me, didn't you, Cherokee?" the face of Chas was surprised, and he held a giant smile, finally laughing. "I knew it."

"Men will call you Bad Chas Bellew after the night. Now it is up to you, Chas?" I said in private, and we walked across the street. I felt the need to introduce my friend and said, "Folks, meet this tall Texas Ranger, Chas Bellew. He is a mean and ugly man. I am taking bets on the wounded Kentucky Kid."

My hat was on my chest, long hair in the wind.

"Well, well, Jackie Ray," said Chas. "What's that saddle doing on your horse, bud?"

Jackie Ray brushed his saddle and flipped his stirrup over the horn.

"I see how you feel about me, Chas. Nearly choked me to death when things got crazy today. To answer your question, my horse is saddled for Kentucky, bud."

"Why?" asked Chas. The man propped his foot to the bottom rail of the corral and watched dozens of horses turn nervously in a circle. "You calling it quits, Jackie Ray? Heading back to Kentucky, huh?"

"Yeah, bud," answered Jackie Ray. "Never thought my best friend would turn on me. Well, it looks like you did in front of the good Padre Ortiz and his Catholic friends. What was that all about?"

"I am truly sorry for my anger, cousin."

I saw them face each other.

"We ain't been ill on each other since we were kids," Jackie Ray said, working with his horse. "We fought about silly frogs and betting on the fastest horse."

"Jackie Ray," said Chas, hand out and face of regret. "Sorry about my temper, and it will never happen again, brother."

"I forgave you when it happened," said Jackie Ray, looking at his friend. He saw Buckskins. Pintos. Quarter Horses. "Do not forget much, though. Talked to Padre Ortiz, and he told me to put it behind me, so I did. I lost my friend somewhere today, and I'm not sure what that means for us right now, at this very moment."

"We are the same two rough men who left Carter County, blood brothers," said Chas. "I know some crazy Voodoo things have happened this year, and we had some bad luck. But, Jackie Ray, listen, we had a lot of good things happen, too. I wouldn't make this journey to Texas with anybody else but you, bud." He slapped his shoulder. "I want you to know the truth, Jackie Ray. On this trip, if anything, we have learned the truth about each other."

"We sure have learned the truth," said Jackie Ray. "You mean that? Do not speak the words if you don't mean it, Chas."

"Yeah, full-on truth, Jackie Ray. I mean it, bud." Chas said, holding out his hand again. "I need a favor."

"What?"

"Need you as my trainer today. All or nothing, we said that when we were kids, still the truth between us."

The two men gripped hands, and Jackie Ray said, "All or nothing, brother. Are you serious about me being your trainer, Chas?"

"Truth."

"It's the way we live, all or nothing, Chas."

That was the day I saw Jackie Ray become a great man.

"Brother," said Jackie Ray, "you just got yourself the meanest dang trainer in the country, cousin." Jackie Ray slapped his back, and the two men hugged. Nobody wants to beat Carl Bellew worse than I do, Chas."

"Time to talk about winning this fight, Trainer J.R. Monroe."

"Got a few ideas of my own," said Jackie Ray, who hung a big smile over his chin. "It's a simple punch and stance. Knock him out."

The year 1871 would not have been remembered if it were not for brokenness and the fight for brotherhood.

OLD SAN ANTONIO ROAD RIVALRY

I laughed and saw Jackie Ray and Chas walk out into the wilderness, far from stirring crowds who cheered for them. They talked about horses and rolling hills, like brothers, and the two men climbed atop a boulder and made a good strategy. They distanced themselves from ugly crowds, spirited women, things of distraction, and people who stood against them. That was the first time Jackie Ray became serious about anything in a long while, which meant a bond to watch out for each other.

My hands turned blue after a short while, and my face was cold. How would they fight in a blanket of snow?

Sunset fell too fast in Texas, and winter filled the valleys in December, and my concern was for my friend. Fingerless gloves and homemade coats were wrapped around women; some had blankets, and men wore long coats and leather boots. When the time of the fight approached, church bells of the Methodists and Catholics sounded beside Presbyterians and Lutherans; all were ready. People rushed out of taverns and ran to the street at Railroad and El Camino, where the sheriff and marshal had outlined the ring in a simple square pattern. One side was defined in blue, and the other side was red. Chas was assigned the blue side, and people shuffled to the side of their favorite fighter. The crowd was split even. Folks hung off balconies and stood on wagons, shoulder-to-shoulder, all together: little kids, proprietors, cattle barons, outlaws, Rough Riders and Cowboys. Beer and wine made them brave, and out of three hundred people that had gathered, no one had fought by half-light.

FIGHT OF HIS LIFE

"Welcome to Crockett, good folks of Texas and beyond!" said Sheriff Ellis, who turned to see who had circled the fighters in the frigid snow, faces he knew and some unknown. His friends shivered; men and women and cold faces stood, nodding and smiling, hands in pockets, and inside, they brewed with beer and anticipation. "I was against this bare-knuckle fight when approached by Padre Ortiz, but when the good folks of this great town had called him to stand as referee, I immediately voted for the bout to happen."

"Let these men fight, sheriff!" said a tall man in glasses.

Carl removed his heavy coat and strutted.

"I am ready to kill him," said Bad Carl, bulbous at the midsection and nearly twice the size of most men there, who thumped his fist into his palm and beat his chest.

Men chanted, and women cheered. Folks whistled from across the street, and most of the women were without beauty or style. The natural thing to do was to stay warm and block the wind, so women huddled around men and for a better seat, some people had no exceptions to the extent of their generosity on Old San Antonio Road.

Chas was ready and handed his hat to Jackie Ray. Both men spun around to the crowd. Half the folks had come to support his sudden prominence as a Texas Ranger and, now, a fighter. I don't know whose idea it was to start such a bare-knuckle fight in Crockett, but the match was sent out on the wire, and folks rode into town on wagons and horseback by sundown. After each round, telegrams were sent to the governor and other stations for a message of update.

"The time to fight is upon us, friends. Okay! Okay! I heard your chants," said Sheriff Ellis, hand raised for a short man. "Our referee, Padre Ortiz, front and center. Let's start this match amid the dead of winter. I'll hand it over to you, sir."

"Sheriff Ellis, it is cold, amigo, very cold," announced the Padre. "This is the first snow fight in the history of bare-knuckle fighting."

The crowd cheered, and he was well received.

The sky spat snow, and the ground, once dusty and rugged, was a white canvas, wavy across the land of East Texas, where footprints and fences, high places like churches and businesses stood. The land was something of a paradise, and the Lord had delivered as He wished. The sheriff shook the minister's hands, and they stood together for the first time. Side-by-side, new brown leather was wrapped firmly to the waist of the sheriff, tied to his leg, armed. His lips were cold and tight, and his eyes shone in the light and looked mean. Padre Ortiz was still in his dark Catholic cassock, even as a professional referee.

"I will cover the rules in a few sentences, fighters!" said Padre Ortiz, who recognized each fighter and checked hands for weapons. We will use the London Prize Ring Rules, and here we go."

"Announce the fighters, Padre," a round man shouted from the back roll.

"Settle down, amigo," said Padre Ortiz, a man who intended to honor rules and traditions. "Yes, we must fight."

I felt Chas would be named first, the underdog, and the smaller of the two, nearly twenty years younger. He had never seen this type of fight before but knew what he had gotten himself into: the main event.

"In the blue corner, standing six foot and one inch," said Padre Ortiz, who waved his arm. "The one and only "Kentucky Kid," now a proud Texas Ranger, Charles "Chas" Bellew!"

Chas stepped, toed the line, and the young man saw features in his uncle's face that reminded him of Chet and Charles. My eyes filled with hope, like a river with many swimming fish, when the crowd cheered for him. Others booed and laughed at the prospect of youth and lack of experience, thinking about betting and how the fight might double the size of their pockets.

Bad Carl stood of his own accord.

"In the red corner, to the Wild West, standing six feet and four in boots, Bad, Bad Carl Bellew," said Padre Ortiz. "This man has fought in two bare-knuckle bouts, one in Wyoming and the second in Colorado, and Carl made himself rich on gold and cattle and by harming innocent people, right?"

He had no answer and turned away.

I noticed the bottom of Carl's traditional leather boots were slick, made for riding, not for the snow. Unlike Chas, who had changed his boots for the bout at the shack. Something Jackie Ray suggested, a change for a better grip and a bit of confidence. Chas had a lot of ground to cover to beat Carl, though, backed by the Cowboys of Dallas and Fort Worth and other towns. Only a few ticks chimed on the pocket of Ortiz before the bout. Chas saw the crowd, faces laughing and talking, cold faces, and he became cold himself. Scared, not of the fight, but of the faces in the crowd. My voice, low to his ear, was not enough at that moment.

"What's wrong?" I asked him.

No words were spoken. No sounds. He captured faces, all the faces, some laughing, some betting, and others drinking. He saw two young boys drawing smokes, thin and rowdy, smoking two cigarettes, one for each lip. Chas remembered himself at the same age, without a care in the world, and he had changed, remembering the bout to be his way out.

"He's just got the first-time jitters," said Jackie Ray, who stood above him and slapped his shoulders. "First fight is nothing, Chas."

I had known Chas all my life and saw him stunned by the mountain lion, but I had never witnessed him that rattled by faces and chants, like a rock inside a tin can.

"Let's get this match started," said Padre Ortiz. The preaching referee raised his hands, waved to each fighter, and said, "Toe the line, fighters!"

The crowd cheered in an endless roar. The town had never seen so many people gathered for an event of this caliber. At the center ring, I stood behind Chas, a face of stone and unsettled man before the fight.

"You sure our fighter is alright, Jackie Ray," I said and tried to have a conversation with him.

In the eyes of Chas, I saw the look of a fish hooked by talons, a fish out of his own element. He was not as confident as the day he fought the bear or the night he stabbed the mountain lion. I saw the sky turn dark, and every other person had lanterns that glowed about their faces, and oil lamps were atop the undriven snow. Hands smacked and rubbed, friends near to the heat. My hands extended on his shoulders, stretched hands that formed wings of protection as promised, and prayed with my eyes closed. I felt the dance in my feet, and the Great Spirit crawled over my skin. I needed Chas back to normal; the Spirit of God was the only way to open his eyes.

Voices and drums pounded inside my head, beating ceaselessly as I danced; sounds rattled, the whistle of the flute was unmatched in the cool air, and the dance continued. I was young again and ran "Into the Woods," it was my namesake, anyway. Silence came over the crowd as they stopped, heads canted and lifted, mouths cocked, and eyes locked upon my dance. A timeless dedication and tradition happened. For a brief moment, I spun and danced, caught in style and rhythm, until the owl sounded. Then, I stopped, became a Ranger again, and realized where I stood, back in Crockett, Texas. No longer was I young and brave. I whispered something to Chas, something from my world, as a young brave and gave advice as an old man, face wrinkled, hands tired, slow of voice, but sincere with all my words. My head sang in my native tongue meaningfully, though the sounds of years had passed; still, I hummed to the beat of a walking bear. The world was blurred, and nothing was clear for my eyes, but my voice was of a stronger and younger man.

"Way heya, heya, heya," I said and started my dance. Chas needed to hear the voice of the Great One, the Holy Spirit and needed a word from Christ Jesus. His ears were dulled by nerves and faces. I hoped he had heard voices, drums, singing, and dancing. I walked between him, and Bad Carl and Chas saw my face. And he was no longer like broken stones, and the last battle cry woke his sleepy eyes.

"Stop that Cherokee, Sheriff!" said a round man. "Marshal, stop Feathers!"

The last thing I remembered was a wallop to my head, and the ground rushed upward. I crawled over to where the two boys smoked, and I sat between them near a warm lantern, and my head was dazed.

"Atohi, Atohi," said Chas. The lively face I once knew was back and smiled.

I waved away the smoke and saw him grinning.

"Chas," I said, fists curled in front of my heart, seated between two young smokers who smiled and welcomed my face. We were friends, and they cheered for Chas and smoked.

"And no hitting below the belt," said Padre Ortiz. "That is every rule I know."

"He is back!" said Jackie Ray, nodding his stern chin and slapping his face.

"I am about to knock him into Laredo!" said Bad Carl with his outreached hands.

"Gentlemen," said Padre Ortiz, extending his arms. "Back to your sides! The fight will start in one minute."

I watched Jackie Ray encourage Chas. I was proud of their sincere reconciliation and hoped they were ready for a battle.

"Fighters!" said Padre Ortiz, "Fighters, toe the line, and knuckle up."

Slick boots or not, Carl swung the first punch in the sawdust. The crowd went silent when Chas landed at my boots, eyes crossed. A sermon by his uncle, the other one, I thought I had forgotten, rolled off my tongue, and I said, "Let him sit alone in silence, for the Lord had laid it on him. Let him bury himself in the dust."

I was surprised that he fell so fast and hard. It was the best I could do on short notice.

"Jeremiah?" said Chas, eyes lifted between my boots, and he finally caught his breath.

"Yeah, my son," I said, laughing. "There may yet be hope for you, Chas, as a minister. Let him offer his cheek to the one who struck him, and ... let him be filled with disgrace. That is all I remember from Jeremiah, Chas. Get up! The bout is more of a standing position than flat-faced."

When my hand was finished lifting his head and a handful of hair, I heard him moan, and his eyes came back to normal.

"That hurt my chin," said Chas, side to side, his jaw pivoted.

"Fighter knocked down," said Padre Ortiz with one hand ticking off the count beside Chas. "Get up, kid. Chas, get the heck up and fight." He counted. "One, two, three, four, five, six."

"Chas," I said. "Stand up!" In my best Cherokee voice, I said, "Fighting is a standing position. More vertical, like trees!"

"Seven, eight, nine," said Padre Ortiz, "Boy, the fight is on your feet."

"Told you so," I said, waving smoke from the fighter's face.

"We have ourselves a fight," said Padre Ortiz.

The minister held the wrists of Chas, and his head was steady, eyes blinked.

"Fighter?" said Padre Ortiz. "Can you continue?"

"He's been fighting all his life," said Jackie Ray, "Tell him, Chas."

"I can fight," said Chas, mumbling low, lip busted. "Let's fight."

"We have first blood!" announced Padre Ortiz, who agitated the crowd.

"Hey, Referee Ortiz," said Sheriff Ellis near Ortiz. "Can that boy stand and fight? He seems unable to proceed with the match."

"I said I can fight!" yelled Chas, eyes cleared and blood removed.

Bad Carl Bellew chuckled and stood cocky in front of the Cowboys. More money was exchanged, and men laughed and caught snowflakes with their mouths like pups.

"He can surely take a punch," said Carl. "Solid hit. His face broke my knuckles."

"When a fighter is knocked down," said Padre Ortiz, arms out, "he has ten seconds to recover. Ranger Chas has recovered. Let's fight."

"Let's fight, you are right," said Marshal Johnson, hand on his collar.

Dressed in a black cassock, Padre Ortiz was chosen by God to minister to the flock and chosen by man to stand between the fighters as a self-proclaimed, semi-pro referee. Without debate, he was the most honest man in Crockett, and Chas was relaxed after his face was dusted by the cold snap of snow and sawdust.

Jackie Ray brushed snow from the fighter's clothes. I laughed, still amid the smoke of young boys, as Chas cleared caked snow from his blood-struck face and waited. The Double 8 Ranch, a place not much more than a dusty corral, rolled out logs and added more sawdust after Chas was knocked down, which were timely benches for entertainers. Ladies paced between rounds. More bets were made with men from the Double 8 Cattle Auction House; ranchers sold more tickets with each round, and the crowd tripled by the fifth round. The wooden corral ring was where the Double 8 Ranchers broke horses and branded cattle for market and was surrounded by spectators. It was said to be a place planned for the railroad connector in 1872. Folks did not believe it would happen, though.

"Make a hit or something," said Jackie Ray. "Sixth round, Chas. Are you tired of being punched in the face yet, buddy?" The trainer pressed his cold shoulders and cleaned his wounds. Fighters sat on round whiskey barrels. Chas was furious between rounds and felt sick. "He keeps hitting me," said Chas, head down, eyes dark.

"Chas, Chas," said Jackie Ray. "It is simple: keep your head away from his knuckles. When you see a punch, step away and dodge the train."

"I'm trying, Jackie Ray!" said Chas. Sweat and snowflakes covered his head. "He's the size of a dang mule and has the reach of a lion."

"Here, fighters," said Padre Ortiz. "To the center, toe the line again."

The lantern was at my feet, and logs were rolled around to make a ring at the eighth round of fighting in the sawdust. The two boys had not spoken but grunted when Chas hit the snow and splashed mud on the crowd. I imagined what the owl had seen from the tree: the blood, the punches, eyes rolled, heads being lifted, and ribs being smashed. From the top of the tree, the owl must have been amused or disgusted, for his head circled after each round.

I poured small rocks and seashells from a leather sack into my cold, large hands and prayed. Some good words would encourage, I thought.

"What are those rocks and shells for, sir?" said the boy who stopped smoking to my right and observed. "I am William, and my twin brother is James. He won't speak much, but he'll smoke all day if you got tobacco in your pockets for him."

"No tobacco," I said with a handful of rocks and shells. "I only have rocks, shells, and a small broken mirror. I have a wooden cross necklace."

"Don't seem like anything to trade on," said William, snowball in his hand.

"I'll be seeing you, William," I said, collecting my items and dusting snow from my long legs. "Smoking is bad for you boys. Better tend to my friend."

"That Ranger is fixin' to get his head knocked off, ain't he?" said William, who crushed snow. "Think I could whip him one-handed," William whispered to his twin brother.

His brother took the tobacco from his lips.

"You could whip him like you did Cousin Aspen last summer," said James with his rough voice when he spoke to his brother.

I saw Chas beaten and stood beside Jackie Ray, who tended to his cut face and bruised eye. He could hardly see out his swollen left eye, and his arms flapped weak and limp. Both men were tired; it was much different than when we rounded up cattle or broke green horses in Denton.

"Can he win?" I said to Jackie Ray.

"Yeah, he can possibly win," Jackie Ray said halfheartedly.

The lovely Mrs. Maria Ortiz, brown hair, long and beautiful in her hands, walked up to my right side and stuck her head close to Chas.

The lady whispered softly, saying, "He can win."

She was the forty-year-old woman, the wife of Padre Ortiz, who had sent his wife to our side of the ring, and at the time, the reason was unknown. The Padre nodded at his wife, and she held the hand of Chas and tended to his cut face with care.

Maria said, "Chas, seven Spanish angels are waving and flirting with you. They would like to double their money and go home with you when you win." Her smile could have been seen by blind man Sammy Summers assuredly. "Some ladies went back home to warm in the tub."

"What does that have to do with me?" said Chas, hand leaning into her voice.

"As cold as it is," said Maria Ortiz, "my people love you. My angels love you, amigo. Just like you, they have traveled a long and broken road on mules, horses, afoot, and now that they are here, especially those tender ladies waving at you, and all need husbands and new friends. Do you know what I am saying? But you must win so I can introduce my sweet Spanish angels to you and your friends."

"This is not going to work, Mrs. Ortiz," I said and helped her back to her seat. "Thanks anyway, Maria."

Jackie Ray hit my shoulders, and we both heard the names of seven beautiful Spanish ladies cheering for Ranger Chas. We did not know where they came from or if it was a some wonderful dream. They were real because I was invited to park between them. My arms became warm when they felt their hands. I did not care that they smiled for Chas. It was a beautiful moment for all of us. With his blue eyes darkened and bruised, the bloody lip raised, cheeks red, and teeth shone, Chas was revived. It was, by some strange miracle, not the seashells left by Sunshine Frenchie.

Mrs. Ortiz returned with another message.

"I just came over here," said Maria Ortiz, voice sweet and low, "well, the women are very cold and want to go inside the house, sit by the fire with the champ." She winked.

Maria Ortiz sat with her Spanish angels, shoulders tucked inside coats, huddled, and three lanterns made their hands and faces warm inside blankets.

"Ready fighters?" said Padre Ortiz. The man winked at Chas and gripped his right hand.

Face swollen and cut, Chas nodded and yelled, "Ready!"

The shells, rocks, and broken mirror story I aimed to tell Chas for inspiration and hope had to be for another day. Away from the ring, Spanish ladies smiled and waved, and I felt they needed a chance to be heard and seen. Jackie Ray spoke with his eyes when he saw the beauty that sat on my arms, not far from the Blue side of the ring. Jackie Ray slapped the shoulders of Chas, who "towed the line" for round nine.

Carl Bellew cocked a smirk on his head and raised his fists, one behind the other, the nature stance of a seasoned bare-knuckle fighter, but his stance was not like Stonewall Jackson.

Chas became a wildcat who was untamed inside the ring. Punch after punch landed, body, head, body, head, and three shots busted the nose of Bad Carl Bellew.

"He may have won this round," I said to Jackie Ray. "Carl's legs are wobbling, but he caught himself."

Chas swung with every pound, arms extended and well-balanced was his position. Carl stumbled.

"Awe!" The crowd stood. "He's hit hard," said one man. "He fell like a tree!"

"Timber!" said James, lips pursed. "Big man Carl went down. He ain't so bad, William."

The lips and chin of William dropped, snow fell from his head, and his eyes popped when he realized his twin brother had watched the entire fight and smoked his last one.

"I am not sure what has gotten into the Kentucky Kid," I said. "Chas is an animal."

"He has a new desire," said Jackie Ray, eyes full of hope. "His aim is better than round three and round seven put together. He has a left jab now." He held the shoulders of Chas.

I grabbed Jackie Ray's shoulder and prayed.

"Carl is down!" I shouted. "Carl is down in the snow."

"His head was knocked back to Waco," said Jackie Ray, arms up, jumping up and down.

The beautiful Spanish angels who had sat so peacefully and quietly for far too long yelled, screamed, and cheered for Chas. My fighter stepped beside Jackie Ray, punching and jumping, and he waited for his opponent to recover. I ran to the side where Big, Bad Carl Bellew had landed and waited for the count. The two boys, William and James, stopped smoking and counted along with Padre Ortiz.

Carl was knocked out.

The long-eared hound owned by Padre Ortiz cocked his leg above the downed fighter, and the snow and Carl Bellew became the color of a summer daisy.

Struck by the hard knuckles of Chas, Bad Carl Bellew was motionless, and the black and tan hound sat beside Chas and Jackie Ray. Padre Ortiz lifted the limp arm of Carl Bellew flat on his face, and he rested in a line of yellow snow.

The owl flew across the sky, just off the roof of the barn at Old San Antonio Road, and a fat rat was balled inside the talons of the strong night owl. The rat was knocked out.

"Let him sleep, Padre," I whispered. "Eyes closed, referee."

The curious crowd became silent and shocked, holding their breath, and their necks hung in suspense. However, less surprisingly, my eyes curled in true happiness. The minister stood, back arched, arms wide, and dropped onto his knees to check the fighter's recovery, who had fallen as hard as any man could drop from over six feet. Padre Ortiz nodded to his wife, saw the Spanish Angels huddled, caught the trader, Sheriff Ellis, and waved over at Marshal Johnson. Both men had lost what they had wagered to yours truly.

Padre Ortiz became silently hopeful and held a tight-lipped smile toward Chas for the second time since he had shared his sandwich with him at Crockett Spring. The cold, blue-curled hand of the referee ascended and descended, deeply breathing and sweaty in his approach. Loud and clear, his voice sounded across the crowd who waited with ripe anticipation for the count and recovery. The fighter, hinged, flat on his wiry face, Carl, down and out in Crockett, Texas, was motionless.

"Get up," said the leader of the Cowboys. "Get up, now!" shouted Rough Riders. "Carl, stand. Get up!" The crowd sounded.

"One, two, three, four, five, six, seven, eight," said Padre Ortiz, looking for any movement from the fighter, "nine," he shouted as loud as any sermon he had preached. "Ten!"

Chas stood in the center of the ring.

"The Champion!" shouted Padre Ortiz. "The Champ!" Hands of both men up. "By a knockout, in the Blue corner, Chas Bellew, the Kentucky Kid, has defeated Bad Carl Bellew, by a knockout on this snowy wonderous night in Crockett, Texas."

Spanish Angels surrounded Chas, and to honor the Champ, a short parade and celebration marched him through the snowy streets of Crockett. I played the harmonica in celebration. Our victorious trainer, Jackie Ray Monroe, swayed and played the piano to a large crowd in the parlor of Crockett Tavern. The Champ, one eye dark by the end of the bout, became the center of attention and was escorted by Spanish Angels every step of the night. My heart and harmonica stopped when they spoke of his next opponent. The rumor was that Chas had a bath of bubbles and champagne, which is why he recovered. Chas soaked up good company and became known as the first Texas Ranger Bare-knuckle Champion in Houston County.

Due to the large crowd that spread about the town, the Texas Traveling Show made their debut in Crockett and opened on the same night as the fight. A Chinese lady, Sarah Sang, held great compassion and sympathy for others and saw the opportunity for her entertainers to tend to the fallen man in the yellow snow, Carl Bellew. They had forgiven Carl for his temper and eagerness to fight, and it was rumored that Bad Carl traded gold for a kiss from Sarah Sang. It was no surprise when Carl had stolen the long-eared hound, a gift carried for a date. Sarah, known as an animal lover, had named the hound Yellow Dog of Round Nine. No one mentioned to Carl about the deposit the long-eared hound had given him and how casually he had cocked his back leg. Ten Cowboys, pockets emptied from betting, threw whiskey bottles at the Texas Traveling Show and were later jailed by the town Marshal Johnson but escaped when Sheriff Ellis left open the doors at midnight. Another truth is that Sheriff Ellis worked underhandedly and was spoken of as a dishonest man.

By the words of an urgent telegraph, Sheriff Dunn wanted to meet the Champ. Last we heard, Ellis had no badge and was headed to El Paso, the last town in the Wild West of Texas.

"Congratulations on your bare-knuckle fight, Chas," said Sheriff Dunn. "You are a true Champion!"

He pointed as we sat in his office. Sheriff Dunn asked everyone but the three Texas Rangers to leave the room.

"The governor has one thing to say to you men," said Sheriff Dunn.

"What's that?" said Chas. He expected good news.

"The assignment was to bring Carl Bellew to justice, right?" said Sheriff Dunn, eyes sharp behind his glasses. "Where is Bad Carl Bellew now, Rangers!"

"He was knocked flat on his face when I was being paraded across Crockett," said Chas with satisfaction.

"Next to death, I bet." Jackie Ray told and turned his gambler hat on his fist.

"Wait a minute, that was the job of Sheriff Ellis, right?" I said, hands up.

"Nope. Bellew was assigned to you. Let me tell you where Carl was last seen," said Sheriff Dunn, who turned the desk over and sat back in his chair. "He rode out last night with a wagon load of entertainers. The man I want to be locked up for life ran off with the Chinese lady, Sarah Sang, and her Texas Traveling Show. Now, how do you like that one, Rangers?"

"Must be heavy tracks," said Chas. "Atohi can scout him."

"Five hundred people left Crockett this morning," said Sheriff Dunn. "How can you track them?"

"He's right. The traveling show has been covered by wagons and horses," I said, legs crossed, hands folded. "They have gone to the next town."

"They could be in Deadwood, South Dakota in a week," said Sheriff Dunn. The man plugged his thumbs down inside his belt bucket. "I need some fresh air, boys. Outside!"

We followed him to the street. Patches of melted snow and poodles of water were left behind by the snowfall, the first good snow of its kind we had seen since we'd left Kentucky.

"Are they still a reward out for Bad Carl, Sheriff Dunn?" I spoke. "I want to hear you say it."

"Yeah, Atohi. 1000 dollars," said Sheriff Dunn. The officer rubbed his rough beard. "But you three Rangers are paid to do a job for Texas, not fight a wanted man in some bare-knuckle competition for popularity and a soapy bath."

"I quit," I said.

"I'm out!" said Jackie Ray.

"I have not trusted the government since the Indian Wars!" I shouted

We handed the sheriff our Texas badges and walked toward the corral, men in a hurry to find our horses.

"Not just anyone will be a fit for a Texas Ranger," Dunn said.

"I know where the badge will fit, Sheriff Dunn!" I told him.

"Are you sure this is the right thing to do, Atohi?" said Chas.

"We are now Bounty Hunters, Chas!" I told him. "Kentucky Bounty Hunters, from here on out. The Great One leads our direction, the Lord Jesus, not betting badges. Three of us headed to the corral. "All or nothing, Chas, remember?"

"Yeah."

"I hope this is a better plan than going to New Orleans," said Jackie Ray. His pride was bruised since he had regrettably handed over his authority and said, "I am no longer law and order. No one can call me Jackie Ranger anymore." His head dropped.

"Sorry about this, Sheriff Dunn," said Chas.

"Do not be sorry, Chas!" I shouted and walked backward.

"Give the governor our best," said Chas, who threw his badge into the dusty Texas sky and walked away.

"You boys are gonna get killed!" yelled Sheriff Dunn. "Don't expect the governor to back you up when Carl Bellew and the Cowboys have you pinned down!"

An owl perched himself on top of the Sheriff's office. Then I whistled. The bird flew and nabbed the cowboy hat from Sheriff Dunn's head.

"Atohi, I know you sent that barn owl!" shouted Sheriff Dunn.

Chapter 24
Thither They Return Again

We rode down a long stretch of road on the 21st day of December, four days before Christmas, and little light was left in the evening as we looked forward to Waco. Chas and Jackie rode slowly, and our faces needed warmth on the trail; the road widened, four tracks or more, heavy wagons ahead, and most of them were pointed north. There was a certain draw about the dusty Town of Waco, something more than other towns in Texas, something I could not figure out until I saw it for myself, collectively and rendered in the light of day. Beneath the small flat, the crest dropped deep, turning north to Hillsboro or south to Waco, a place of stories and legends and a community we had heard about for years.

"We made it to Waco, men," I told my closest friends.

"Dang it, bud!" said Jackie Ray. "I reckon we have."

All the words in the English and Cherokee language, Jackie Ray picked those unique words when we crested the hill.

"Let's explore this town," said Chas.

The town stood proudly before our weary eyes was a beauty. The road narrowed down into the water, and on the banks were chunks of thin ice, broken and melted, the size and shape of hymn books. Rain from the north had left a muddy watermark, and the river had cleared somewhat. I had predicted much worse in McLennan County days earlier, but I was no Claire Voyance, like Jackie Ray's lady.

"Chas, the sun rises hot," I said. "And goes down cold, same as anywhere else, I guess. Wait. South of here, my telescope shows a good-sized structure in the distance."

"Bridge?" said Chas.

Chas passed the telescope on to Jackie Ray, and we all witnessed Waco for the first time through the small lens of the telescope and felt good about being in Central Texas.

"Yeah. Industry. Bricks. Cables. Steel." I said, eyes held in amazement. My cold hand collapsed the telescope and tucked it inside my saddlebags. I tied down the leather bag, draped the bags on my shoulders, and prepared to stay the night. The first thing we wanted to do was bathe and repack our food supply.

"I want to see a gypsy lady and ….."Jackie Ray took off his gambler's and placed it on his chest. "And find a talking parrot!"

"Why do I even bother, Chas?" I said. "A parrot?"

"Yeah. I have always wanted to talk frankly to a parrot and a gypsy." Jackie Ray told, roping his horse to a tree.

"I hope we find them. See what you would do," I said, peering down at him.

"It ain't no dang bother to see a gypsy and hold a parrot. You got to do it in that order, or it's bad luck, bud." Jackie Ray said very kindly.

"Can't promise we'll find you one," I said, rolling my eyes.

The piano man, Jackie Ray Monroe, was the best of the bunch when it came to supplies and music, but his superstitions were something to be desired. As often as I could, we let him know what an outstanding job he had done as a trainer for Chas, backing the fighter in Crockett. Both men proved to have their own ways, different ways, and beliefs.

"This is the mighty Brazos River, the one Uncle Chet spoke about in his letters and diary," said Chas with a map tucked in his pocket. "Let's camp here just like he did. We can hunt for Carl Bellew when we get to Waco in the morning."

"What?" said Jackie Ray, face shocked. "Why not cross the dang bridge, find a fire, and get out of this cold weather, huh?"

"A blanket of stars will keep you warm," I said. "Enjoy the fine dirt of Waco. Dream of your gypsy and parrot, bud."

"We will camp here tonight," said Chas. Eyes shaded black, and the prizefighter had not yet healed. "Leave, Jackie Ray, if you don't like our ideas."

"Ridin' into town!" Jackie Ray jumped on his horse. "Catch up with you fellers in the morning. Goodnight."

"The 'all or nothing, brotherly love' was short-lived, boys," I said, "This fighting and bickering will end tonight, gentlemen!" My hand pointed at each young man. "Got it?"

Jackie Ray was mad when he rode to the bridge.

Neither young man said a word, and I felt serious, fatherly love. Minutes later, Jackie Ray returned to our warm campfire and stood, face of regret, and smiled.

"Get killed sneaking up on a man, Jackie Ray," I said, whispering, and held a knife to his neck.

"Hey, I-I-I am sorry, Atohi," Jackie Ray said, catching his breath. "Big toll road at the bridge. No money."

Boots near the flames, Chas rolled over and laughed 'til he cried aloud, and I know that he was thinking of what he would say to a gypsy and a parrot when he found one.

I warmed my hands.

"Sorry about the temper, boys," I said as I held my blade. "Must have left my patience in Crockett."

We talked for a while and made friends again. And they appreciated my skills, and we spoke about Jackie Ray having a parrot as a pet on the horn of his saddle.

"Preacher Chet said the word Brazos means, The Arms of God, men," said Chas. "Thank God for Jesus and Winchester rifles in Texas."

"We will see how it goes," I said, eyes closed, flat on my back. "Way too early to tell. Be nice to find some hidden gold on the Brazos riverbank. Seen more Winchesters than I have Jesus and parrots on this trip."

We rolled and laughed.

"Yeah. I would agree with him," said Jackie Ray, boots off, drying his cold feet. "Tired after a three-day ride. I sure need a gypsy, and my luck is running out until I see a parrot."

"Chet spoke often of his missionary time in Waco," I said. It was late evening when I stood at the river bend and searched for a good place to cross the river at sunup. "Your uncle spoke of good people and good churches in this town, too. Lots of smoky chimneys and taverns."

Through the fire, I saw Jackie Ray light up his tobacco.

"Might be Spanish Angels in this town," said Jackie Ray, poking at the fire. "I can play piano, too, and give us some luck."

"Some people like your style of playing," I said.

"I could use a drink right now," said Jackie Ray. Dropped his hat and threw it to the ground. "Where is my whiskey? Bottle is empty, huh?" kicking the dirt. "Can't sleep a wink without it."

Each man had his own ritual before bed. After dinner, Chas was known to write, and I had watched him write on a dozen nights since the spring. He had no idea of my book, the one I held dear. Fireside was the time to close our weary eyes, a time for prayer, and a time to give thanks. More times than not, Jackie Ray, who talked most of the time, cursed the day he left behind and disrespected what part of the world he'd been handed. I had read all the theology books Preacher Chet had on his shelves, and Chet said, "To bend your ear to nature may save your life, Atohi." I listened to more than voices, lent myself to natural things, and enjoyed the peace of God and my part in it.

"Did you hear that coyote?" I said, laughing. "One howl of a coyote means the food supply is low, but many howls from many coyotes means the food supply is high."

"Did you see the hundreds of cattle tracks in the mud?" said Chas, who grunted, head atop his saddle, wrapped in a thick coat and blanket roll. "Looks like plenty of beef in Texas and lots of trails turned north of the Brazos River."

"Maybe we should turn north to the stockyards of Fort Worth, huh?" said Jackie Ray with a sincere voice.

The piano man spoke as if he had rejected the thought of seeing Waco. He changed his mind about being a bounty hunter, seeing a gypsy, and touching a parrot.

"I'm looking forward to seeing Waco in the morning," said Chas, voice stern. "Promised Padre Ortiz that I would find his daughter, and that's just what we'll do."

"You made that promise as a Texas Ranger, Charles Bellew," said Jackie Ray, rolling over. "Not as a Bounty Hunter. The table has turned."

"My promise was not about being a Ranger," said Chas, and he sat tall. "The promise was made as a Christian man. Be it in El Paso or Del Rio, I made the promise to the Ortiz family."

"I am with you, Chas," I said. "Keep your word, disciple."

"How much is he paying you to search for his daughter, Chas?" said Jackie Ray, one eye open. His face turned to his friend, a smile glowing in the firelight.

"One day, you will have a daughter or a wife, Jackie Ray," said Chas, elbow on his saddle. "If you ever lose one of them, housefire, shootout, or captured by outlaws, like the Cowboys or Carl Bellew, you'll miss them more than anything. Every man gets back what he plants, Jackie Ray."

"One day, it might be your lost daughter or lost your parrot," I said, hand pointed. "That's enough talk, go to bed, bounty hunters. We are in the arms of God."

It was the most peace I had ever felt at night.

The wind whipped across Waco at first light, but hot coffee warmed our bones. Chas, head down, sketched the entrance of the Victorian-style bridge; two columns that looked like a castle and a toll road were on paper, the ideal rendering when finished. Carefully, Chas tucked away his drawings into his saddle bags, and his drawings held pieces of our treasured journey together.

We followed the river trail to the bridge and etched on the prior page, Edwards Plateau, a final drawing by Preacher Chet, who rendered Waco before the Civil War some years early. The lazy river was unchanged, hill country and plateau, shadowed by clouds, the sky drifted no differently some years later, a timeless passage. The Brazos River had dropped to normal overnight, less swift, and Jackie Ray watered and fed the horses while Chas sketched him by the Brazos River. Then, we met the Wall Bridge Company authorities at the entrance, a post-War toll toad. The day was cold in December, and smoke lifted high above the countryside. Jackie Ray had not spoken much to anyone since the disagreement by the campfire, still a bit unsettled without his parrot.

"Welcome to Waco, boys," said Chas, a smile broke beyond his cold frown.

"Thank Jesus and Winchester!" said Jackie Ray.

BRAZOS RIVER AT WACO

The toll bridge was unlocked and open at sunup. We agreed Chas was first, and I followed Jackie Ray across the Brazos River, a long span, newly built structure of brick and stone, a mighty structure of cable, lined with steel, stretched over the river and between patches of wildflowers.

"Morning, sir," said Chas, spoken in peace, hat tipped.

"Good morning, youngster, where are you men from?" said the toll worker. "The accent?"

"O' Kentucky," said Jackie Ray, and saw the man drink his coffee, who hesitated to let three riders from the Bluegrass State cross his bridge until he saw some money.

"How much?" said Chas, hand out.

"One animal and one rider will cost you a dime, times three," said the man. Arms crossed, he moved slowly and steadily. "Thirty cents to cross my bridge into Waco, gentlemen."

"What are those long, purple flowers in bloom?" I said and watched songbirds fly around the crest of the woods. I pointed across the river and backed up the horse.

The toll worker stood where he could see the wildflowers better, tipped his glasses, and said, "My wife calls them Gayfeather flowers, which bloom in the winter, draw butterflies, hummingbirds, and more songbirds than I can count on warm days. We use the roots to treat snake bites. And don't take all our snakes, fellas." He laughed and collected our money. "Enjoy our fine town, gentlemen."

"Good day, sir," I told him.

"Let's find a corral for the horses," said Chas, who crossed the bridge first. "Wash up, get breakfast, and hunt down Carl Bellew. Maybe we can find Isa Ortiz in this town and not have to ride to Del Rio or down in The Valley. Jackie Ray, hope you know we might not make it back to Kentucky."

"I knew that much when I signed up for this long ride," Jackie Ray said.

"Not guaranteed one minute in this forsaken world!" Chas yelled.

Jackie Ray brought his horse up beside Chas, and I listened.

"Chas, bud," said Jackie Ray, voice low. "Wait. Wait."

"What happened? Did ya see a gypsy?" I said, stopping my horse.

"If you don't mind, cousin," voice sincere, eyes tight, " I'd like you to do something for me?"

"What now?" said Chas with his eyes on Jackie Ray.

"If you say no, well, that's just fine." Jackie Ray told him, unbuttoning his shirt. "But would you baptize me in the Brazos River, underneath the bridge?"

"You want to be baptized in the dead of winter!" yelled Chas, still on horseback.

"Jesus, Jackie Ray," I said. "You see that ice on the riverbanks? Can't you wait until springtime? Jesus knows your heart."

Jackie Ray jumped off his horse and said: "The Lord hit me this morning. I am a man of repentance and conviction. I request to be baptized and saved in water, down yonder. If you can't, ya can't. I'll forgive your shortcomings. We all fall short, brother Chas."

"Where did the Lord hit you, Jackie Ray?" Chas jumped off his horse. I saw his big grin, slipping off his boots.

"I don't see any marks," I said and held my smile.

"This ain't no laughing matter, bud, it's a spiritual moment!" said Jackie Ray, hand on his hips. "Are ya gonna baptize me or not, huh?" He dropped to his knees and said, "Lord, please forgive my raging mouth."

"Guess I got to, Jackie Ray, " said Chas, sleeves rolled up. "But no minister, and the water won't save ya, bud. You know that, right? Sinners are saved by grace through faith, not by river water and work."

"Hot dang!" He jumped and ran to the water. "Thank you, brother Chas. I sought redemption from my awful ways last night and had some faith and belief in the Lord, a good bit of it." Jackie Ray held out his hands over the water. His body was half submerged. "That is like ice," and his teeth chattered. "The Lord could've made His call on my life on a warm, warmer day." His mouth shook, eyes searching the clouds.

"I should've charged you three dollars to baptize an idiot!" shouted the man atop the tool bridge. "But I am a godly man."

"The man on the bridge thinks we're nuts," I held the horses. "Baptizing him in December, that is crazy. President Grant said the Cherokee people are wild and unruly. Believe your insanity has us beat."

I tied the three horses to the end of the bridge and hurriedly sketched my friend amid the Brazos River before Chas knew it. Padre Ortiz had given Chas the pad that Chet Bellew had left behind years ago.

"This water is like ice," said Chas, feet in the water. "Soon as we find a minister, we can come back, Jackie Ray."

"Nope. Today is the day," said Jackie Ray, shivering. "I swear to you, Chas, you have been my minister all my life. I need you to be the minister of the river."

"Okay. Okay. You are one crazy person." Chas tightened his belt and said, "Let's hurry and do this before we both die. Hurry up. It's cold."

"Well, Chas…" said Jackie Ray, head cocked, and he leaned back and said, "Are you gonna say some words to the Holy Spirit or throw some water or something? Don't just stand there, bud."

I sat on the riverbank and rolled and laughed.

"You don't want to hear what I'd like to say, Jackie Ray," said Chas, and they gripped hands.

"Yeah, Chas, I do," said Jackie Ray, eyes open. "Dang it, say something, for-for-for God-God's sake."

"Jackie Ray Monroe," said Chas, "do you take the Lord as your personal Savior in this river, named Brazos, the Arms of God?"

Chas held his cousin's back as the water bent and splashed.

"Yeah. But it's Jackie Raymont Monroe."

"Raymont? Your middle name is Raymont?" Chas caught his grin. "Well, Jackie Raymont Monroe," said Chas, "do you take the Lord as your personal Savior in this river, named Brazos, the Arms of God?"

"I do. I will." Raymont crossed his arms over his chest and declared, "I am here, ain't I, Lord. You got me?"

Jackie Raymont held his nose and closed his eyes.

"Then, with the power vested in me by the Church of Uncle Chet, I, Chas Bellew, baptize you, Jackie Raymont Monroe, in the name of the Father, and of the Son, and of the Holy Spirit."

Chas plunged sinner Raymont beneath the torrents that swept gently around them. I stood and watched Jackie Raymont vanish amid the muddy Brazos River, where a splash of bubbles surfaced for a moment. I felt the grace of God. All of a sudden, doves flew from the wildflowers and crest of the riverbank; the sinner became a true saint. I sketched the baptism and saw "faith and hope," the two doves that flew across the river were drafted on paper above their head. The spiritual act, the baptism, and the way Jackie Raymont's eyes opened from the chilling water caused the two men on the toll bridge to break out in song.

"Amazing Grace," said the men, "how sweet the sound that saved a wretch like Raymont."

I joined the singing, knew the words John Newton had written by heart, and said, "Once was lost, but now I'm found, was blind, but now I see." I shouted it. "I once was lost, but now I'm found, t'was blind, but now I see." And I hummed and thought of Sammy Summers, and I knew his Heavenly eyes; for the first time, the man saw the Baptism at Brazos River.

Chas walked out of the water beside Jackie Ray, and they sang with heavenly voices, echoing across the small valley and beneath the bridge. From the bridge to the river, five of us sang at first light, and the morning sun lined easterly down the length of the Brazos River; it was truly "The Arms of God" who embraced us on our first glorious morning in Waco.

When the men sang the hymn a second time, I felt the Lord tug on my heart and soul. I rode my horse to where the steep trail turned into a river.

"Chas," I said and shook hands with the saintly men, and Heaven must have cheered. "I am the next sinner."

"Are you serious, Atohi?" Chas replied and searched my face.

"Well, I'll be a monkey's uncle," said Jackie Ray. My friend smiled. "He looks serious, don't he, Brother Chas? He needeth redemption in the river."

"This ain't no game, Atohi," said Chas. "Now, the Lord is watching us with a fist full of lightning."

I sat, removed my boots, and stepped into the water.

"What's wrong, Brother Atohi?" said Chas, halfway in the water.

"Water is too cold, Chas!" I said, teeth chattering. "Wait until summer. The Lord can wait until a warmer day if he wants to see me saved by grace and Baptized."

"I told you the water is chill, chill, chilly, Chas-Chas Bellew," said Jackie Ray, coat over his back.

We bent; five men laughed, and all sold out to God by the Brazos River. Jackie Ray's teeth chattered, and he fell into the mud.

"The water is chill, chill, chilly!" I said.

While I hugged both my friends for the first time ever, thoughts rolled about the Town of Waco, and I had not mentioned it to anyone. Other than the river, it was a warm and welcoming town, a spiritual place surrounded by wildflowers, butterflies, men of song, and doves of pearl, and something of a revelation filled my heart. I felt good on the first day and remembered that morning, bright on my face, teeth shone, and how the wet eyes of Preacher Chet crossed my weary mind when Waco, Texas was spoken about. The morning of the Baptism and celebratory singing was for the Great One, no one else. I will not forget the river of inspiration and how two young men followed in the footsteps of a great man of faith, Chet Bellew, and became votary.

SUNDAY RAIN

We rode to the corral, a place new and well-kept, horses tied. Inside were dozens of strong horses, muscular and shiny: Appaloosa, Mustangs, Paso Fino, Morgan, and the smaller of the horses, Shetland. Working the horses alone, with excellence, labored a Spanish man, fifty-something, dark skin and hair of gray, who was thin, and the horses trusted him, a man careful with animals. Amused for a half hour, he knew we were in a good corral, and respect was granted.

"Welcome, amigos, David!" said the handler, lively, as he brushed each horse and shared his scent with each animal. "How long do you three men plan to stay in Waco?"

"Not sure yet," Chas said.

"My brother, Padre Ortiz, said you are really good men and would help us."

"Your brother, Padre Ortiz, is a godly man," said Jackie Ray, smiling. "He sent you a telegram, huh?"

"Si," said David Ortiz, hand out. "Padre Ortiz is the best man I know, and he did say one of you is a chimp."

"Monkey?" said Jackey Ray, who laughed at himself. "We ain't no monkeys, David."

"Luchador. Fighter. Black eye!" said David, hands out like a boxer. "The champ."

With his humor, all of us had made friends. We pushed the shoulder of the fighter, eyes turned to Champ Chas, black eye tan, who grinned and ignored our celebration.

"I can guess this man..." David said. "Luchador Bellew."

"Bounty hunter, now," said Chas, who brushed his horse and fed him grain. "But this trip is to hunt down a man, not to fight in a Waco boxing ring."

"I know the fighting story," said David, eyes bright. Some told by telegram. But, men, Bad Carl Bellew holds my niece captive, Chas Bellew."

We all sat in the corral, voices low and only a few feet apart; we spoke for a short while and warmed by the fire.

"How do you know that, for sure, David?" I said and listened.

"The entertainers are in Waco," David said in private. "Sarah Sang and her entertainers are working in town."

"The prettiest Chinese lady in the country and some weird men who travel together are here, in Waco?" said Jackie Ray. "Where can we find the Chinese lady? I fear she is without Christ Jesus."

"Let's not talk here, amigos," said David, hand over his face. A small map was stuffed into the shirt of Chas. "You will stay with my family until we have trained men to defend themselves. "We need to move Carl Bellew onto the next life."

"Your men are no bounty hunters, David?" I said, head turned. "We need men who can shoot and ride, men of bravery and skill, not planters and men who work with brick."

"You take what I have, or you leave, and leave now," said David, neck red. The man's hand held his dark mustache, and his hands switched in wait, and he read our faces. "So, do we have a deal, amigos? My brother said you were good men."

"We are Bounty Hunters and not a bunch of planters and rope makers," Jackie Ray said, and his foot kicked sawdust.

"How many men have you caught, Bounty Hunters, huh?" said David, and his eyes caught the faces of his new friends. "How many men?"

"None," Chas spoke first.

"So, I am not sure you are real Bounty Hunters," David said, face satisfied. "I need men who can fight, not a bunch of Kentucky farmers, just hill bullies and a Cherokee. You are just men on horseback, toting guns and rifles, playing in El campo. Okay. I have gathered men, brave men who will join up with you. Are we together…. in this deal? There was a promise and a handshake to my brother, right, Chas?"

"Yeah. We hold to our promises. You are right, David," said Chas, who leaned over and said, "We will meet with you and your men." The look on his face told me that Chas trusted David. "Later tonight, far from the Town of Waco."

Tipping his hat, David said, "You stay on my farm outside Waco; Go to Rock Creek Road and wait."

"We will see you before sunset," I said.

Movement of a large herd of cattle, fifty head or more, men paid the toll and crossed the suspension bridge. Several men drove the cattle toward the corral and stables. They headed to market, where David and his men worked horses and cattle and acted as if we had only spoken of business.

We nodded and walked away.

"You will have your horses back after lunch!" yelled David.

"Gracias, amigo!" Chas turned and waved.

Chas paid David well for his loyalty and his partnership. My friends did not know if they could hunt down Bad Carl Bellew in his hometown and take him back to Jasper, Texas, or not. We were unsure about men who could not handle weapons, but they were unsure about men who could not speak their language. David's men were tough-looking and angry enough to volunteer to help Padre Ortiz get his daughter back to Crockett, though. I was once that type of man, young and brave, and compassion was given with grace when someone rescued this hungry writer from Mingo Falls.

Several hotels, one-man clinics, dentists, restaurants, and small schools lined the streets of Waco. The city had more than 3500 people by the 1870 census, two thousand people of which had moved to Waco after the Civil War. Waco was a busy town of construction and commerce, but we were not in town to admire business practices and trade routes as we first planned. Our purpose had changed drastically and became a life-or-death ride across Texas.

We met David Ortiz that evening in Rock Creek, and he was grateful for the union. His men were there, all of them eager men, and we had drinks and plenty of food and good stories to tell. Their wives and children stayed behind and worked in a nearby community. At the same time, we walked out to see his horses and visit an empty chapel.

"This is a small and beautiful church," said Chas. My friend felt at home with the woodwork, ten pews, handcrafted, and a pulpit that had been used only a few dozen times since the Civil War had ended.

"Many of the men who built this church did not return from the War," said David, who stood and held the pulpit with both hands and rocked by and forth. "Your uncle Chet Bellew preached here for fifty-three days in a row, and the old timers still speak about his sermons and ask about him to this day. How is that old goat doing?" He raised his hand, and his face was happy, and said, "You should have brought him back to Waco."

"He was killed, David," said Chas, who slapped his friend's shoulder. "Shot by a man who had been stealing from him. Uncle Chet aimed to let the thief escape, but the man seemed scared and turned and shot him. My uncle returned fire. Both men died that night on our farm in Denton, Kentucky."

"I am sorry, and my family loved him very much. Chet brought many of my friends to know the Lord," said David, and he touched his eyes.

The Spanish man walked to where we sat in the pews, held his lantern, and said, "I do not comprehend why God leaves a nasty man, like Bad Carl, and takes a good man, like Preacher Chet."

"To lose him," said Chas, "the man I trusted and respected was difficult. Many people knew him and loved him. He had traveled to many places with the Good News and had many friends."

Like many men of Spanish descent, his accent was broken, but his voice was sincere in any language.

"My wife will be heartbroken," said David. The lantern hung on a post, and the man struck a match and lit three more lanterns, warming our hands and faces. The church glowed like a hot stove in late December. "More men will show up, good men. I told them we are here. I hope your belly was well-fed tonight. We have excellent meals at Rock Creek Farm."

"I know I speak for all of us," said Chas, his voice deep and mature, "the beans and beef, mixed with ground red peppers, were hot and spicy, my friend. The potatoes and hot butter were my favorite. Coffee, perfecto, amigo."

"Coffee and bunuelos were divine," I said, holding my belt.

"Christmas is a good time for bunuelos," said David, smiling. "And good coffee."

"I am not supposed to say this because of the new acceptance of the Lord and being inside a chapel of God," said Jackie Ray, holding his vest, "but the tequila and pineapples were my first time to such a sweet dessert, and you tell the wife, my head is spinning."

"Camila will be happy," David said, whistling, and made his way outside to meet his amigos.

Within an hour, forty-one men held torches. All of them spoke Spanish, few words of English and Cherokee were spoken. His men were educated in different ways. I met teachers, missionaries, clinic workers, farmers, and some men who cooked in restaurants. All brought guns and rifles to the church. We stayed at the church and made it our home, eating and sleeping, and taught the men how to shoot better than when they first arrived. Of the forty-one men, twenty-two stayed and volunteered to fight Bad Carl Bellew. The others prayed for victory and left the day before Feliz Navidad to serve their family and friends.

DAVID AND HIS FIGHTING MEN

Twenty-five men, guns and rifles packed and loaded, three from Kentucky and twenty-two from Texas, sat as brothers in arms, huddled inside the Rock Creek Missionary Church, and had spent days training with weapons. I even trained in hand-to-hand combat, just as the Cherokee trained in the mountains of North Carolina, a tradition of fighting, learned and shared among the amigos, as well. I planned how we would attack the Cowboys and Bad Carl Bellew, even scouted his land. I returned with a map of his ranch, South of Waco, hidden in Hewitt.

"I feel my men are ready," David said, a man proud of our union.

We stood beside Chas, and he led the group.

"Atohi," said Jackie Ray. "When will we attack?"

I stepped in front of the men and named each man, men whom I had trained and trusted, mainly in a week's time. Men of all ages, seventeen to fifty-three, and many of them became our close brothers days later.

EVE OF NEW YEAR'S EVE, 1871

"Some of you will die on New Year's Eve," I said, face concerned. "Some of you will be heroes. All of you will be brothers of heroes and heroes of brothers. Most of all, you will be Bounty Hunters tomorrow night."

The church became loud with celebration.

"My men are prepared to die, Atohi," David said, directing his hand at each man.

"Mio Bueno," I said. The men laughed and liked my long Cherokee face. "I like you men. I will not marry you, but I like you." That was the day I became a man of many hugs and handshakes and gained many friends in Texas.

We had a long table at the Rock Creek Missionary Church, and it was time for a fiesta. The celebration was held at sunset, and the table had more food and drinks than we had ever witnessed on one occasion. All the men were friendly, but one man, a caballero, Edwardo, and I intended to find out why. After dinner, he smoked alone, and I walked the field until I found him.

My black hair was long and braided by a lovely lady at the ranch whom I had known one night, and my clothes were handmade by friends of David, even down to my boots. I trained them how to shoot and fight, but beyond warfare and combat, I knew little about them in less than a week's time.

"The coyotes howl in packs in Texas," I said. "Much different than in Kentucky."

"What do you need, Atohi?" said Edwardo, the man who was fifty-three years old and spoke in a cold, distant voice.

"Why did you sign up for this if you have no desire to help find Isa Ortiz?" I asked, arms crossed.

He turned with a cigarette, lips tight, eyes cold, like a man from a funeral who had lost a loved one, and held his hand across his stomach.

"I do not speak much about finding Isa Ortiz or hunting this man Carl Bellew, but out there… somewhere," waving with his cigarette hand, "someone has my only daughter, too. I am here and can do some good for one man's daughter, at least. This is not my first time to kill a man or hunt for my daughter, Atohi."

"Where is she?" I cried and held a face of deep compassion.

"I do not know," said the man. "She disappeared at the same time Isa Ortiz was gone. So, I have become jealous that no Bounty Hunters or men of law have joined my family to hunt for my lost daughter. It is rare that a Cherokee and two white men, men with no children, far from Kentucky, who take an interest in hunting people. There must be a good reward for such a daughter, one pretty, like Isa Ortiz, Atohi, right?" He turned to the purple and orange sky, back to my face, and smoked. "See, Atohi, I have no money to offer Bounty Hunters. No money for a good reward or to borrow a man's time to track and hunt. She has been gone for almost a year now. If I seem different from the rest of the men, it's because I'm angry inside. I must go now."

He wept and walked away. I stopped him, hand about his shoulder as I seldom do to Chas, an angry man. His dark eyes raised under his salt and pepper hair, and his cheeks became red at what I had done.

"Takes no money to have us hunt for your daughter, Edwardo," I told the man.

"Did your friend fight for no money?" Edwardo said.

"Chas will not accept money to recover Isa Ortiz or your daughter, sir. That's my promise, Edwardo. What is her name?"

"Valeria Julieta Espinosa. She's beautiful," said Edwardo. "Her absence has broken my wife's heart. I am the same."

Edwardo Espinosa walked back to his bunkhouse.

The next morning, I read the *Waco Era* newspaper to all the men, and we had a good breakfast at the long table, one designed to hold twenty-five men. The news column spoke of an invitation-only party being held at the ranch of Mr. Carl Bellew, Hewitt, Texas.

We readied every man, pistol, rifle, and knife and packed enough ammo for another big Civil War. I saddled up twenty-one men, Bounty Hunters, and aimed our horses toward Hewitt, Texas. My good friend and the man I had coffee with that morning, Edwardo Espinosa, returned home and did not ride with us. He had his reasons, and not because I was Cherokee or because my friends were white; it was more personal. I found out it was because his heart hurt for his daughter, and he had no spirit to fight, inside or outside. Halfway to Hewitt, I rode beside Chas, who was the leader, and everyone knew it. Jackie Ray trailed, and half the men rode with him to see if we were being followed.

The land was dry, and the day turned cold. I imagined myself being back in Kentucky, resting beside the warm fire alone, listening to the briskness of the winter wind and calling birds.

"My plan is good," I said to Chas, just south of Waco. "We will detour horses and wagons from the party until we have handled our business and taken care of Bad Carl Bellew and his gang."

"I will pound Carl into gunpowder," said Chas, and his eyes were held forward as we rode. "He will tell us where Isa Ortiz is being held."

We rode fast, and the men thundered across the land.

After lunch on New Year's Eve, long before anyone had arrived, the men had cornbread and water and rested on a rim of grass, and the eagle screamed above the mesquite trees. The evening was so quiet we could hear the breath of the horses, and a flock of wild turkeys had disappeared into the woods. I used the telescope, took the same map route, and spotted the servants' quarters, the windmill, and the large ranch house. The barn was west of Hewitt; three men rode in from the east, heavily armed.

"Carl is on the front porch," I said. The telescope was in my hands, and I saw the land he owned. "Three mounted riders kept on riding after they spoke to Carl, headed out west."

"Did the men leave the ranch?" Chas said, eye on the telescope.

"Let's attack now, Chas," I said, checking my ammo out of habit and tradition. Each man did the same and stayed behind the grassy hillside, hidden in the shadows of low mesquite.

"I will take Carl, and you hunt for the girl," Chas said and commanded the men.

"What do you want from my men?" said David, who squatted to the right flank, voices low.

"Take half east and half west," I said, pointing in each direction. Our hands shared the map in the dirt, and our faces were ready to attack. "Close the gap slowly on each side, and we'll win. We want to leave here with every man we have in the group."

David's mighty men rode to their positions, half cut through the woods, and others rode down a steep hill into the valley to where the stream turned beside the house.

"I have the buildings scouted," I said and mounted up.

"I will check the ranch house," Chas said, voice low.

We were halfway to the house, and Jackie Ray rode over the hill. His horse stood broadsided in a clearing and made himself a target for Bad Carl Bellew.

"What the heck is he doing, Atohi?" said Chas. "He's rearing his horse, like Stonewall Jackson did. The man will get us all killed."

"Not sure why you brought him to Texas, Chas," I said, and held my horses and rolled my eyes.

"Thought you told him to ride with us," said Chas.

"Look!" I yelled and pointed at the porch. "Carl Bellew has a rifle on the front porch."

"The fight just started again, Champ!" I yelled and fired. Carl was hit in the leg and ran inside the house.

"Jackie Ray is charging down the hill," said Chas. "Out of position!"

David's mighty men moved in as directed. I heard a whistle from Chas, the same call that meant trouble in New Orleans. Jackie Ray ran to where we were positioned. Carl Bellew had fired three more rounds and hit three of David's men.

"Where did you all go?" said Jackie Ray, breathing hard and smelled like tequila.

"Thought you were with David and his men, huh?" said Chas, pointing. "Atohi took off for the servants' quarters."

"No. I am here and a hundred yards away from the porch," said Jackie Ray, face sick. "Chas, Carl is surrounded. Let's smoke him out again, make him pay."

Flat on his back, Jackie Ray closed his eyes and was sick.

"Are you on opium again or drunk, Jackie Ray?" said Chas, holding his head. "Don't fire that dynamite!"

"I drank too much and can't see straight, Brother Chas. The whole ranch is a white cloud, and I'm scared I won't find a gypsy and a parrot!" Jackie Ray covered his eyes with his gambler's hat and rested. "Nerves."

"That's fog! Just stay low," said Chas on the ground. "Wait until I whistle. Drink some water and stay flat on your back."

I saw Chas take his position near the front porch, pistol in hand and a good knife on his side. No guests had arrived by lunch. Lots of folks were on their way. Fifty or more people, couples, we had heard.

"Carl! Carl Bellew!" sounded Chas. "Come on out. You are a dead man!"

"Come in and get me, dirty trader!" yelled Carl. "You'll be my first guest for the evening. My brother would be ashamed if he knew you were hunting his own blood down, wouldn't he?"

"Chet is dead!" Chas told him. "He hoped you would get right with God, but you are the devil's brother."

Chas fired a torch, broke the window, and moved to the front door. The house was locked, and windows were on each side of the door. David flagged his men and held their position. Chas was close enough to sneak inside the ranch house and take him by surprise.

I was at the servants' quarters, knocked several doors off the hinges, and searched for anyone that Carl Bellew and his Cowboys had tied to the wall.

"Hey, anybody in here?" I checked rooms, built half underground; golden grassy sod was atop the homes. The door fell on the floor of the last room, but I had made it uncontested. The cool air had left my lungs, and I searched and pounded. I heard someone jump and rounds fired in the distance at the ranch house, and the person was afraid. I saw Jackie Ray, flat on his back in the grass. Sick. He was no help. I worked my way upright and held my Colt.

"Hey!" I pushed back the curtain. "Who's in here?"

A pretty lady was tied up in the room, and tears rolled down her red cheeks. I wasn't sure who she was or where she was from, but she was safe in my arms. Her dark eyes spoke from her soul for help, but her red face trusted no man, even a good man.

"I'm here to help you." I moved slowly and spoke low.

She did not move. Suddenly, she sprung with her fist and ran out the door.

"Jackie Ray, get her!" I yelled and held my busted lip.

"Isa Ortiz!" yelled David, who ran through the grass for his sweet niece.

"Pow!"

The gunshot came from the ranch house. David went down, and his hands reached for hers, inches away.

"Uncle David!" she cried out.

Suddenly, Chas jumped through the window, glass shattering, and the action surprised Bad Carl Bellew. Two more shots were fired inside the ranch house. I ran to the long porch, and Carl staggered to the front door. Blood ran down his face, and his side was red like a bear had attacked the man.

Chas was down.

"Atohi!" yelled Carl. "Where are you, Cherokee! It's time to die, Cherokee!"

"Chas, get up!" I yelled, pistol low, and he stumbled.

In my lifetime, there were no sons of my own blood. My mind was clouded. Chas was no different than my own son. Suddenly, Chas ran out the front door and knocked Bad Carl to the ground. Blood was on the face of Chas, and the face of Carl was blood red.

Suddenly, the evil man raised his long knife to stab his nephew, and both men fell to the ground. I ran closer. David's mighty men circled the house; three needed medical attention. The other Spanish men, who rode in from the west side, rushed to find David, shot and blood-soaked.

"Get this pig off of me!" said Chas, kicking both legs around.

Four of David's sons pulled Carl Bellew from atop Chas, and both men were severely stabbed. Carl Bellew's wound was fatal, and he was no longer Bad. He was dead, cut deep, from a knife that I had brought Chas in Waco on Christmas Eve. The first time the knife was used happened that day.

"He's alive!" I said, kneeling beside Chas, my best friend.

Late that night, David's sons told their mother how he was killed, and the world of laughter they had the night before, smiling faces, eyes full of love, hands held close, had changed to tears.

The small mirror I had clung to all those years, a glass used for a thousand moments of vanity I now hated, remnants of pride, chards of a selfish life, shattered with it. Fallen faces of the hurting, hearts broken by war and law, wounded friends, close ones, and loved ones, became more important than my own vanity. My heart felt a revelation that changed the course of my life – I knew the rest of my life was meant to share the Lord.

On the crest of that Christmas, I understood what it meant to not have a father around and knew the difference between men and mankind.

David's wife, Camila, screamed and fell into the arms of her oldest son, who carried her inside, far from the darkness of the world.

Chas found where Edwardo Espinoza had moved to since his daughter was gone. I rode alone and knocked on his door long before midnight, and the door slowly opened. The man was half asleep and recognized my face.

"Amigo, Edwardo, you awake?" I said, face serious.

I stood in front of his humble home, felt small, ashamed of how I had pushed him to become a fighter, and had a heart full of regret.

"It's too late, Atohi."

"We found your daughter's ribbon, sir," I told the man.

He held his face, and his eyes bent in pain.

"Valeria's red ribbon," Edwardo said.

"Daddy!" Valerie shouted. "I love you, Papi. Tie the ribbon in my hair."

Valeria stepped from behind my horse and walked into the light of his lantern. Her mother ran faster than any human I'd ever seen.

They wept. I did my part, and we all held each other.

"Valeria!" said his wife. "My baby!" eyes soaked.

"I owe you my life, Atohi!" Edwardo said and held his daughter.

"I'll take coffee instead, mi amigo."

He bent my shoulder with a giant hug.

"Mi amigo," Edwardo said. "Hermano."

"We are blood brothers," I said, and we talked over fresh coffee.

I listened, and no more vanity crossed my heart. For the first time in a long while, I felt the love of family.

His wife placed a white candle on the table and surrounded the candle with lentils, beans, rice, corn, and flour; the kitchen smelled like cinnamon in a short while. We smoked and had red wine, and at midnight, Edwardo finally tied the ribbon into Valeria's long, thick hair.

It was a New Year, 1872.

The girl was a beautiful teenager. Her father handed Valeria a present from Christmas, and she held her dress, new shoes, and a giant smile. We had a late-night meal: thick cheese, eggs, beans, avocados, sausage, and tortillas. The house smelled like a grill in a fine Waco restaurant. I felt more welcome than any place I had ever been.

"I must go, Edwardo," I told the man and hugged his family.

"You are welcome in my home," Edwardo said. "Stay anytime, Atohi."

"Happy New Year, Edwardo!"

"Atohi, Feliz año nuevo."

DEAD OR ALIVE

On the 1st day of January 1872, a celebration occurred; some felt sadness, and others felt jovial. Two Texas Rangers, the town sheriff, the marshal, and the Waco undertaker, showed up. The first telegram from my hands made it to Austin, a message that told about the death and burial of Carl Bellew. In reading the same message, Sheriff Dunn of Jasper, Texas, kindly agreed to wire 1000 dollars to Chas Bellew, Bounty Hunter, who had kept the law and his promise.

Two days later, dinner was served by the Governor of Texas, held in Waco, who had offered us our old jobs back as Texas Rangers. He promised to hold three positions for five years, that is if we ever wanted to work in the State of Texas again. We made small amounts of money along the way, bought new clothes and boots, traded, and dined as well as the governor for a few days and met more good people, too. The governor was well thought of in Texas and encouraged us to have a family. He wanted to know about my father and mother, and without a temper, the truth about the Trail of Tears was spoken. But we had other things on our mind, different than law and order, far across the country. With three hands counted, the decision was made to return to Kentucky.

Our next stop was in Crockett, Texas. Chas knocked on the shack door and said, "Padre Orlando Manuel Ortiz, toe the line, father!"

"Champ!" said Padre Ortiz. "How was Waco?"

"Good," Chas said, face long, hands open. "We found the ribbon of your daughter, part of her dress, too. I wish we..."

Running to her parents, "Papi! Madre!"

She couldn't wait to see her mother and father.

"Your hound followed us," I said, and the family embraced the dog and the girl.

I became a man who learned to embrace others and gave of myself without vanity. Isa Ortiz wept and shouted, and so did her parents. The second promise was fulfilled, and the surprise was the return of his hound. The Ortiz farmhouse, the one I had burned down with arrows, the three of us became carpenters alongside many Catholic brothers and sisters, and the home was rebuilt. No more bare-knuckle fights were held in 1872, and Chas was remembered as the "Campeon of Crockett Spring."

The smell of supper waved through the crack in the door. We were welcomed at the Butterfly Farm of the Orphans and saw Lucy Goodman, where we left half of our reward money to the little girls for education and meals. We promised more money would follow, and it did. Chas had to see the butterflies, and Jackie Ray thought Lucy was an angel sent down from above. He had bought Lucy a parrot and left it for her. We would never make it to Kentucky by springtime with those two sightseers.

By 6 March 1872, three unshaven Rough Riders had weathered the storm across Kentucky. Our clothes were worn and tested by snow and the elements, and we had not tasted a decent meal since Arkansas. We kept pace to make Louisville, three weary men who had made it by sundown.

"I swear my hands are naturally cold and curled, gone," said Chas. "One good thing: we should see Sherri at the hotel and get a hot meal and some drinks."

"Tail is stuck to my saddle," said Jackie Ray. "Frozen and mounted."

Jackie Ray fell off his horse when I unhooked his saddle. Chas propped his head against a barn post, and a goat ran after him, horns down.

"The goat loves you, Jackie Ray," said Chas.

"You two make me cry," I said, and my grin doubled. "Thirty years ago, my grandfather and thousands of Cherokees walked from North Carolina to some flat and dry, nowhere land in the middle of Oklahoma, and you two haven't seen a rough day yet. I know for sure because I raised both of you on goat's milk."

Chas and Sherri spent the day at dinner, and stories were told about our journey. We rode the popular Louisville Street Trolley System and toured the town. In every town we visited, Chas and Jackie Ray made friends, like two homeless pups, held in the hands of compassionate and wealthy people. Our trousers were tight when we rode out of Louisville, and our horses fully rested and ready for another trail ride across Kentucky.

YOU CAN GO HOME AGAIN

Back in Grayson, Reese Johnson and wife received their 300 dollars back from the York Brothers. In Denton, I dressed in my best clothes and walked to Straight Creek Presbyterian Church. I knocked, and a strong welcoming wind opened the door and the spring shower had ended.

"Hello?" I said and held my hat. "I am glad to be home."

No one answered. I hoped for a familiar face, but no one was there. I went inside and knelt to pray for the kind people we had left behind. I thought of friends: Sherri, Marie Laveau, Millie, beautiful orphans, Sunshine Frenchie, Meli, Sammy Summers, and the good men from the blacksmith shop in New Orleans. Many great friends filled my heart, like David and his mighty men, Padre Ortiz and his family, Edwardo, Isa, Valerie, and the Texas governor and the men who served beneath him. I prayed for the men and women we lost and their families along the way. My hope was to see Meli again with our horses.

Later, I remembered the man who held the pulpit, Preacher Chet Bellew, who said, "With pride, I hope to have God on my side, but I must have Kentucky. And as we try to overcome loss, Heaven must be a Denton, Kentucky kind of a place." I hoped it would be.

I found the pews unoccupied and realized someone had followed me inside Straight Creek Presbyterian Church.

"I rode a train," said the tall man. "I rode a horse, and a man named Chas Bellew said he knew where I could find a Cherokee brave inside a Presbyterian church."

"Father!" I found vanity did not exist when you loved someone more than yourself. We laughed, and we wept. In that grand moment of my life, we held each other for a very long time. Then, he sat on the first pew, and I proudly rested beside him.

"How's mother?"

His eyes were closed, head bent, and air left his lungs. I knew she was gone. We walked outside, stood atop the steps of the church, and witnessed the evergreen of Denton. We had new hope between us on that day. My father spoke of many things he would like to do in the mountains. He walked with strength, still upright and confident, and his long gray hair waved in the breeze. His face was aged and wrinkled, mostly because of the brokenness in Oklahoma. He told about how he fought the wild bears with a spear when he was a young brave and won. We spoke of love and loss. My father spoke of the two wolves that lived inside each man and how the woodpecker was a carpenter and flute maker. He remembered many stories. I listened.

"I have good friends I want you to meet, Father," I said.

"I met Jackie Raymont Monroe," said my father. "He talks more than any man I know. Or woman, for that matter. I met Chas Bellew and Kate when I rode up the hill. Chas told me where I could find you inside the church, and he spoke the truth."

We walked and traded stories. He held his arms behind his back and had a wonderful laugh about him, and our voices were the same and echoed across the mountains.

"It's your turn to lead the Cherokee Nation, Atohi," he said, and I knew what he meant.

That evening after dinner, Kate, Chas, Alice, and Jackie Raymont joined my campfire, and my father told many wonderful old stories, some of war, some of the Cherokee Nation, and how he was not fond of Andrew Jackson but met George Armstrong Custer. The only thing wonderful about him was his yellow head.

He told about the Legends of the Cherokee and battles against other tribes, and he spoke about the Indian Wars.

"Luchador?" said Jackie Raymont.

"What language does he speak?" my father said.

We laughed, smoked, ate, and told him about the bare-knuckle fight and our attack on Bad Carl Bellew. My father was proud.

"I wish we could have fought together, Atohi." My father held my neck, and his smile divided him from all other men. A tear broke free from his eye.

"It would have been a glorious day."

He made us Chiefs of the Denton Tribe, and my father sounded with a strong war cry that echoed throughout the valley.

"And remember this, Atohi," he said, "you became the wolf you feed, good or evil."

"I remembered that as a young brave," I said and finished the story for him.

We saw his long face glow in happiness when I became the storyteller of the family, just as he was among friends.

My father turned to my friends and said, "Let me tell you about the Great Spirit: He rides a white horse whose rider is called Faithful and True." He went on to say, "He treads the winepress of the fury of God Almighty. On his robe and on his thigh, he has the name written: KING OF KINGS AND LORD OF LORDS."

"The Book of Revelation," I said, surprised.

"Yeah. I love you, son," he said in front of everyone." He hugged greatly as fathers often do.

"I love you, father." I held him as a son should, caught in deep admiration.

I rose early; the ember of the flame had gone away, living in a dark shadow. Then, I heard the coral cry of the cock and brewed his favorite drink.

"Coffee, father?" He had his hands folded on his chest. "Father?"

My father fell asleep that night forever.

"Let's bury your father beside our fathers," said Chas. My friend stood in the doorway. Jackie Raymont wept and nodded.

"My father would be honored," I said, eyes wet. "Are you crying, Jackie Ray?"

"No," Jackie Ray said. "That's the grace of Sunday rain."

And so it happened that way in the mountains, both life and death, the ages falling like withered leaves at the end of a lengthy season and finally at rest. Our mornings were spent brooding those we'd loved and lost.

For us, death, but on the contrary, hands kept calloused and heads arched beyond the hills, still captivated with faraway places. Large junctions of water poured pure and natural, and we were left to assume, as Chas and I did, that some had yet to meet our brand of coffee or tea. Each one lit his own lantern and had a maddening hunger to begin again. We'd heard old-time stories and sermons about the Lord Christ Jesus, beckoning messages of hope scattered about by a timeless divinity, and we had not heard them all.

Not all could say they lived in the high country, where acorns became shady oaks, snowflakes formed roaring rivers, and before the mountains were the words of God. Written in the pages of newspapers, the names of our fathers, men no longer dusted by the cares of this world. Horses readied for the next incredible journey, youth full of ambition, and we spoke of tomorrow's wonder. On days so stunning in the hills, we were out there, and on Sundays, we learned what we could with the beauty of its language.

About the Author

Photo credit: Debra Lester. Thanksgiving 2021, Tybee Island, GA.

PETE was born and raised in West Virginia, alumni of Baileysville High School (Home of the Rough Riders), in Wyoming County; and holds degrees from Concord University, Liberty University, and a Doctorate from Tennessee Temple University. Pete is a U.S. Army veteran and an award-winning painter and international artist.

SOUTHERN FICTION NOVELS: *The Tobacco Barn* (2019), Amazon Top #600, August 2019, *When Geese Fly South* (2021).

WESTERN NOVELS: *Saddles of Barringer* (2021), *Sunday Rain* (2023). In 2023, Pete was inducted into the Western Writers Hall of Fame, Buffalo Center of the West, McCracken Library, Cody, Wyoming.

MEMBERSHIPS: Western Writers of America, Hemingway Society; F. Scott Fitzgerald Society, Thomas Wolfe Society.

Made in the USA
Middletown, DE
24 February 2024

49857756R00179